Dreams of You

Tina Wainscott

St. Martin's Paperbacks

DREAMS OF YOU

Copyright © 1996 by Tina Wainscott.

ISBN: 0-312-95979-6

Printed in the United States of America

St. Martin's Paperbacks edition/October 1996

10 9 8 7 6 5 4 3 2

Acknowledgments

My sincere gratitude to John Sciarrino for bringing the magic of photography to life for me and making sure I had it right.

And my thanks to the people who took the time to write about the homeless so that I could see what their lives were like, even if a little.

Dreams
of
You

Prologue

Three years earlier:

The sky blackened, making the wind gust wickedly through the palm trees. Not exactly the Hawaii one pictured, but Adrian Wilde was on a roll, quite literally. Supermodel Ellie Marlow held her long hair out of her face, frowning at the camera.

Adrian tilted his head. "Come on, Ellie. Just a few more shots." He lifted his hands to the roiling clouds above. "Can't you feel the excitement in the air, the danger? It's perfect."

"It's insane! We're going to be electrocuted."

As if the sorceress had summoned it, lightning cracked across the clouds, puncturing the blackness with wicked fingers. A second later thunder shattered the air.

"Just two more shots and we're out of here," he called over the wind. "And let go of the hair. Please," he added with a smile.

After a pause, she let her brown hair whip across her face, walking toward him with a jaunty cant, her finger in her mouth.

"Perfect, Ellie. This is going to be the shot of a lifetime."

For a second, the hairs on his body shot to attention. The

air tingled. In a single flash of light and a loud crash, he was knocked backward. Vibrations charged through his body. He could hear Ellie scream, but he couldn't move or speak. Darkness swirled around him, as if those spikes of light had pulled him right up into that black mass.

"He's not breathing!" he heard someone scream.

The twisting mass formed a tunnel, and at the end a brilliant light pulsed, waiting for him. He moved toward that light as a roller coaster screams across the tracks. Images flashed past him, vivid and full of life.

Only it wasn't his life.

A young girl made a sandcastle on the beach, patting the sides with infinite care until a boy with dark hair stalked over and kicked it in. That same girl, now a lovely teenager, standing on a sea wall, her golden blond curls dancing in the breeze as she looked out to a cerulean ocean. Her arms were crossed in front of her, slender hands on her throat. And then the same girl, now a woman, driving through town in a white Mercedes convertible on a summer day.

He kept rushing through space without time or thought. The woman's image flashed in front of him again. She was walking out of a pristine mansion. Storm clouds darkened the sky there, too, but he hardly had time to notice. If he kept going, he was going to crash into her. She didn't see him coming right at her, right . . .

He was expelled into a thicker darkness, a liquid warmth that flowed all around him. Blood pumping through his veins, a muffled thunder that pulsed through the thickness. A heartbeat. Her heartbeat. He was inside her.

And then everything exploded, worse than the thunder, more painful than the lightning. Fire, the smell of smoke, flames on his skin, searing pain, so much fear and panic! All he could see was the venomous orange burst that surrounded the woman. Her thoughts were louder than the roar of flames. *What is happening? Mother! I've got to get out and find her.*

"He's got a heartbeat!" a voice said from some far outer place.

Adrian jumped with a start, rolling on the sand in a desperate attempt to smother the flames. Hands were everywhere on him, holding him down as he struggled. He opened his eyes. The crew. The people he'd left behind what seemed like hours ago. They stood around him, confusion and concern in their eyes.

"He's alive!" Ellie breathed, squeezing his arm.

He looked around. No fire. Only the rain, gushing from the sky.

Two of the men helped him to his feet as he struggled to stand. His shoes had been knocked off, and his feet felt like two balls of fire. They looked as if he'd been standing in a frying pan.

"Let's get you out of the rain. Geez, are you all right? You gave us a helluva scare."

Adrian's breath came in heavy gasps. His body felt like liquid. When he reached the nearest palm, he held onto it.

"Get away from that tree, Wilde," Bob said. "You want to get hit by lightning again?"

"Is that what happened to me?" He saw his camera lying on the sand, scorched and now wet. "Where was the fire? I felt flames, smelled smoke."

Ellie pulled him to the van, where he dropped down onto the floor. "There was no fire, love," she said, wiping his shoulder-length dark hair out of his eyes. "It must have been the lightning you felt. You were dead, you know. Margot performed CPR and got your heart beating again."

"I was dead," he said softly, looking at the place where he'd been thrown. He closed his eyes, settling his forehead in his hand. Flashes of the tunnel ripped through the blackness behind his eyes. Dead. He had heard of the tunnel, of people seeing their life flash before them. But who was the woman? Why had her life exploded?

Chapter 1

Just because no one will listen does not make me silent.

Cold water engulfed Adrian, pulling him down, down to some hellish oblivion beneath the sea. He heard the wild beating of his heart and the sound of air as it escaped his lips in the last bubbles of hope. Blackness surrounded him. He held his breath until his lungs threatened to burst. Breathe, he had to breathe. No air. He inhaled cold water into his lungs. Panic froze him. He took two short gasps. More water rushed in, crushing his chest.

"No!" He heard his own voice tear the word from his mouth in one long wail of agony. Fear raged through his veins as he caught his breath in gasps. He looked desperately around for a way to escape, his survival instinct strong and fierce. But there was nothing.

The water and fury disappeared, leaving only the cool darkness of a November New York night. The sounds of the city far below assured him that life progressed—taxi drivers honked their horns, music drifted from somewhere. He wasn't dying. Yet

"My God, Adrian, what were you dreaming about?" Rita's voice whispered from the dark.

He'd forgotten she had wormed an overnight invitation.

She reached over and turned on the soft light over the bed. He studied his outstretched arms and hands, the bed around him. No water, except for the dampness on his body. A faucet leaked in the bathroom, the *drip*, *drip* chilling him all over again. He rubbed his long fingers over his face, trying to erase his expression of fear.

Rita touched the tensed muscle of his arm, then wiped the perspiration that covered him onto the silk sheets. "Are you all right? Geez, you're soaked!" She tucked a lock of his hair back from his face.

He finally felt composed enough to turn at the concern in her voice. Her black mane of curls tumbled around her face, wildly framing dark eyes and olive skin. She always looked camera ready. Adrian smoothed back his damp hair, dark as her own.

"It was just a nightmare. Go back to sleep." But his voice betrayed him, cracking softly.

How long would he keep having this nightmare? It was worse than the fire he'd experienced through Madame Blue's eyes, and no less vivid. Since the moment of his death three years earlier, his life had never been the same.

Adrian rolled out of bed and walked over to the black lacquer dresser, leaning on the slick, uncluttered surface. In the mirror he could see the green light spilling from beneath the pedestal of the black bed like a mystical fog, and Rita sitting there watching him. The air chilled his damp skin, every inch exposed. He lit a cigarette, took two drags, and crushed it out in the blue glass ashtray.

"Why don't you just quit cold turkey?" she asked.

"I'll quit the way I want." That reminded him why he didn't want anything permanent with a woman. Nagging. So, he wasted money. Last month he took five drags before putting it out. Last week, three.

Rita's voice softened, and suddenly she stood behind

him, her body pressed against his back. "Adrian, talk to me. It'll help."

"No," he answered with finality, moving away from her. He would never share his after death experience. He had, in fact, only shared it with one other person, the only person who wouldn't think he was crazy.

It wasn't just the strange journey death had taken him on, but what that journey had started. Visions. Whatever happened that day connected his soul with that mysterious woman's soul. He could *feel* her emotions. During brief flashes, like those images in the tunnel, her delight, or sadness, or acute loneliness reached out to him. That's why she became his Madame Blue. He could feel what she felt, see what she saw, but he couldn't see her. Sometimes it was the ocean, other times it was an art gallery someplace.

"Adrian, did you hear me?" Rita's voice penetrated his thoughts. "Don't shut me out."

He shook his head, straightening. "Go back to sleep. I'm going to get some work done."

It wasn't the first time he'd spent half the night printing photographs after a nightmare. But the watery dream was far different from any ordinary nightmare. Although he had experienced a fiery explosion through Madame Blue, his nightmares were the final moments of her life. If this woman existed, what had the fire done to her? He would never know the truth because he knew nothing about her, not even her name. Not even, for sure, if she really existed beyond his soul.

After taking a cold shower, he threw on some baggy cotton pants, pulled his thick hair into a ponytail, and walked into his studio. The bright lights and faint vinegar smell of darkroom chemicals brought the comfort he wanted. He thought of Rita sitting there in his bed wanting to comfort him. As one of the most sought after fashion photographers in the business, Adrian considered emotional involvement with a woman hazardous. Frequent travel and work with beautiful women didn't lend themselves to the average dating scenario.

Throwing a Moody Blues CD into the stereo system, he took the negatives still hanging in the drying cabinet and closed himself in the darkroom. He laid the strips on the contact easel and shot the contact sheets for the black and whites he'd taken last week in Palm Beach for Guess. Although he'd never been to the area before, it had felt eerily familiar to him. He still couldn't shake the feeling.

Adrian worked for hours, hoping that when he emerged daylight would be a rising force and the long night far behind him. The contact sheets came alive in the developer, and as always, he was pleased with the results. Mari Flannegan, a new star he had discovered, looked fresh and innocent in the foamy waves, like a Norma Jean for the nineties. Behind her, the Atlantic Ocean shimmered like a blanket of diamonds in the sun. Adrian smiled. This was his life—nothing meant more to him than his photography.

The shot of Mari holding a wad of seaweed with a grimace on her face wasn't planned, but he would recommend it be the first one in the series. He pulled the sheet out of the wash, squeegeed it, and hung it up to dry, pleased with the spontaneous side of his work.

Adrian never kidded himself that he didn't have miles to go before becoming the best of the best. When he reached that pinnacle, then what? For now, he had everything he wanted, mostly the security that he would never worry again about losing his home or not having food for dinner. All that was in the faraway past before he had any control over his life. This was enough, he told himself. A penthouse in downtown New York City, travel to exotic places, working with gorgeous women . . . what more could he want? What else could there possibly be?

He started the last contact sheet, feeling lack of sleep

creeping up on his features. So far most of the shots looked perfect, except for the blurry one when the bedraggled Spanish girl tugged at his sleeve just as he was making the exposure. Adrian told her to leave, then felt so bad at her obvious disappointment, he played sucker and bought one of the shell necklaces dangling over her arm.

When he had put the last contact sheet in the fix, he snapped on the light and surveyed the shots. His gaze rested on the last one. Mari gave the camera a sensational smile, probably glad she was almost done with her part and could get out of the nippy sea air that pinkened her nose. The beach curved away behind her. Mari wore a gold tank top and skin-tight blue jean shorts, trying to pretend it was a summer day for the June campaign. The mist that enveloped the background made it seem surreal—a perfect shot. But . . . wait a minute. Something showed up in the background that he'd clearly missed when taking the shot.

Adrian squinted, making out a lone figure of a woman standing on the beach. Judging by the drab attire and general appearance, she looked to be a ragamuffin, a homeless person. His face went red with frustration even as his mind worked on how to cut that part out. He decided the figure could be airbrushed so that it would blend in with the mist.

"Damn," he muttered, leaving the darkroom to let the pictures dry and grab a bite to eat. He hated missing details like that.

Rita chewed on a bagel, sitting at the slate gray counter that separated the kitchen from the dining area. She wrinkled up the note she'd been writing when he walked out of his studio.

"Hi, darling. Wasn't sure if I'd see you before I left."

"Aren't those bagels stale?" He wanted to avoid "morning after" conversation. Sometimes that could be stale too.

"It's fine." She wrenched another bite free with her

straight, white teeth. "You've been working since that nightmare?"

"Got a lot done. The shots for Guess came out great. Well, except for a few of the them."

He poured himself a cup of the almond coffee Rita had brewed. He didn't care for fancy coffees, but as long as it was fresh and potent, he could live with nuts in his java.

Rita smiled over her cup, letting her gaze linger on his bare chest. "You should do some modeling, Adrian. With those eyes, that mouth . . . you'd be a magazine ad god."

"Humph," he replied. "I have no desire to be on the other side of the camera, thank you."

With a loud meow, Oscar, his white cat, made a grand entrance. He walked over to the super-size cat food bowl and sniffed at its emptiness. Rita opened the cabinet door and filled the bowl.

"Do you think Giovanni will ever come back from Australia and get Oscar?" she asked, stroking his soft fur.

He smiled, remembering Giovanni's plea for Adrian to watch his cat while he "found himself" in the Outback. He found himself all right, along with a lucrative contract for *National Geographic*. Adrian didn't keep pets or plants, since he was gone a lot, but he'd agreed to his good friend's request. A year later, Oscar was still in residence, and Rita took care of him while Adrian was away.

"Probably not. The last letter I got from him detailed his new life with some Aborigine tribe, with a three-hundred-dollar check for Oscar's upkeep. And of course, lots of buttering up for not sticking him in the pound."

"Ah, you wouldn't do that, would you?"

He raised an eyebrow. "Only if he does his business in my clean clothes again."

Rita laughed. "In protest for his owner leaving him, I'm sure. He's been good ever since, hasn't he?"

"He's been fine."

Oscar, as if sensing his existence being discussed, wandered over to Adrian and rubbed against his leg. Adrian leaned down and scratched his head.

"Yeah, yeah, I hear you."

Rita leaned on her elbows, looking up at him under thick, dark lashes. "If I behave, will you keep me too?"

Adrian closed his eyes, too tired to deal with this again. He made it a point never to lead a woman on, just as he never lied to them. "Rita . . ."

"I know, I know. You're too busy to have a relationship. Adrian, I wonder if you're capable of loving someone, even if you did have time. Lucky Oscar here, the only reason he gets to stay is because he was foisted on you. Is that the only way to get to you?" She took a sip of her coffee, keeping her eyes on him. "What if I got pregnant?"

Adrian dropped his cup on the counter, splashing coffee on the gray-flecked surface. "Don't even think about it, Rita. The only way that's going to happen is if you poke a hole in my condoms. If I catch you anywhere near my drawer with a needle, we're over. Understand?"

She understood, all right. Her eyes narrowed, as catlike as Oscar's. With a lift of her chin, she said, "I wouldn't do that. But I could still get pregnant, you know? Those things aren't a hundred percent. Even with the foam."

"Then maybe we'd better stop fooling around, just to make sure."

Rita pushed her coffee cup away and gathered her overnight bag. "I'm out of here." At the door, she paused. "See you later?"

His fingers still tensed on the counter at her subtle threat. He lit a cigarette, taking his two drags before crushing it out. "Sometime." Then he walked into the bedroom to get dressed.

*   *   *

By the time Adrian returned to the darkroom, he'd forgotten about both Rita and the ragamuffin. He aimed the remote at the central music system, and piano sounds boomed throughout the apartment. The Bang and Olufsen stereo system wired into every room had sold Adrian on the place.

He sat at his white table, the contact sheets spread out before him. A yellow pencil marked the ones he would recommend to Guess. He picked up the last contact sheet and stared at the figure in the background. Holding it under the bright studio light, he automatically reached for the loupe. Something about the woman's posture sent a funny feeling curling through his insides. Even magnified, the woman still looked obscure.

Adrian decided to blow up that shot to see if he could make her out. Even with the negative in the enlarger and the head extended all the way to the top, he still couldn't get the magnification he was after, so he reached for the 130-millimeter lens. The negative's image projected onto the easel, and he shifted it to capture just the woman in the background. After testing, he set the exposure for ten seconds and dropped the print in the developer, watching the figure instantly appear as he pushed it around with the tongs. Magic. That was what photography was: magic.

Fingers of déjà vu gripped his heart in a tight hold as he examined the print in its bath of fix. What he could see of her features beneath the scarf was delicate, her lips sensual and full. She seemed oblivious to all the activity further down the beach as she looked out at the ocean. His fingers trembled as he transferred the print to the wash, then held it beneath the blow dryer. He knew this woman with her arms crossed protectively in front of her, fingers up by her throat. She had haunted his life for three years. *Madame Blue!*

As he started from the table, he shook his head and calmed down. Lack of sleep was catching up to him. Looking at the print again, he reasoned that it couldn't be her. In his visions, Madame Blue lived in a mansion on the ocean, drove a Mercedes Benz, and was exquisite. This woman appeared to be homeless, with her shabby coat and faded scarf.

Adrian set the photograph on the corner of his table and looked through the other shots on the contact sheets. As if a ghost, the woman didn't appear anywhere else. It was crazy to even think she was Madame Blue.

Adrian sorted through the prints, focusing on his work and not on his notions. But his attention kept drifting to the woman. Something deep within him felt it was her. The feeling persisted throughout the morning and afternoon. Time and again he picked up the print and held it under the light. He brought it with him to the glass dining table while he ate his lunch of a stale bagel loaded with lox and cream cheese. His fingers held it when he walked to the window and looked at the cityscape.

Adrian remembered the flashed image of Madame Blue standing on a lawn of manicured grass, her blond hair flowing out behind her as she looked out to the ocean. She did that a lot, looked out at some body of water.

He wondered if some force larger than himself wouldn't let him dismiss that photograph. He glanced upward, then back at the print. Adrian was sure he'd seen her in this exact pose in that tunnel. While he'd always believed his visions to be real, he hadn't been able to prove it. This photograph certainly wasn't proof, not to anyone but him. But it explained his feeling of familiarity with Palm Beach, especially now as he remembered the palm trees and mansions facing the ocean.

What if it was her? The possibility sent pinpricks down his spine. What if that fiery event had somehow turned her life upside down and made her a ragamuffin? And worst of all, what if he airbrushed her and never found out?

He dropped down into one of the leather seats behind him, letting out the deep breath he'd been holding. The thought was incredibly exciting. But another more foreboding thought crept in. His Aunt Stella's prediction.

Stella was the only person he had ever confided his strange experience in. Those images haunted him afterwards, and the nightmares about drowning had gripped him in fear and panic every night for months.

His mother scoffed at her sister's psychic abilities, calling Stella a phony every time her name came up. Adrian wasn't inclined to believe in things paranormal, but he knew he'd go crazy if he didn't talk to someone.

"Do we have to do this here?" he'd asked, feeling uncomfortable in her shop with the red velvet drapes obliterating the light outside.

"Good a place as any. Stop being silly." She rubbed her hands with a lotion from a ruby red jar. "Something is troubling you."

"I was hit by lightning a few months ago. That's when it started."

She took his hand in hers, and he swore that it tingled. "Yes, I know. Your mother told me." Her fingers fluttered across his palm. Her eyes were closed, face relaxed. Suddenly her eyes opened again. "Did you die? I mean, did your heart stop beating for any length of time?"

"Yes. For a few minutes. Why?"

"Something very strange happened while you were dead."

He felt a tightness in his chest. "Yes," he whispered.

Stella's eyes closed again, and her hand tightened on his. "This is very strange. I've never felt anything like this before. I can feel your life force, very strong. But there is another force, fainter, inside yours. Your soul left your body . . . and connected with another soul. A woman."

Adrian hadn't realized his eyes had drifted shut until

they snapped open. "Yes! Can you see her? Who is she?"

Stella raised her other hand, issuing a command of silence. Her eyes remained closed, but a muscle above her lip twitched. "She has golden blond hair, and is quite lovely. But there is much pain."

"From what?"

Her brows furrowed, and lines gathered around her eyes as she concentrated. "Heat. Fire. Some kind of explosion."

He couldn't believe it. Stella could not know about Madame Blue, unless she was really a psychic. "Where is she now?"

"I see water. I can still feel pain, but this is a different kind. More inside, like the heart." Her eyes opened, and she blinked. "I lost her."

"You said our souls connected. What did you mean?"

"When we die, our souls leave our bodies and start down that final pathway to heaven. Sometimes they return to our bodies before reaching their destination. But something else happened to you. Your soul went to hers. At the moment you were hit by lightning, she was experiencing something just as traumatic. Perhaps it was that connection that united your souls."

"I see through her eyes, feel what she feels. It's like I'm inside her. It only lasts for a second."

Stella's eyes closed, and her fingers slid over his palm again. "Your destiny is entwined with this woman of the golden tresses and eyes the color of a stormy sky. Her life is in danger. If you seek her out, you may be able to save her. Or you may bring her even more risk."

"What kind of risk?"

Stella shook her head, coming out of her trance again. "I don't know. All I see is water."

He sat up straighter. "Water? Maybe that has something to do with a nightmare I keep having. I'm inside her soul, and suddenly I plunge into water. I fight to stay afloat, but eventually I tire out and sink into the blackness. When I can't hold my breath any longer, I feel the cold water rush into my lungs." He could feel the panic constricting his chest. "Then I wake up."

Stella's expression looked haunted. "The water I keep seeing is your nightmare. You're seeing her death."

Adrian snapped out of the memory, taking in a deep breath of air. He looked at the photograph again. Would she drown because of him, or could he save her? If Madame Blue existed, then he would find her. He realized then that he had no choice but to try. Adrian walked to the phone and set his travel agent to work.

The roar of flames engulfed Nikki Madsen, making her gasp great breaths as oxygen burned away. *It's only a nightmare,* her conscience intoned through the horror. *Wake up, Nikki; control the dream.*

She jerked awake, inhaling the clean air around her. Despite three years' distance, still she kept reliving the horror over and over again. Now the images came just once a month, the ripping heat of the orange fireball as it ravaged her, the feel of the dirt as she dropped into a bed of petunias and rolled the flames out. The sound of her cries filled her ears as she screamed for her mother, saw her engulfed in flames. The worst part was not being able to breathe; even in her dream, the choking sensation panicked her.

Nikki snapped on a switch and grabbed her teddy bear to cuddle in the pool of light that encompassed her bed. Trying to push away the memories, she pulled out the leather-bound journal that had indirectly saved her life that day. If she hadn't forgotten it, hadn't started leaving the car before it exploded, then her life would have been shattered into blazing bits like her mother's. If her father had been alive then, he would have been killed too. He had loved the fair, where they were headed, though Mother seemed only to indulge their whims.

The webbed scar tissue on the back of her hand looked faint now, but the memories would never fade. Her fingers caressed the blue leather covered with tiny cracks. Scarred, too, but from age. She felt more aged and worn than the journal would ever look.

Nikki had always been a vivid dreamer. At thirteen, she'd decided to learn more about the dream world and what it meant. That's when her dream journal came into existence, where she recorded the strangest of her dreams in order to decipher them. A few years ago she had mastered lucid dreaming, the ability to control her dreams and redirect them.

The journal had been the subject of one of her last conversations with her mother, Blossom. More like an argument, really. Now it seemed so silly to have argued over the journal and what it represented, but neither of them could have known how their lives would be ripped apart only days later.

Blossom had been sitting on the edge of Nikki's bed when she returned from one of her photography forays. Her mother hardly ever came in her room, but there she sat, holding Nikki's journal in her hands. Nikki felt violated and defensive as she set her camera on the dresser.

Blossom stood, wearing a cream silk pantsuit. Those beautiful eyes of hers took her daughter in and then seemed to spit her out. She set the journal on the bed and walked forward, taking Nikki's hands in her smooth ones.

"Nikki, Nikki, Nikki," she intoned through perfectly red lips. "You are my daughter."

Nikki had heard that tone in her voice before. "Yes, Mother."

"And you are a beautiful young lady—"

"I'm not beautiful. I'm okay."

Blossom's eyebrow, arched dramatically with a brown pencil, quivered. "Nikki, hear your mother out. I have been patiently waiting for my daughter to bloom. You're twenty-three now, and look at you. You're dressed like a homeless person! What would my friends say if they saw you like this? They'd say, 'Doesn't Blossom buy her daughter clothes? Hasn't Blossom schooled her daughter, given her an education and the opportunity to meet wealthy, ambitious young men?' Have I failed you in some way? Have I not set a good example for you to follow?"

Nikki walked over and picked up the journal. "What were you doing with this?"

For a moment Blossom had the dignity to look a little embarrassed. "I was merely cleaning up in here after coming up and finding you gone. I saw that and was curious."

"Why don't you just admit you were snooping?"

Her mother looked away for a moment. "If I was, it was for your own good. I worry about you, darling."

Nikki glanced down at her drab clothes. "Because I don't dress as nice as you do? I can't walk around taking photographs dressed in silk and linen. I have to blend in. Besides, it's impractical." She could never tell her mother just where she'd been taking photographs and why she had to blend in.

"But honey, you shouldn't have to be practical. You're a Madsen, poised to inherit millions in a few years. You should be dating, finding a nice man to marry. Then you can photograph your vacations and babies."

Nikki rolled her eyes. "I want a career in photography. I don't want to marry any one of those snobs from the country club. I want to be respected for my mind, for who I am, not for how pretty I can look at social functions." That was her mother's expertise. "Or for my bank account."

Blossom walked to the window with a long-suffering

sigh, watching the waves wash in from the Atlantic Ocean. "Your father would be so disappointed."

Nikki whirled around. "My father would be proud of me," her throaty voice said. "He was proud of my photography and encouraged me to pursue it." Even ten years after his death, she could still feel his encouragement from above.

.Blossom had turned at the fiery tone in Nikki's voice. "He was just humoring you. He wanted for you what I want."

"And exactly what is that, Mother?"

Blossom cocked her head and smiled. "You spend so much time alone; you don't date, you're consumed with this photography thing, you seem to live in this—this dream world." She gestured toward Nikki's journal. "We just want you to fit in, darling. That's all we've ever wanted."

Nikki laughed, though the words hurt. "You send me away for my high school years, then off to college, and you expect me to come back and fit right in?"

Her mother did her best at a laugh. "Darling, you've never fit in. Even when you were young, you never wore all those ruffly dresses I bought you, never had a lot of friends, never went to the school dances. I just wanted the best for you. And I still do. Your brother may be an idiot, but at least he's trying to fit into the Madsen mold, trying to follow in his father's footsteps. You should do the same."

Nikki saw how the pressure to fit that mold had made Devlin a little crazy, reckless even. He wanted too badly to prove himself, but he just didn't have the business sense their father had. She took the journal and returned it to the place her mother just happened to find it: tucked beneath her mattress.

"I don't want to fit the Madsen mold. I've got to live my life my way. I'm really sorry I let you down." Her voice caught in her throat, and she cleared it. "But I can't be the person you want me to be. The men you approve of bore me to death, and the others just want to get their hands on my money. I can't pretend to like dressing up for stuffy parties where everyone tries to outdo the other, where even the conversation is a put-on to sound impressive. Do you want that for me, Mother, to be married to a proper man I don't love, to exist in a place where I'm not happy, but you are?"

Blossom walked through the doorway and turned around. "I just want you to fit in where you belong. You've always been a rebel, Nikki. You need to grow up and join the real world."

Nikki tucked the book away, leaning her forehead against the leather. Maybe there was no place for her to fit in. Maybe she was destined to be a misfit her whole life. Or, did she fit in here? No, not even here. She lived a lie. What would her mother think now?

She smiled faintly, picturing the horror on her mother's porcelain face as Nikki changed from her silk nightgown into baggy denim pants and the faded lumberjack's shirt she'd bought at Goodwill. Peering out the tiny side window, she could see the first hint of the sun's rising. *What would you think now, Mother?*

Time to go before she was caught.

Nikki grabbed the glass cleaner and climbed out the back door of the plain, brown van parked at the rear of a used car lot in West Palm Beach. With three quick strokes, she wiped off the outrageous numbers she'd written in shoe polish the night before. Back inside, her fingers deftly pinned her long, blond curls back, tying a scarf over her head. She poured bottled water into a basin and brushed her teeth, tossing the foamy water out the back, then made her minuscule bed. After climbing into the driver's seat, she pulled out of the lot a full hour before it opened. Some of the used lots erected barbed-wire fences around their perimeters, limiting where she could park at night without being detected or towed away. She rotated between seven different spots, including alleys and hotel parking lots, to be sure she didn't arouse any attention.

Nikki pulled her camera from its hiding place beneath a towel and tucked it in the seat beside her. She had ten more shots to take before she could develop the roll.

Seamus, a skinny old man who was a regular in her photographs, was already out from whatever crevice he slept in at night. His white whiskers stood out against his dark skin. Beside him sat the baby stroller in which he toted all his worldly possessions. Nikki parked around back of the shopping center, nearly half vacant, and walked to where Seamus stood. His foot was propped on a bench, and he gestured during an animated conversation he had with no one. Sometimes he was lucid, and then there were days like this. She snapped a couple shots, showing that there was no one listening to his serious talk about the irony of war. She would call it, *Just because no one will listen does not make me silent.*

Chapter 2

Love is only a dream that death has shattered.

Adrian drove along Oceanview Drive with the top down on his rented Mustang, even though a cold front had blown in the night before. To a New Yorker, driving a convertible in November was like cheating Mother Nature. The sun-washed sky melded into the teal ocean, itself covered in white caps. On the left, Palm Beach's mansions of glory rose tall and proud to take in the view.

Palm fronds whipped in the stiff breeze, reminding him of a little girl making a sandcastle. Adrian pulled into the drive-way of the house he'd rented for his assignment last week. Everything was just as he'd left it a few days ago; even the shell necklace the Spanish girl had sold him still hung from the key hook. He wondered if he would have ended up like that, selling trinkets for money; his mother believed marrying Elio had saved them from that fate. Which fate was worse? Being homeless or getting beaten up?

Adrian sectioned off the map of the area, then pulled the four sheets of yellowed paper from his briefcase. He'd done the drawings a year ago when he worried that he might someday forget what Madame Blue looked like. They were all he had of her. Them, and the gallery he'd seen her walk into in one of his visions. That's where he would start.

It took only a few questions of the locals to pinpoint where the gallery was. The Wharf was what he would call an artsy-fartsy tourist stop with quaint souvenir shops, galleries, and cafes. It was in West Palm Beach and, despite the name and dockside appearance, actually sat across the street from the Intracoastal. Weathered gray planking and railings were accented by groups of pilings roped together and occasionally topped with a pelican, real or otherwise.

He had never seen the name of the gallery, but there were only five of them in the plaza. He spotted the fishing nets, the green Chinese float, and the basket of painted sand dollars out front. The Garcia Gallery.

This was it. Adrian had been here before, through Madame Blue's eyes. He buried his hands in the pockets of his leather jacket and walked inside. A string of silver bells on the door tinkled as they announced his entrance. The disappointment he felt as he looked around the cozy shop made him realize he'd subconsciously been expecting to see Madame Blue behind the white counter. The Latin man in his forties, straightening a painting in the far corner, was a poor substitute. But maybe he could help find her. The thin man turned at the sound of the bells and walked over to greet him.

"Hello, welcome to my gallery. I am Ulyssis Garcia. If you have any questions, please ask. Everything is done by local artists. A lot of talent, eh?" he asked, proudly gesturing with his arms.

Adrian nodded, reaching into the band of his jeans to pull out the sketches.

"Ah, you are an artist?" Ulyssis asked.

Adrian couldn't help the smile. "No, these aren't nearly good enough to sell. I'm a photographer from New York, and I met a young woman while on a shoot here about four years ago." Adrian touched his hand to his heart. "I haven't forgotten her, and now that I'm back in the area, I wanted to look her up. Unfortunately, I've lost her name and address. All I know is that she brought me here once. I thought perhaps you could help."

"Anything to help lovers," he said, leaning over to look at the drawings.

Adrian pulled the sketch of Madame Blue's face from the bottom. He hadn't brought the photograph because it was so obscured. "Have you seen her lately?"

Ulyssis's pleasant expression dripped away with such suddenness, Adrian pulled the sketch away. The owner grabbed a nearby rag and turned to dust the frame behind him. His profile revealed a sharp nose and tightened lips.

"No, I have never seen anyone like that." After a second, he turned back to face Adrian. With a wave of his hand, he said, "A thousand people come through here every week. If that woman did come in, especially four years ago, I don't remember."

Ulyssis seemed to put on a polite mask, but his posture remained rigid. Adrian leaned against the counter casually, not wanting to upset the man or sound like a cop.

"Sure, I understand. How long have you owned this shop, anyway?"

"Ten years." Ulyssis kept wiping the top of the gold frame over and over.

"Does anyone work for you?"

Ulyssis gave him a sidelong glance. "In season I hire someone to open up for me a couple of days a week." He nodded toward the sketch and shook his head. "I have never hired anyone who looked like that."

Adrian slowly folded the sketches again, forcing a smile. "You should. It might help business." He casually perused the wall of paintings beside him. Instinct told Adrian to drop the subject. Even with his back to Ulyssis, he could feel the man's eyes on him.

Adrian made his slow way around the gallery, and with a sigh, turned toward the door. Just a few feet away, a collection of black-and-white photographs caught his eye. An eerie feeling of familiarity washed over him. The prints themselves were poignant—the human side of the homeless. Uncomfortable to him particularly, because it was a state he and his mother had come close to after his father died. A peach card stated the photographer as Nicolina.

Ulyssis was furiously wiping at a spot on the counter when Adrian turned to ask, "Who is this Nicolina?"

"I don't remember. Those pictures have been there for five years." The man flipped his hand as if to dismiss them.

Adrian cocked an eyebrow. "And you've kept them up there all this time?"

"I've sold a few. The woman never came back to pick up her money." Ulyssis took a quick, impatient breath. "Why take them down? I might as well try to sell them."

"They're good. Very good. She's got some admirable techniques. I'd like to meet her, exchange ideas."

"I told you, she hasn't come back in almost five years. I have no idea where she is."

Adrian reached up and pulled one of the black frames off the wall. An old black man stood next to a baby stroller filled with what looked like his life possessions: a cup, a book, and some clothing. He had one foot propped on an old bench and was conversing with absolutely no one. The words at the bottom made his throat go dry. *Just because no one will listen does not make me silent.* A shiver worked its way down his back.

"I'll take this one."

Ulyssis tensed, as if he contemplated whether to sell it to him.

"It is for sale, isn't it?" Adrian pushed, pulling out a fifty from his eel skin wallet and setting it on the counter.

"Of course. It . . . it just happens to be my favorite. I

mean, I've gotten so used to it being there all these years."

Ulyssis placed the picture gently in tissue and handed Adrian the sealed box.

"I hope you enjoy it. And I'm sorry I couldn't help you with . . ." He nodded toward Adrian's stomach, where the sketches lay against his skin. "Perhaps she was just a tourist."

Ulyssis's smile was far from the genuine one Adrian had received when he first walked in the gallery. The man was hiding something, and Adrian had a feeling it had to do with Madame Blue. The thought made him crazy.

As soon as he reached his car, Adrian opened the box and looked at the picture again. Something about it reached out and took his heart in a firm hold. He stepped out of the car and walked back to the gallery. The bells on the door tinkled pleasantly. Ulyssis's smile faded when he saw who his customer was.

"I want the rest of them."

Ulyssis's dark brown eyes widened. "Of those?" He pointed to the collection of nine pictures with a gaping hole in the middle.

"Yes."

"I see. Well, of course. I will wrap them up for you."

Ulyssis slid a glance to Adrian every few minutes as he wrapped up each picture and set it in a larger box. He quickly taped the box shut and handed it to Adrian along with a receipt.

"I hope you enjoy them," he said with a forced politeness.

Adrian gave his most charming smile and said in a soft voice, "I will." Then he reached into his pocket and pulled out a business card. "If for some reason Nicolina shows up, will you give this to her? She has talent, and I can make her very successful with it."

Ulyssis gave the card a thorough once-over. "I doubt

she'll come in," he said, tucking the card beneath the cash register.

"You just never know."

Nikki wrapped her gray wool coat close around her as the frigid wind blasted her from over the ocean. The waves crashed in, creeping close to her faded boat shoes. The leather was already brittle from age and other assaults from salt water. They were the only shoes she had, save for a white pair of Keds.

She closed her eyes, smiling, ignoring her shivers. It wasn't often that her long hair was loose and free to be caressed by the wind. After a few moments her fear won over, and she tied a band around it and tucked it under the hood of her shawl again. If someone recognized her . . . she didn't want to think about that. Nikki knew she should cut her hair short, but she couldn't bear to part with that one little bit of her identity. The rest of her had been stripped away in the space of a minute.

The worst part was that she hadn't made peace with her mother before she'd died. The day before, Nikki had talked of moving out of the family mansion, and again, Blossom had used every manipulative power she possessed to get Nikki to stay a little longer. Why did she want Nikki to stay if she disgraced her mother so? She should have asked. But Nikki had been afraid that the answer wouldn't be the affirmation she sought so desperately from Blossom.

That morning as they left for the fair, with the vibes so stressed between her and Blossom, Nikki had resolved to reach out to her again, try to make her understand, to risk the rejection Blossom so readily dispensed. She'd planned to take her mother's hand at the fair and give her a smile that showed she loved her. If only she'd had a few more hours with her, if only she'd known . . .

She pushed that thought from her mind, reminding herself that it was peace she sought at the ocean, not regrets. It was a risk going there, she knew that. It was only a few days ago that she'd been down there, but the ocean called to her so often. Here, she fit in. The ocean, the seagulls, and the strangers never judged her, never expected anything from her. This was where she belonged.

Last time it had been sunny and cheerful, but today the late afternoon clouds cast a gloomy air over the beach. And last time there had been more people there. The crowd that gathered between her and the lifeguard station had put her on alert. She'd been too busy watching the restless waves to look ahead, and the crowd hadn't been there when she'd arrived four hours before.

At first Nikki thought it might be an accident, with onlookers circling others who were moving around with some kind of purpose. She had pulled her faded coat closer, hoping to become invisible. Most people didn't pay much attention to her anyway.

When she got closer, it became apparent that it wasn't an accident at all, but a photography shoot. Even though the winter winds whipped, the pictures were obviously being taken for a summer advertisement; the models were wearing gold Lycra bikini tops and jean shorts. They wore alluring smiles, but Nikki could well imagine the goosebumps the camera wouldn't pick up.

She had intended to keep walking by, but instead became one of the curious spectators. Glamour was something she hadn't been around in two years, and the women with makeup and windswept hair sparked a twinge of envy. Not that she'd ever been glamorous, but putting on makeup and dressing up now seemed as far-fetched as catching a ride on a spaceship to some distant planet.

Then a male voice, clear and deep, made a tomboyish girl leap from her spot behind the camera. "Get that seaweed out of here, Tracy. That stuff stinks."

Tracy collected the piles of seaweed as if it were discarded underwear, with the very tips of her fingers and a grimace. Nikki remembered Devlin, her brother, flinging the smelly tangles on her as a child, just to see her scream and cry. Then she got smart and learned that seaweed wasn't so bad. Well, so long as nothing was living in it. Or dead in it. When she didn't scream, he stopped throwing it on her. One of the models picked up a tangled mass and made a face, which the photographer caught on film.

Nikki could see only the photographer's back as his velvety voice coaxed the models into changing for the next set. He was tall, with wide shoulders, and he wore a leather cap over his dark hair. His baggy leather jacket enhanced the tightness of his jeans. He was wearing what looked like expensive leather shoes without socks, and on the beach yet!

"Come on, ladies. This is the last change, and we're done. Give me another smile. Ah, that's better."

A lanky blond put her hand on her almost nonexistent hip. "Easy for you to say, honey. You're wearing a jacket."

Without a word, he slipped out of his jacket to expose his black sweatshirt, and lifted his hands as if to say, 'See, I can handle it too.' The blond smiled theatrically and whirled around to join her two companions in the tiny cabana erected for the shoot. The photographer shook his head and continued adjusting his camera. It looked like a Hasselblad, similar to her own only newer. Her hand went to the square lump beneath her coat. She couldn't bear to watch any more and had slid from the group unnoticed.

Nikki shook herself out of her reverie. Would she ever feel pretty again? She pulled her coat tighter, taking a last deep breath of salty air before heading back. She needed a friend, and in her life, there were precious few of them.

Ceil was probably at the grocery store scarfing free samples or at the Lord's Shelter. That left Ulyssis.

Ulyssis grinned as Nikki stepped inside the art gallery. Beyond his smile, though, she could sense something amiss. Three silver-haired ladies were admiring a flowery painting of a little girl by a pond. Nikki wandered toward the back corner, aware of how out of place she looked in the gallery. *You'll never fit in, Nikki*, she could hear her mother's voice saying. Why couldn't she hear the nice things her mother had said, instead of being haunted by her condescending words? When the ladies left, she turned to Ulyssis.

"Did they even look at my pictures?" she asked, staring up at her collection—or where her collection had been. "Wait a minute. Did you move them?" Her heart felt a stabbing pain. "Or don't you want to carry them anymore?" More than pain, she felt panic. Those pictures were her only income, and even that was sparse sometimes.

Ulyssis walked over and stood next to her, wringing his hands nervously. He was going to tell her that he didn't have room for her shots anymore. They were too depressing, too real. Nikki swallowed hard, gathering her courage to face his words.

Finally he touched her arm with his incredibly smooth hand. "Of course I want to show them, Nicolina. Your pictures may not appeal to every buyer, but they catch the attention and curiosity of everyone who sees them."

She forced a smile, then gave a puzzling look at the blank space covered with ten hooks. "What happened to them?"

"I sold them."

Her eyes widened. "All of them? At one time, to one buyer?"

"Yes," he said, still strangely solemn.

She grasped his hands and jumped up and down a little. "That's wonderful!"

"It's the man who bought them that has me a little worried."

He held out the business card, an opaque plastic material with a modern typeface. *A. Wilde, Visions, Inc.* She fingered the raised blue ink, giving him a shrug.

"What has you worried?" she asked.

"Have you ever heard of him?"

"No. He's from New York. I've only met a few photographers, and they were local."

"He came in asking about a woman he'd met four years ago. She'd brought him in this gallery, he said. He showed me a sketch he'd made of her. Nicolina, it was you."

That familiar ache began forming in the pit of her stomach. Fear, the feeling of being prey. Her voice cracked as it left trembling lips. "Me? It couldn't have been. I wasn't seeing anyone four years ago, especially not someone from New York. He must have met someone who looked like me. It was only a sketch, Ulyssis."

"That's what I thought too. And as he was about to leave, he stopped and looked right at your collection. He stood there for a long time just looking at them, and when he turned around, it was as if he'd seen a ghost. Then he asked me if I knew the photographer. I told him those had been there for years, and I hadn't heard from Nicolina in a long time. He bought one, the old black man with the stroller. Then he came back a few minutes later and bought the rest. He left me his card and said that if you were to come in by chance, that he could make you successful."

The business card dropped from her fingers, and Ulyssis picked it up. Nikki realized that her mouth was hanging open, and she quickly closed it. "But there couldn't be a connection. He doesn't know me, and even if he was hired to find me, how could he think I took those shots? Ulyssis,

I never told anyone but you that I took pictures of the homeless. God, Mother would have had me quietly institutionalized if she knew I went to that side of town." Nikki swallowed the lump that had formed in her throat. "There's no way he could connect me to those pictures. You're the only one who calls me Nicolina." She didn't want to believe that someone was after her again, not after all this time. For two years, after the investigation and trial, she had lived on the streets. Her sentence was two more years, and ironically, it was the only place she felt safe.

When Ulyssis handed Nikki her part of the sale, his thin hand held hers. He looked relieved. "You're right, of course. I'm just being paranoid. I'm sorry to worry you. After all, he didn't seem to connect your pictures with the girl in the sketch, who probably just looked a little like you. And if he were hired to find you, he would have pictures of you, not just a sketch. Besides, I called the number. It seems to be legitimate. The answering service said that Visions, Inc. has been around for five years. Don't give it another thought. You know I worry too much about you. But be careful, maybe a little more than usual, okay?"

She thought of her recent forays to the beach, but didn't mention them. "I will, I promise."

"Good." He looked at the card. "If he is legit, maybe you should keep his card. In two years, when you're free to return to society, you might want to call him up."

She took the card. "Maybe. It can't hurt, anyway."

"Your latest batch is probably dry by now. Choose the next ten you want displayed, and I'll frame them for you."

"Thanks," she said, meaning it in many ways. She headed to the darkroom Ulyssis had set up for her two years ago when she realized she had to trust someone from the other world. He had proven to be a trustworthy friend, and without him, she would be picking through dumpsters and living on samples like Seamus and Ceil. As she pulled her prints down from the clips, she wondered about the mysterious man who had bought her pictures. She couldn't think of anything that would give her away. The man didn't have a photograph of her, nor did he use her name. If he were hired, surely he would have given Ulyssis that information.

Nikki walked into the back room to her drying cabinet, fashioned from a hanging wardrobe closet. She tried not to think of Devlin, but sometimes she remembered him at the oddest moments. Like now, as she pulled the photographs down from her clothespins, she remembered finding Devlin in her makeshift darkroom at the mansion, looking at the drying prints.

"What are you doing here?" she'd asked, annoyed that he'd trespassed in her private sanctuary. Even Blossom didn't venture into that wing. Nikki was just glad that particular batch wasn't of the homeless area.

He looked a little startled, but recovered quickly. With his dark brown hair and beady eyes of the same color, he looked nothing like her, but just like their mother. Nikki had her father's light coloring.

"I just wanted to see what you were up to, what you do when you hide out over here."

"I don't hide out." Why did she always sound so defensive? She smiled to diffuse the words. "I just need peace and quiet when I work."

Devlin wandered over to a table where she laid out her photographs to choose which ones she'd try to consign at Ulyssis's gallery, another secret. She wished he'd leave so she wouldn't feel scrutinized.

"You're actually pretty good, kid."

She stood there, waiting for the punch line. It didn't come.

"Y-you think so?"

"Well, I'm no expert, but they're good as far as I can

tell. You should try to sell them.''

She had been selling them, but she'd never shared her small triumphs with her family. Devlin wasn't putting her on. It was the first time she could ever remember him complimenting her.

''Maybe I'll do that. Thank you.''

He started to leave, but turned and leaned against the doorway. ''You really love doing that, don't you?'' he asked, nodding toward the table.

''Yes, I do.'' It seemed so strange to talk about what she loved with her brother.

''Mother seems to think your photography is silly, but you're serious about it.''

''Very.''

''Well, I have to give you one thing: You're doing what you want, not what Mother wants.''

Nikki had never felt close to Devlin, but for some reason she felt compelled to open a tiny bit of herself to him. ''And my prize for doing that is I eternally disappoint her.''

''Everyone disappoints her.'' His lips thinned, then he smiled. ''I got to thinking that I've never seen your work. I don't even know what you take pictures of. So I came up here to see.''

''I didn't think anyone cared to see my work, so I only showed them to Dad.''

''You miss him, don't you?''

''More than anyone will ever know.''

''You were his favorite. I could always tell that.'' At her protest he said, ''It's okay. I got used to it.'' He smiled, not that persuasive or cocky smile, but a genuine one. ''I don't even know you. I knew you took pictures, but didn't realize how much it meant to you until I saw that look on your face when you saw me up here.''

''We live separate lives, even though we live under the same roof.''

"When Jack and I get together, he tells me this and that about you, and it sounds like he's talking about a stranger. Maybe we can remedy that before one or both of us finally gets enough nerve to move out of this house and loses complete touch."

"Okay," she'd whispered, totally stunned.

That was three months before her life was ripped apart. She'd never been able to figure out exactly what he'd been getting at.

Adrian sat at the oak table, his black boots propped on the edge, studying the black-and-white prints. His gaze kept wandering back to the picture he'd taken of Madame Blue—Nicolina.

"This is crazy, Wilde." He stood, pacing the tile floor. "I'm a thousand miles from what I should be doing, asking about some woman whose soul is supposedly connected to mine. Maybe my aunt is crazy, like Ma's been saying all these years." His ride through the tunnel, his feeling as though he had sunk through Nicolina's flesh and into her bloodstream, and the visions he'd had through her eyes since, they were real. He glanced at Nicolina again. Though her face was somewhat obscured, he knew—*knew*—it was her. He looked at the photographs again. And he also knew, somehow, that she'd taken these pictures. So maybe he was crazy.

Adrian dropped down in the chair with a sigh. His fingers found the print again. If he could find her, just to know that she really existed, then he could go back to his life. He would just leave it at that.

The ten framed pictures were scattered over the table's surface. Adrian picked up the one of the black man having an animated conversation with the air. The man at the art gallery said the pictures had been there for years. His strange behavior from the moment he'd seen the sketch had

Adrian wondering. And the man had actually seemed reluctant to part with the pictures that should have been an eyesore after all that time with no sales.

The glass in the picture reflected Adrian's face, showing his thick eyebrows furrowed in thought. He picked up another picture, a run-down building with boarded up storefronts and two doors flung open. Inside two black people sat on folding chairs, dressed in their Sunday best. Above the doorway a sign read, "The Dedicated Deliverance Church of Jesus, Inc."

Besides theme, the photographs all seemed to have something else in common: location. They were taken in a deserted-looking area of town, maybe across the waterway in nearby West Palm Beach. Another picture showed an impromptu sidewalk sale in front of a used car lot. In the background an old Buick was pulling out of the lot. It was obviously not a test drive, because the car had a license plate.

Adrian held the picture closer, trying to read the date on the expiration sticker. If only he could get a handle on how long ago these had been taken, he could believe the gallery owner and assume Nicolina had taken off for parts unknown. He extracted the print from the frame, then removed his loupe from the camera bag. Holding it under the bright lights in the kitchen, he studied the numbers. His heartbeat stopped for a second. The tag expired the following year. These prints had been taken recently.

Within a few minutes, Adrian was in his rental car, the framed photographs on the seat beside him. It only took a few inquiries to ascertain the area where they had been taken. He left the clean, pristine area of Palm Beach and drove into West Palm Beach just a few minutes away. Not far from the mansions and elegance lurked the poor area of town. His sense of familiarity came from the pictures he'd studied. Many of the stores were permanently closed and boarded up, with weeds growing rampant where landscaping had once flourished.

When Adrian passed the black man with the stroller, he nearly slammed on his brakes. He pulled into the nearest parking lot and grabbed the photograph Nicolina had taken of him. Pulling on his leather jacket, Adrian stepped out of his Mustang and walked over to the man who was humming faintly.

"Hello?" he asked. "Excuse me?"

The black man slowly turned his head to Adrian, then smiled absently. Adrian noticed first the stench of the man, who hadn't bathed in some time. The man was wearing a dingy, worn sweater, and shivered from time to time in the chilly air. Adrian didn't want to notice anything else, and pulled the print from behind him.

"Who took this picture of you?"

The man squinted, his watery brown eyes trying to focus. "It was warmer back then. Gets colder every year."

Adrian glanced at the photograph. "How long ago was this taken? Do you remember a pretty lady taking this picture of you?"

The man smiled, though Adrian couldn't tell if it was because he remembered her, or for some reason unknown to Adrian. He did look at the picture again, his yellow teeth showing in his smile.

"Pretty," he said.

"Yes, she's very pretty." Adrian pulled out the sketch he'd drawn. "She looks like this. Have you seen her? Listen, I don't want to hurt her. I . . . I just want to find her."

The man smiled again, then scratched his oily hair with grimy fingers. "Camera," he stated, as if proud he could remember the name.

"Yes, camera." Adrian took out his own camera and took a picture, hoping to jar the man's memory more. "She took a picture of you like this.'' He looked around. ''Maybe right here. This picture.''

The man didn't look at Nicolina's picture, but seemed fascinated with Adrian's camera. As his gnarled fingers reached for the shiny equipment, Adrian pulled it away.

''Picture. Pretty.'' Then his smiled disappeared, and the yellowed whites showed when his eyes widened. His voice rose. ''Ship capsized. Men screaming. Pray. Pray!'' He dropped his head down. ''Nothing left.''

Adrian didn't know what to say to the man, but somehow didn't feel right just walking away from him. ''Are you all right?''

''All dead.'' He looked down at his trembling fingers. ''Seamus hungry,'' he said in a plaintive voice, his hand over his stomach. Then he clutched the cracked handles of his baby stroller and turned away, mumbling.

Adrian had always been annoyed by beggars, but this man wasn't begging. He caught up with Seamus and handed him a ten-dollar bill. The man looked questioningly at Adrian.

''Get something to eat,'' Adrian ordered, then quickly returned to his car.

He sat there for a few minutes, staring at the photograph of the man who called himself Seamus. Adrian had worked hard for financial security, wanting to get as far away from his past and those fears as he could. But what if his mind went and he squandered his money? He shook away the fears and pulled out of the parking lot.

Adrian returned to the pink house he'd rented, exhausted after hours of walking the streets. He didn't care about the hundred dollars he'd paid for information, but it had reaped nothing but dead ends. And there was the streetwalker who'd been pissed off because he'd asked her about another woman instead of taking her up on a twenty-five-dollar blow job. Most people had nothing to say to him, scared off by his outsider looks. He looked down at his designer jeans, his leather boots and jacket. No, he didn't fit in. He didn't want to fit in.

Adrian got a cold chill when he realized something. What would Nicolina's reaction be to him when or if he found her? He looked at her picture. She obviously lived somewhere down there, though it was still hard to believe after seeing the mansion in that tunnel. But she was there somewhere, and that gallery owner was lying to cover her existence. Why? Had that explosion of heat and fury shattered her life and sent her to the streets?

He looked at the prints again, knowing the answer to finding Nicolina lay in them. The only way to get any answers on her whereabouts was to become one of them, to blend in. His Uncle Carlo had taught him about blending into the background when he followed fraudulent workers' compensation claimants. Adrian's fingers clenched on the leather armchair at the thought of living that life, even if only in pretend. To occupy them, he pulled a cigarette out of the pack and lit it with the gold lighter Rita had given him for Christmas, even allowing himself a third drag before crushing it out.

He stood up and walked to the window, looking at the lighted yard across the street from him. Here beauty and cleanliness surrounded him—everything he'd been used to for the last several years. There, on the streets of West Palm Beach, he would be surrounded by the fears that haunted his early childhood.

He thought of Seamus, the hooker, and the dozen characters he'd asked about Nicolina. Could he really live among them, as if he were one of them? It seemed so much easier to go back to New York City. Back to his life, his job. Surely Stan Fiske, his agent, would be having fits by now, realizing Adrian was out of town without a trace. But if he called Stan, he'd have to give him some explanation, and Adrian didn't feel like inventing some cockeyed story for him at that moment.

Adrian also knew that he couldn't walk away from Madame Blue. Not now, when he'd found she really existed. He at least had to find her, to satisfy his years of curiosity. It was easier to forget and go back home, but Adrian knew that wasn't a choice. So tomorrow, he would become a homeless person and find Nicolina.

Chapter 3

What is dark and scary to you is my home; though you call it ugly and dangerous, it is my sanctuary.

In two days Adrian had the makings of a beard and a new wardrobe from Goodwill. He'd had everything washed twice, raising more than one eyebrow as he'd taken the ratty clothes to a laundromat to wash and fold the clothes for him. When he'd handed the girl behind the counter a fifty, his hand was shaking a little.

That morning he put on the old blue jeans, faded black shirt, and worn sneakers. The only things he left on from his normal life were his Calvin Klein briefs and his gold chain with the cross on it. Fingering the cross, given to him by his Aunt Stella, Adrian figured he could use all the help he could get.

It was a chilly morning, though he still put the top down on his convertible. His hair was loose, and he absently scratched at the beard to which he was unaccustomed. He drove down Oceanview Drive, drawing in the salty air as one does before entering an airless place. He found a busy parking lot not far from Nicolina's part of town and walked the several blocks to the city.

Even though he had purpose in being there, it couldn't

appear that way. Most of the people who stood around looked as though they were waiting for the earth to drop out and swallow them. Adrian slowed his pace and took a deep breath.

A big black man leaned against a bundle of garbage bags that Adrian assumed was out for trash pickup. As Adrian walked by, he realized that bundle was the man's life, his very existence. He eyed Adrian suspiciously as he walked by, spreading his bulk a little more over his bags.

The Lord's Shelter was Adrian's first stop. The front door was open, but he was met by a man his age wearing a sweater and dress pants. He had blond hair and wore glasses, maybe an associate preacher or the like.

"I'm sorry, but we're at capacity right now," he told Adrian in a soft, sympathetic voice. "But we're serving soup and hot biscuits at noon if you'd like to come back then."

"Th-thank you, I appreciate that." Adrian felt silly standing there, perceived as a beggar grateful for soup, when he had a thick steak waiting at home for him. "I'm looking for someone; can I take a look around to see if she's here?"

"She?" the man asked, a surprised expression on his face.

"Yes. I met her here a few years ago, and wondered if she was still in the area."

The man seemed to think about that, then stepped aside. "You're welcome to take a look around for a minute. We don't allow anyone in the sleeping quarters after eight o'clock in the morning, so she'll be in the main area if she's here. But please, only a minute."

Adrian put his hand on the man's shoulder as he walked in. "Thank you."

He walked inside, confirming his first thought that this had been a church before. In the main room tables were scattered about, and the people sitting at those tables had listless expressions on their faces. Sad faces. Adrian wished he'd brought his camera, and he now understood why Nicolina photographed the homeless. Their hopelessness was a sad reminder of this part of society. Sunlight streamed in through the jalousie windows on both sides, giving millions of dust motes a stage in which to dance. Adrian scanned the room, but didn't see Nicolina anywhere. As he headed out, the apparent manager of the mission called out, "Don't forget lunch! Hot soup."

Adrian nodded, wondering if maybe Nicolina might be there for some soup later. He stepped over a sleeping man and continued down the sidewalk.

By afternoon, he had visited the other shelters in the area, and although they were all full, he was allowed in to have a cup of coffee and take a look around. He returned to the Lord's Shelter for a bowl of soup and another look. As he ate the tasteless broth and chunks of vegetables, he thought of a recent dinner he'd had at Carmine's in New York, the table covered with huge plates of bountiful Italian dishes. So much food, it went to waste.

"We have a men's Bible study tonight," a voice said from behind.

Adrian turned around to see the man he'd met earlier. "No, thanks. I'm looking for a woman." At the man's shocked expression, he added, "That friend I mentioned earlier. I . . . er, just moved down from New Jersey, for a job that didn't materialize. I know my friend used to live around here."

The man sat down next to him. "I'm Dave, by the way. I run this place. What's your friend's name? Maybe I can help."

"No, that's all right." Adrian stood up. "Thanks for the soup."

"You're welcome. If you change your mind about the

Bible study, we meet here at seven, after the evening meal. Come for spaghetti and learn about the Bible with us. If you find your friend, why don't you invite her to join our women's study group. We don't have many, as you can see.''

Dave gestured toward the place the pulpit used to be. A table and group of chairs sat beneath a large gold cross and stained glass windows. And sitting at that table alone, in a shower of muted colors cast by the sun, a woman leaned over a Bible. Her long, blond hair hung in curls like a curtain around her, and a slender hand swept a strand of it behind her ear.

Adrian stood mesmerized by the woman, his heart crushing under a great pressure. Dave turned to follow his gaze, breaking Adrian out of his spell. He cleared his throat.

"Maybe I will come back for that Bible study, Dave. What time did you say it met?''

Dave's fair face lit into a smile. "Seven.''

Adrian nodded toward the woman. "She's the only one in the women's Bible study group?''

"Sometimes we have two or three. There aren't as many women on the streets as there are men. She comes every week and reads the Word for an hour, no matter how many people come.''

"Who is she?'' Adrian's voice had lowered to a whisper, and he cleared his throat again.

"Nikki.'' Dave shrugged. "Don't know her last name. I don't think I know anyone's last name around here.''

Adrian held out his hand to Dave. "My name's Adrian. Adrian Nash.'' He doubted anyone around here had heard of his photography, but he didn't want to take any chances, especially now that he'd found her. Nicolina. Nikki. *She really exists.*

"Welcome, Adrian. I'm Dave Watts.''

Adrian pulled his gaze away from Nikki again, focusing

on Dave. "Wish we were meeting under better circumstances."

"I hope you get another job soon. Until then, we're here if you need us." He glanced around at the room. "There's room now if you want to hang out and read. We've got books and magazines over there on the shelves. Beds are given on a first come, first get basis tonight if you need a place to sleep." Dave smiled, then walked over to the shelves to help an elderly woman who was trying to reach a book.

Adrian watched Nikki, letting it sink in that he'd found her. Wasn't that what he wanted, just to find her, to know she existed? He took a step closer, feeling it somehow appropriate to find her in this holy place. He clenched his fingers, watching her lean back in her chair. He could hear the memory of her heartbeat as he'd passed from the tunnel into her soul. Was finding her enough? Could he walk away now? He took another step closer, finding it difficult to breathe. No. It wasn't enough.

Stella's words drifted through his mind. *Your destiny is entwined with this woman of the golden tresses and eyes the color of a stormy sky. Her life is in danger. If you seek her out, you may be able to save her. Or you may bring her even more risk.*

Her life was in danger. Was that why she hid on the streets? Could he risk bringing her more danger? Walk away, that's what he should do. He turned around, closing his eyes for a moment. That horrible drowning nightmare lurked ever near to his conscious, and he thought of that angelic woman breathing in the cold water. His presence in her life might bring that death to her, or it might save her. Walk away or face his destiny. His hands felt clammy, his throat dry. Walk away or stay?

He turned around again. She was immersed in her reading, not even noticing his struggle. He walked nearer, and his breathing eased. She looked up briefly, then burrowed back in the Bible, obviously ignoring him or probably hoping he wasn't approaching her. Adrian remained there, feeling an enormous sense of déjà vu as he watched her. Those images in the tunnel flashed through his mind like a movie. She was the woman in those images, and she was the woman in the photograph.

He wanted to reach out and touch her hair, touch her skin, her hand, anything, just to make sure she was real. He also knew that would violate any trust she might ever have in him, so he remained there waiting for her to acknowledge him. Every second seemed balanced on a fine wire. To say a word, to move any closer, would shatter that balance.

Adrian didn't have to say anything. Nikki's fingers nervously toyed with the edge of the delicate paper, then she looked up at him. The blast of emotion at seeing her for the first time in the flesh made him take a step back. Part of her soul lived within his; he had felt her heartbeat surrounding him. She was more beautiful than he ever imagined. Her haunting green eyes seemed filled with all the mysteries of the rain forest, tinged with the gray of rain clouds. Her full lips were slightly parted in surprise, as if she were about to say something but nothing would come. He found that suddenly his voice didn't work either.

More unnerving than the feeling you were being watched was looking up to find the watcher standing only a few feet away blatantly staring at you. Nikki looked at the man who stood by the cherry wood railing and who appeared as surprised as she felt. Even more unnerving was that he had the most gorgeous eyes she had ever seen. It seemed insane to even notice something like that after all this time. Bedroom eyes, dark brown, sloped to give them warmth. Dark, straight eyebrows formed a ridge above them.

Her first instinct was to look away and ignore the man,

as she had ignored the many men who strayed in here from time to time. She felt paralyzed, unable to draw her gaze away from him. There was something about him, something undefinable that shivered through her body and made her heart quicken. Then he smiled. He had sensuous lips surrounded by a soft-looking beard, and a smile that filled his eyes with compassion.

"Is this where the Bible study meets?" he asked in a velvety voice.

She blinked, trying to break out of his spell, and glanced down at the Bible in her hands. "Uh, this group is for women only." Nikki glanced at the empty chairs. "It's a small group today."

He smiled again. "I can see that."

"I think the men's group meets later tonight. You can ask Dave about it. He's the guy in the white sweater."

"I'll do that." But he didn't leave.

What was it about him that gave her a funny feeling inside? When he finally lifted himself from the railing, she felt a peculiar longing and buried herself back in her Bible. The man walked around and sat by her at the table. Despite her strange feelings, she wished he would go away. In her world, she could trust no one, not even if he was handsome and had compassionate eyes. For some reason, the rudeness she was always able to summon did not come. She wanted to ignore him, but she found herself looking at him.

"I'm Adrian Nash." He held out his hand to her.

She looked at his hand, large and strong, suspended over the table. When she had decided to ignore the gesture, her hand moved hesitantly to his without her permission. His hand was warm and soft, and that warmth seeped down her arm and into her stomach.

"I'm Nikki," she almost whispered back, finding the will to look back at the pages. The words swam in front of her. Her hand tingled from his touch. She couldn't remember ever having that happen, even when her life was normal. Even when she'd first met Jack Barton.

His finger grazed the binding on the Bible. That action made her stomach clench, as if he were touching her.

"Have you ever read this from front to back?" he asked.

She shook her head, pushing away her mind's straying thoughts. "No. Have you?"

"Yep. My father made me when I was a kid."

She lifted an eyebrow. "Are you a preacher?"

He laughed out loud, lighting up his whole face. She noticed slight dimples that disappeared beneath his brown beard. "No, not quite. I'm a construction worker. I came down here because a friend said there was plenty of work. When I got here, there was no work and no friend. I guess he went somewhere else looking for work. Right now I have nothing. I sold what little I had to come down here. I figured I could hang out with him until I found a job and a place of my own."

From his build and olive skin, she could believe he was a construction worker much more easily than she could imagine him a preacher. "You should go somewhere else. You don't want to live here like this." She gestured vaguely behind her. She'd seen some of them come and stay for years, living on nothing more than hope. "You don't seem like one of the usuals around here."

He looked thoughtful at that, tapping his long fingers on the table. The waves of his dark hair looked soft and shiny and made her think of an advertisement she'd seen in a magazine recently. She noticed the muscles at his wide, masculine jawbone tense.

"You don't seem like a usual around here either."

Nikki stood then, gently closing the Bible and placing it on the battered table. "I have to go." She really had to go. The way he made her feel . . . it was too eerie.

He stood, too, but didn't try to keep her there. "Don't you stay here?"

"No. Goodbye."

Every part of her wanted to go back, but she couldn't trust anyone, not even those who drew her to them. Besides, the feeling was probably because it had been a long time since she'd seen a gorgeous man up close. It couldn't be anything else. Without looking back, she left the Lord's Shelter and headed toward her own shelter parked behind the building.

The next morning Nikki foisted the plastic bag with her dirty clothes onto the dryer with a resounding thud. The laundromat was open-aired, with only a roof for protection from the elements. Still, the equipment was stained with rust, though whoever owned it kept it running and clean inside and out. The snack machines had been removed a year ago when vandals kept smashing the glass and making off with the goodies inside. She longed for a good old Snickers bar.

After sorting the darks and whites, she put a dollar's worth of quarters into the slots and started the first machine. Four years ago, she'd never even smelled laundry detergent; the maid seemed like an elf, whisking away their dirty clothes and returning them in neat piles or on hangers.

When she heard the scuffling noise, Nikki whirled around. "Crackers!" She knelt down to the mutt and scratched his head, then pulled out the food for which he'd been named. Crackers was only a puppy, a lab mix, she guessed, the mix being some smaller dog. He lived somewhere in the area, though he wore no tag and always looked a little bony. She scratched his head as he slurped on another cracker.

"You sure make my laundry days nicer, sweetie." His tail whipped from side to side, carrying his whole back end with it. "I wish I could keep you, but it would be impossible."

She hugged him, despite the fact that he was dirty and probably riddled with fleas. That summer she'd give him a few impromptu baths beneath a faucet out back. He'd been so soft and clean afterward, and she swore he looked happier for it. Now it was too cold to get him wet.

After the food was gone, Crackers wandered around sniffing the area, and Nikki searched through the library of books that had been forming for the last year. Thank goodness thieves didn't consider books worth stealing. Nikki had started the library, installing a shelf and donating the first paperback. The following week, the book was gone, and she was disappointed that her idea wasn't going to make it. The next week, another book had appeared, and after that, the little library had built so that there was always a new book to read while she waited for her laundry to get done. She wrapped her coat around herself and settled in a plastic chair with a new Judith McNaught romance.

She was two chapters into the book when Crackers barked sharply and started running through the empty lot toward the road. A scruffy-looking cat on the other side sauntered toward the shopping center and jumped on a window ledge, but that didn't deter Crackers any. It was an overcast day, and the puppy's beige coat blended in with the dirt he was running over. When Nikki heard the car's engine, her heart jumped.

A white Mustang pulled around the corner. The car wasn't going very fast, and perhaps if he'd been going faster, Crackers would have made it across the street safely. Nikki screamed as she watched the car swerve. Crackers hit the bumper and was knocked across the street where he lay on the dirt. She ran crying across the empty lot, calling Crackers's name, and watching the car continue around the corner. She didn't have enough time for anger that the driver didn't stop. The dog lay still, his leg at an odd angle and bloodied. She cradled him in her arms, and he whimpered softly.

"Crackers, don't die. Please don't die." He was a mangy mutt to anyone else, but he was a friend to Nikki.

"Nikki, what happened?" She looked up to see Adrian running across the lot toward her, his face white.

"Someone hit Crackers," she said through her tears. "And then they just left." She stroked the dog's snout, her fingers trembling.

He moved her hand away. "He might bite you. Not on purpose, but because he's scared." Adrian reached down and grabbed hold of the shirt he wore beneath his blue sweater, ripping the bottom portion off. He wrapped it around Crackers's mouth, then knelt down and inspected him. "I don't see anything too serious. His leg might be broken. Let me get him to a vet. Do you know where the closest one is?"

She had already been thinking that, and quickly said, "The animal hospital is about ten blocks away. I can take you there."

He looked at her, and she didn't care if he thought she was silly. She didn't realize how much Crackers had come to mean to her. Taking her by surprise, he reached over and wiped away her tears with his thumb.

"Don't worry. We're going to do everything we can to save him." Then that compassion she'd seen in his eyes turned to business as he scanned the area. "I need a board to put him on in case he has a back injury."

Nikki ran to the laundromat structure where the old sign still leaned against the back wall. With supreme gentleness, Adrian slid the pup onto the board, then hefted both. His muscles strained the material of the bulky sweater he was wearing.

"Do you want me to help carry him?" she asked as they

headed in the direction she'd indicated.

"No, I've got him. Just . . . hold his paw or something.''

She kept stroking Crackers's head and whispering sweetly as they hurriedly walked the ten blocks to the hospital. Adrian felt like the biggest goon on earth. That dog had come out of nowhere, and he'd tried so hard to miss him. His heart had sunk when he'd heard the thump. But he'd also heard Nikki's scream, and when he saw her running toward the puppy, he had to keep going. How could he explain driving a rental car like that if he didn't have a job? So he did the next best thing, which was pull into a back alley behind some brown van and pretend that he'd just been walking by. Her crying nearly crushed him inside.

"He didn't even stop," she was saying, shaking her head. "It wasn't his fault, but he could have stopped."

Adrian stepped up their pace, feeling guilt press down on him. Was this foreshadowing the risk he would bring to her? "Maybe he was in a hurry or didn't really know he'd hit him. You said he swerved."

She let out a sigh, continuing to pet the puppy. "Yeah, maybe. But if I ever see that car again, I'm going to throttle the driver."

"Did you see who was driving? Was it a man or a woman?"

"I'm not sure. All I could see was dark hair—like yours. It was sort of long, so maybe it was a woman."

Adrian sniffed; his hair was only just past his shoulder. "Well, you know those women drivers." She eyed him, but didn't respond. Her attention was fully absorbed by the pup.

"It doesn't matter what gender they were," she said, still looking at the dog. Her lower lip trembled. "Why couldn't they have stopped? What is wrong with people? Why are they so cruel? People just don't care about anything anymore! A human life, or the life of an innocent animal, is nothing to them!'' Her eyes narrowed, and she was staring into the distance. ''Especially if they gain something from it.''

Adrian knew her anger went far deeper than some uncaring heel not stopping after hitting a dog. He paused, but it took her several moments to realize he had. She turned around, seeming to focus in on the present.

''Nikki, are you all right? No one hit this dog to gain anything by it.''

She wrapped her arms around herself and glanced down. ''I know that.''

Nikki started walking again, very slowly. After a minute Adrian picked up his pace. When they reached the hospital, the doctor took the puppy in right away. Nikki paced like a worried parent, and Adrian stood at the window cursing himself for not swerving fast enough, and for the charade that wouldn't let him just drive them to the hospital. He wanted a cigarette badly, and was almost desperate enough for something in his mouth that the dog biscuits on the counter looked tempting.

''You don't have to wait here with me,'' she said, breaking him out of his trance of guilt. ''I mean, I appreciate your help. I'm not sure I could have carried him all this way without collapsing.''

He was sure she couldn't; Crackers was a big puppy, especially when he was dead weight. Unconscious weight, he quickly corrected.

''I don't mind. I know you're worried.''

She was worried sick, he could tell. She twisted her hands and paced, glancing at the door Crackers had been taken through. He wanted to make sure the puppy was all right so he could see relief replace the grief on her expression. Red tear tracks marred her lovely skin, and red rimmed her green eyes. Her wavy hair was braided in the back; she'd had it tucked beneath her coat earlier. He noticed then that she had blood on her hands.

He took her hand, but she jerked away from him. The mistrust in her eyes nailed a spike through his heart, though he couldn't blame her. He just wanted to help her; nothing more.

"You've got blood on your hands," he said, and she lifted them. "I didn't mean to startle you."

"I should wash them," she said, her voice an unnatural pitch. She asked an employee where the bathroom was and disappeared inside.

Adrian quickly walked up to the counter. "I want to pay for the bill, but I don't want her to know." He nodded toward the bathroom. Handing the receptionist a hundred-dollar bill, he said, "Put this toward the bill. If it's more, I'll come back in tomorrow and pay the rest."

The pretty blond eyed him as she took his money. "Is the dog yours? Or hers?"

"Neither. But she cares about that dog, and I don't want her to feel responsible for the bill. Just tell her there's no charge since the dog's not hers, or whatever you want."

The woman smiled, but he didn't miss the appraisal she gave his attire. He didn't care, as long as that dog was all right.

It had been a long time since Nikki had experienced this kind of agonized wait in a sterile place. Last time it was in a courthouse, two years ago, with reporters clamoring for a juicy tidbit and everyone else looking at her with pity. She forced herself to sit down on the black leather couch, but watching Adrian pace near the desk didn't settle her nerves at all. His hands were jammed in his pockets, stretching the faded linen of his blue pants tightly across his buttocks. He had taken his sweater off and rolled the sleeves up on his too-large white shirt, showing strong fore-arms. He glanced at her every few minutes, and she quickly averted her gaze, pretending for the umpteenth time to study the chart of dog breeds on the wall.

It was silly to even notice a man that way. More so, it was rarer yet to find such a specimen in her world. Most of the men her age who came through this part of town were into drugs, evident by trembling hands and the glazed look in their eyes. Adrian was healthy, and his warm, brown eyes were filled with life. Why was he so healthy, and yet on the streets? She remembered that he'd come down for a job that didn't materialize. Okay then, why was he still around? Certainly not for her. He'd said she didn't fit in there. This was the one place her life depended on fitting in.

Nikki had to admit it was fortunate that he happened to be around the corner when Crackers got hit. Suspicion made her heartbeat slow. Or was it just fortune? She looked at Adrian through wary eyes, trying to see some sign of deceit. What had Ulyssis said about the man who had come into the gallery with a sketch that looked like her? She couldn't remember him saying anything about him. She did remember the name on the card, though: A. Wilde. A as in Adrian, maybe? Still, A. Wilde had only asked about a woman who looked like her. It had to be a coincidence that he'd also bought her collection.

When Nikki glanced up at Adrian again, she felt silly for her thoughts. He was rubbing his temple, an expression of worry on his handsome face. Most hired killers didn't give a whit about people, much less animals. Physically Adrian could fit the bill: strong, large, with an air of determination about him. Something in her heart stirred, a strange ticklish feeling, as he turned to catch her staring at him. She looked down at her fidgeting hands, though it took all her will to tear her gaze away.

The door behind Adrian opened, and a short, thin man walked out. Both Nikki and Adrian walked up to him, and the man backed up a little, taking in their homeless garb.

"You brought in the dog that was hit by a car?"

Nikki saw Adrian wince slightly before saying, "Yes, we did. Is he okay?"

"He's fine. And very lucky." He glanced at his papers. "Cracker?"

"Crackers," Nikki quickly corrected, though she didn't know why. Other than her name for him, the dog was a Rover Doe.

"Crackers only sustained a broken right leg. It was a simple break. Do you own this dog?"

"No," she answered quietly. "I think he's a stray."

"Oh." The doctor's expression looked grave. "In that case, I'll call the Humane Society. He's going to need some care before he's healed."

"I'll take care of him," Nikki found herself volunteering. At once she wanted to take those words back. How would she be able to take care of a dog when she lived in a van? Even as a puppy, Crackers would take up half the floor space. Still, she couldn't bear the thought of his absence at the laundromat, or the thought that he'd be put to sleep.

The doctor seemed to sense her hesitation, but after a moment he said, "Okay, if that's what you want to do. I'm going to have to give him his vaccines, though. If he's a stray, I'm sure he hasn't had them. The anesthesia should wear off soon, and then I can release him. Keep a close eye on him and check his excretions for blood. That would indicate internal injuries, though the X rays didn't show any. Don't let him play or jump around, even though his leg is in a cast. Bring him back in two weeks for a follow-up."

"How long will he need the cast?" Nikki asked.

"About four to six weeks, depending on how fast it heals."

When he handed the paperwork to the woman behind the counter, Nikki suddenly realized there would be a bill to pay. From her recent sale, she had enough to live on for a few months, even with Crackers's extra food added on. One vet bill could deplete the whole thing, and most homeless shelters didn't give extra food for pets.

"How much do I owe you?" she asked softly, cringing in anticipation.

The woman glanced at Adrian, then said, "The dog isn't yours, is he?"

"No, he's a stray. But I brought him here."

"We always allow a certain amount each month to take care of strays. Luckily, we haven't used this month's kitty yet, so you're covered."

"Oh. Thank you."

An hour later, the doctor reappeared with Crackers in his arms. The dog's head lolled to the side, and his tongue stuck out between his teeth. Adrian took the dog gently into his arms.

"He's still a little out of it, but I think he's fine to go home now."

"Thank you," Nikki said to both the doctor and the woman. She walked up to Crackers and stroked his head. When her fingers grazed Adrian's skin, she felt a jolt of electricity and jerked her hand away.

"Is something wrong?" Adrian asked.

"No, just static electricity. Must be the cold weather."

As they left the veterinarian's office, Adrian said, "I hope you don't live far from here. I think this dog has gained five pounds since we brought him in."

With a cold chill, she realized she had a problem: how to get the dog home without revealing to Adrian where she lived. And without seeming overly suspicious.

"I, uh, don't—the shelter! Let's take him to the Lord's Shelter." Her mind was working frantically as she walked beside him. She reached up and touched Crackers's limp paw bouncing in sync with Adrian's steps.

When they reached the shelter, she said, "Wait here while I talk to Dave. I know he's not going to like this, but it's only for a short time."

Lunch was being served, and the smell of vegetable soup reminded her stomach that it hadn't been fed yet today. She found Dave behind the long, stainless-steel counter dishing up soup to the line of cold, hungry people. He noticed her frantic expression and motioned for her to come around behind him.

"What's wrong?"

"I need to ask you a big favor." She looked down, hating to give away anything of her life, even to kindly Dave. "I saw a dog get hit by a car today—he's okay," she added quickly at Dave's expression of surprise. "But I've got to take care of him until his leg heals."

"You know we can't allow pets in here, Nikki," he said in that kind but authoritarian tone of his.

"I know, and I wouldn't ask you that. I just need to leave him here for a little while, until I can pick him up. It's too far to carry him to where I live."

"Only for a little while? You'll be back today?"

"Yes, I promise."

"Take him into my office, and use the entrance outside. He doesn't have fleas, does he?"

She twisted her lips, not wanting to lie to the man who was studying for the ministry. "If any get in your office, I'll hunt them down myself and remove them from the premises."

He laughed, dishing another bowl of soup. "Okay, you have a deal."

Dave's office looked dim and orangey from the sparse light filtering through the curtains. Nikki grabbed some towels from the back room and made a little bed in the corner.

Adrian knelt down and settled Crackers on the pile of old towels. The dog whimpered softly, but his eyes remained closed. Adrian felt a stab of guilt again, wishing for the umpteenth time that he'd taken another route to his secret parking spot.

Nikki knelt down beside him, stroking the pup's paw with her slender fingers. Adrian turned, finding her closer than he'd thought. The sleeve of her coat touched his sleeve, though he was sure she didn't know. Even bundled in her drab coat with her hair pulled back, the orange glow of sunlight streaming down over her made her look like an angel. For an unguarded moment, as she gazed at the sleeping puppy, her green eyes were filled with emotion. Her lower lip trembled so slightly that if he hadn't been crouched only inches from her face, he would have missed it.

"He'll be all right," Adrian assured her softly, feeling a strange urge to take her in his arms and comfort her. Instead, he placed his hand very slowly over hers as it rested on the dog's paw.

She didn't move away, as he expected, but he heard her slight intake of breath. The warmth between their hands intensified, and she looked up at him. There was such question in her eyes, and he wished he could answer whatever it was that she wondered. She moved her hand from beneath his, but he couldn't pull his gaze from hers.

"Thanks for your help," she whispered. She stood up quickly and turned around. "I have to go now, but I'll be back later." She glanced at the puppy, then back to him. "Good-bye."

Adrian knew she meant that word in more than a casual sense. It would be easier for him to bid her the same and return to his normal life. This woman of mystery, his Madame Blue, did not seem to want his help, or his friendship. She avoided his gaze every time he looked at her, crossed her arms in front of herself—everything to tell him to keep his distance. He closed the door behind them, stepping out into the afternoon sun. Nikki crossed quickly to the sidewalk and turned right, probably heading back to the laundromat to get her clothes.

In the sun, her hair had a strawberry hue beneath the webbed strands of the shawl still covering it. She didn't look back at him, but cautiously glanced behind her before disappearing around the building. He couldn't just leave her, not until he found out why she was in danger. Maybe he could help, once he'd gained her trust. He followed the direction she had taken, taking his time so she would pass where his rental car was hidden.

Nikki closed her eyes briefly as she walked, enjoying the feel of the sun on her face. She held her hand to her cheek, her fingers still tingling from Adrian's touch. Then she shook it, chastising herself for the silly notion. Perhaps he was just a friendly transient, a handsome man who cared about animals just as she did. Soon he would be gone, and judging from the way her heart's rhythm had shot up when he'd touched her, the sooner the better. In any case, she couldn't afford to befriend him.

When she glanced behind her, she saw him following a block behind. That cold fear crawled through her veins. She had long ago learned not to show dread to the young men who hung on the street corners looking for customers, like the man on her left. They had stopped bothering her shortly after her arrival. But the handsome man who had come out of nowhere, who was following her, struck real fear into her. She glanced back again—he was still there.

"Want some hashish, pretty lady?" the man called to her as she approached.

Nikki wasn't worried about Adrian's seeing her going to the laundromat to retrieve her laundry, if it hadn't been stolen already. But her next stop was her van, parked in an alley nearby. She had to get Crackers, and she couldn't let anybody see her get into that van.

As she passed the drug dealer, she whispered, "Ask that man back there. He was looking for some." That should hold him up for a minute or two.

Chapter 4

Love, to me, is like touching the stars.

When Adrian saw the sleazy man speak to Nikki, his protective instinct urged him to rush up and guard her against the filth. His common sense stopped him as his muscles tensed for action. After all, she had lived there for however long, and seemed capable of taking care of herself. She actually looked more concerned about him, evidenced by her worried glances backward. Sure, he wanted to know where she slept at night, just to make sure it was someplace safe. But right now his concern was getting to his car before she saw him anywhere near it. His plan was to take off just as she disappeared around the corner before crossing the empty lot. Then he would drive in the opposite direction, this time keeping a careful lookout for dogs.

The man ambled up slowly, purposely intersecting Adrian's path on the cracked sidewalk. Adrian glanced at the storefronts to his right, considering walking into a store before reaching trouble. The entire strip was vacated, the only sign of life being the piles of newspapers the homeless used when they slept in the alcoves at night. Rearing up to his full height of six foot two, much taller than the man, he charged ahead.

"You want hashish," the man stated. "I got the best, the purest. Come 'round back with me."

The man was now right up on Adrian, close enough for his week-old sweat to taint the air. He started to touch Adrian's arm, as if to escort him around back of the building he'd indicated with a nod of his head.

Adrian lifted his arm, giving the man a look that instantly made him back away. "Don't touch me. I'm not interested."

He raised his arms. "Sorry, man. The girl said you wanted something."

Adrian glanced up at Nikki, who was now reaching the alley where his car was parked. He nodded in her direction. "*That* girl?"

"Uh-huh. You a cop or something?" The man backed further away, tensed to run.

Adrian was too baffled to care. He looked at Nikki again, who was staring into the alleyway, her posture stiff. She'd seen his car, no doubt. But why had she even bothered to look, especially if she was telling drug dealers he was interested so she could get away from him? Glancing back at him, she started, then continued across the street.

It bothered Adrian that she was that afraid of him. What had he done to produce that kind of distrust? The second she rounded the corner, he shot into action, turning down the alley and jumping into his car. The van was still parked there, but he scarcely took note except to assure himself he hadn't blocked it in.

He quickly combed his hair into a ponytail and slipped on his sunglasses before pulling out. Instead of staying on the main street, he went a block west, into a lower-class neighborhood, and then south. Most of the houses in the area were tiny, smaller than his studio back home. The bars on the windows and patched wooden fences attested to the safety of the area. It was with great relief that he drove over the bridge leading to prestigious Palm Beach a few minutes later. Freshly painted plazas were filled with shops and people carrying designer shopping bags.

This is crazy, Wilde. She obviously doesn't want you around. It's a god-awful place to be. Go home. Forget about her.

But as he drove down the street of perfectly trimmed hedges and swaying palm trees, he muttered, "I wish I could." The decision was already beyond his control.

The bells tinkled softly as Nikki slipped into the Garcia Gallery later that day. Ulyssis was intently studying something on the counter, but looked up and smiled when he saw her.

"I didn't expect to see you so soon, Nicolina. You didn't spend all that money already, did you?"

"No, I just . . . I don't know, I'm just restless, I guess."

She walked over to inspect the new collection of photographs by the mysterious Nicolina. Ulyssis had framed them beautifully, as always, using an understated gray with white matting. They always sold for reasonable prices, and Ulyssis only deducted the cost of the frame. That was something she insisted on, otherwise he would have given her all the money. And she always took Ceil out to dinner at the Seashell Diner with the first of her profits, sort of a tithe. But Ceil hadn't been around lately.

"They came out nice, yes?"

"Yes." She turned to him. "Has that man been back? The one who bought the last collection."

"No, no sign of him. It was probably nothing more than my suspicions, as you said."

"I have a pet," she said, wanting to change the subject. "A puppy. Crackers."

He raised a thin, dark eyebrow. "How can you keep a pet in your van? Especially a dog."

"A big dog, or he will be. But I'm not keeping him, just nursing him back to health." She told him about the accident. "A man helped me. He came to our rescue, carrying Crackers all the way to the animal hospital."

Ulyssis eyed her strangely. "A man?"

"Yes, a man. He's very nice, and I could tell he cared about the puppy's welfare. Don't worry, I didn't let him carry Crackers to my van. We took him to the shelter until I could get back to pick him up."

"Who is this man?"

"His name is Adrian Nash. He came from New Jersey for a job his friend had told him about, but they were both gone when he got here. I guess he sleeps at the shelter."

"Why are you smiling like that? I've haven't seen you smile that way in a long, long time."

Nikki tried to wipe any expression from her face, not even realizing she had been smiling. "It's not like that, Ulyssis. Yes, he's handsome. I guess I haven't seen a man like that in a long, long time. He'll be gone soon, I'm sure."

"Be careful, Nicolina."

"It would be ridiculous to get involved with anyone in my situation!" She gestured emphatically with her arms, then dropped them to her sides. "Even if I could forget I'm being hunted, that I live in a van. He has no home, no job. We'd go nowhere."

"What does this man look like?"

"He's very tall, with dark, curlyish hair to his shoulders and brown eyes." Nikki realized then that she *was* smiling and stopped immediately. Ridiculous, she repeated in her mind. Dangerous. "Are you thinking of A. Wilde?"

"You know exactly what I'm thinking. He was tall, though his hair was straight and shorter I believe."

"Did he have a beard?"

"No, but a man can grow a beard if he needs to." Ulyssis rubbed his own long chin. "Well, some men can. Where did he say he was from?"

"New Jersey, not New York." She also realized then that she didn't want Adrian to be after her. Not anyone, but especially not him.

"They're close, Nicolina. Very close."

"Let's call the number on the card again and ask for Adrian Wilde." She pulled the card out of her pocket and recited the number while Ulyssis dialed.

"May I speak with Adrian Wilde, please?" he said, then nodded solemnly. "I see. And do you know where he is? Okay. Thank you."

Nikki's heart dropped as Ulyssis hung up the phone. "Same name?"

"Yes."

"Maybe it's still a coincidence."

"Perhaps, but doubtful. Adrian isn't exactly a common name."

Nikki sighed, leaning on the counter. "I know. But how could the man who came in here have connected me with those photographs? It's impossible!"

"I don't know, Nicolina. I don't know. Please be very careful. Stay away from this man. Isn't it strange that a man comes in asking about a woman who looks just like you, buys your photographs, and then soon after another man with similar features and the same first name shows up on the streets?"

"Maybe." She took a deep breath, feeling a tremor inside. "Don't worry. He may be handsome, but I'm not in love with him or anything like that."

"Then stop smiling every time you speak about him."

"I'm only smiling because I'm glad you worry about me. At least someone does." She squeezed his hands, knowing she was lying. "I don't plan to see him again, okay? I'm going to avoid that area for the next day or so, and he'll probably be gone when I return."

"Check in with me next week, just so I know you're still alive. I worry about you out there by yourself. I wish you'd just move into my apartment and hide out there."

"I'm not by myself. Right now I have a puppy, though he's hardly a threat when all he wants to do is lick my face and cuddle in my lap." She already knew it was going to be hard to put him back on the streets again when his leg healed. "And I can't move in with you. I refuse to disrupt your life like that. We've already talked about it."

"I know, I know. Be careful, Nicolina." He leaned over and kissed her forehead. "Don't let him into your heart."

"What the hell are you doing down there? We've got enough muff up here in New York City to last you a life-time. You don't need to go down South for it."

Adrian held the phone away from his ear for a second, picturing the short, balding man with the horn-rimmed glasses he considered a fashion statement. "Stan," Adrian tried to cut into the Stanley Fiske tirade. He was the man-ager of Dreams in Color, the ad agency Adrian did most of his work through. "I am not chasing muff. Geez, is that all you ever think about?"

"No, I also think a great deal about money. Making it, specifically. But we're not talking about what I'm thinking about, we're talking about what *you're* thinking about. What *are* you thinking about? Why aren't you in New York City making thousands of dollars a week for us?"

"Aren't I entitled to take a vacation?"

"Sure you are," he said sweetly. "When you give me a week's notice!" His voice bellowed. "I've been calling your place for the last two days every ten minutes, and you just now decide to call and let me know you're in the mid-dle of some cockeyed vacation? It's crazy!"

"This is why I'm self-employed, Stan. So I don't have to answer to anybody."

"You're self-employed so you can make a fortune and become the best damn photographer in the business. That means being available, and giving people notice when you decide it's time for a break."

Adrian laughed, refusing to let the little son of a bitch get to him. "Have you been drinking darkroom chemicals again, Stan? Geez, you're uptight."

"I'll have you know I haven't touched a drink for five days. That's a record, but if you keep this up, I'll have to make myself a martini within ten minutes. You want to ruin my wagon record?"

"Don't give me that—what's going on?"

"All right," Stan said, taking a calming breath. "Calvin Klein wants you to do the next layout for their briefs. They're talking to Tom Cruise and Paulina. How often do you have a chance to get a megastar like Cruise to pose in his briefs, and you get to be a part of it. They *want* you to be a part of it. Be back in the City tomorrow morning. They want to meet with you and brainstorm some ideas. Get this: They want something bold this time."

Adrian sipped a glass of wine, enjoying the feel of his silk shirt and the heavy fragrance of Obsession he'd over-dosed on after scrubbing away all the sadness and hope-lessness that had touched him that day. He glanced at the old clothes he'd discarded the minute he'd stepped into the house, still lying in a heap on the tile by the front door. But to return to the high life wasn't tempting enough to leave Nikki without at least trying to help her.

"Stanley, put them off for a week. They can wait. Or they can have someone else do the layout. I've got some emergency business to take care of."

Stanley put on the whiny voice he used when he really got desperate, like in those early days when it was tampons they wanted photographed, not pretty women. "Adrian, they want you. I told them they could have you, and tomorrow is the day they chose. How can I go back to them and say you changed your mind?"

"Temperamental artist?" he suggested, deciding not to point out that Stan had no business sealing deals without consulting him. "Tell them my wife left me and my dog died."

Stan laughed without humor. "Now you sound like a country music song. Adrian . . ."

"Stan, I'll be back next Wednesday night. First thing Thursday we'll do the brainstorming." That would give him a week to accomplish his goal. He didn't think he could handle much more than that.

Stan paused before speaking. "What time are you flying in?"

Adrian grabbed the note pad that actually had nothing written on it because he hadn't made a return flight. "Nine."

"Good. Be ready to meet with them at nine-thirty."

"Ten. I'll meet them at my studio." Adrian knew his quick agreement would irritate Stan. Stan liked to wrangle compromises.

"All right then. So, is everything all right?"

"Too late to ask now. I already know how much you care." Adrian leaned the note pad on his knee, jotting down the information.

Stan's tone lightened. "You know I do, Adrian. You got me worried, taking off like this. You just don't do this kind of thing. So really, is everything all right?"

"I told you, it's the wife and dog thing."

"You don't have a wife," Stan said, as if the statement would surprise Adrian.

"No, and I don't have a dog, either," he said, though he thought of Crackers. "Bye, Stan."

His next call was to Rita. When he'd left, it was with only a quick call to ask her to watch Oscar and a promise to take her out to dinner when he returned, which he'd left vague. Now that he had a deadline of sorts, he could firm things up with her.

Rita's answering machine kicked on, and Adrian felt a bit of relief at not having to answer any of her questions. Her breathy message came to an end, and he readied himself to leave instructions.

"Hi, it's Adrian. I'll be back in town—"

"Hi, darling!" her voice abruptly answered. "Did you say you were back in town?"

"No, I was about to say I'd be back in town next Wednesday night, about nine o'clock." He made a note to call his travel agent to see if there even was such a flight.

"A whole week from now?" she said, her voice taking on that whine he hated. She must have remembered that, because she changed tone. "Great! I'll pick you up at the airport and we'll have that dinner you promised me."

"Can't do it. Stan's set me up for a meeting right after I get in, and I'm not exactly sure when that is yet. I'll just get a limo."

That disappointed pause. "Okay. How about dinner the following night?"

"Fine. Listen, thanks again for taking care of Oscar. Sure you don't want a cat?"

She laughed. "Oh, no, you don't! He's my best reason for seeing you these days." Her tone became serious again. "Adrian, what are you doing?"

"Taking care of business," he said, refusing to lie to her. Equally refusing to answer her.

"Are you staying at a hotel where I can reach you?"

"No, I had to rent this house for the whole month when I came down for the shoot, so I'm using the rest of the time."

"Adrian, did you meet someone while you were down there? I know I have no rights to you, but I'd like to know."

"Rita, the answer to that is yes and no. I did, but it's not what you think. I met up with an old friend who needs some help. That's all I'm saying, so don't ask any more questions. Thanks, Rita."

The next morning Adrian reluctantly slipped out of his thick terry robe and into brown corduroys and a brand new undershirt beneath the faded black sweatshirt. He ruffled his fingers through his hair, mussing it slightly. As he passed the hall mirror, he did what he'd promised himself he wouldn't do: look. Cringing, he rubbed his beard and studied himself. Well, he fit into the homeless class all right. Except for the hopelessness. Even when he had been on the verge of homelessness, and too young to do anything about it, he had never lost his hope. Even when Elio had kicked him around some and his mother never said a word to stop him, Adrian harbored only hatred and a fierce desire to free himself as soon as he could. He had never lost hope. Only his pride. With a smirk, Adrian realized he was losing that now, too. He shook his head, and left.

Adrian got a little taste of hopelessness as the hours of the morning slipped by with no sign of Nikki. He roamed all over, stopped for lunch at McDonald's, then roamed more. Dave hadn't seen her all day, though he'd said that wasn't unusual. Then he'd asked why Adrian has missed the Wednesday Bible class. Adrian wanted to tell him that it wasn't his soul he was worried about, it was his head. He made up some other excuse instead, finding all this necessary lying coming a little easier each time.

By late afternoon, his feet ached. He'd run into Seamus, who spoke so highly of Mama Jam's Jamaican beef patties that he bought six for both of them. Seamus wolfed his down within seconds; Adrian had watched him work those dirty fingers deftly to shove them in his mouth. Losing his appetite, he'd given Seamus his three as well.

Now, grumpy and hungry, Adrian wandered over to a makeshift bench that faced the port of Palm Beach to watch a barge come in. He rubbed his fingers down his face, letting his body relax for the first time in hours. But within a few minutes he was tense again as a man sat down beside him. He was in his sixties, with a large belly and grizzled gray beard, and he nodded silently at Adrian as he settled onto the bench perched atop two halves of a green oil drum.

Adrian felt instantly uncomfortable; not out of fear, but for some other reason he didn't feel like delving into at the time. Still, he didn't get up right away. The strange sense of social obligation seemed terribly out of place.

"New 'round here, aren't you?" the man asked, though he kept looking ahead at the incoming barge.

"Just passing through."

The man nodded. "I thought that too, when I first got here. That was ten years ago."

Adrian looked at him, a clammy feeling in his stomach. All he wanted to do was get up and leave, but the words came out unbidden. "What happened?"

"Ah, it's a long story, you probably don't want to hear it. Used to work on a ship. Much bigger than that thing over there." He pointed to a large, steel ship in the distance. "I was the captain," he said proudly, raising his shoulders. "Captain Charlie. Made a lot of money, had respect." He looked down at himself with a melancholy smile. "Hard to believe now."

Adrian was already leaning over the bench, but something in the man's voice made him sit back again. He reached in his pocket for his lighter and fired up a cigarette. Charlie's eyes lit up, and with the speed of a ferret, he was holding the gold lighter in his liver-spotted hands.

"Nice lighter." Charlie eyed Adrian. "Where'd you get something like this?"

Adrian retrieved it, hiding it in his pocket. *Stupid move, Wilde. Nash. Get a Bic.* "Friend gave it to me. A long time ago."

"Oh." Then Charlie's eyes widened again as Adrian dropped his cigarette after two drags and stepped on the butt. "No! What are you doing?"

Despite his rotund appearance, Charlie could move if he had to. Apparently, he did, because within a second he was down on his knees reaching for the cigarette with one hand and holding Adrian's sneaker with the other. The cigarette was flat, but Charlie tenderly fingered it until it was oval at best.

"How can you waste a whole cigarette like that?" After patting his pocket, he turned and asked, "Can I have a light off that pretty lighter of yours?"

Adrian lit the squashed cigarette for him, holding tight to the lighter this time. Another mistake. Bums didn't waste cigarettes or liquor, not for any reason. He'd have to save his lighting up for private moments, and leave the gold lighter at home.

"So, what happened? When you were the respected captain?"

"I made a stupid mistake. Got drunk one night and rammed the ship onto some shoals. They fired me, but good. My wife divorced me in shame, and I left town." He shrugged, taking a deep drag off the cigarette. "Not much work for a drunk sailor these days."

"Maybe you should get off the booze," Adrian said, not feeling much pity for the man now.

Charlie turned to him, his watery gray eyes stern. "I haven't had a drink in ten years, since that night. All it takes is one mistake in that industry, and you're gone. I tried everything I could, but I just couldn't make ends meet.

Now I have nothing. But I tried. Once, I had it all.''

Adrian sat there, letting the man's pride settle in the chilly air. Even a man like that had pride. It surprised him. And once, he'd had it all. Adrian shivered, realizing that's where he was now. Could something happen, something devastating that could ruin his career in one swift moment of poor judgment? He thought of Stan's urgency in returning to New York City to talk to Calvin Klein. Nah, they would wait. Still, Adrian stood, feeling uncomfortable. He slipped his hands into his pockets and started walking away. Then, he turned around, pulled out the lighter, and tossed it to the man.

''Good-bye, Charlie.''

''And that horrible car was right there behind my van in the alley! Can you believe that?''

Ceil leaned over the formica table, absorbed in Nikki's story about Crackers's accident. She fingered the chopped strands of her bright red hair. ''Are you sure it was the same car?''

''No, that's why I didn't take a rock to the windshield. I couldn't wait around for the driver, either.''

Ceil's gray eyes widened. ''Why not? I'd have spied on the car,'' she whispered conspiratorially. ''You want me to spy on it?''

Nikki waved her hand. ''Nah, it's gone now.''

''And what about that guy, Arian?''

''Adrian,'' Nikki corrected.

Sometimes, though Ceil was in her midthirties by her own best guess, she acted like a young girl. The young girl she had never been able to enjoy being, because her stepfather molested her. Then her mother had kicked her out of the house when Ceil finally gathered the courage to tell her. It had been one hell after another for her; ending with the state taking her children after her husband deserted her for a young waitress. Now she lived at the Lord's Shelter, where Nikki had found her this afternoon.

"So, what happened with him?"

"Nothing! He's probably gone by now." Nikki glanced around the Seashell Diner. There was no one quite that handsome anywhere in sight.

Ceil smiled, looking up at her through her red eyelashes. "You like him, don't you?"

"Ceil!" Nikki said, then lowered her voice when she realized how loud it was. "I don't like him. I mean, he was nice, but that's all. Things like that don't happen down here. Besides, I can't trust anyone."

That's all Ceil knew about Nikki: that she was hiding from something or someone, and that she lived in her van. Sometimes Nikki even let Ceil drive it around when the cops harassed her. Because of Ceil's appearance, they seemed to think she was a hooker. Nikki hoped not.

"Is he cute?"

Nikki rolled her eyes, not wanting to talk about the mysterious stranger anymore. "No, he's not cute." At Ceil's surprised expression, she added, "He's handsome. He has these gorgeous brown eyes that seem to pull you in when he looks at you." She thought of how gently he'd handled Crackers, how he'd carried him ten blocks to the animal clinic. "And he's noble."

"What's noble?" Ceil asked, still smiling dreamily at Adrian's description.

Nikki frowned, saddened that Ceil knew nothing about nobility and chivalry. "It's being good and tender."

"Oh. Did you kiss him?" Ceil asked with a mischievous smile.

Nikki threw a wadded napkin at her. "Stop it!"

Ceil broke out into a fit of giggles, nearly knocking over her root beer float. When she finally settled down, her face sobered. "You're too pretty to be down here, Nikki."

Nikki leaned forward. "So are you."

Ceil blushed furiously, highlighting every red freckle on her face. "Get out of here!"

"I'm serious." Nikki had already vowed to bring Ceil with her when she left this horrible place that had become her home. With an emotional overhaul, Ceil might be all right.

"Has the puppy pooped in your van yet?"

Nikki whirled at the sudden change in conversation, but was glad to be off the subject of Adrian. "No, he's been very good. Poor thing, though. You should see him limping around with that cast on his leg."

Ceil hunched over, digging in her dirty parachute bag that used to be white. Then she proudly brought out three bottle caps: Arizona tea, New York Seltzer Water, and a white, flat one. She picked up the Arizona one.

"This was raspberry flavored. Very good. A little boy left half of it at the mall yesterday. It was still cold when I took it out of the garbage. Kids leave the best food. Remember that. Follow a big family, and you're set for food for a week. Fanny Farmer's was giving out free samples of their butter toffee. Yum! You should come with me sometime. There's all kinds of goodies at the mall."

"Maybe sometime."

Ceil scooped her caps up and deposited them with the many others she toted around in her sack. They were as valuable as gold to her, and she shared them only with Nikki.

"Nikki, tell me about Adrian again. Tell me what he looks like, and I'll spy on him for you. Maybe he's an alien or something. Someone should keep an eye on him."

Chapter 5

You see me as homeless, but I am a survivor.

"Wait!" Nikki scooted toward Crackers and pulled the two yellow flowers from between the cracks of the asphalt before the puppy sprayed them. She smelled the tiny bouquet, remembering the fresh flowers the maid had put in her room every morning when she lived in the mansion. Nikki didn't particularly miss the jewels in her box, the fancy clothes, or especially the droll parties where everyone tried to outdo each other with dress and drunkenness. She did miss silly little things, like the flowers . . . and Häagen-Dasz ice cream. And bubble baths. She returned to the van, putting those flowers in a cup of water. Because the flowers didn't smell, she lifted the cap off her Opium perfume bottle and inhaled. And then, just for the heck of it, she deposited a tiny drop on her wrist.

Nikki, why don't you like dressing up like other girls? You've got a whole wardrobe of beautiful things, dresses that would make any girl green with envy.

Mother, I don't like dressing up like that all the time. What's wrong with dressing like this?

She glanced down at her fuzzy robe and slippers, then up where that remembered conversation hovered. "What do you think, Mother? Understated with a traditional flair?'' Lowering her gaze, she added, "Sorry, Mother. I've probably disgraced you beyond forgiveness, anyway. I just hope you understand that I have to do this, that I have no choice."

She removed the robe, then her silk nightgown, and put on her wool sweater and jeans. Over all that she put on her shawl to hide her braided hair and the overcoat. Grabbing her camera, she rejoined Crackers where she'd tied him to the bumper.

Her main purpose in life was surviving, but beyond that, taking pictures filled the greatest moments. The rest was an empty space that dreams had left behind. If she could spend every waking hour taking photographs, she would. But that was impractical, and expensive. Last night, as she'd lay in her bed tossing and turning, she'd thought of some great shots with a crippled puppy in them. Today, she would turn those thoughts into film.

The cold front had swept through the night before, bringing with it rain and even colder air. Wispy clouds moved swiftly across the sky, leaving streaks of blue where they thinned the most. Soon they would dissipate altogether, leaving a glorious day. For now, the weather would be a good backdrop for her pictures.

Midmorning, when the sun began to dominate the sky, Nikki was still posing Crackers, this time in Seamus's baby stroller. She knew he allowed it only because he was far into another world today, and hadn't realized what she'd asked. That was why she wanted to get the shot quickly and be on her way. Now that her creativity was percolating with ideas, she wanted to find Ceil and pose her with Crackers, sharing a treat together. That was what she wanted her photographs to show, that the homeless were people too, and that they enjoyed the same simple pleasures everyone else did.

"You're going to spoil that puppy crazy," a low voice said behind her, and she jumped just as she made the exposure.

Whirling around with her hand on her heart, she stood to face Adrian standing just behind her. He looked extraordinarily handsome at that moment, with the sun gleaming off his almost black hair and a devilish smile on his face. She looked away, not wanting to notice those things about him.

"I was just posing him."

Crackers had already struggled out of the stroller, and waddled over to Adrian, obviously recognizing him as his savior. Adrian knelt down and scratched under the puppy's chin. In a sweatshirt, his chest looked even larger than before; she could imagine him wrapping his arms about a woman and making her feel very, very secure. Her hand went to her lips at the feelings that thought invoked. Not this woman, Nikki reminded herself, looking away. The feeling lingered, though. It had been so long since a man had held her. Just the thought of it seemed like heaven.

"He looks happy. You must be a great nurse."

"Okay, I am spoiling him rotten, and he loves it." Her voice grew soft. "I doubt anyone's ever spoiled him before." She couldn't help but smile at Crackers's tail, wildly swinging every time Adrian spoke.

He held the pup's chin and said directly to him, "You don't know how lucky you are, little fellow."

Nikki pulled on the leash she'd fashioned from a couple of belts and started walking away. She could hear Adrian stand and follow behind her.

"Did I say something wrong?" he asked in that velvety voice of his.

"No. It's just that I ... have to go now. I have to get Crackers back. ...'' She'd started to say home, but let the sentence hang. "He's been on his leg all morning."

"Can I walk with you?"

"It's probably best if you don't." *Adrian Wilde. Adrian Nash.* The words filtered through her mind, along with Ulyssis's warning to be careful. Still, she turned and asked him, "Do you like to photograph things, Adrian?" Damn, but she liked the feel of his name on her tongue.

He gave her an odd look, but answered, "Yes, but I'm not very good. There wasn't much to do where I grew up, so when my Uncle Carlo gave me one of his cameras he'd outgrown with his private investigator practice, it gave me something to do with my time."

Nikki found herself smiling, picturing him as a kid with a camera. In spite of herself, she wanted to know more about him. "What kinds of things did you take pictures of?"

"At first everything, but my newspaper delivery business could hardly support my habit. I always looked for the story behind the photograph."

Like her, Nikki mused. "And you didn't do anything with it? For a job, I mean."

He shrugged. "If you can count working with my uncle catching illicit cheaters for rankled spouses. Even then, I always went for the artistic angles." He reached for the camera in her hands, and she reluctantly let him take it. That he would steal it was the least of her worries.

"A Hasselblad. It's a good camera, isn't it?" He handed it back to her.

"I suppose. I've ... had it for a while." A gift from her mother who always insisted on the best. When her mother thought it was all just a hobby.

As he looked into her eyes, she felt such a poignancy, she could hardly pull her gaze away from his. Once again she forced herself to turn away from him, wondering if he was lying about his mild interest in photography. She tucked her camera in the folds of her coat to hide it from any other interested individuals who wanted to do more than compliment her taste in equipment.

When he spoke, his voice was a short distance behind her, and she knew he had remained where he was. Crackers was straining against his homemade collar, trying to go back to him.

"Nikki, let me buy you lunch. Crackers too."

"I don't need your charity," she said, still looking ahead. Her voice trembled, and she cleared her throat. "But thank you anyway."

He laughed, though not in a mocking way. "I'm not offering you charity. I just want to buy you lunch. You can tell me about your hobby."

When she turned around, he was standing there with his hands in his pockets, leaning his weight on one leg. He smiled, such an innocent smile. If he were hired to find her, or to kill her, he was probably the best in the business. And her brother, Devlin, would hire the best.

Crackers continued to strain as she fought with herself over something as silly as whether to have lunch with this man. The two belts came undone, and the pup hobbled eagerly over to Adrian. She found herself ironically glad that she'd given Crackers a sponge bath now that Adrian was rubbing his cheek against the top of the dog's head. Something in that small action tugged at her resistance, and she stepped forward to retrieve her puppy.

"I guess I'm outvoted."

He smiled up at her. "Looks like it."

Adrian reattached the belts and carried the dog several blocks to a restaurant called Mama Jam's. She paused warily outside, already smelling the jerk spices.

"Haven't you ever eaten here?" he asked. "Or have you, and that's why you're looking like that?"

"No, I've never eaten here."

He looked up at the peeling paint of the sideboards and the jaunty sign over the door depicting a round black woman with fruit on her head. "I didn't think I'd ever eat at a place like this either, but Seamus talked me into it. They have great Jamaican meat patties." Adrian tied Crackers up to the black bars on the window in a shady spot.

Her eyes widened. "Seamus? You and Seamus had lunch here?"

"Sure. What's so strange about that?"

She shook her head, walking closer. "I just can't imagine you and him having lunch together. Does he talk to you?"

"He told me about his wife and little girl, and how they died in a car accident."

"I didn't know," she said softly, walking inside as he held the door for her.

"Maybe it helped him to talk about it."

Island music played in the background, and a large black lady waved them vaguely to sit wherever they wanted. Nikki wondered if the woman was the model for the sign, though she wasn't wearing any fruit. Adrian led her to a small homemade table near the back and against the window. It overlooked an empty lot thriving with weeds and chunks of cement where a building had once been rooted.

Once the hot tea had been brought to the table, Nikki was glad to occupy herself with preparing it. Adrian dumped one packet of sugar in his and stirred it, but he was looking at her. She could tell, though she stared into her cup and watched the amber liquid make little whirl-pools. He was leaned back in the simple wooden chair, one leg stretched out so that it extended to her side of the table. It seemed to her that his presence overwhelmed the tiny place. When she finally had to look up at him, he didn't quickly look away. Instead, he smiled. The strange feeling in her stomach made her wish he would have looked away.

"I thought you'd be gone by now," she said, trying hard not to make it sound like she cared one way or the other.

"Not yet. I'm looking for work in the area. I like it here."

The way he was looking at her made her feel fidgety. So, he wasn't going away anytime soon. A tiny feeling of elation overruled her sense of security.

"Where do you go at night?" she found herself asking.

"To sleep."

He looked a little surprised at her question. For a second, Nikki panicked. Damn, it had been so long since she'd had a conversation like this. She'd forgotten the rules. Then again, there were no rules on the streets.

He shrugged. "Sometimes at the shelter. Sometimes they're full, so I go elsewhere. Where do you go? You said you didn't stay at the shelter."

"Here and there," she said quickly. Too quickly, but she didn't add anything else.

"Tell me about your photography. How long have you been doing it?"

It seemed so strange to be asked about herself, her hobby. With Ceil she shared tidbits of her days. With Ulyssis, she was vague so that he didn't worry too much about her.

"Since I was a teenager." Like Adrian, she had used it as an escape.

The woman brought plates of meat patties and red beans and rice to the table. The fried pastry and spicy beans smelled delicious, and she dug right in. Aside from her occasional meals at the diner, the rest of her food she cooked on her one portable burner.

"Did you grow up around here?" Adrian asked her.

"Yes."

She didn't want to give him too much information. If he were a hired killer, maybe it was his way to get to know his victim, to befriend them. Then, at the appropriate time, in a dark alley or private place, he would pull the gun equipped with a silencer, and she would be dead. Her hand trembled as she reached for a piece of bread.

"You don't talk much," he said, diffusing the words with a smile.

She looked away. "No."

That only made him smile more. He picked at his food while she ate continuously, more out of nervousness than hunger. She wondered if he had a gun hidden beneath his sweatshirt. Like the little Davis thirty-two caliber hidden in the pocket of her coat, the one Ulyssis had insisted she take after she'd been robbed early on.

"Nikki, what's wrong?"

She blinked, wondering what expression had been on her face. "Nothing." *Are you here to kill me? Did Devlin send you here?* She wanted to occupy her attention with food, but it was all gone.

"Is something bothering you? Are you uncomfortable?"

"Yes," she answered honestly.

He leaned forward, only a foot away from her face. "Why?"

"I don't know." It was too complicated to explain, even to herself. She leaned back, uneasy with his closeness. *You're too close, too handsome, too dangerous. It scares me to feel this way.*

He leaned back again, but his voice retained that intimate softness. "I don't want to make you feel uncomfortable. Just tell me what I'm doing, and I'll stop."

"I think I should go." She stood, gathering her coat and slipping it over her arms. "Thank you for lunch."

She quickly walked out of the restaurant, hoping to gain time while he paid the bill. Unfortunately, the clever knot Adrian had tied to secure Crackers kept her standing there long enough for him to walk over.

"Wait a minute." Instead of demanding to know why

she'd walked out so suddenly, he knelt down and opened a package of crinkly white paper. "I promised Crackers lunch, remember?"

She looked down at him, holding the meat pattie for Crackers to take, which he did in two bites. How could a man who remembered promises to dogs be a hired killer? She felt a tug at her heart, watching him. He stood, wiping his hands on his pants. In half a second, he freed the belt from the black iron and handed it to her. She felt warmth creeping up her cheeks at her rudeness. How long had it been since she'd had to apologize to someone? Probably two years. Nikki smiled, as close as she could come to an apology, and turned away. Crackers still gave resistance, tugging back toward Adrian.

Exasperated, she said, "Crackers, I'm going to leave you here if you don't behave!" She yanked on the leash, and the belts came apart again.

Adrian put them together, then nodded toward the small general store one block up. "Why don't we get him a real leash?"

"No, I can't afford it. That's why I'm using this . . . thing."

"I'll buy one. They can't be that much."

She narrowed her eyes at him. "You spend a lot of money for someone down here."

That smile of his was disarming, and he knew it. "I'm not a drug runner, if that's what you're thinking. Actually, I had a bartending job last night. Made a few extra bucks because their regular guy was out sick."

Nikki wasn't sure whether to buy that or not, but decided it didn't matter anyway. She had too much to lose by trusting this man. Still, she found herself walking with him to the general store to buy a leash for a dog she wouldn't have around much longer. How could two different creatures ingrain themselves in her very private life like this? Adrian with his smiles, and Crackers with his puppyish self. Except for Ceil and Ulyssis, Nikki had let no one near her.

When Adrian reached for the belts, his fingers touched hers, and that electric jolt shot through her. He let them linger for a second too long before taking the leash from her. He knelt down again and measured the length they needed. When he handed it back to her, she purposely reached far below his grip.

"Be right back."

She pretended not to watch him through the dusty panes of glass fitted with metal bars. He studied the different leashes on a far aisle, then walked to the register. When he emerged, she quickly looked away to ensure him that she had not been watching.

He'd purchased a purple leash and collar to match. She held tight to the belts, even as Adrian knelt down and freed Crackers from the makeshift leash. When he stood, she was staring right at his chest. Despite her wish not to, she looked up into those brown eyes of his. Her heart tightened, aching from some need she refused to acknowledge. A cool breeze ruffled his dark waves and caused a strand of her own hair to tickle her cheek.

He reached slowly out and brushed it away, his fingers lingering against her skin, then moving to beneath her chin. She knew she must move, turn away, and leave. If she could breath, or swallow. If her heart hadn't stopped beating altogether.

"You are beautiful," he said, his smooth voice almost a whisper. "Too beautiful to be down here."

The warmth from his fingers spread to her entire body, and his words caressed her soul. To be touched, to be beautiful again . . . to be held in those strong arms, against that massive chest, and be held, just held. She shivered, and his hand moved away. Nikki wrapped her coat tightly around her, looking everywhere but at him.

"I must go." *Before I cry. Why do I want to cry? And if I did, would he hold me?* "Good-bye." Her voice trembled, and she cursed it. Crackers seemed to sense her distress, for he followed with only the slightest tug backward, as if he were only looking back.

"Good-bye, Nikki," he said from a short distance.

So, he wasn't following her. Thank God. Her hands trembled, and she wanted to run, to get as far away from Adrian as she could. Crackers wouldn't cooperate, and it wasn't until she was several minutes away that she allowed herself to look back—only at the dog. The pup was hobbling more, favoring his broken leg. From her peripheral vision, she saw Adrian still standing outside the store, watching her.

"Crackers, just one more minute."

Eyeing the end of the strip of stores, she sped up a little and took the corner with a sigh of relief. Leaning against the cracking paint, she caught her breath, wrapping her arms around herself. Not because she was cold; warmth surged through her. She took a deep breath, then knelt down and scooped Crackers up into her arms. After scanning the back of the building for lurkers, she circled around to where her van was parked in an alley. Even struggling with the dog's unwieldy weight in her arms, she felt a profound loneliness descend upon her.

She let herself wonder, for a minute, what it would have been like if she'd met him three years ago on one of her photography forays. She would have been afraid of him for different reasons, but she would have been swept up easily in those eyes of his. Nikki smiled as she imagined bringing him home to meet Mother and what her expression would look like. Horror, no doubt. Risking her mother's disapproval was something Nikki could handle in those days, especially for love. Love? Had she really thought that? That was something she couldn't afford, not for a long while.

*   *   *

Adrian watched Nikki walk quickly away, Crackers hobbling along behind her and looking back every two seconds. He shrugged, as if to let the dog know he was as confused as Crackers was. Confused at his own action more than her reaction. His fingers still tingled where they'd touched her cheek. He was doing this all wrong. He didn't want to scare her away; he just wanted to help her. When she looked up at him, the moment before he'd touched her cheek, all he wanted to do was pull her into his arms and hold her, protect her from whatever she was hiding from.

He lit a cigarette with his red plastic lighter, took two deep drags and stomped it out. The light fragrance of her perfume still lingered in the air. He'd noticed it right away, that musky warm scent of Opium. As beautiful as she was, it seemed strangely out of place here. And she was beautiful, though nothing like the woman he'd seen driving the Mercedes. Without any makeup, with her long hair hidden beneath her shawl and hood, her eyes still rivaled any model's.

The camera reinforced the fact that Nikki definitely came from a lot of money. Hasse's were the Rolls-Royce of cameras, even for the pros. For an amateur to have one was almost unthinkable. Adrian had splurged for his own just a few years ago.

He went over what he'd told her about his own photography. She seemed overly interested, as if she weighed every word. He was pretty sure he hadn't given anything away. He couldn't tell her the part about Uncle Carlo being so impressed with his work that he'd shoo'd him out the door with an invitation to meet a photographer's agent with whom he played poker. Stan had snapped him up instantly, and things had just gotten better and better.

As Nikki turned the corner and disappeared from sight, he felt a deep urge to follow her, to do just what he wanted to do—hold her and take her away from all this. Her green eyes said so much, and through the jumble of emotions he could read only one clearly: fear. Not fear of him, but fear of trusting him. Adrian only hoped his impatience wouldn't blow his cover.

Nikki was nearly out of breath when she approached her van. Crackers was struggling too, feeling her grip slipping beneath him. She finally set him down and let him hobble safely toward his temporary home. His tail wagged when he saw the van, and he sped up.

She lifted him into the van and closed the door behind her. This was only a vehicle, a shell with those few personal items and luxuries from that other life, but it was her home. She dropped down on her tiny bed and sighed. The only sound she heard was Crackers lapping his water. She had never had pets; her mother despised animal hair in the house. Her father let her have a hamster once, but Sunny died four months later, and her mother said no more pets, claiming to have smelled the soiled cedar chips from the hallway.

A sharp pounding jerked her from her reverie. Nikki jumped up and peered out the window. Could Adrian have found her safe harbor? The sight of Ceil, her red hair gleaming in the sun, eased Nikki's heart back from where it had lodged in her throat. She slid the door open. Ceil looked around as if she was being followed.

"Are the police hassling you again?" Nikki asked.

Ceil looked sheepish. She reached out and touched Nikki's cheek. "I saw him touch you. You like him. He's beautiful, isn't he? That's the man you told me about, isn't it? He's beautiful. And so big. You do like him, don't you? He won't take you away from me, will he? Will he make you go with him?"

Ceil's face had undergone several amazing transformations during her speech, ending with a pout. Nikki didn't much care that Ceil had seen Adrian touch her cheek, but she did mind the blush that stole across her skin.

Sure that Ceil had made her way to Nikki's van unfollowed, she gestured for the redhead to come in. Ceil was the only person, besides Ulyssis, she allowed to see the inside. Ceil's expression was always one of awe, and she touched the silk gown hanging on a hook by the makeshift bathroom.

"Ooh, so soft. He doesn't know where you live, does he?"

"Who, Adrian?"

Ceil smiled dreamily. "Yes, Adrian. He's beautiful, Nikki. Beautiful."

Nikki grinned at Ceil's choice of words, the same word he'd just used for her. "Yes, he is beautiful. And big. No, he doesn't know where I live, and no, he won't take me away from here or you."

Ceil settled on the floor with her knees up and arms wrapped around them. She smiled. "Good. I'd miss you. But you like him, don't you?"

Nikki shook her head. "I can't like him, Ceil. I can't like anybody, except for you."

"He likes you." Ceil nodded with certainty. "I saw him watching you when you walked away. He just kept watching you."

"Did he follow me?"

"No, he just kept watching. And he lit up a cigarette. Then you know what he did? You'll never guess." Ceil's enthusiasm was like a child's.

"What did he do?"

"He took two drags and put it out. Just dropped it and stepped on it. It was flatter than a squashed bottle cap. Couldn't even light it."

"You don't smoke, Ceil."

"I know, but I wanted to see if I could light it. Almost the whole cigarette, Nikki." Her expression became serious, with her lower lip pouting out. "Be careful of him. You should follow him. Just to see where he goes. Want me to follow him? I will. I'm good at it."

"I know you are." One of Ceil's three children lived in a nearby neighborhood, and she often spied on the girl. Luckily, the child looked happy and well taken care of. One of Nikki's most poignant pictures was taken one time Ceil had asked her to go along. The raw emotion on Ceil's face as she saw her little girl was heartrending. Nikki would never sell that picture; it was too personal. "No, you don't need to watch Adrian. I'll do it." She nodded, knowing it was the answer to finding out who he was. "I'll do it."

The sun was beginning to set in the western sky. Without a cloud in sight, the horizon looked to be the color of orange juice, fading to blue at the edges. The air was cooling fast, sneaking through the fibers of Adrian's sweatshirt. After Nikki had walked away from him, he'd spent the rest of the afternoon trying to figure out where she spent her nights. Now he walked around the old Riviera building, which had been a theater a long time ago.

The deep alcove was littered with trash and newspapers, evidence of those who sought shelter there at night. The ticket windows were boarded up, the billboard frames empty. What about the inside? Was it empty as well, or did Nikki find solace behind the old theater curtain? He cased the building, testing the boards all around that covered up who knew what. All the doors were secured, and not even butting his shoulders against the boards would budge them. He stepped over an old, stained mattress lying out back, knowing somehow that Nikki would never sleep on something like that. Wherever she slept, and lived, she was safe and protected. She kept herself clean, and even smelled nice.

It was when he walked around to the front that he felt as though he were being watched. Wearing his sunglasses, he could appear to be looking in one direction and study another. A cloaked figured peered around the side of a building across the street. He knew—could *feel*—it was Nikki. She ducked around the corner as he slowly moved his head in her direction. So, she didn't want him to see her. He wanted to walk over to her, but he didn't. Instead, he walked along the sidewalk in the direction of the parking lot where he kept his car.

Maybe she didn't want him to see where she slept at night. He would keep going, she could go to the place she slept, and he would be able to pinpoint closer where that was. Sticking his hands in his pockets, he braced against the wind that had kicked up since the sunset and headed on. Every few minutes, he would stop and look in a store window. In the reflection he could see her lurking in the background. He took off his sunglasses and tucked them in his pocket, realizing he'd look sinister if he kept them on any longer.

Three blocks later, and she still tailed him. The reason behind it perplexed him, but he didn't give away the fact that he knew she was there. He stared into an empty store, as if wondering how to get inside where it was warm. The street lights kicked on, those that worked, and gave the dreary city a foreboding look. A couple of young men stood on a street corner, probably looking for trouble. Adrian was more worried about Nikki's safety than his own. He could take care of himself. When he thought of the way she'd looked earlier that day, he felt a surge of protectiveness. But he had to remember that she'd been here for a while, and she'd survived so far.

The light of day was long gone. He had two choices, as

he saw it. One was to lose Nikki and quickly get back to his car. He didn't know his way around the area as well as she did, but he was fairly sure he could manage it. If he did that, she might think he was doing just that. She'd distrust him even more than she already did.

The other choice was to prove to her that he was what he said he was. If he were really homeless, where would he sleep? A spotlight lit up the Lord's Shelter sign one block ahead. He remembered Dave's invitation, if there were enough beds. If he went there, Nikki would go home, wherever that was. At least she'd be off the streets.

Despite his determination, Adrian paused on the sidewalk in front of the shelter. No wine or steak or hot shower. He'd be taking a bed from someone else in the deal, while his large bed remained empty all night. Adrian ran his fingers through his hair, hating the deception and what it was making him do. Or could he do it?

Chapter 6

Love is but a memory to my frozen heart.

Adrian took the steps to the door, still feeing Nikki's presence behind him somewhere. The smell of food reminded him that he hadn't eaten since the lunch he and Nikki had shared.

He reached for the door and opened it. The room to his left was filled with people at tables scooping beef and vegetables into their hungry mouths. A few looked up at him, then returned to their business. A line formed from the metal counter where food was being unceremoniously slopped on plastic plates. His appetite fled from his knotted stomach.

"Adrian, wasn't it?" Dave's voice said from Adrian's right.

"Yes. I've . . . come for a place to sleep."

Dave gave him an understanding smile, though Adrian knew he'd never understand if he knew the truth. "Of course. We only have a few beds left. I'll take you to the room."

Adrian followed him to a large room filled with cots. Several were already occupied by sleeping men. Adrian shivered, looking around at the high ceiling dusted with cobwebs. Some of the beds were made up with thinning blankets and lumpy pillows.

"Find one that's still made and turn it down to signal that it's taken, then join us for dinner."

Adrian quickly shook his head. "No dinner, thanks. I'm feeling a bit queasy at the moment. I think I'll just lie down."

"Okay. We stop serving in an hour, so if you change your mind before then, come on in."

The room smelled of a mixture of food, old wood, and sweat. Adrian picked the bed closest to the door, and pulled the gray blanket down to indicate it was taken. Then he walked over to the windows that ran along the entire wall of the room, almost too high to see out of. He pulled the heavy material aside and looked out. Shrubs moved in the breeze outside, scratching against the building. He didn't see Nikki anywhere. Maybe she had already gone home. Adrian thought of leaving now, maybe out a back door. If she saw him, she would know he wasn't homeless. No, he had to stay.

Adrian found the Bible Nikki had been reading, and settled into bed with it. He fingered the gold cross beneath his sweatshirt as he read. Within an hour, men started filtering into the room. A few were his age, and he wondered how they ended up there.

Conversation came in fits and spurts. According to the sign outside the shelter, drunks were not allowed. Adrian saw that some of these men at least had been drunk during the day. Their eyes were bloodshot, their movements groggy.

A large black man shuffled over and stood looming over Adrian's bed. He tried to ignore the shadow cast over the pages in front of him, but it was the man's smell that made Adrian finally look up. The man was probably in his thirties, had not lacked food obviously, and was staring right at Adrian.

"Can I help you with something?" Adrian asked, not moving.

"That's ma bed," he said simply, pointing at the bed.

Adrian set the Bible down and peered over the edge. "Don't see your name on it. Guess it's mine tonight."

"I mean, that's the bed I alway sleep on."

Adrian wasn't giving up the bed closest to the door. "You can have it back tomorrow, okay? I'm not moving."

When the man didn't budge, Adrian stood up. Though the man was large, Adrian's height exceeded his.

"You can have the bed tomorrow," Adrian stated again. "That one over there looks more comfortable anyway. I suggest you take it."

The man stared, as if he couldn't believe Adrian had defied him. Then he looked at the bed Adrian stood next to. Without saying a word, he shuffled over to another bed several yards away and dropped down on it with all his weight, making the bed creak and groan.

Adrian sat back down on "his" bed. Just as he found his spot again in the book, Dave's voice sounded at the doorway.

"Ten minutes before lights out." At the grumble, he added, "You know the rules, men."

Adrian set the book down on the floor beside him and reluctantly laid back on the pillow. This was crazy. In exactly ten minutes, the lights went out. A few men still moved about in the darkness, bumping into other beds with a loud *ow!* The man he'd displaced was still grumbling. Adrian lay on his side, waiting for his eyes to adjust to the complete darkness around him. A chorus of snoring took precedence over the mumbling in the far corner. One man was fighting a war in his sleep.

"Get his gun! He's an enemy soldier, get his gun!"

Adrian's ears perked to the slightest of sounds, especially those indicating that someone was approaching him. Springs creaked whenever someone shifted in their bed. He heard someone crying softly, muffled as the man gasped into his pillow. What made a man cry, he wondered. Losing his job? His family? Everything?

Adrian shuddered, knowing he was living his worst nightmare. This was what he'd thought of when his mother told him they were going to become homeless if she didn't get a good job soon. He'd worked damned hard and invested every penny so that this would never happen to him. Now, here he was, right in the middle of it.

He should just get the hell out of there, pack his stuff and get back to New York. Sure, he would wonder what had made Madame Blue go to the streets, and how she was doing. But he'd forget about her over time. With a sigh, Adrian pulled the blanket over him. It just wasn't that simple.

When Adrian woke, it was still dark. The only noise he heard was the cacophony of snoring around him. He sat up, rubbing his face, then walked over to the window and peered out. The street lights lit up the front area of the shelter, but beyond that light darkness lay in wait. Holding his watch up to the light, he saw that it was five o'clock. Moving quickly, he opened the door and slipped outside to the hallway. The large room where he'd first found Nikki was pitch black. He was sure she wouldn't still be outside. The front door was locked, and he unlocked it and walked out into the crisp, clean air.

Adrian headed toward his car, still several blocks away. He sucked in the air around him, glad to have someplace to go at night besides a shelter. It wasn't disgust that he felt for those men back there—it was pity. Even for that big, black man who'd wanted the bed Adrian had chosen.

That was probably all that man had, some bed he could call his own if he made it to the shelter early enough. It wasn't always because they didn't want to work. Some of the men in the shelter had spoken about their jobs, but it just wasn't enough. Some of them had mental problems, like Seamus. Some, like Charlie, had just fallen on bad luck and never recovered.

Adrian touched the gold cross that lay against his chest, thanking God for his good fortune, praying it would never run out. He stepped into his rental car, enjoying the new car smell. The heater kicked in quickly. He pulled out of the parking lot and headed for his cozy house near the beach.

Nikki was a different story than the rest of those poor souls. She didn't belong down there anymore than he did. Something had driven her there, and he had to find out what it was. If he could set things right, he could leave knowing she was safe and back in society. That's all he wanted to do, make sure she was safe. He ignored Stella's prediction that he would bring her risk. Nikki was already in danger.

Nikki smiled as the shots on the contact sheets came to life beneath the solution. Magic, that's what it was. Even though Crackers in the baby stroller was hopelessly blurred, she thought of Adrian standing behind her, speaking in that soft voice of his. She finished developing the rest and hung them up to dry. The ones of Crackers and Ceil came out great: a homeless woman enjoying the attention of a puppy, sharing an ice cream cone with him. She'd call it *Simple pleasures*.

Ulyssis was finishing up with a client when she emerged from the back room. She waited until the well-dressed woman left. Nikki had noticed that one of her pictures was missing, and it pleased her immensely. Because she still had money left over from the last huge sale, she allowed herself to think of her photography as something of pleasure, not necessity.

"It's so nice to see you smiling, Nicolina."

"My photographs came out wonderfully. Wait until you see them."

"Did you happen to take a picture of the man you spoke of last time you were here? Maybe I can tell you once and for all if he's the man who came with the sketches."

Nikki rolled her eyes. "No, I didn't take a picture of him. He's not . . . homeless enough."

Ulyssis looked skeptical. "So, you're still seeing him?"

She laughed at his term. "I'm not *seeing* him, no. We're not dating or anything." Just using the word *dating* seemed strange after all this time. "But he's around, yes."

"Is he the reason you're smiling?"

"He told me I was beautiful," she blurted out, realizing then how silly it sounded.

"Nicolina, don't buy into this guy. He might be a pimp for all you know!"

"He's not a pimp. You should see how tender he is with Crackers. And he's not the man who came in here, either. I followed him last night, just to see where he went. He spent the night at the shelter. I believe that he's just down on his luck."

Ulyssis smiled. "You are beautiful, Nicolina. Even like this." He gestured at her general appearance. "Be careful."

"I appreciate your concern. I'll be okay." Her voice softened. "He'll go on his way soon, I'm sure. He's looking for a job."

"Don't trust your judgment when your heart is involved."

She tweaked his cheek, and they both looked surprised. She hadn't done that since before the explosion.

"Nicolina, it is good to see you like this. But there is

something else I should tell you that might change your mood.''

She frowned. "What?"

"Jack came in the other day."

Nikki felt a yank on her heart. "Jack? My Jack?"

"Yes, if you wish to call him that." Ulyssis had never thought much of Jack, though he could never give Nikki a solid reason. "It's the first time since the trial that I've seen him at all."

"What did he want?"

"He wandered around a little, asked if I'd seen or heard from you."

Nikki hoped that Jack had obeyed his promise and never mentioned her dealings with Ulyssis to Devlin.

"Did he look at my pictures?"

"Only with a passing interest. Not like the first man."

Nikki didn't have to ask Ulyssis what he'd told Jack. She trusted that he'd said nothing. "How did he look?"

Ulyssis shrugged. "The way he always looked. Intense, dressed nice."

Nikki leaned against the wall. "I almost married that man. Life would have been so different if . . ." Her voice trailed off, not wanting to say the words.

"Don't forget that you had second thoughts, even before . . .''

Even Ulyssis couldn't say it. She stood and headed to the door. "I know. He was hurt when I wouldn't let him take care of me after the trial. Hurt that I wouldn't trust him with my life."

"You can only trust yourself, Nicolina."

She winked. "And you." Then she walked out the door.

As she drove through town to one of the places she hid her van, she saw Adrian walking down the sidewalk. Shrinking down in her seat, even behind the tinted glass, she drove quickly past him. Crackers sat in the passenger seat, and she called to get his attention. Too late. He saw Adrian and, tail whipping through the air, barked happily. Adrian looked up and watched her turn the corner. Inside, her heart was beating the same rhythm Crackers's tail was swinging.

She went several blocks before turning right and back-tracking. When she emerged on the sidewalk with Crackers, Adrian was heading toward the laundromat where he'd helped her the second time they'd met. He had a small bag in his hand, probably his laundry. He moved with such grace and pride, despite where he headed.

The day was warm and sunny, a welcome break to those who lived on the streets. The radio newscaster said it might reach eighty. She felt the tug of the beach calling her. Even though it was close to her old home, Nikki felt the most freedom when she walked on the beach.

She realized she was walking slowly toward the laundromat. Adrian was in the middle of the vacant lot now. Crackers saw him and started to run, forgetting the leash his idol had bought for him.

"That's what got you into this mess in the first place," she said to him.

Still, the pup pulled against the leash, hobbling along on his three good legs. When the tugging didn't work, he started barking. Adrian turned around and smiled. Even from a distance, that smile did strange things to her heart. Different things than Jack had ever done.

When Nikki reached the border of the lot, safely across the street, she let Crackers go. He bounded awkwardly to Adrian, who knelt instantly to pet him. But his gaze remained on her approach. When she got near, he stood. He always took her by surprise when she stood close to him. He was so tall and built, and just being next to him made her feel somehow safe.

"Hi, there."

"Good morning," she said, her voice going soft on her.

She could tell that he hadn't seen her following him last night. He probably would have thought she was strange. His smile was free from any suspicion.

"You know, I thought I heard this little guy barking as a van went by. I mean, from inside the van."

"Was it a brown van?"

"Yeah."

She nodded, hoping her expression wouldn't give her away. "We heard it too. Crackers went nuts."

Adrian seemed to buy her story. "I was just going to get some clothes done." He nodded toward his small bag. "What little I have." Then he looked up at the cloudless sky. "But it's so nice out. Since there's nothing in the paper today jobwise, I have a better idea. Want to go down to the beach?"

She must have looked surprised, because she could hardly hide her reaction to what he'd said. "H-how would we get there?"

He shrugged. "I've still got a little of that money left from my bartending job. I talked to the guy yesterday, and he might need me again. We could take a cab."

Nikki felt giddy, something she hadn't felt for a long, long time. Of all the places to suggest, he'd chosen the place she most wanted to go. And she would be safe with him. She felt silly, taking a cab when her van was right around the corner. Still, she couldn't take the chance.

"Okay." Was it a date? No, not here. People on the streets didn't have dates. Nor did they fall in love, she firmly told herself.

"We can bring Crackers. I doubt there'll be anyone down there, or at least not anyone who'll have the authority to kick us off."

"I know a place we can go where hardly anyone goes." They would have to go there. It was the only place on the beach where she felt isolated, and none of her family's friends lived near it.

"Sounds like a plan."

They hailed a cab, and Adrian paid with a handful of faded ones. The brisk wind slapped at her, but sunshine poured down like liquid warmth. They walked for several minutes, way past the few people who were watching the waves crash in. Probably tourists. Crackers strained on his leash toward the people, but Nikki pulled him close to her. The group of people *ooh'd* and *ahh'd* at the pup's bandaged leg, but when they looked up to see who the dog was with, they quickly turned away. Adrian didn't seem to care at all. He planted the two bottles of water he'd bought in a shady spot, and then pulled off his jacket and set it on the light brown sand, gesturing for her to sit on it.

Nikki almost laughed at the gesture, but managed to curb it into a smile. God, but it had been so long since that kind of chivalry had been shown to her. Even Jack had been too selfish to do such a thing. She sat down, pulling off her own coat and hugging her knees to her chest. Adrian took off his shoes and socks and leaned back, letting the sun caress his face. His dark curls danced in the breeze, and she fought an irresistible urge to reach out and touch them. They looked soft and silky.

Sunlight glistened off the cerulean blue water, a thousand diamonds scattered for the taking. Waves lapped up the sand, washing up with a *shwoosh*, then retreating silently. White clouds rolled swiftly by above them, and a gust of wind roared in her ears.

She let her head roll back and closed her eyes, smiling up at the sun. Oh, but it was strange and wonderful to feel this way! She felt young again, as young as her twenty-six years, instead of the old lady she looked and felt like in her daily existence. When she opened her eyes again, Adrian was leaning on his side watching her. In those brown eyes lingered a smile, the same one that was on his sensual lips.

"You're enjoying yourself," he stated.

She nodded. "I love coming down here."

"I know. I mean, I could tell. I'll bet you were a real beach bunny once."

She looked at him, wondering how he could ever guess that. "I was down here all the time, if that's what you mean." Almost every day when she was young, building sandcastles or playing out Barbie adventures.

"That's what I mean."

He rubbed a hand across his forehead, then pulled off his sweater. Beneath he wore just a T-shirt, and it stretched across his chest. His arms were tan and muscular. She caught herself staring and looked at Crackers busily sniffing around some piles of seaweed.

"You said you were in construction. What kind?"

He took a stick and made lines in the sand. "Mostly houses. Some remodeling." He looked at her, his gaze holding hers. "What about you? What did you do before . . ." He vaguely gestured, but she knew what he was talking about.

"I wanted to be a professional photographer." She looked out at the ocean, narrowing her eyes. "Then I went through some tough times and had to stop."

Tough times! How could she call what she'd been through tough times? When your mother is blown to bits in front of you, and you think you're going to die too. She shook her head, disgusted.

The touch of his hand on hers jerked her back to the present. "Are you all right?"

She nodded, not wanting those memories to spoil her wonderful day. She had plenty of time to think about that. His finger caressed the mottled skin on the back of her hand. She pulled it back, not wanting him to see the ugly scar tissue.

"Does that scar have anything to do with your tough times?"

"No," she answered too quickly. "Yes. But I don't want to talk about it."

"I understand."

And when she looked at him, she did see understanding in his eyes. Something else too. Something fierce and determined, just for a second. Then he took her hand, that scarred hand, and pressed it to his lips. His kiss sent shock waves through her body, but she didn't pull it back. Three years ago flames had licked at her hand, and now they were again. This time they were blissful, but just as searing. He kept his gaze on hers and she wondered what he saw.

His chest rose and fell deeply, though she could hardly catch her breath. Still holding her hand in his, he grazed her cheek with the back of his other hand. Her lips were trembling, and she only hoped he couldn't see it. Her heartbeat pounded through her as he moved closer. He reached behind her and pulled the ponytail holder from the bottom of her braid, then massaged his fingers through it to free her hair. The wind pulled it gently over her shoulders.

The hand he still held now burned hot beneath his touch. With the other hand he drew his fingers up the length of her neck until they reached her chin. His lips looked soft. His hand felt soft. He was looking right into her soul, she was sure of it. She swallowed hard. He leaned forward, very slowly, and captured her lips with his. They lingered for two seconds, then he moved back a couple of inches.

"You are so beautiful," she found herself whispering, though she'd meant to keep the words to herself.

She didn't have long to be embarrassed at their sound. He leaned forward and kissed her again, this time a little harder. His lips caught her lower lip in a tender grasp, and he slipped his tongue between. She opened her mouth, just a little, and he took her invitation without hesitating. His breath hitched slightly, and his hand slipped up to caress her jaw as they kissed. Instantly she was lost as their tongues danced together. She was in a dream world, a love story. And Adrian was her hero.

It seemed like they kissed for hours, but at last he ended the kiss and looked at her. Framing her face with his hands, he said, "*You* are beautiful." Then he kissed her again, with even more passion than before. There were places in her body tingling with warmth that she'd almost forgotten about. She felt dizzy with it all, and this time it was she who moved away.

"Let's go for a walk," she said, hearing her breathlessness and hoping he did not.

She expected an argument from him, but he stood, then offered her his hand. She took it, reaching up with her scarred hand and for the first time, didn't worry about it.

He let go of her hand when she gained her balance, and they walked side by side toward the mist beyond. She found herself smiling. This all felt so *normal*, walking with a man down the beach. For a little while, she could pretend her life wasn't in danger, that she didn't fully trust the man beside her, and that she lived in a van.

Adrian seemed deep in thought, looking out over the waves while the wind whipped at his hair. Nikki's own thoughts were a jumble of doubts, hopes, passion. Her lips still tingled, and she caught her fingers grazing them, remembering their kiss.

"How long have you lived on the streets?"

His voice, soft and low, rocked her out of her thoughts. He was looking at her, his eyes inquisitive. She wrapped her arms around herself.

"Two years." After the trial . . . which was a year after the explosion.

"Have you ever thought of going back? To society, I mean."

She shook her head vehemently. "Not now. Maybe later."

"How much later?"

She stopped, looking at him. "You can't save me, Adrian. I mean, if that's what you're thinking."

He smiled, though there wasn't denial on his face or in his voice. "Why not?"

"You just can't." She looked away, then returned her gaze to him. It surprised her that she wanted to tell him why he couldn't help her. Would it scare him away? Or did he already know? "What about you?"

"I plan to spend as little time here as possible. Sharing a room with forty other men isn't my idea of the good life. I've had roommates before, but they smelled a lot better."

"Women?" she asked, wishing instantly to take the word back.

He shook his head. "No, I've never lived with a woman."

Despite her agitation at her forwardness, she found herself smiling. It was foolish, really. Soon he would be gone, and she'd be long out of his mind. She thought of the last time she'd looked in a mirror. Her eyes seemed dull, no makeup on her skin, ragged nails. Well, at least she was clean. Nikki couldn't imagine anyone even thinking about kissing her. But he had. . . .

"What about you?"

She jerked out of her thoughts, finding her fingers combing through her windblown hair. "Me?"

"Ever lived with a guy? Or been married?"

"Engaged. A couple of years ago."

"And what happened? Cold feet?"

It was an innocent question, but she shivered anyway. "No. Well, yes, in a way. He wanted to get married right away, and I wasn't ready. We—oh, you don't want to hear all this." She really didn't want to tell him.

"Sure, I do."

"Well, we argued a lot about it, because we'd only known each other for a few months. I didn't want to be pressured, so I gave him his ring back." And then her life exploded.

"He's not the reason you live on the streets, is he?"

"No."

Adrian had started walking again, and she picked up his pace.

"Are you hiding from someone?"

She looked at him, feeling her suspicion rise. But if he were hired to find and kill her, wouldn't he already know all this? "Why do you ask that?"

He shrugged. "I'm just guessing, really. I think something happened to you, something terrible and frightening, and you're hiding on the streets. Am I close?"

Nikki didn't want to meet his eyes, but they drew her gaze and held it. "Too close."

"You've lived here for two years, by yourself. And you're afraid to go back to where you came from."

"Can't we talk about you?" She tried valiantly to keep her tone light and change the subject.

Adrian laughed. "Oh, no, you're much more interesting." He stopped again, holding her forearms lightly. His laughter left his features. "Will you tell me what you're afraid of? Maybe I can help you."

"No one can help me," she said, her voice in a whisper.

"Talk to me, Nikki. Try me."

Parts of her soul cried out to tell him everything and unload her burden. Despite his touch and the earnest look on his handsome face, the sensible part dominated.

"There's nothing you can do. Please, don't ask."

He nodded, letting her arms go. "I'm sorry."

Looking out to the ocean, he ran his fingers roughly through his hair. She could see the frustration in his eyes, and it baffled her that he wanted to help her. Why? She linked her fingers together, twisting them. In the last three years, she had worked hard to shut everyone out of her life. During the trial she had been a protected witness. Most of that time, she'd been in the hospital getting the many surgeries needed to restore her skin. After that, when Devlin had been acquitted, she'd gone into hiding.

"Why do you want to help me?"

Adrian turned around, and there was a strange light in his eyes. "I can't explain it. I just do."

She nodded, understanding not being able to explain things. What she did not understand were the feelings this man invoked in her. It was hopeless to feel giddy, flushed . . . hope*ful*. What could she possibly hope for? He couldn't save her. He wouldn't stay around. Yet, she found herself hoping that he'd kiss her again. Ah, it had felt so wonderful to be kissed, to be touched.

Adrian suddenly dropped down to the beach, scooping moist sand into a pile. A slice of skin showed between his T-shirt and jeans as he worked.

"What are you doing?"

He sat up. "What does it look like? I'm building a sand-castle."

Chapter 7

Can I dare to hope, to dream, to love?

Adrian loved the sound of her laughter as she watched him shape the large mound that would be the main part of the castle. One of the images in the tunnel showed Nikki doing this very thing. Who was that boy kicking in her sandcastle? He wanted to know, but couldn't ask.

Now she watched him with a reminiscent look on her face. A minute later, she knelt across from him and started pushing sand toward the mound. Sure, it was silly. Adrian wasn't even sure what had possessed him to do it. In fact, he was still stunned at his last impulsive move—kissing her. He didn't want to get involved with Nikki, beyond trying to help her. Stella had said their destinies were entwined, not that they would be lovers. Besides, Nikki had squelched his attempt to help her. So, why was he building a sandcastle with her? He should be going back to the house and packing, arranging for an earlier flight back to New York. He should certainly not be kissing her . . . or thinking of kissing her again.

She looked up at him, green eyes sparkling. Realizing he'd been staring at her, he dove back into the work at hand, shaping the first turret. Nikki watched him, then started building one on the other side. Her teeth were white as she smiled at him. She took good care of them, he could tell. And she always smelled clean, though today he couldn't detect the musky perfume she'd had on before. Her blond hair hung over her shoulders in soft waves, dragging in the sand when she leaned forward. A faint smile tinged her features as she busily worked at their creation. Crackers wandered over to investigate, but Adrian threw a stick to distract him, not wanting this sandcastle destroyed.

Nikki had to be one tough kid to survive for two years on the streets by herself. But right now, she seemed like a china doll, the sun reflecting off her pale skin. Her delicate fingers worked with precision, making the turret just perfect.

When she started to look up, he turned and searched in the immediate area for shells. He pressed them into the sides of the castle, just as she had done years ago. She watched him, a dazed expression on her face.

"What's wrong?" he asked, though he knew what she was thinking.

She shook her head faintly, then reached over and took a few of his shells to stick on her turret. When they finished the last two turrets, they decorated the inside courtyard with twigs and colorful coquina shells. Adrian laid on his stomach, working intently on one of the turrets. With a tiny stick, he drew a window, carving out a tiny hole.

"What's that?" she asked, leaning over his shoulder. Her hair tickled across his arm.

"This is where the princess is kept prisoner."

She raised an eyebrow, but didn't say anything at first. After a minute, she asked, "And where is the prince who will come to save her?"

He turned, his cheek less than an inch from hers, and softly, said, "Right here."

Her reaction made him regret saying the words, though

he hadn't planned to say them at all. Nikki's eyes closed, and she moved away, crossing her arms in front of her. He stood up, brushing the sand off, giving her a moment to herself. After a minute, he couldn't stand the silence.

"I think we should go for a swim."

She swiped her hair out of her eyes, looking at the aqua waters rushing in. "Be my guest."

He walked nearer to her. "How cold do you think it is? Can't be that cold."

"Warm enough for the tourists from Canada, maybe."

Adrian grabbed her around the waist, lifted her, and readied himself to hoist her into the water. She wriggled violently, though he was surprised at how light she was. And how thin.

"No! Put me down!"

He was standing in ankle-deep water with her in his arms. She had ceased her struggle, probably realizing it was safer to stay calm.

"On the count of three. Ready?"

"No!" She screamed, though her voice was filled with laughter, when she saw the teasing smile on his face.

"One." He started swinging her. "Two." She started struggling again. "Three!"

The nightmare flashed in his mind, the feeling of sucking in cold water instead of air, drowning. The water he saw through Nikki's eyes was black, so she would not drown with the sun sparkling through the ocean. Still, he swung her upright instead of out, holding her squarely around the hips to keep her feet out of the swirling water. She looked down at him, haloed by the sun behind her. Her fingers clenched on his shoulders, and her breath came heavily.

"Okay, maybe I won't."

He held onto her and walked back up to the beach. Her fingers relaxed their hold, and his shoulders felt warm where she touched them. She appeared uncertain as he stood there looking up at her. With her hair falling forward to frame her face, she looked childlike and free. Then he saw her shoulder, bared as her sweater had skewed from her struggle. A lacework of scars covered it. He let her slide slowly down in front of him, but she had already adjusted her sweater to hide her shoulder. She didn't meet his gaze, and he knew she'd seen him looking at it. When she started turning away, he pulled her back.

"Nikki . . ."

"Please . . . ," she said, trying to turn away again.

He saw shame on her face, and couldn't imagine why such a thing should make her feel ashamed. Adrian didn't let go of her arm. *Nikki, tell me about the fire. I felt it too.*

"Tell me what happened."

She shook her head, biting her lower lip. "No."

He pressed her scarred hand to his lips again, then held it up, studying the disfigured skin as it disappeared beneath her sleeve. Did it go all the way up to her shoulder? And where else? Not that it mattered.

"Fire," he stated.

"Adrian, please."

She pulled her arm, but he wouldn't let go. Instead, he turned the palm toward him and kissed it gently. Closing his eyes, he kissed each finger, savoring the feel of her skin, scarred or not. Beneath the screech of a seagull, he heard her breath catch. The wind whispered, but he paid no heed to its warnings not to continue. *You may bring her even more risk.*

When he opened his eyes, Nikki's were closed. Her head was tilted slightly back, her lips parted. He could not resist that invitation, those hungry lips. It had not been so long since he'd kissed a woman, but nothing felt the way kissing Nikki did. He wanted more.

Adrian pressed her hand against his chest and kissed her. She started slightly, but didn't move away. Her eyes remained closed as he continued to kiss her. Her tongue hungrily sought his, and he obliged her with equal passion. Touching the line of her jaw, he deepened their kiss. Her free hand joined the one on his chest, and they both slid upward to his shoulders. Adrian wanted to crush her to him, to hold her close and take away all her shame and fear. He remembered, though, how fragile she seemed, so he ran his fingers along her arms instead.

Tenderness warred with heat inside him as his body awakened. Her fingers curled through his hair at the nape of his neck, and he shivered at her touch. He wanted to comfort her, but he also wanted to lay her down on the warm sand and make love to her. The thought jarred him, making love to Madame Blue after all these years.

Crackers started barking, and Adrian instinctively looked up. Nikki backed away, wrapping her arms around herself in that protective manner. A couple approached, holding hands and enjoying that kind of intimacy only long-term couples shared. For the first time ever, Adrian envied them that.

"Crackers! Come here, silly dog," he bellowed.

Crackers made his way to Adrian, all the while keeping his eye on the couple as they walked past. His tail flipped through the air so fast, it almost became invisible.

When Adrian looked up, he saw Nikki walking back toward their coats. He motioned for Crackers to follow and caught up with her. She looked straight ahead. Even though her expression was sober, her skin was divinely flushed. He walked beside her.

"We shouldn't have done that," she said.

"Maybe not."

She faced him then. "Adrian, this will lead nowhere."

"You're right."

"It's pointless!"

"Probably."

She raised her arms, then dropped them with a long sigh.
"Will you do it again?"

The instant Adrian pulled her into his arms, Nikki melted
in his warmth. His lips hungrily devoured hers, swallowing
her up. After a few moments, he took a shuddering breath
and held her tight, enveloping her completely in his embrace. Oh, to be held like this! She felt completely safe,
warm, and loved. Loved? No, not that. But everything that
went along with it. She felt his breath on top of her head,
then the touch of his cheek resting there. Was it possible
to make this moment last forever? If only she could somehow suspend it on film.

Her arms had slid automatically around his waist, and
her cheek rested against his hard chest. The worn fibers of
his T-shirt were soft against her skin. His body radiated
heat, like a mist of male scent mixed with spicy deodorant
or cologne. She wanted to scream, to cry, to laugh—all at
once! The feelings rushed in over her on the sound of the
waves behind them. Sun-warmed sand crept up between her
toes. She felt tiny wrapped in his arms, like some small
creature seeking solace from the cold, harsh world around
them. His heart beat steady and strong; her own pounded
out an exotic rhythm.

After several minutes, she expected him to get tired of
standing there like that. He didn't indicate it, if he did.
Nikki could have stayed there all day, all night. Maybe all
month. She didn't want to feel that way. Well, parts of her
did, but not the sensible part. Of course, if she'd been sensible at all, she wouldn't have let him kiss her the first time,
much less all the others. Despite her self-chastising, she
found herself smiling. Okay, she could be sensible later,
when it counted.

It was Adrian who finally broke the spell, moving back
a foot. His finger trailed down the side of her cheek. "I'm
afraid if we stay like this much longer, I'll find myself in

an embarrassing and uncomfortable predicament.''

She flushed, fighting that involuntary urge to look down. Being held felt so innocent and wonderful, but Adrian was a man, after all. A man. What would he think if he knew she was a virgin? He pulled his T-shirt low over his jeans, then reached out for her hand. She noticed the trembling in her fingers as she slid them into his warm grasp.

Sure, Jack had tried his best to make their engagement more solidified. They did the petting thing, but something always held Nikki back. She'd never even told him that he would have been her first. Jack was so into the whole social scene, Nikki was sure he wouldn't understand how she didn't fit in or didn't want to. The more Mother pressured her to be social, the more Nikki shrunk into herself.

Adrian helped her into her coat, and they walked up to catch a taxi. Nikki didn't braid her hair, but tucked it back and slid her hood on. He watched her with curiosity, but didn't say anything. His strong arms scooped Crackers up as they headed toward the stairs to hail the cab.

It was late afternoon when the cab dropped them off in the city. Crackers had fallen asleep with his head on her lap on the ride back. He hardly moved at all when Adrian pulled him out and set him down on the sidewalk.

''I'd better get going,'' she said, though her heart told her to stay.

He looked as if he wanted to say something, but only nodded.

She looked at Crackers. ''Come on.'' As she started walking away, Adrian's laugh made her turn around.

''I don't think he's going anywhere.''

Crackers was lying down, snout between his paws. Bits of sand jumped each time he exhaled through his floppy lips. Nikki snapped the leash on him and pulled, but he didn't budge. She thought of the exhausting trip she'd made carrying him the last time. She was even farther from her van now.

"Nikki, I realize you don't want me to know where you stay. But if you want me to carry him somewhere, I will. You can pick him up later."

So, he'd figured that out. She doubted Dave would let her leave the pup in his office again. If she tied him up somewhere, someone could hurt him or take him before she returned with the van. Nikki looked at Adrian who was fully aware of her predicament. Could she . . . dare she trust him? The memory of his kisses clouded her senses.

"Follow me."

He effortlessly scooped up Crackers and walked beside her. All the way back to the alley her van was parked in, she debated on letting him know where she lived. Of course, she never left her van in the same spot. She moved it throughout the day and parked it in different spots every night. A man who held a dog like that couldn't be a killer, or a double-crosser. He just couldn't.

When they rounded the corner and walked into the alleyway, Adrian stopped. He looked at the brown van, then at her.

"This is where you live?"

"Uh-huh."

He followed her to the van, where she slid open the door and stepped aside so Adrian could set the dog down on the pillow bed she'd made. He looked around at her abode as he did so, taking in the orange carpet, brown carpeted walls, and all the tiny things that made it home to her.

"Wow." He nodded. "This is really something."

She couldn't believe his look of admiration. Sure, it was neat and efficient, but it was only a van. Her Steiff bear sat on the tiny bed, as if waiting for her return.

Adrian smiled. "Well, at least I know you're relatively safe at night."

That made her smile. He cared that she was safe. A warm rush of tickles washed over her. She thought of inviting him inside, but in this mood, she was likely to crawl back into his arms. Not that that was so bad, but she knew it would lead to more. She was already in enough trouble as it was. Her heart pitter-pattered when he touched her chin.

"See you later, okay?" His eyes told her he would hold her to that no matter if she agreed or not.

She could only nod. His fingers remained against her skin for a moment as he looked into her eyes.

"Take care of yourself," he said; then he turned and walked away. Nikki watched him go, noting his graceful walk filled with confidence.

She climbed into her van, slid the door closed, and sat down on her bed, hugging her teddy bear close. No, this couldn't be happening to her. She couldn't be feeling dangerously close to falling in love. He was homeless, she was hiding for her life.

Nikki realized it was already too late. She couldn't wait to see him tomorrow. She couldn't wait to feel his lips against hers again. When Ulyssis warned her to stay away from Adrian, he had no idea how right he was.

Rita paced back and forth with each empty ring. Damn, where was Adrian, and what was he doing? Men were so rude, taking off and not telling the women who loved them why. She had wrangled the phone number and address from Stanley, with the promise to get him back earlier for that Calvin Klein meeting. Hmm, maybe she could sweet-talk Adrian into using her for the layout. There were definite advantages to having a hot photographer as a lover. If only he would give his heart to her, then she'd have it made, in more ways than one.

After the twentieth ring, Rita hit the off button and dropped the phone onto the couch. Either he was out, or he wasn't answering. Well, whatever he was doing, maybe he could use a little company. She glanced in the mirror, fluffing her hair. What if she showed up on his doorstep and surprised him? Rita smiled, imagining his pleasantly astonished expression when he walked in and found her naked on his bed, or maybe wearing an apron and nothing else, cooking a nice little meal for him. Maybe his guard would be down.

Oscar meowed loudly until she poured cat food into his white bowl. He rubbed against her leg, then walked over to check out the contents. If only Adrian were that simple, she thought with a sigh. Satisfy him, and he'd eat out of her hand. Not a chance!

Rita picked up the phone and made another call, this time to her travel agent. This would be a surprise visit Adrian wasn't likely to forget in a long time.

The next morning Adrian stood in front of the large bathroom mirror, combing his beard. He now wished he hadn't adopted the damn thing for a disguise, although it might seem suspicious that a homeless man would be clean shaven every day. It was worth it if the beard helped Nikki believe his lie.

He sighed, leaning on the counter. Adrian hated lying. Every time he had to tell an untruth to support his original lie, it killed him. He realized now that Nikki never would have let him near her, though, if she suspected anything but that he was temporarily homeless and out of luck. She was beginning to trust him, though Adrian knew it was the last thing she wanted to do. And she'd let him kiss her, though it was the last thing he'd expected to do. She did kiss nicely . . . very nicely.

The time was coming to tell her the truth. How could he really help her without doing so? He had no idea how she'd take it, but it was far better for him to tell her than for her to find out on her own. Nikki didn't belong on the streets anymore than he did, and he intended to do everything he could to get her off them.

Even if she was penniless, she had a great deal of talent. Perhaps he could bring her to New York and hone that talent to something more commercial and lucrative. A mental picture flashed into his mind of Nikki sitting at his dinette table, the city of New York behind her, drinking coffee and going over contact sheets with him. It was a cozy picture, and gave him a warm feeling inside. Strange, but he'd never gotten into cozy domestic scenes before. Why, he'd even seen Crackers lying at her feet.

Adrian shook his head, not sure if he was ready for all that yet. What he did know was he wanted to save Nikki from whatever she was hiding from, and he was getting closer to finding out what that was. Once that was done, then he'd see about the rest of it. The first order of business was finding her this morning and taking her out for breakfast.

Rita pounded on the door, then tried all the windows of the charming two-story house where Adrian was staying. Her five-inch heels sunk into the grass with every step as she tromped through the foliage which was still lush and green, even in November.

Her black hair snagged on a branch overhead, and she gently disentangled it before trying the window around back. With a gleam in her eye, she realized the catch was loose. She jimmied the window, and it slid free. It was impossible to climb in a window wearing a miniskirt and fur coat with any amount of grace. She removed her shoes and threw them in first, then climbed after them.

"I hope no one calls the cops. This could be very embarrassing," she muttered, half in and half out.

When she regained her balance, she realized she was in a bedroom, but one that wasn't being used. Rita found the master bedroom quickly. It was light and airy, with a ceiling fan and two picture windows. And a nice, large bed. Adrian's silk robe was thrown haphazardly over a stuffed chair.

In the bathroom, she got all kinds of delicious thoughts when she saw the large, marble tub. There was even a separate glassed-in shower stall, big enough for two. The sink was still wet, though there was no trace of those tiny hairs left over from his morning shave. Most importantly, though, Rita found nothing to indicate that a woman also shared that bedroom with Adrian.

She hadn't let herself think of finding him here with another woman, but her enormous sigh of relief let on that her subconscious had thought of little else. Which led her to the question foremost in her mind: What was he doing here?

What she did find baffled her even more. In the closet were the clothes she expected to find. But in the drawers were the grungiest things she'd ever seen. Oh, they were clean, but stained and faded and just plain old. Rita assumed that they had been left here by the previous renter, but even that left the question: Why would anyone able to rent a place like this wear clothes like that?

The photographs were a mystery too. Framed pictures of homeless people were spread all over the dining tabletop. Rita sat down at the place where Adrian obviously ate— alone—and picked up one of the pictures. These people were the real thing too. There was another one without a frame. It was a homeless woman on the beach, all covered in a cloak.

Then Rita smiled, figuring out the big mystery. Adrian was working on a project, photographing homeless people for some reason known only to him, apparently. Not that Adrian was the most open of men anyway. She remembered the nightmare he'd had and wouldn't share with her.

Her frown turned back into a smile as she looked at the pictures again. This wasn't the kind of work Adrian usually did, and it couldn't be all that profitable. So he was keeping it a secret from everyone, even her. It was the perfect opportunity to show him she could be trusted.

Rita's plans of sprawling herself out on his bed wearing a sexy teddy turned into a nap as she grew bored waiting for him. When she woke up, she looked in the mirror and made a face. She looked terrible, not at all what she wanted Adrian to see when he came home. She'd been there for three hours already, and she'd be the picture of boredom by the time he returned, whenever that was.

Rita walked over to the pictures again, picking up the one with the old building made into a church. This is where he was, she knew it. He was taking photographs. Now, wouldn't he be surprised if she showed up there? She went back into the bedroom and put on her black velvet jeans, a puffy sweater, and those heels. Then she slipped into her fur coat, because it was the only coat she'd brought. She took off all her jewelry, not wanting to attract too much attention in an undesirable part of town. A laugh escaped her lips as she looked in the mirror. How could she not attract attention?

She was feeling very clever and pleased with herself as she took the picture of the church into a convenience store and asked where it was located. The clerk pointed her in the right direction with a red marker on her map, but warned her about going there alone.

"Oh, I have a friend who's down there right now. He's big and strong, and he'll save me if I run into trouble." And, of course, she didn't plan on getting out of her car until she saw him.

She couldn't wait to see the expression on his face when she found him. Wasn't he going to be impressed?

Chapter 8

Deceit wins no lovers or friends.

Rita cruised through town a few times before she spotted Adrian. Or she thought it was him, anyway. He was tall and had dark hair. He wore it loose, like he did when they made love, and it was curly, the way it looked before he blew it straight. But he had a beard, something she'd never seen on him. And he was wearing the most god-awful clothes she had ever seen on anybody, much less a fashionable man like Adrian. Still, it had to be him. But who was the woman walking with him?

She pulled around the corner and got out, fluffing her hair. Then she walked around the building to the sidewalk. Closer up, she knew it was Adrian. She'd recognize those eyes anywhere. What she didn't like was the way they took in the woman beside him. She was obviously a homeless person, though she had a fresh prettiness about her and a nice smile that she flashed at Adrian.

It was insane to feel threatened by this woman, but Rita did. She would not lose the man she loved to a street waif. What could he be thinking? Not about photography—no camera in sight.

They were almost upon her when she gathered her wits

about her. Her voice didn't come out as casually and normal as she would have liked.

"Adrian?"

He looked up at her then, and she waited for a flash of recognition and surprise, hopefully a smile. She got nothing.

"Do I know you?"

He gave her such a blank look that Rita began to doubt it was him after all. "Aren't you Adrian Wilde?"

"No, my last name is Nash. You have the wrong person. Excuse us."

He walked on, never even looking back. Rita stood there with her mouth open, staring after them. She wanted to scream at him for pretending not to know her. As if he was ashamed to know her! Maybe he'd hit his head and really didn't remember who he was. No, he looked perfectly healthy. The woman with him glanced back for a second, her expression filled with question. Rita was sure hers looked the same.

"She's still standing there," Nikki said, watching Adrian's face carefully.

He shrugged. "They say we all have a twin somewhere. Mine must have the same first name too. But I don't know her."

It wasn't the first name that bothered Nikki tremendously. It was the last name. Just a coincidence that this Adrian Nash looked like Adrian Wilde, who had gone into the gallery searching for a woman who looked like her? Her throat tightened, but she pretended to remain calm.

Nikki glanced back, saw the woman walking to a nice rental car. She certainly wasn't from this area. That fur was real. In fact, the woman reeked of New York City.

Adrian looked deep in thought, but not apparently about the woman; he hadn't looked back even once. She looked at Adrian, who smiled at her. He said something about all the empty stores in the area, but her mind was clicking at high gear with her suspicions. Adrian had lied to her, had looked for her, and now had touched her heart. But why? If he was working for Devlin, why hadn't he killed her already?

Her heart was being crushed under the weight of her thoughts. *Adrian Wilde, who are you?* Tremors ran through her body, reaching all the way down to her toes. She had only been worried about his breaking her heart before; now she also had to worry about his taking her life.

"Are you all right? You look pale," he said, still looking as concerned as he always looked.

She smiled, willing the color to return to her face. "I'm okay. Maybe I'm just coming down with something."

"Do you want to go back to the van?"

She nodded, grabbing at any excuse to get away from him. Above all, she couldn't let on that she suspected anything. Instead of running away, she let him walk with her back to her van. As soon as he was gone, she would leave the area. Then she remembered Ceil's words: Spy on him. Nikki had tried that before, and he'd gone exactly where she had expected him to go. But could he have known she followed him? She had to find out who he was before she just disappeared. Every instinct told her to run far away, but her heart cried out to know who this man was.

Crackers slid out from beneath the van, his pink tongue hanging out. In her mind, Nikki could see Adrian gently carrying the pup to the animal hospital, pacing as he waited with her to hear if the pup was all right. No, he couldn't be working for Devlin! She looked at him, knowing her heart was breaking into a thousand bits. If he was, he was damn good at his job. And damn slow at it too.

Nikki untied Crackers and unlocked the door. "See you later," she said, wishing she meant it.

"You going to be all right? I can stay with you if you'd like."

She shook her head. "I'll be fine."

"Can I get you anything?"

Why did he have to look so concerned, so genuine? "No, thank you."

"Would you like to get together later?"

"I'm just going to relax tonight. Maybe tomorrow."

"Sure."

He left, and Nikki leaned against the side of the van. Where would he go now? There was one way to find out. This time she would make sure he didn't notice her. She went inside and put on a gray raincoat and boots. She retied Crackers to the bumper and walked down the alley. He was walking south.

Nikki slid out of the alley and ducked into an indented storefront. He didn't look back, though. In fact, it was several blocks before he did turn around. She quickly turned and pretended to look in the little food store, scrunching down to appear shorter. When she glanced at him, he was gone. She quickly walked to where he had disappeared, peering cautiously around the side of the building. Nikki wondered if he stayed in the apartments around the corner.

She heard a car start, and ducked back as a white convertible Mustang pulled out of its parking space. Somehow, she knew it was him even before she saw him. She also knew it was the same car that hit Crackers. Of course, he couldn't blow his cover by admitting it, or stopping when it happened.

Nikki felt a sharp pain in her chest, and all the energy drained out of her. She slid down to the sidewalk, drawing her knees up in front of her. She wanted to scream, to cry, to hit something, but all those took more strength than she had. Now there was no doubt Adrian had lied to her. The question remained: Why? Was he going to Devlin's right now, to report on the latest? Perhaps if she knew for sure, she could put him behind her and disappear. She had to know if Adrian was connected to her brother. And she planned to find out tomorrow night.

When Adrian returned to his rental house, he found Rita leaning against a rental car out front. She'd probably blown the whole thing by showing up like that. Anger burned inside him, but he tamped it down. She looked confused, but her eyes widened when she saw him pull in. He didn't want to explain anything to her; she had no right to be there, and he owed her nothing. What he didn't want was for her to run back and tell Stanley he'd lost it. Stanley would be here in five minutes, begging him to regain his sanity. What a mess. He only hoped Nikki really hadn't felt well, and wasn't blowing him off.

"It *was* you!" she said accusingly, walking toward the garage where he parked his car.

"Yes, it was me. What the hell are you doing here, anyway?"

"I wanted to surprise you."

"Well, you did that."

She followed him into the house, and he saw immediately that she'd already been inside. She replaced one of the pictures she had with her, putting it back exactly where it had been on the table.

"Adrian, I know about your secret project. You don't have to worry about me telling anyone. It's our secret."

"My secret . . ." He followed her gaze to the pictures. "Oh, that secret project." She'd just given him a way out.

"It just makes me sad that you didn't tell me about it." She inched closer, putting her hands on his shoulders. "Didn't you trust me?"

He moved her hands away. "It's personal, that's why. I'm trying to blend in with those people, and you show up and blow my cover. And you wonder why I didn't tell you."

He regretted the words when she looked so hurt. "If I knew, I wouldn't have gone there. I just saw these pictures and thought you might be down there. I'm sorry, Adrian. I'll stay right here out of your way."

"You're going back to New York."

"But why? I came all the way down here to spend some time with you."

"If you'll recall, I didn't invite you. I'm not here at the house very much, and you'd be bored anyway."

She smiled. "I could have dinner waiting for you when you get home."

Adrian sat down with a sigh, rubbing his face. "I don't always come home for dinner."

"Do you have dinner with that woman you were with?"

Adrian heard the jealousy lacing her voice, just as he heard her attempt to hide it. "Sometimes. Look, Rita—"

"I know, I know. I have no right to ask. But a girl's got a right to know about her competition."

The thought of Nikki and Rita in competition was ludicrous. Nikki was Madame Blue, not his girlfriend. And neither was Rita.

"She's a friend," he said simply.

She nodded slowly. "I see."

They sat in strained silence for a few moments, and he didn't like that much more than their previous conversation. "Who's watching Oscar?"

"Morty. I told her I'd only be gone a day or two." She looked at him hopefully.

"Well, won't she be surprised when you return early."

"Adrian," she whined. Kneeling before him, she stroked her long fingers down his faded jeans. "Let's have some fun for a couple of days. Then I'll leave, and you can go back to your project."

He stood and stripped off his shirt, then unzipped his jeans and stepped out of them. He hated wearing those grungy clothes any longer than he had to.

"Mmm, now that's more like the Adrian I know. The beard is, well . . . I like it. It's different, but it gives you a whole new look."

Just the mention of it made his chin itch. "I hate it, but it goes with the whole costume."

Rita licked her lips, letting her gaze roam down his body. She was never shy about her intentions, he had to give her that. And that might be all he was giving her. His body didn't seem interested in the prospect of cozying up with Rita in that big bed in there. It had sure worked the day before, and he'd only been kissing Nikki. But the whole package with someone else didn't excite him. This was the strangest thing he'd ever encountered.

"I'm going to take a shower, then we'll go out for an early dinner. You can stay tonight, but tomorrow you have to go back to New York. Got it?"

She looked slighted, her lip pouting out and eyebrows drawn together. "Okay, Adrian, I'll take the proffered crumb."

"Rita, I didn't invite you here, remember?"

"I know. Want some company in the shower? Or, I noticed that nice big tub in the master bath."

He didn't hide his irritation at her having snooped through the house. Probably looking for signs of a female companion. Adrian couldn't imagine how such a beautiful woman could be so insecure.

"Go ahead and take a bath. I'm just going to take a quick shower. By myself." *How do you tell a woman you're not interested in a nice way?* Well, he'd have to figure out a way if she was going to stay the night.

*   *   *

"Ceil, do you know how to break into a car?"

Ceil giggled, looking for a second like a schoolgirl. "Well, kind of. There was a guy around here who showed me how to do it. I have the tool."

"You have the tool? How did you get it?"

"When they came and arrested him, he gave it to me to hide." She patted her big bag on the seat next to her. "Right in here."

"Do you use it?"

"Oh, no! I just like to keep it with me. Jake showed me how to use it. Nikki, he was so fast. I timed him once. One minute, twenty-two alligator seconds."

"Can you show me?"

Her eyes widened, as if realizing now what Nikki was asking. "*You* want to break into a car?"

"Yes. Adrian's car."

"He has a car? I thought—"

"So did I. I have to find out who he really is. I spied on him, Ceil, just like you said to. And I found out he keeps a car hidden at an apartment complex nearby."

"Ooh, he's such a liar!"

"He's that, and maybe more. I'm going to get in his car and see where he goes. Can you help?"

"Of course I can help. Did you see him smoke a cigarette like I was telling you?"

"No, I've never seen him smoke at all. There's a lot to him I don't know. But I'm going to find out."

Nikki had lunch at a diner with Adrian the next day. She did her best to be animated and act as normal as she could.

"Well, you look like you're feeling better," he said with a smile after they'd finished eating.

"Yes, I am." Actually, she felt horrible, especially when she looked at his lips and thought of their kisses. She cursed her body for wanting more of them. "Sorry I was such a dud."

"I understand." He leaned his elbows on the table, resting his chin on his folded hands. "Nikki, let's go down to the beach tonight. You have a little barbecue grill, right?" She nodded slowly. "I'll bring some hamburgers and we'll cook them on the beach. I want to talk with you tonight. About something important."

Her heart lurched. "Won't it be cold?"

"It's only supposed to get to the midsixties tonight, but we'll go at sunset so it'll be warmer. If it gets too cold, we can go back to the shelter and read or something."

"I don't know." She searched his eyes for any sign of malice, but found nothing.

"What's the matter? Don't you trust me?"

Nikki almost choked on the soda she was taking a sip of. "Of c-course I do." She gave him her best imitation of a sheepish smile. "Why, shouldn't I?"

A pained look flashed briefly across his features. He took her hands in his, soft hands that couldn't belong to a construction worker. "You can trust me with your life."

She couldn't breathe for a moment as she looked into his brown eyes. If she didn't know better, she would have believed him. Her heart wanted to believe him, dangerously disillusioned thing that it was. It all made her so angry, that he had come here and stolen her heart under false pretenses, that he might be a killer. She hid her anger behind another phony smile.

"Dinner on the beach sounds nice. Why don't we meet here at six?"

He smiled, probably glad his plan was working so well. Get her alone on a darkened beach and kill her. Maybe after seducing her. She should be angry at him, but what she felt most was the pain that she had fallen in love with a man who was not what he pretended to be. If he was a killer, he wasn't going to get a chance to perform his job on her. By seeing where he went, she would be able to tell who he was and what his motives were. Not that it mattered. Even if he weren't a killer, he had lied to her for some reason. That was enough to make her disappear from his life forever.

Nikki made a quick exit after lunch, pretending to have a lot of things to do. Actually, she had nothing to do but wait until six. Then she would put her own plan into action and get some answers.

From across the street, Nikki saw Adrian glance at his watch again. He wore loose white pants and a long-sleeved shirt that was untucked. She chastised herself for admiring those broad shoulders, and especially for remembering all too vividly how it felt to be held in those arms. It just wasn't fair! But, she reminded herself, she knew to keep her heart away from him right from the beginning. She deserved every ache inside, every twist of her stomach.

What bothered her most as she slipped from her vantage point and headed toward his car was that he looked worried. Genuinely worried, but not irritated that his plan wasn't working. Her emotions were playing tricks on her perception. Or he was a better actor than even she gave him credit for.

The jimmy Ceil had given her worked on the second try, and she quickly climbed in the back and crammed herself behind the passenger seat. She hoped he would give up on her showing soon, before her joints permanently locked in this position.

Unfortunately, it was more than an hour before he returned to the car. Nikki was sure the pounding of her heart would give her presence away as the blood pumped loudly in her ears. Light filled the interior for a second, filling her with dread at the same time. Adrian closed the door, but didn't start the car right away. The faint smell of cologne drifted through the tiny space as he let out a sigh.

"Nikki, where are you?" he whispered, making her heart ache with the emotion in his words. Maybe he had convinced himself that he cared about her.

It was several minutes before he even started the engine, and then he slowly pulled out and drove around for a while. The only part of her that showed beneath her coat and hood was her eyes. From her spot, she could only see lights above the stores, and had no idea where they were. He was driving slowly, though, indicating that he was searching for her. She only hoped he wouldn't find her van, though she was fairly certain he wouldn't think of looking in a used car lot. With the price written on the windshield, and parked in the darkest spot in back, she doubted he'd even notice.

Nikki's legs were numb by the time he stopped the car again. She heard a door slide open, then he pulled in a car's length. By the echo of the car engine, she knew they were inside somewhere. Maybe a garage. The engine cut to silence, and still Adrian sat in the car for a few minutes. Again, dreadful light filled the inside, and she shrunk down in her hood. A second later the door slammed shut, making her ears ring with the sudden change of pressure. She heard another door close behind her, guessing that he had walked inside a house.

Nikki waited a few minutes before daring an attempt at extricating herself from the tiny space. The numbness in her legs turned to a tingling ache, but she was glad to know they were still alive. The garage was dark, though she could see the fine line of light beneath the door leading inside. She stretched her legs on the backseat, remaining low just in case he decided to come out to the garage again.

After a while, she drifted off to sleep, bored from waiting in the dark. When she woke again, she had no idea how much time had passed, but it felt late somehow. The light beneath the door was out, and the garage was almost completely dark. She quietly got out of the car, noticing when the interior light came on that it was nearly two in the morning.

Putting her ear to the door, she couldn't hear any sound inside. All the crazy thoughts she should have considered before rushed into her mind. What if he had turned an alarm on when he went to bed? What if he were awake, sitting right on the other side of the door reading the paper? What if the door was locked? She had no idea where she even was, what with all his driving around. Though if he did work for Devlin, he probably would be staying somewhere near the mansion.

Nikki listened for the tiniest sound, even the rustle of a page of newspaper being turned. Black shadows moved before her eyes, the dark playing tricks on her. All she could hear was the sound of her heartbeat. Her fingers trembled as she wrapped them one by one around the cold doorknob. The metal warmed beneath her touch, then became slippery with her perspiration before she even attempted to turn it. Her life hung in the balance at what she would find on the other side. Especially if it was him.

She rustled up memories of Adrian with Crackers, gently carrying him, keeping his promise of buying him lunch. Other unwanted memories came too, though. His kisses, gentle and filled with promise. She was sure that he hadn't intended to kiss her by the surprise on his expression. He had touched her, had asked softly about her scars, but hadn't pressed for answers. She shook her head, expelling those last memories and the rush of feelings that came with them. That was when he thought she believed his charade. If he found her here, he would know that she knew it was all a lie. And if he were here to kill her, he would have to go through with it, or know he couldn't finish the job because she would disappear.

She turned the knob a fraction. Then another. It wasn't locked. He might not notice the knob turning, but he would sure notice when the door cracked open. She remembered the lack of light beneath the door, and it gave her the courage to turn the knob another inch. He couldn't be sitting in the dark reading, now could he? Though he could be just sitting there, wondering why she had stood him up. And she would walk right into a situation that could end her life and make her two years of hiding in vain. The next turn of the knob released the door, and she held her breath before pulling it open.

Chapter 9

Life is too precious to trust to the heart.

Darkness greeted Nikki, and nothing else. She released her breath, but remained on the step. After a few seconds of listening to the silence around her, she stepped inside, leaving the door open. Not for a quick escape, since the garage was sealed. No, she would have to leave through the front entrance. Then, even if she woke him, she could disappear outside before he could get to the door.

In what looked like the living room, a light shone dimly. Nikki held her breath again and walked into the dark part of the kitchen where she could see into the lighted room. The coral-colored couch was empty, and beyond that was a darkened hallway. She had to hope that Adrian was in bed. There was, of course, one way to find out. With that assurance, she could roam around and try to get a clue as to who Adrian really was.

She felt exposed as she walked through the lighted room, but knew she would attract more attention if she turned the light off. There were no personal items in the living room, only a newspaper. A staircase led up to what had to be more rooms, and she only hoped Adrian slept on the lower floor. Stairs could creak, and in the quiet, it would be a dead giveaway. Dead. She swallowed the lump that already had begun forming in her throat.

Nikki walked across the cool tile toward the hallway. The first door was half open, and moonlight poured in through the sheers above the bed. The bedroom was large, with a king-sized bed in the middle and two dressers. It smelled faintly of Obsession. Her heart jumped when she saw Adrian lying in a tangle of sheets. They were thrown off his chest, as if he'd been tossing and turning in his sleep. She found herself drifting across the tile toward the bed, standing only a few feet away from him. The sheets rode low on his hip, and the flush of heat at the realization that he was naked surprised her.

She wanted to feel anger toward him, sleeping here in this beautiful house while pretending to be homeless. He must have known she was following him that night he'd slept in the shelter. How he must have hated that. She smirked at him, but felt it turn into a faint smile. Nikki remembered telling him that he was beautiful. He was, no doubt about it. His arms were strong, even relaxed in sleep, and his wide chest tapered down to that slim, bare hip. She had just been too vulnerable, and he knew how to touch all the right buttons. No matter how foolish she had been, she had to get smart about it now. And find out who he was.

The robe draped over a chair in the corner was silk, as she found out when she touched it on the way out of the bedroom. Did he live here? she wondered. It didn't look personal enough for a permanent residence. She remembered the man who had come into Ulyssis's shop asking for her. He had been from New York. She turned and narrowed her eyes at Adrian. *Who are you?* she mouthed silently.

Nikki walked back to the kitchen. Judging the angles, she knew turning on a light wouldn't affect the hallway. Light filled the kitchen area, making her blink while her eyes adjusted. The kitchen was well stocked, but the sticker on the wall instructing how to use the coffeemaker. clued her in that this house was not a permanent residence. He made coffee and ate bagels just like any normal person. What did he think about when he stood here in the morning waiting for the coffee to brew? How to kill her? She couldn't be sure, but what other reason would a man have for hunting down a woman he had never met before?

A box of gourmet cookies sat on the counter, and in the garbage she saw the remains of a lobster. The refrigerator revealed more delectables: fresh mushrooms, two steaks, a package from the store labeled shark. He ate well for a man who was jobless.

What she found on the kitchen table both cleared things up and confused her more. Laid over the surface were her framed photographs of the homeless, the collection from the gallery. It still didn't make any sense that he would buy her entire collection of photographs. She looked at them, as if they would give her a clue. Perhaps they had given him the clue he needed to find her. After all, they were taken in her world. But how had he connected them with Nikki Madsen?

Another photograph lay on top of one of hers, this one unframed. She held it under the light, annoyed that her fingers trembled. It was her, on the beach. It could not have been taken that long ago. Nikki thought of her recent visits to the beach, obviously foolish risks. Of course, the last visit with Adrian popped into her mind first, and she quickly dismissed it. She knew he didn't have a camera with him.

The picture slid from her fingers as she remembered the fashion shoot over a week ago. It was him! She hadn't seen his face, but remembered that smooth voice coaxing the models into changing for the next shot. How could he have known she would be down there? How? There was no earthly way! Even the photograph showed but a little of her face. She stared at it, her eyes wide in confusion.

Would he have set up this phony shoot just to snap a picture of her to show Devlin as identification? She knew even Devlin wouldn't have recognized her from that picture. Nikki had risked her life to come here and find out who Adrian was, and she had at least done that. But now she was even more confused about why he was there.

She looked around the kitchen for more clues. A camera sat on the edge of the counter, and she walked over to pick it up. It was a Hasselblad, like hers, only his was much more sophisticated. This wasn't the kind of camera an amateur would buy for a cover. Of course, he could be a private investigator. Hadn't he said his uncle owned an agency?

On the other side of a bottle of wine was a note pad. She walked over to read the words scribbled there. "Calvin Klein. 10:00 meeting next week. Tom Cruise and Paulina." Next to that was some flight information and a little drawing of a short, balding man with glasses. It didn't look anything like Devlin, that was for sure.

Nikki rubbed her fingers down her face, thoroughly confused. She picked up the Hasselblad and studied it again. When she turned it upside down, she saw an identification label: "Adrian Wilde, Visions, Inc." along with a New York address. The same as the business card. Adrian Wilde. Seeing the whole name spelled out like that made something niggle at her memory, and she made a mental note to check on it later. Her gaze remained on the words *Calvin Klein.* Adrian was real. Why in the world was he looking for her, lying about who he was? It had to be in conjunction with Devlin. There was no other plausible explanation. But what was the connection between a New York fashion photographer and her brother? The lack of plausibility baffled her.

She wished she could somehow tie up Adrian without waking him and ask all the questions that bombarded her mind and heart. That was impossible, she knew that. She shook her head, knowing the frustration she would always live with not knowing the answers.

When she turned around, her elbow bumped one of the framed photographs and it fell from the table. It seemed to be in slow motion as it fell to the tile floor. Her hands fumbled, catching it, losing it, then gripping it just before it hit the floor. Her heart raced, paralyzed her as she listened for sounds of Adrian waking up from the small noise. After a moment, she let out her breath.

She took another look around, overwhelmed by the different view she now had of Adrian. Obviously well off, a famous photographer who enjoyed the finer things in life, yet had dressed like a homeless person to get to her. Why?

It was time to leave. She'd been lucky so far, but her luck was bound to run out. As she turned to go, she saw a shell necklace hanging from the key rack. Her hand reached for it of its own will and took it. She slipped it over her head as she headed toward the front door. A reminder. Of her own foolishness, she added to her thoughts.

Her fingers tightened around the knob as her other hand turned the dead bolt and slowly opened the door. No alarm went off, and she silently slipped outside and closed the door behind her. She found herself trying to find a way to lock it from the outside, then chastised herself for worrying about Adrian's safety.

The smell of the ocean assailed her senses along with the salty breeze. She was near the mansion, she knew it. The sound of the waves washed over her, sending chills through her just as the cold water would. It would be a long trek back to her van. While Palm Beach would be safe, at this time of the night her own neighborhood would not.

Nikki always stayed in her van after eleven, her own self-imposed curfew. The drug dealers slithered out into the night to peddle their wares as did the hookers. And if the night people didn't play by the rules, they were shot. Still, she was safer there than in Adrian's arms, despite that wonderful illusion of warmth and safety. She pulled her coat tighter around her, taking on the stiff gait of a tough young man as she walked through the prestigious neighborhood that used to be home.

An hour and a half later she stepped wearily into her van. Since she would have to move it soon anyway, she drove to a nearby alley, too tired to even remove the shoe polish numbers on the windshield. More tired than her legs and feet, her mind was exhausted from trying to figure out Adrian Wilde. It was no use. Only he could answer for himself, and she wasn't about to give him that opportunity, not now.

Acting on her earlier hunch, she opened a trunk and dug through the personal items she'd taken from the mansion before going into hiding. One folder was filled with tips on photography and terrific examples she'd taken from magazines. Her fingers, still stiff from the cold, fumbled through the clippings and loose pages until she found the one she'd thought of earlier. It was the winner of *PHOTOgraphic Magazine's* amateur photographer contest ten years ago. She was so impressed with the shot, and the photographer, that she'd written the magazine to get his address. Unfortunately, the magazine couldn't give out that information. It was that picture that made her search for deeper subjects than sunsets, and eventually led her to the homeless.

The picture was a black and white of a black saxophone player in a smoky jazz club. The surroundings were drab, as were his clothes, but the pure pleasure on his face as he gave himself to the music was mesmerizing. She could still feel that poignancy she had felt the first time she'd seen it.

And beneath the shot was congratulations to the winner: Adrian Wilde. He was nineteen years old then, and the little picture accompanying the article showed a handsome young man. Nikki had been intrigued, filled with notions of becoming his pen pal, then maybe meeting him someday. He lived in New York and worked with his uncle at a private investigation agency.

Nikki felt the chills wash over her as she stared at the article. They had almost connected ten years earlier and now their paths had crossed again. But Adrian had made sure they crossed under the guise of luck-run-bad. Surely her letter hadn't triggered this, because she doubted he'd ever seen it. Maybe the magazine had sent it on to him, but why would he seek her out now if he hadn't even bothered to write her back then? No, it just didn't make sense. She rubbed her fingers over her aching temples. Nothing did.

Worn down by her questions, she flopped down on her little bed. Ever since she'd met Adrian, she had gone against common sense—by showing him where she lived, by letting him kiss her. Look where her heart had led her, into a pit of confusion. Now, danger screamed at her from all directions, and she couldn't ignore it. She knew she had to hide out until he gave up and went back to New York. She also knew how hard it was going to be to walk away from Adrian Wilde.

The roar of water surrounded Adrian, chilling his skin. He held his breath as he sunk deeper and deeper, farther from air and light. All he could hear was his heartbeat and the sound of bubbles as precious air escaped his lips. His lungs tightened, and he opened his mouth, sucking cold water into his lungs. He gasped for breath as he clawed out of the water to consciousness. His body was covered with perspiration, and he took deep breaths.

It was only a nightmare, something to be grateful for. He had tossed and turned all night, worrying about Nikki. She had been acting a little strange the last time he saw her, but he could have been acting strange too. After all, he hadn't expected or wanted what was growing between them. His life was too busy to get involved with anyone, especially someone like Nikki. Maybe Rita's appearance had made her suspicious, though Nikki had acted as though she'd believed him.

Later Adrian took a sip of coffee and glanced at the calendar hanging on the kitchen wall. Today he was scheduled to return to New York and talk with Calvin Klein's people. If Nikki had blown him off purposely, he could return to his life of luxury and forget about her. If he could be sure of that. Stanley would just have to be pissed when Adrian told him he'd be staying another few days.

When he turned, he saw that the door to the garage was open. He walked over and peered into the dimness. Everything seemed normal, and he closed the door, believing that he hadn't closed it well enough the night before. He had, after all, been preoccupied by Nikki's mysterious absence.

Dressed in his homeless garb, he reached for his car keys and looked at the empty pegs next to them. It took a minute to realize what looked different. The shell necklace was gone. Not that it mattered, but it struck him as being odd that it was now missing. He looked on the floor and the counter, but didn't see it. Maybe he'd thrown it away during the last week and didn't remember.

When he noticed the front door was unlocked, he really began to question his sanity. "What the heck is wrong with me?" he mumbled as he threw the dead bolt. This whole business was driving him crazy. He walked out to the garage, testing the door's closing to reenact the catch not holding. It closed soundly each time. He shook his head.

While Adrian drove to West Palm Beach, he thought of the nightmare again. He had to find her and tell her the truth. He'd planned on doing that the night before, but she'd stood him up. Or been held up. This charade had gone on too long, for him and for her. He hated deceiving her, and more than that, hated living this awful life of the homeless.

As he walked the now familiar streets, he detected a decidedly different atmosphere. Seamus wouldn't even look at him, wouldn't take him up on a meat pattie later on. Most of the regulars had seen him with Nikki at one time or another, and so when he asked Charlie if he'd seen her, the plump man's vague answer perplexed Adrian. He didn't talk about his days on the ship as he usually did.

Leaning against a post, Adrian lit a cigarette and took a drag. A woman with short, bright red hair peered around the side of a building across the street. Her eyes were wide, like a child sneaking around. Except that she was looking right at him. He took his second drag and dropped the cigarette, too annoyed at everything to care if someone saw him. It didn't seem to matter anyway. After stepping on the live butt, he looked up to find the odd woman gone.

Dave's reaction totally baffled him. It was almost lunchtime when Adrian arrived at the shelter. The day was overcast and colder than it had been the whole time Adrian had been there. The shelter was packed with the homeless seeking a bit of food and warmth in that room where he had first seen Nikki.

Dave was at the door, greeting an old man warmly as he invited him in for some chicken noodle soup and pumpkin pie. Adrian walked up the steps, his hands in his pockets.

"Hi, Dave."

Dave moved in front of the doorway as if to block Adrian's entrance. Adrian tried to circumvent him, but Dave just moved to the left to block him again.

"We have no use for your kind here," he stated simply, starting to turn around and close the door in Adrian's face.

Adrian pushed the door back, and Dave was no match for Adrian's strength. "Excuse me?"

"You heard me. I don't know what your purpose is, but I don't want you here. And I don't want any trouble, so why don't you just go on your way. The cops show up quickly if I call them."

"I don't know what you're talking about. There's been a misunderstanding."

"I don't think so."

Adrian was baffled by everyone's change in behavior toward him. "Can you tell me what's going on here?"

Dave crossed his arms over his chest. "You know perfectly well."

Adrian realized he would get nowhere with this man. "Okay, fine. Just tell me if you've seen Nikki since yesterday. I'm worried about her."

"Oh, I'm sure you are. She's gone."

"Gone?"

"Left. Something about going north. She didn't explain, that's all she said."

Dave closed the large wooden door, and Adrian was too confused to even stop him this time. Not that it mattered. Dave obviously wasn't going to tell him a thing. But why the change? It was as if everyone knew he wasn't what he pretended to be. But how could they know? He was very careful to park the car far away from this area. Had Nikki heard whatever they had heard?

Adrian walked around for another two hours before giving up on the area. She could be anywhere, but she wasn't here. He drove around, combing the area surrounding West Palm Beach until late that night, but there was no sign of Nikki's van. Frustration mounted inside him; he hated feeling helpless.

He was pretty sure Dave had been lying about Nikki going north. It was obvious that she had gone somewhere, though. Why couldn't he just go back to New York and get on with his life? Sounded easy enough. He pulled into the garage, pounding on the steering wheel. If he'd only told her the truth earlier . . . then what? She might have run away then too. But he had to talk to her, at least one more time.

He stripped out of his homeless garb as he usually did, leaving the clothes in a heap by the door. Starting a pot of coffee, he dropped down into a chair at the table and looked at her photographs again. The room filled with the aroma of brewing coffee. When he stood to fix a cup, he saw the photograph of Nikki lying on the floor. He picked it up and dropped it on the table.

"Nikki, what is going on with you?" he said, his voice almost startling him in the silence. It had been so long since he'd spoken to anyone. He hadn't even listened to the radio as he'd driven around. "Be there tomorrow."

By noon the next day, Adrian knew Nikki wasn't going to be making an appearance in her usual places. She and Crackers had virtually disappeared. Tired from another night of tossing and turning and worrying, he returned to the house and had lunch.

He had ended up talking to the Calvin Klein people himself yesterday, explaining Stanley's tendency to firm up assignments before consulting with him. They were understanding, if only a little irritated about the whole matter. They'd ended up brainstorming a few ideas right there on the phone, and they were so impressed, they agreed to wait another week until their meeting. Adrian had let Stanley sweat it out until that morning before telling him everything was still on.

Now, as Adrian sat at the table with his feet propped up

on the edge, he wondered if he should just give up on Nikki and go home. It was a thought that continually came to mind, but there was some other part of him that didn't buy into it. He leaned his head back, letting out a long sigh.

"Nikki, where are you?" Before he'd had the photographs to clue him in on her whereabouts. Now he had nothing. He lifted his head. Or did he? He had the visions, didn't he? It had never occurred to him to actually try bringing on a vision. Usually it just happened, once in a while. It was his last hope, unless he wanted to stay in the area indefinitely, which he didn't.

Adrian closed his eyes and concentrated on Nikki. It was surprising how easily he could conjure her smells, the sound of her voice. But those were only memories. He tried harder, picturing her clearly in his mind, feeling her skin and the way she felt in his arms. Still, nothing came. He rested his head on the table, feeling the cool smoothness of the wood against his forehead. His hands clenched on his thighs, trying to force something. Nothing.

It was when he gave up and started to stand that it happened the way it usually did. First the emotion, this time confusion; it always seemed that a strong emotion connected the two of them. Then a smell that didn't belong in his kitchen mixed with the aroma of coffee: salty ocean air. Through her eyes, for just an instant, he saw the waves lapping on the shore and the sound of a gull screeching indignantly.

His gaze rested on the photograph he'd taken of her. He could never see her in these visions, because he always saw through her eyes. But he was sure she stood just like that, arms crossed in front of her, hands up by her throat. He put his faded clothes on in the chance that she hadn't heard anything to make her doubt his story, at least until he told her the truth.

She wasn't at the beach they had gone to, the beach

where they'd shared that first kiss. Nor was she at any of the beaches nearby. He kept stopping at every pass, even illegally parking to get to the private beaches used only by the people who lived on them.

Adrian had found an empty lot where a house had recently stood. The churned up dirt held chunks of old concrete. The gate was closed, but there was just enough room to park his car and climb through a small section that had been knocked down during the destruction.

He enjoyed the two customary drags of his cigarette before stepping from the car. There was no way he was cutting down to one drag now. It was everything he could do to keep from increasing to fifteen.

The sun was trying to peek through the hazy cover of clouds, but it was still overcast. The wind blew in off the water, chilling him even through his jacket.

As soon as he stepped onto the beach, he saw Nikki in her unusual stance, watching the waves crash in. His heart tightened, and he told himself it was only because he didn't know what to expect. Would she let him explain?

Nikki saw him before he reached her, and glanced nervously behind her. She was obviously judging whether she could outrun him back to wherever she had hidden her van. Then she turned to face him as he neared her, standing tall. Adrian felt disheartened to see her take such a defensive posture toward him. The anger in her green eyes almost made him wince. Something had happened.

"Nikki, why did you stand me up? Did I do something to make you angry?"

"Oh, I don't know. Let's see." Sarcasm dripped from her voice. "You came here looking for me, hunted me down, lied to me about who you were. You . . ." Her eyes grew misty for a second, and she swiped angrily at them. "You kissed me, made me trust you."

That's when he saw it. The shell necklace peeking out

of the collar of her coat. His heart started moving up toward his throat as he walked closer to her. It all made sense now: the open door, the missing necklace.

His voice seemed suspended in his throat, but he forced the words out. "You've been at my house." It wasn't a question.

"Yes, Adrian Wilde, I have been at your house only blocks from the beach. Not bad for a guy down on his luck. Or did that nice guy who's been letting you bartend for him offer you his place too?"

Adrian dropped his head, cursing himself for not telling her the truth earlier. "Nikki, let me explain."

"Just tell me one thing. You owe me one bit of truth. Did Devlin send you to find me?"

"Who's Devlin?"

She studied him, as if weighing the truth of his words. "Damn you, Adrian, don't lie to me about this. My life depends on it."

"I don't know any Devlin. Nikki, I wanted to tell you the truth, but you wouldn't have come near me if I'd told you who I really was and why I came here looking for you. That three years ago I was struck by lightning and died for a few minutes, and during that time it was your life I saw, not mine. That our souls connected, that I experienced that explosion with you, the fire and smoke and fear. I came here to see if you really existed after I found you in the background of one of my shots. You hardly trusted me with a believable story."

The red of her anger disappeared as he spoke, leaving her face pale. "What do you mean, you saw my life?"

"You know the old saying that when you die, your whole life flashes before you? It was your life flashing by me. I saw you building a sandcastle when you were a girl, and a boy kicked it in, and you cried. I saw you walking on a sea wall behind a huge mansion, saw you driving your

Mercedes convertible. And then . . . I don't know how to describe it, but it felt like I was going *into* you, just before you experienced whatever put those scars on you. I was there with you. I felt everything you felt."

"You were hit by lightning," she said, her eyes wide. "You were feeling the lightning."

He shook his head. "I know it sounds crazy, but it was real. After the explosion you kept thinking that you had to get to your mother. Over and over you kept thinking it, and everything was orange around you, hot and burning, and you couldn't breathe because of the heat searing your lungs. Then I came back to my body. But there's more." He had to keep talking to her, make her believe. "Since then, I've been . . . connected to you. I call them visions, and they've happened a dozen times. When I have these visions, it's through your eyes. I can feel what you're feeling, see what you're seeing. Sometimes it's the ocean you're looking at, and you're afraid and angry at the same time. Once you were lying on the ground, watching a man run away with something that belonged to you. You felt violated and vulnerable."

She backed away from him, shaking her head. "No. No, it can't be. You just know these things; someone's told you."

"I saw you going to the art gallery. That's how I found your photographs. I knew you'd taken them, even though the owner tried to tell me otherwise. I've been there with you. No one told me. Nikki, let me help you." He held his hand out to her. "Trust me."

Her lips trembled as she shook her head. Her voice stretched thin with impending tears. "You hit Crackers."

He dropped his head, feeling that tormenting guilt wash over him again. "I didn't mean to. He was suddenly there in front of the car."

"And you couldn't tell me, because you were lying to me!"

"I know. But I explained why. I had no choice. Would you have given me the time of day if I'd come up to you and said, 'Hey, our souls have been connected since that terrible explosion three years ago. Can we talk?' Let me help you, Nikki."

She walked further away, never taking her eyes from him. "I can't trust you. Not with my life. I can't. If you want to help me, go away. If you're working for Devlin, go back and tell him you couldn't find me." He saw a tear snake down her cheek. "I can't." She shook her head and ran up the beach.

He couldn't chase her; it would only scare her more. What would he do, pin her down until he could convince her he meant her no harm? And it seemed that he couldn't help her. Stella was right; she was in danger. But from what? And who was Devlin?

Nikki's retreating figure disappeared. Now she knew the truth about him. She probably thought he was a kook. Just the expression on her face indicated she didn't believe in such strange things as visions and souls being connected. He was beginning to doubt his own sanity. Adrian stared out to the ocean, hands on his hips. He might not ever be able to find Nikki again. He might lose what could be the most lucrative contract in his career. It didn't matter, because he was a man sinking in quicksand. All the money, his reputation, his fancy apartment—none of it mattered if he returned to it knowing Nikki was in danger.

He turned around to head back to the car. A skinny young man was clipping hedges in the backyard of the mansion behind him. Adrian watched him thoughtfully, remembering the mansion he'd seen Nikki standing behind in that pose that had identified her in the photograph. He had tried to find the mansion before, but he hadn't tried

hard enough. Holding the memory of it in the foreground
of his mind, Adrian started walking down the beach, stopping at each mansion and comparing it.

He paid for his venture with chapped lips and chafed
skin, but it was well worth it when he found Nikki's old
home an hour later. It was less majestic now, less pristine.
He couldn't tell whether someone was home, and didn't
even know what he intended to say when he knocked on
the door. All he knew was that he had to get another angle
on Nikki, see if her family still lived there.

As he started up the incline toward the stone steps, he
caught sight of his shabby sweatshirt. He looked like some
derelict looking for a handout. This would never work. Taking note of the house's characteristics, he walked back to
the car and changed into the sweater he kept in the backseat. The jeans would have to do; by the time he walked
to the mansion's grand entrance, he at least looked like a
normal guy on vacation.

The ornate, faded sign at the entrance said MADSEN. That
was next to the other sign saying, NO TRESPASSERS. When
he pulled around the driveway, he knew he'd seen this
place before. Nikki had walked out of that front door just
before the explosion. The distant roar of flames filled his
mind.

Adrian pulled the tarnished brass knocker and let it slam
back against the door. After another try, the door opened.
A man about his age stood there, looking somewhat annoyed and curious at the same time. He had slick, black
hair and wore glasses.

"Can I help you?"

"Yes, I hope so." Adrian put on his most charming
smile. He hoped the line worked better than it had last time
he used it. "I was vacationing here about four years ago,
and met a lovely young lady named Nikki. I'm back in

town for a couple of days and wondered if she still lived here.''

The man's face paled even more than it already was. ''My sister,'' he said on a quick breath. ''She doesn't live here anymore.''

Adrian knew the man would have left it at that, but he couldn't let it go now that he had a lead. ''Does she still live in the area? Maybe I could give her a call and take her to lunch.''

The man's dark brown eyes seemed focused on something behind Adrian. His voice was thin. ''I don't know where she lives. She left a few years ago.'' He shrugged, bringing his focus back to Adrian. ''Sorry, I can't help you.''

Adrian wanted to ask about the explosion, but the man was already taking a step back into the house. ''I'm sorry too. She was a sweet lady. I do remember her talking about you. You're . . .'' He snapped his fingers, as if the man's name was on the tip of his tongue.

''Devlin,'' he supplied, taking another step back and holding the door's edge. ''Good-bye.''

The name stuck Adrian like a knife. Devlin, the man Nikki thought had hired him to find her. He seemed harmless enough, and none too happy. Could the man be hunting his sister down? Adrian returned to his house, dumping the homeless garb by the door for the last time. He stood there in his briefs, staring at the pitiful pile. Now what? He hadn't come all this way to find his Madame Blue alive and in danger, just to go back home. He was going to help her, whether she liked it or not. Now all he had to do was keep his heart out of it. This was enough of a mess as it was.

Chapter 10

He's everywhere I go, in my heart always.

"Visions, Inc. May I help you?"

Nikki cleared her throat. "I need to speak with Adrian Wilde, please. It's rather urgent."

"He's out of town right now. I can take a message, or you can talk to his agent, Stanley Fisk."

"I'll talk to Stanley." Nikki didn't know what she would say when she wrote down the number on the phone booth wall. She didn't even know what she was looking for exactly.

"This is Stanley," a whiny kind of voice answered.

"I'm looking for Adrian Wilde. It's important that I speak with him right away."

"Well, that's two of us who feel that way, sweetheart. Unfortunately, the man has decided to take some emergency vacation or something. I'm afraid I don't know when he'll be back, though God willing, it'll be soon. I can relay a message to him next time he calls."

"Uh, do you know where he is?"

"Somewhere in Palm Beach. On some mysterious mission. Don't you think his agent should know about these things?" The exasperation in the man's voice was clear.

Nikki shook her head. "I-I'm not sure."

"You're not a model, are you?"

"No, sir. Just . . . an old friend. I'll try to catch him later. Thanks for your help."

She hung up, leaning her forehead against the phone. *Adrian, who are you really? Why are you here?* Nothing added up with him. He was a photographer from New York, that much was true. And then there were the visions he'd told her about. She shivered, still hearing his words as he told her about getting struck by lightning and seeing the images of her, and then going inside her. It sounded so bizarre, and yet, it could explain the pull she had felt for him even that first time she saw him.

She hurried back to her van parked in the Fort Lauderdale Hilton's lot. Devlin could have told Adrian about the sandcastle, though she couldn't think of a reason he'd pick that particular incident. But what about her loneliness? No one knew how lonely she had been in that wealthy, privileged world. Yet Adrian had.

She closed her eyes, feeling an immense pain shiver through her body. He said he'd been there when the car exploded. Her fingers traced the network of scars on her shoulder that would forever remind her of that horrible day. Nikki could still see Adrian touching her shoulder at the beach, kissing the scars on the back of her hand. That hand went to her mouth, to lips that could still feel his kisses. Her eyes widened.

"Oh no, I'm in love with him. No, I can't be!" But her heart told her differently. "No, I am not in love with him. He lied to me. No matter what he said about his visions, he still lied. I can't trust him."

At the sound of her voice, Crackers got up from the little bed she'd made for him and hobbled over. When she started scratching his head, he curled up beside her and sighed contentedly.

"Crackers, you're the only male I can trust, besides Ulyssis. Even if you do like that . . . that man. At least I know you're legit."

The pup licked at her finger, then closed his eyes. When she had walked him earlier, after her flight from Palm Beach, she'd noticed him looking for Adrian. She was looking for him too, but for other reasons. He'd never find her here. Maybe after a few days of not seeing her, he'd give up and go back to New York. Crackers was due back at the vet for a checkup in a day or so, but Nikki planned to wait another two days before returning to the area. She'd go to another vet, but she didn't have the money; the checkup was included with the first visit.

And now that her suspicious mind was at work, she wondered if Adrian hadn't paid for that bill. Probably out of guilt. As well he should, she thought, lifting her head. If he hadn't been sneaking around, he wouldn't have hit Crackers.

She stroked the pup's soft fur, wondering how she was going to put him back out on the streets when he healed. Though her life was definitely not set up for having a dog, she had to admit to enjoying his company. Especially during those lonely nights. Against her will, she thought of the time Adrian held her down at the beach. She gave Crackers a little squeeze. It wasn't the same, but it would have to do. She couldn't let Adrian near enough to do that again, not ever.

For two days Adrian pored over the entire Palm Beach area looking for Nikki. He decided that she had picked the best place to hide from her brother, even if he was only a few minutes from there. The people of the street blended into the background—because people wanted them to be invisible. Adrian used to feel that way too. He didn't want to see them because they reminded him of what he was once afraid of becoming. For a little while, he *had* been one of them. They weren't just nuisances or blotches on the face of society. They were people, human beings who had run out of luck and hope. He would never look at them the same way again, not here or in New York.

Adrian parked outside the Lord's Shelter. It was a bright, sunny day, and he felt like a completely different man than the Adrian Nash who had gone there to spend the night. He looked different too, with crisp designer jeans and a bulky sweater he'd picked up in France a year ago. His hair was combed straight and tied back, and his face clean shaven. Strangely, he didn't feel as out of place as he looked.

When Dave saw him walk inside, his friendly expression turned curious, then to that hostile tone it had held the last time Adrian was there. He walked right over to where Adrian stood, just inside the front doors.

Before Dave could say anything, Adrian said, "Hello, I'm Adrian Wilde." He handed him a business card, turning Dave's expression back to curious. "Can I talk to you for a minute?"

Dave looked him over, then shrugged. "Follow me to my office."

Adrian remembered the office well, though they'd gone in a different way. He could still see Nikki standing there with the orange light all around her making her look like an angel. Dave took a seat behind his battered desk, but Adrian remained standing. Dave read the business card.

"You're here to take pictures of the homeless? Is that what this has been about?"

"No, not at all. I told you the truth when I said I was looking for a woman I had known. Nikki is that woman. I don't know what she told you about me, but she's right about one thing. I did lie about who I was. It's not because I'm on some devious mission." Adrian leaned against the desk. "How much do you know about Nikki?"

Dave shrugged. "Not much. Most people who come in here don't volunteer much about themselves."

"I suppose not. But there's something different about Nikki. I'm sure you've noticed."

Adrian swore that Dave's light skin blushed at that. "Of course. She's a lovely girl who certainly doesn't belong here. But she's never asked for help, and our policy here is not to push it on anyone."

"It wouldn't have mattered, because Nikki wouldn't have taken your help anyway. She's in danger. I can't tell you much more than that, because I don't know. All I know is that I have to help her."

"She knows you lied about your identity."

"She also knows who I really am and why I'm here. Whether she believes the latter part, I don't know." He wasn't about to explain it all to Dave. "I've looked all over for her, but I can't find her anywhere. I'd like to help out here, so if she comes in, I'll be able to talk to her. That's all I want to do, is just see her and try to help her." At Dave's hesitation, he added, "I know you have no reason to trust me, but I'm all Nikki has right now. You'll be here to make sure I don't throw her over my shoulder and haul off with her." The thought did have some appeal, but Adrian shrugged it off. He raised his hands. "I can ladle soup real good."

Dave seemed to contemplate the whole thing, tapping his fingers on the desktop. Finally he said, "Okay. But if there's even the inkling of trouble—"

"I know, the cops respond quickly when you call them."

Both men smiled, and Dave said, "Okay, you got the hint last time." He looked at his watch, getting up. "It's about lunchtime. Let's see if we can find an apron that'll fit you."

"I'll risk my jeans, thank you."

As the line of familiar faces filed past him, Adrian's gaze kept drifting toward the door. He smiled at the people with whom he'd spoken, but they only gave him curious glances. Adrian wasn't sure they'd even recognize him without the beard, but he didn't much care. There was only one thing he cared about. Well, two. One was small and fuzzy.

Nikki had finagled the phone number to the rental house under the pretext of having left an item there while friends had rented it a month ago. Though the agent insisted they'd never found a camera, she sweet-talked the man into letting her phone the current resident just to take a quick look in one of the upstairs rooms where the cleaning people may have missed it.

No one had picked up the phone in two days. When the answering machine picked up, it was just a generic voice announcing the guests were out seeing the sights and would she like to leave a message. She realized she'd hoped to hear Adrian's voice, and shook her head in disgust.

Nikki didn't dare drive by the house, but even calls late at night yielded no answer. She wondered if he'd given up and gone back to New York. For some odd reason, that thought made her feel lonely, rather than safe. He could have been some madman, or a murderer. Still, the words he'd spoken at the beach haunted her all the time. *It felt like I was going into you, just before you experienced whatever put those scars on you. I was there with you. I felt everything you felt.*

She shivered, wondering if his voice would ever go away. He had described her experience, what she'd seen and felt. Maybe he'd guessed what it was like to get caught in an explosion. But knowing that she thought only of her mother, and seeing the man who had mugged her, taking her wallet and leaving her feeling violated, how did he know that?

It was late afternoon before Nikki got up the courage to drive back into West Palm Beach. She parked behind the veterinarian's office and quickly walked inside with Crackers. The same pretty blond was behind the counter, and she greeted Crackers and gave him a dog biscuit.

When she returned from letting the doctor know Nikki was there, Nikki leaned against the counter and asked, "When I was here before, did the man who was with me pay Crackers's bill?" The blond seemed to weigh her answer, and Nikki added, "You can tell me the truth. I won't tell him."

That much was true.

"Yes, he did pay the bill. He even came back in and paid the balance." The woman smiled. "He's very handsome. He was in a few days ago to see if you'd brought the puppy back in for his checkup."

Nikki's face went pale. "He was just in?"

"Like I said, it was a couple of days ago. I guess you haven't seen him for a while, huh?"

"No," Nikki said, grateful that the doctor walked out just then to take them back to the examining room.

Crackers got a clean bill of health, another dog biscuit, and good news that in two weeks the cast would come off. She didn't make an appointment, just in case Adrian was still in town and came in again.

"I'm parked out back. Is there an exit back there?"

The woman gave her an odd look, then nodded. "Sure. Follow me." When she opened the door, she added, "And good luck with your fellow. You're one lucky lady."

"Yeah. Lucky," Nikki said, walking out.

After looking around a little for Ceil, Nikki decided to check the Lord's Shelter for her. It was getting late, and the nights were cold now that it got dark so early. Nikki was pretty sure Ceil would be sleeping at the shelter, if she got there early enough. A bowl of chicken noodle soup might help the chill in her heart too. It helped everything else, didn't it?

Nikki wrapped her arms around herself as she hurried up the front steps to the shelter. It had been a while since she'd been there, and it gave her an odd sense of comfort as she pushed open the heavy door. The line of hungry people nearly reached the entry, but she wanted to find Ceil first.

When Nikki walked past the kitchen, she nearly dropped dead in a faint. She couldn't believe what she saw, and blinked her eyes several times. Adrian stood behind the counter, dishing out bowls of soup to the hungry bunch in front of him. Or at least she thought it was Adrian. At first she thought her mind was playing tricks on her.

He was clean shaven, and his hair was straight, pulled back in a discreet ponytail. His rich burgundy sweater hugged the width of his chest. But it was his eyes that solidified the fact that it was indeed Adrian Wilde. She'd never forget those gorgeous brown eyes. As she stood with her mouth agape, she saw his eyebrows knit together a second before he turned in her direction.

She ducked out of view before he saw her, leaning against a bookcase in the now deserted reading area. Her heart was pounding like a jackhammer. After taking a second to catch her breath, she slipped down the hallway to Dave's office. It was dark and cold, but she was glad it was unlocked. She shut the door and locked it, leaning against the wood. Her hand was pressed against her heart as if that could calm its frantic beating. After a time, she let herself feel some amount of relief that he hadn't seen her.

The last time she'd been in this office, Adrian had been with her, carrying an injured Crackers. She remembered how concerned he'd been, and realized that was guilt. She had seen it again at the beach. But whether it had been concern or guilt, she knew it was real. Her heart whispered that a killer wouldn't have felt either for a dog, but she ignored it. How could she have let him get so close to her? How could she have trusted him?

But she already knew the answers to those questions. The way he'd made her feel, the way he'd listened to her talk. He'd told her that she was too pretty to be on the streets, and she knew, deep in her heart, that he'd meant it. Nikki wrapped her arms around herself, remembering how wonderful it felt to have Adrian's arms around her. If only she could trust him. She knew she should run far, far away from here, somewhere he could never find her. If only she had enough courage to leave.

"You've got to go to school. You don't want to spend the rest of your life here, do you?"

Pedro vehemently shook his head, sending his silky black hair spraying. Adrian had seen himself in the Cuban boy and finally had gathered the courage to face the ghost of what he might have been. Pedro's mother was fired from her job as housekeeper, where she and her son lived. Now the boy was out of the school district he'd been in, and not going to school at all.

Adrian heard Dave's angry voice at the door and excused himself to see what was going on. The front door closed, and Dave balled his fists up in silent fury.

"What's wrong?" Adrian asked as he approached, but Dave shook his head.

"Nothing." He looked at a few of the homeless who had gathered upon hearing the confrontation. Shaking his head again, he headed down the hallway to his office. Adrian followed, too stubborn ever to take the hint.

"So tell me what that was all about."

Dave gestured for him to close the door. "The city officials want to close us down. We have two weeks to fix our code violations before the doors are shut. This isn't the first time they've been here. The problem is, we have no money. We barely have enough to get by as it is. Why do you think we only serve biscuits and soup? I've been trying to keep it all together on a dime budget, but this is going to blow the roof off.'' His long fingers grasped at his blond hair, pulling it tight in frustration. ''There's nothing I can do about it.''

''What will happen to all the people who eat and sleep here?'' Adrian was thinking about Pedro particularly.

''They'll go back to the streets, sleep in cardboard boxes and alleys. The city just wants us out of here. They figure if the shelter goes, so will the homeless. It doesn't work that way.''

''What needs to be done?''

''The two biggies are a better roof and a larger kitchen. Heck, this kitchen was made for little church functions, heating coffee, things like that. But it's all we have.''

Adrian looked out the window through the coating of grime. If he never saw Nikki again, he would worry about her night and day. Was she safe? Well fed? He wouldn't be able to help her with the first concern, but if the shelter was here, she would at least have a place to go for a hot meal. He thought of Seamus, Charlie, and all the others who relied on the Lord's Shelter. If he were homeless, this would be a place of solace and comfort. He wanted to make sure it was there for them, now and always.

''Well, it looks like we have a lot of work to do, then.'' Adrian smiled at Dave's confused expression.

''What do you mean?''

''I mean, we have to meet with a contractor to see what kind of work we're talking about here. Then we'll all pitch in to get it fixed.''

''You didn't hear me. That all takes money, and we have exactly two hundred dollars in the emergency fund. That won't even buy a new stove.''

"We're not going to touch the emergency fund. I happen to know a wealthy businessman who could use a good tax write-off. I have a feeling that he'd have a special interest in this project. What are you sitting there with your mouth open for? Get the phone book out and start calling contractors!"

When word spread that the shelter was in danger of being shut down, everybody who called it home pitched in to help. Charlie had been in construction briefly after the shipping accident and had a little handyman experience. Even Pedro was eager to help, as much as a twelve-year-old could. The contractor took care of the electrical and plumbing, and everyone helped with hanging drywall, painting, and cleaning up. Adrian supplied hamburgers to all the help, since the kitchen was inoperable.

The roof was handled simultaneously by professionals, but Adrian kept on top of everything, pretending he knew more about the business than he did. Rock and roll music blared from morning to dusk and into the evening hours after the construction crew left for the day. Adrian, Dave, and a handful of other men and women continued their work, furiously protecting their home.

For six days Adrian worked from sunup till late at night, breaking only after Dave insisted. More than protecting the shelter from being shut down, all the hard work kept Nikki from Adrian's mind. Thoughts of her only crept in when he paused for a few minutes, or when he went back to the house at night. Sometimes he showered at the shelter and stayed up talking with Dave until they were both half asleep.

That was the case tonight, and when Dave's eyes started drooping, Adrian reluctantly pulled his boots from the corner of the desk and stood up. Unlike Dave, and despite the days of hard work, he was restless tonight.

"Well, I'll let you get some sleep. I think that shower woke me up for a while."

"If you want to keep shooting the bull, I can stay up if you can."

Dave was not the sort of guy Adrian would have hung around with in New York, but the hard work and common goal had brought them together like old friends. And despite the fact that Adrian stuck with the story of a business acquaintance footing the bill for the construction, he suspected Dave knew it was his money.

"Nah, I'm sure I'll drop dead as soon as I get home. See you bright and early tomorrow. We're almost done."

"Thanks to you, we are."

"I'll pass the thanks on to my friend."

Dave winked and gave Adrian a knowing smile. "Sure, you do that."

Adrian wore only a white cotton T-shirt and blue jeans to his car, not bothering to put a sweater on for just a minute or two. He left the windows open as he drove back to the house, his radio blaring jazz to counteract the overdose of rock and roll.

When he walked into the house, he sensed immediately that something wasn't right. It only took him a second to find just the opposite was true—something was very right. The shell necklace was hanging from the peg, and Nikki was sound asleep on the sofa in the living room. His heart lurched crazily inside him, but he told himself it was just because he was glad she was safe. Right there on his couch. He took the necklace off the peg and walked into the living room.

Crackers's tail thumped against the throw rug as he struggled to his feet when he saw Adrian. He stroked the pup's head, but his gaze remained on Nikki. She was wearing a long skirt and a black sweater, and her long, blond curls flowed freely around her face and shoulders. He couldn't take his eyes off her. God, she was beautiful. She looked so peaceful, so content. And she was safe. But he couldn't deny that his feelings for her went deeper than relief. The overwhelming need to protect her, to hold her in his arms again and keep her safe and warm, engulfed him. Remembering the taste of her lips muddled his feelings, and he pushed them aside.

Breaking out of his spell, Adrian kicked off his shoes and walked closer to the couch, kneeling down beside her. He set the necklace on the table. He didn't want to disturb her sleep, but thoughtfulness was overcome by the curiosity that invaded him. She was curled up under an afghan, and her hands were tucked beneath her cheek. Thoughts of kissing her seemed ludicrous, like kissing a child or an angel. He reached up and touched her cheek, and she stirred from a deep sleep. Her green eyes widened, then rested upon him. Like a little girl, she rubbed them sleepily, sitting up.

"I didn't expect to find an angel on my couch when I came back. I would have returned earlier." He spoke softly, as if not to jar the delicacy of the moment.

"I hope you don't mind that we came in. I waited out front for a while, but it got so late. There was a window in back that was unlocked."

Rita, he thought with chagrin. "I don't mind. I'm glad you're here. I've been worried about you."

She smiled, becoming more awake. "You've been too busy to worry about me."

"Oh, you mean the shelter. If it weren't for that, I'd go crazy."

"I thought you would be gone by now."

He touched her cheek again. "You can't get rid of me that easily."

"I can see that." She looked around for a moment, then back at him. "I don't even know why I'm here. I shouldn't be."

"Do you still think I'm working for Devlin?"

She started at his familiar use of the name, but shook her head. "No. I don't know." Her voice grew very small. "Adrian, please hold me."

He gathered her in his arms, holding himself back lest he crush her. She felt small and delicate, and he had to remind himself just how tough she really was.

"Let me help you," he said into the mass of her hair.

She pulled out of his embrace, facing him. "You can't help me. I wish you could understand, but no one can help me. I just have to wait."

"I want to understand, Nikki. Tell me what we're up against." At her puzzled look, he added, "I told you, we're in this together. If something happens to you, I think a part of me will die too." He would never tell her about the drowning nightmares and what they foretold. If she drowned, and he experienced it with her, would he also die?

She rocked back and forth a little, her lips in a tight line. "I haven't talked about it since the trial. I don't even think about it, except for the nightmares."

Her hand subconsciously went to her scarred shoulder. Her eyes focused elsewhere, somewhere beyond him. He sat next to her on the couch, Crackers at his feet.

"The day you felt the explosion . . . that was when my whole world shattered."

Chapter 11

No regrets, no doubts.

Nikki couldn't believe she was sharing this with anyone, much less someone she couldn't completely trust. Yet, as she looked into Adrian's warm eyes filled with sympathy and understanding, she continued what she had started.

"Three years ago . . . it seems like yesterday when it all happened. My life seemed to be going okay for the first time. It wasn't what you would think, with the money and the mansion on the beach. I didn't fit into all that, and I knew I'd let my mother down because I was different. I tried, for most of my young life, to fit her mold. She set a great example: beautiful, active in the social and charity thing, but it just wasn't me.

"Much to my mother's chagrin, I hadn't planned on marrying one of her friends' sons and settling down. I had gotten into photography and wanted to travel and take pictures of real life. No one knew that I took photographs of the homeless. I was happy with who I was and what I was doing with my life. I was dating a handsome man who wanted to marry me.

"There was never peace in my family, between me, Devlin, and my mother. You see, Dad had left both Devlin and me two million dollars in trust funds, which we would inherit when we turned twenty-eight. Even with two years to go, Devlin was impatient, so he kept borrowing money from Mother, promising he would pay her back when he inherited. He figured that since she had plenty of her own money, she would give him whatever he wanted, so he kept investing in all these business ventures that flopped. Mother would get angry at him for squandering away the money he'd be inheriting. They would go on for hours sometimes. He was under a lot of pressure to fill Dad's shoes, but he just didn't have enough business sense. The worst part was he kept trying.

"I know he resented the fact that even though he was twenty-six years old, she controlled the money. That's why he was so desperate to get out from under that control." Nikki turned to him. "Mother was a good woman, but she liked to control her children. We were all she had, and she reminded us of that often. She controlled me with guilt, but even she couldn't make me live the kind of life she thought I should. She controlled my brother with money. She was his sole source of income, and if he did something that displeased her, she'd cut him off. He'd get back in her good graces, then search for some way to get some money of his own so he could do what he wanted."

She took a drink of the glass of water she'd fixed earlier. Adrian's posture was relaxed, but his eyes were focused on her every move and word. She continued.

"It was a grand day, and Jack had invited all of us to a big fair in Miami. It sounded like fun, and I hadn't spent much time with Jack because of my photography. The plan was that he would meet us at the house, and he and I would ride together so we could spend some time alone.

"Jack had this bad habit of arriving late, and he was right in character that day. Devlin said I should teach him a lesson and be gone when he got there, so he would have to meet us at the fair. I was kind of irked about it, so I agreed. We gave him fifteen minutes, and then we decided to leave him a note and go. I got in the back, Mother got in the passenger seat, and Devlin got in the driver's side. Just before he started the car, he said he'd forgotten his sunglasses and got out. It was a hot day, so he tossed the keys to Mother and told her to start the car to get the air cooling down.''

Nikki squeezed her eyes shut, knowing the pain that would come in telling the next part. Adrian touched her hand, giving her strength. His voice sounded soft and smooth.

"If it's too hard to talk about, you don't have to finish. I might expire from suspense, but I won't mind.''

"I talked about it so much to the police and then in court, but I haven't said anything about it since then. Maybe it'll be good to talk about it again. Maybe it'll make the nightmares go away.'' She took a deep breath. "I remembered that I'd left my dream journal on the table. I'd planned to take it to the fair with me.''

"What's a dream journal?''

"It's a journal that I logged my dreams in. I . . . I learned how to dream lucidly, and would record the stranger ones.'' She took a breath. "So I started to get out of the car just as Mother was starting it. I almost yelled for Devlin to grab my journal for me, but I figured he'd be too nosy to resist reading my personal scribblings. Thank you, God, that I didn't ask him. I would have stayed in the car. And I would have died.

"It all happened so quickly. At first I didn't believe that it *was* happening. I thought the car was really loud when it started. It was like a roar, and suddenly there was this hot, orange cloud surrounding me, pushing me back.'' She looked at him. "I remember thinking that I had to get out and save Mother.''

Nikki remembered everything so vividly, she could feel the flames licking at her skin. She wrapped her arms around herself, trying to protect herself from the viciousness of the memory.

"I knew I had to get out of there if I was going to live. I could hardly breathe, and the air seared my lungs. I crawled out of the car, and realized that my right side was on fire. There was a bed of petunias right in front of me, so I dropped down into it and started rubbing the flames off. I didn't see Mother in the car, which was totally engulfed in flames by then. I made my way around to the passenger side of the car.

"That's when I saw Devlin. He was just standing there on the front walk. I screamed for him to help me find Mother, but he just kept standing there. So I walked around, and that's when I saw her lying on the driveway."

Adrian wiped the tear from her cheek with his thumb, roughened from his work on the shelter. "You don't have to tell me about your mother."

She nodded. "I do, I do. Because I keep seeing her there, just like she was that day. She was completely covered in flames, but she wasn't trying to extinguish them. The police said later that she was already dead. I didn't even look at my own body. Maybe I was afraid of what I would find, I don't know. I didn't know what to do to help her, so I started throwing dirt on her body to put out the flames. She looked terrible, covered with dirt and black. When I had the flames out, I dropped down next to her and tried to shake her, begged and pleaded for her to be alive. I couldn't see the huge gash in her back. When I looked up, I saw Devlin still standing there with his mouth open. I screamed, 'Devlin, call nine-one-one! Now!' He finally went inside and called an ambulance.

"I could feel myself fainting, but something told me not to lose consciousness, not until help came. By then, Jack

pulled up and some of the neighbors had come running over
to see what the noise and smoke were about. A huge black
cloud filled the sky. The car was still burning, but it was
already destroyed. Then I heard the ambulance, and everything went black.''

"God, Nikki, I never imagined it was that bad. I knew
you were hurt and scared, but I . . .'' He just shook his
head, then reached for that scarred hand and pressed it to
his lips. She shivered from his touch, but didn't move away.

"If I hadn't been half out of the car, the police think I
would have been killed too. I went through four operations
for my burns.''

"Nikki, do you remember the date the explosion happened?''

"Are you kidding? I'll never forget September twentieth.
Why?''

He looked thoughtful for a moment. ''That's the same
day I was struck by lightning. So I did actually experience
the explosion the moment you did. At least I got to return
to my life. You had to live through hell, the burns, losing
your mother.''

"But that wasn't the worst of it. The police suspected
Devlin and started investigating him. He had all the motive
and opportunity they needed. Mother had finally cut him
off financially, and he was furious about that.

"Jack had some kind of business offer for him, and Devlin couldn't raise the money to take advantage of it. With
Mother gone, he was due to inherit over six million dollars
in two years. And he would get a regular living allowance
that her will stipulated if she were to die before we turned
twenty-eight.''

Adrian squeezed her hand tighter. She knew by the tragic
look in his eyes that he knew nothing about the explosion.

"I didn't want to believe that my own brother could kill
our mother. But the evidence kept piling up. The arguments

he'd had with Mother in the preceding months, the way he just stood there when the bomb went off. Adrian, the police told me that pipe bombs are the weapons of cowards; my brother is the biggest coward I know.

"He had also dabbled with explosives when he was a teenager. Nothing serious, just a few rockets and stuff. The police were sure he would be convicted, and they had me convinced too. I was devastated that he had killed our mother for money. I hated him, and I still do. But he and his top-notch defense team somehow convinced the jury that he was a victim, not a murderer. They painted him as a mama's boy, a man who lived for his mother, who adored her. Witnesses corroborated their story, neighbors and friends who'd seen Devlin kowtowing to please Mother so she'd give him a loan. Sure, there were witnesses who'd seen the fights between them, but the defense lawyer explained them away as normal fights in a wealthy family. I couldn't believe it. The prosecution's one big hole was they couldn't prove Devlin had bought the pipe. No one could place him at a hardware or plumbing store, otherwise I think they would have convicted him.

"When it was over, he told me, 'I plan to straighten this out between us.' I was terrified. Still, the district attorney believed that if they found the right kind of evidence, they could bring a civil case against him. That could get him twenty-five years for each offense, plus state charges of handling explosives. They thought it would be only a couple of months before that happened.

"I took what he said to me as a threat on my life, though I couldn't prove it. I didn't think he'd really try anything, especially since the trial had put the whole horrible ordeal in the spotlight. Jack wanted me to move in with him so he could take care of me. He admitted that he wasn't sure if Devlin was responsible and tried to convince me to see what the jury saw. I knew Jack and Devlin were friends, but I still resented the fact that he took Devlin's side once the trial was over. It wasn't that I didn't trust him, but with Devlin's threat, I didn't want to be connected with anything from my life. So I moved to another part of town, trying to work it all out in my head. That's when I found out I was wrong.''

"Wrong about what?''

"That Devlin wouldn't try anything. Three weeks after I'd moved in, I found a rattlesnake in my bedroom. The police thought I was a little paranoid, that maybe it had gotten in somehow on its own.

"The following week I was nearly hit by a car. There were no witnesses, but the police took me a little more seriously that time. They checked with Devlin, even with Jack, since they were friends, but Jack had been on the phone and Devlin was at a bar when the car tried to run me down. The police offered a reward to anyone who had been paid to try to hit me, but no one came forward. They offered to protect me, but for how long? I couldn't hide out in my room wondering when the force couldn't provide protection for me anymore. So I hid in the one place no one knew about—the streets.

"I had already been taking photographs there for months, working on a project I kept secret from my family, even from Jack. I knew they wouldn't understand. So that's where I went, thinking it would only be for a few months while the district attorney dug up more evidence. I've called several times in the last two years, but they tell me that there are just too many crimes in the city to devote anymore time to this one. The further away we get from the crime, the harder it is to find evidence. The more I pushed them, the more excuses I got. So here I am, waiting until I turn twenty-eight so I can claim my inheritance and give it to charity.

"The money doesn't mean anything to me, but my life

does. If I die before I inherit, Devlin gets my half. I won't let him take my life, or my mother's money. They found a twenty-four-pound pipe bomb wedged inside the console. Whoever planted that bomb had no mercy or compassion. I'm not going to give him the chance to do it again.''

Adrian looked mesmerized and angry at the same time. She didn't want to drag him into her problems, yet she felt hundreds of pounds lighter for telling him. He still held her hand, stroking the back of it with his thumb. Her heart wanted to trust him, but it was so hard to trust anyone after all this time.

"I'm sorry, Nikki," he whispered. "I'm sorry I couldn't have somehow found you then. I wasn't even sure it was real.''

"The saddest part was that Mother and I had been arguing a lot before then." She smiled faintly. "It seemed we were always disagreeing about something. I just wish I could have said, 'I'm sorry.' ''

"Everyone argues sometimes,''

She shook her head. "Not for arguing. For not living up to her expectations.''

"How many people live up to their parents' expectations?''

"I felt as if I was the only one in the world who didn't.''

He touched her cheek. "And who says we have to live up to their expectations, anyway? Only you can set your goals and dreams.''

"That's easy for you to say, Mr. Bigshot Photographer. I'm sure you didn't have that problem.''

His expression grew dark briefly, but he lightened it with a soft smile. "My father died before he could even have hopes for his son. My mother and I grew apart after she married an overbearing tyrant. I don't even know if she expected more than for me to just survive. I never got to make peace with her, either. She had died from cancer three days before my stepfather bothered to find me in New York and tell me. I don't know what I would have said to her anyway." His smile deepened when he pinched her cheek. "And I'm not a bigshot. Yet."

"Yeah, right."

He took her hand, pressing gently on her fingers. She couldn't identify the strange light in this eyes.

"Maybe I am a bigshot. I've done covers for *Cosmopolitan*, *Vogue*, and others; won Picture of the Year. I've had my work exhibited in the Whitney Museum of American Art, the Getty Museum, even been featured at photography festivals in France and England." He kept pressing her fingertips while he spoke in a soft voice devoid of bragging. "I work with some of the most beautiful, famous people in the world. I make enough money to never have to worry about living without it." He stopped moving his fingers. "But I'm going to tell you something I've never told anyone—it's not enough. Something's still missing."

Nikki knew that feeling well. But she didn't know what to say to the admission he had made to her alone.

"I wanted to be a professional photographer, but more for the artistic end," she said at last. "I can't imagine making it as far as you have."

"What did your mother want for you?"

"To marry some rich guy, have his babies, do the social thing. I couldn't settle for that."

"I'll bet she was proud of you, even if she didn't tell you. You're an excellent photographer. She could hardly deny that."

Nikki smiled. "Thank you. She did grudgingly admit once that my work was good; what I showed her of it, anyway. But she thought it should be directed to babies and glamorous vacations, not ordinary strangers in sad or touching circumstances. And that's all your fault, you know."

"My fault?"

"Yes. That jazz singer. The photograph that took first place in *PHOTOgraphic Magazine*."

His baffled expression took on incredulity. "From ten years ago?"

"Yep. There was nothing elegant or beautiful about that picture, but I was so touched by what you captured that I started looking for that kind of soul in my shots. That's how I came to photograph the homeless."

"I can't believe you remember that photograph."

"Remember it? I've still got it. When I found out your real name, I went on a hunch and looked in my file. There you were. The funny part was, I wrote to the magazine to get your address. They wouldn't send it to me, but if they had, I would have written you. We almost connected all those years ago."

His lips looked soft and warm, and she remembered all too clearly how they felt against her own. A pressure was slowly building inside her as she looked into his eyes filled with compassion and something else too. Something she couldn't identify.

He squeezed her hand. "A photograph almost brought us together ten years ago. This time it worked. I wasn't sure you were even real until I saw you in the background of one of my shots. Even then, I couldn't be completely sure I wasn't losing my mind. But I had to find out."

She held her lower lip between her teeth. "You came here because of a picture? That picture of me on the table, the one you told me about on the beach?" She nodded toward the kitchen.

"Yes. I know, it sounds crazy. That's why I couldn't tell you the truth when I first found you." His smile made her heart melt. "Do you believe me, or do you think I'm a kook?"

"Both," she said with a grin. Her hand felt hot where

he held it with his large hand. "So what are you doing down at the shelter?"

He shrugged those massive shoulders of his. "We've been working to get it up to the city's standards so they won't shut it down. I started helping out in the kitchen because I hoped you would come in again, so I could talk to you."

"I did."

His eyebrow raised. "I didn't see you."

"No. I saw you first and left. All I knew was that you had lied to me, that you weren't what you claimed to be."

He touched her chin with his fingers. "Do you trust me now?"

The pressure inside her kept growing with every touch, with every word he uttered in that velvety voice. She closed her eyes, wanting to trust him completely. Her life for the last two years had been a lie, yet she couldn't lie now. Not even to the man who had deceived her. "I want to, Adrian. I'm not sure if I know how."

His fingers tightened on her chin, then he let his hand drop. "I understand. Nikki, I want you to know something, because I want no more secrets between us. Not on my side, anyway. I've lied to you enough already, but there's no need to lie anymore. I went to see Devlin after I saw you at the beach."

She sucked in a quick breath, panic assailing her. Adrian's hand gripped hers, assuring her that he wouldn't let her move away.

"I went there because that's all I had, his name. I found the mansion and walked up to the door, telling him that I'd met you four years ago while on vacation. He said you were gone, and that he didn't know where you were. He looked rather sad, empty. Don't worry, I told him nothing more than that, not even my name. I wanted to see what I could find out about you."

Her muscles relaxed a bit, but she shook her head. "He's probably sad because he can't find me anywhere. Don't let him fool you. He's a killer. You should have seen him at the trial, bereft, crying over Mother's death. Three weeks later he tried to kill me."

"Nikki, you're the bravest woman I have ever known."

She knew he meant those words. With one hand he took the shell necklace she had returned and put it over her head. The pressure inside her kept building, leaving a tingling trail of anticipation in its wake as it traveled to her extremities. Anticipation of what? The answer to that made her heartbeat quicken. She wanted him to kiss her again, to hold her in that strong embrace. But there were other feelings racing inside her too. Feelings she was afraid to even think about.

But she was no longer afraid of Adrian, of his presence or his intentions. Her thoughts were suspended on a blissful plane that pushed away all the pain and fear she had lived with for the past three years. Here in front of her was the man who had come for her because of visions. Sitting across from him on the sofa, she had never felt so safe and secure . . . not ever. The warmth and fire in his eyes comforted and teased at the same time.

He turned the hand that had been holding hers so that their palms pressed together. Hers felt moist, and a small tremor moved down her arm and into her fingertips. She moved her other hand up, and he met hers. She looked at their hands, pressed together as if glass separated them. But it did not. His hands were so much larger than hers, his fingers extending far beyond her own. She looked small, frail. Her gaze traveled down his arms, to his shoulders. For the first time in so long, she could let herself feel frail and delicate and feminine.

Adrian entwined their fingers and pulled her gently toward him. She freed her fingers and wrapped her arms

around his shoulders. The cotton T-shirt felt soft against
her arms. His hair was tied back, and the softness of it
brushed against her fingers. He framed her face with his
hands and just looked at her for a few minutes, as if he
couldn't believe she was really there. Was she? Oh, yes.
Nikki had never felt so alive before.

He pulled her close and pressed his lips against hers. Just
tasting, pulling her lower lip between his. Then his tongue
slipped along her lip, leaving a warm, moist trail. She felt
her breath catch and fought to keep the trembling at bay.
His tongue teased, flicking in and out, touching her front
teeth. When she couldn't stand it anymore, she opened her
mouth and kissed him fully. Adrian's sigh seemed to emanate from deep within his soul as he pulled her tighter
against him. His thumbs stroked her cheeks, close to her
lips, and then his fingers moved through her hair.

. A spear of panic trembled through her at the realization
that this would probably lead to making love with Adrian.
Making love. For the first time. Nothing in her life had ever
felt so right as that thought, and she realized the panic was
only because this would be her first time. She also knew
that no matter what happened later, she would never regret
it.

Just kissing Adrian was like making love in itself, with
their tongues moving together in perfect synchronization,
exploring every crevice. She loosened his ponytail and let
his hair flow free over his shoulders. It felt soft and silky
as her fingers moved through it. She heard a low growl
emanate from him, like a tiger. The sound made her heart
race faster, sending an animal-like ferocity through her
bloodstream. She heard herself growl back as he tilted her
head and started kissing and nibbling down her throat.

Nikki was burning up in her sweatshirt, steaming beneath
Adrian's lips as they kissed all around her neck and to her
collar. She leaned back on the couch as he crouched over

her. Parts of her body crackled with electricity as they came to life. Her hands ran along his shoulders and down the hard plane of his chest and stomach. She ventured to his hips where she could feel his hip bones beneath the thick jean material.

It didn't matter that she was dressed in faded clothes, or that she had no makeup on. The way he looked at her made her feel more beautiful than any woman on earth. Adrian smelled of soap and shampoo, but his own essence was there too, more intoxicating than any fancy cologne.

He lifted her sweatshirt off, and she gladly surrendered it. She didn't think about her scars, because in his eyes she felt flawless. Beneath it she wore one of her silk bras, faded peach, but still her prettiest one. Adrian's eyes seemed to soak in every inch of her bare skin, stroking it with his gaze and his fingers. They roamed over her stomach, down to her sides, and skimmed across her breasts. That one simple touch shot fire through her body. She reveled in the newness of the feelings, and of having saved it for this moment.

Adrian bent down and kissed her again, wet and languorous. His eyes were brilliant with desire, and his breath came quickly. She could hardly catch hers after that last long kiss.

He looked at her for the longest time, as if searching her eyes for something. She hid nothing from him, letting everything in her heart shine through. He slid his hand down the side of her face. "If you don't want me as much as I want you, Nikki, you'd better tell me now. Before it's too late."

This was it. But there was only one answer to that. She hardly recognized her own voice as she spoke, it was so breathy and worldly sounding. "Make love to me, Adrian."

He wasted not a second in swooping her up into his arms and taking her into his bedroom where she had once seen him sleeping. He sat her gently down on the king-sized bed, then knelt down in front of her. Adrian took her scarred hand and kissed it with a gentleness that belied the fire in his eyes. He kissed up the length of her arm, taking his agonizingly slow time, before finally kissing across the fabric of her bra and unhooking the clasp. When her bra dropped over her shoulders, he caressed each breast with one hand and kissed them with infinite delicacy. When his tongue brushed her already sensitized nipple, she sucked in a breath. He kept teasing, first one, then the other, then back again, leaving a wet trail in the valley between them.

"Adrian, you're driving me absolutely crazy," she whispered when she couldn't handle another second. Her toes curled up.

He grinned at her. "Good." Then he went right back to teasing her.

Nikki had read the novels, seen the movies. The first time a couple made love, it was usually fast and furious. Why was Adrian taking his ever-loving time? He couldn't possibly know she was a virgin. Or could he?

When Nikki started squirming, he stood up, then took her hands and pulled her to her feet. While he was kissing her crazy, his hands deftly unzipped her skirt. She felt it drop down to her bare feet with a soft whisper a second before his fingers slid beneath the band of her silk panties. But he didn't take them off as quickly as the skirt. Adrian slid his fingers down over her buttocks, lightly grazing her skin before sliding around to the front and mingling with her hair. She could hardly focus on the kiss with his fingers snaking down to barely touch her most sensitive area.

She couldn't take any more. This definitely wasn't fair. Nikki tugged at his T-shirt, forcing Adrian to stop what he was doing to oblige her as she pulled it over his head. Before he could toss the shirt aside, she had already started to unbutton his jeans. His bare chest distracted her, and she started kissing down the indent before giving him a taste of his own medicine.

Her tongue snaked along his hardened nipple, raising the tiny hairs surrounding it into goosebumps. Adrian rocked his head back, eyes closed. She pressed up against him, feeling just how ready he was, despite his teasing. Her hands roamed along the curve of his back and down over his blue-jeaned derriere. She was sure he had the nicest one she had ever seen . . . tight, small, firm. With his jeans unzipped and loose, she was able to slip her fingers beneath his briefs to the soft skin beneath.

Adrian's muscles tensed beneath her touch, and she realized that every muscle in his body was rigid and ready. Every muscle. Nikki slid his jeans down over his hips, and he stepped out of them. His briefs had also slid down with them, and with a startled realization, Nikki was standing there with a completely naked man. And a gorgeous one! She could only stare at his body with all its curves, muscles, and tan skin.

Adrian took this moment to slide her panties down and pull her against him. His flesh was hot, wet where she had plied him with her tongue. Pressed hard against his nakedness, she was all too aware of his desire. He held her tight, as he had on the beach, and she held him just as tight.

After a minute, he leaned back a little and touched her cheek. His eyes were intense as they took her in. "Madame Blue," he whispered. She took a deep breath, fighting the trembling that shook her insides. *Madame Blue*. Those words echoed through her soul.

He kissed her again, with more passion than she had ever felt before. While he kissed, he turned her toward the bed and laid her gently down, following a second later. His hands touched her everywhere, and she explored him in the same way, all while they kissed.

He touched her inner thighs, pushing them gently apart,

then trailed his fingers in the most highly charged part of her body. She sucked in a deep breath at his touch as the bubbles of a thousand bottles of champagne burst inside her. Still he stroked, though she knew he must be in agony with waiting. His maleness rubbed against her stomach, leaving a sticky trail. Nikki thought about touching him, but decided he might not be able to handle much more. So she stroked down the length of his back and buttocks, listening to his groan of pleasure.

When he entered her, Nikki readied herself for a sharp jolt of pain. Strangely, it was at that moment that she realized she loved him. She was so tight, he couldn't move easily inside her at first. It didn't take long for her body to adjust to his size and accommodate him. He moved gently, then faster. The rush of feelings she'd experienced before couldn't begin to compare to the volcano building inside her.

Nikki wrapped her legs around his hips and moved with him, feeling the volcano inside him too. They moved in rhythm, every stroke feeding the volcano, pushing it closer to the surface. He kissed her just as hers erupted, shattering her insides into a million pieces of starlight. She felt the tremor through his body, and he squeezed her so tight she thought she might break. But she didn't, and his grip relaxed as he let out a long breath.

He cradled her face, then kissed her fiercely when she expected a softer kiss. Nikki felt him throbbing inside her, sending the vibration through her entire body. No regrets, no doubts. Nothing had ever felt so right.

There were emotions shooting through Adrian's mind that he had never felt before. Nothing to do with lovemaking itself, but . . . love? Adrian wasn't even sure what that emotion was, or if it was valid. Nikki looked up at him, her eyes filled with wonder. Their bodies were slick with sweat where they bonded together. Her blond hair was splayed out all over the pillow around her, reminding him of an angel again. She wasn't an angel anymore. And he was pretty sure she wasn't as innocent as she had been an hour before.

He let out a satisfied groan as he pulled her close in his arms. Fearing he would crush her, he rolled her over so she lay on top of him. She snuggled into his shoulder where she fit perfectly. Her hair washed down over her shoulders and tickled his chest. He touched a strand of it.

"Nikki, you are so beautiful."

She smiled. "Why did you call me Madame Blue?"

"That's what I always called you before I knew your name. Did you think it was some other woman's name I was calling out?"

She shook her head. "No. I knew it was me. I don't know why, but I just knew."

"Good, because I couldn't have thought about anyone else but you." He didn't want to think about anyone else ever again. But he had to know. . . . "Nikki, did I hurt you?"

"No, it was wonderful. Well, maybe a little, right at the beginning." She looked at him strangely, tilting her head. "Could you tell? That it was the first time for me?"

His heart clenched inside him. "I wondered . . . because you were so tight. It never occurred to me before then."

She smiled, those soft lips looking tantalizing. "You were so gentle. You took your time, even though I knew you wanted to . . ." She nodded her head.

He didn't exactly want to tell her that he wasn't like that with other women. He didn't want to even think about them. "I don't know why I took my time. Something held me back."

He traced a finger down her slick skin, between her lovely breasts to her belly button. The shell necklace made her look exotic. "You were incredible." He gave her stomach a gentle pinch. "Especially for a first-timer. I hope I didn't hurt you."

"You didn't. It was worth it, believe me."

He kneaded his forehead, something from reality forcing itself into his conscience. "We didn't use anything. I'm sorry, I just didn't come here expecting to—" He'd almost said fall in love, but he couldn't have meant that—could he? "—seduce you. I just wanted to see if you were real. And then when I found you, I wanted to help you. I still do, Nikki."

"You can't help me, Adrian. There's nothing you can do."

"I'm not leaving you alone here."

"You have to. Remember, I've been surviving by myself on the streets for two years now. In two more years I'll be free, if I can remember how to live in society again. Maybe . . ."

He took her hand and squeezed it. "Maybe you'll look me up then? Is that what you were going to say?" She shrugged. "Nikki, you're coming back to New York with me. Don't argue about it. I'm not leaving you here."

"Why, so I can live as a homeless person there?"

"Of course not. You'll stay in my apartment with me. That's far enough away from here."

"I can't take the chance. Devlin has a lot of connections. I wouldn't feel safe."

"I wouldn't let anything happen to you, Nikki."

"So what would you do, make sure there weren't any pipe bombs in your car every time you started it? Check the apartment every day just to make sure there was nothing planted there? I'm not going to drag you into this. I'm worth six million dollars to him. He's already killed his own mother for money, and he tried to kill me too. He's sent someone searching for me before. I'd be looking over my shoulder all the time."

"But you're closer to him here."

"But he'd never think of looking for me here. Especially in the streets. I know you don't understand, but I'm truly safer here. I wouldn't feel safe in New York, not even with you."

He wasn't giving up that easily. Now that he had her trust, he could convince her to come back to New York with him, someway, somehow. There would be time to argue about it later. Right now he just wanted to cuddle up in bed with her and hold her. And he realized she had his trust too. He'd never admitted to anyone that his success wasn't enough—not even to himself.

After they washed up and shared a piece of chocolate cake in the fridge, they settled back into bed. Nikki drifted right off to sleep, and Adrian followed her shortly. As tired as he was, though, he woke up a few hours later, sometime before dawn. She was lying only a few inches away, on her side, facing him. He wanted to touch her, but didn't want to wake her. There would be time for that later.

He realized that the fierce protectiveness inside him came from something deeper than humanity. She was special, delicate and brave. For some reason beyond their understanding, their souls were connected on a plane far above this one. That connection had led him here to help her, he had to believe that. She needed him, even if she didn't know it yet.

He found himself envisioning her in his apartment in New York, fixing coffee for him, wearing one of his white terry robes. The scary part was that she fit into that picture so well. He had never imagined a woman in his life, because he'd never *wanted* to imagine one there. Having a woman—a wife—meant trusting her with all his inner secrets and fears, meant being trustworthy as well. He had never wanted to expend that effort because it never seemed worth it before. Now, as he looked at Nikki, he wondered if he'd now found a woman who was worth it. She already knew his deepest secret. Heck, she *was* his deepest secret. Maybe he knew hers too.

Adrian wanted more than anything else to give her a life again. What he did know for sure was that he was willing to do anything it took to accomplish that. Then they could see what was left for them. He shook his head, surprised at his thoughts. When he looked at Nikki, he saw a lonely person struggling to stay alive, living through the days without love. Adrian realized then that when he looked in the mirror, he saw the same thing.

Chapter 12

Just listen with your heart and you'll hear it.

What a wonderful dream, Nikki thought as the sun woke her up. Then she felt the weight of an arm slung possessively across her middle. She slowly turned her head and found Adrian asleep beside her. There was nothing innocent or angelic about him, not even in sleep. She felt strange, waking up next to a gorgeous, naked man with whom she'd made love the night before. But now what? He couldn't stay here, and she couldn't stay either. Not in his house. She felt an ache in her heart, wondering if falling in love with Adrian wasn't the dumbest thing she'd ever done. As if she had a choice, she thought with a smirk.

She thought of a finger of lightning shooting down from a stormy Hawaiian sky, stilling his heart long enough for his soul to travel to hers during the moment her life shattered.

Adrian's thick, dark lashes opened. He smiled sleepily at her, reaching out to touch her cheek. She touched his too, feeling the beginnings of that beard he used to wear. Nikki liked him shaven.

"Stay here," he said without prelude. "I don't want you to go back to the city."

"Adrian, I can't."

"I'll buy a place somewhere else, then. Farther away from your old house. Wherever you want."

"I can't do that. I know it's hard to believe, but I feel secure where I live now. I couldn't feel that way anywhere else. I've got two more years to go, and then I'll be safe." It was hard to imagine living in the real world anymore.

"So you want me to wait around for two years?"

"No, I don't. I can't. I know you have to go back to New York."

"Yes, I do."

Nikki felt a strange disappointment in that, though it had to be. She started to get out of bed, but he pulled her back into his arms.

"Nikki, how can I help you, short of proving Devlin guilty? Is that the only way?"

"No! Don't go near him. Adrian, promise me you won't see him again."

After a pause, he nodded. "So there's nothing I can do?"

"I'm afraid not. But thank you for trying to be my knight in shining armor. I've never had one of those before." She smiled, trying to shove the dark mood away. The memory of the maiden in the sandcastle waiting for her prince shot into her mind, and she closed her eyes for a second. She hadn't known then just what a prince he was.

Crackers put his paws up on the side of the bed, ears perked up. Adrian leaned over to pet him, and Nikki could swear the dog was smiling.

"I'd better go." She searched for her clothes on the floor. Thoughts of the night before rushed like fire through her body. "I have to drop off some film." She also had to move her van from the country club parking lot at the end of the street.

Adrian sat up, combing his fingers through his silky dark hair. "As much as I'd love to convince you to stay, I promised Dave I'd be at the shelter early this morning." He glanced at the clock. "I'm already late. I've got some bagels for breakfast."

She knew she should go, and that he should too. "Okay."

They sat at the table covered with her photographs and ate toasted bagels with cream cheese and lox. It was a luxury she hadn't experienced in a while. Adrian wore baggy white pants and a sweatshirt that made his shoulders look broader, strong enough to hold the weight of the world on them. Oh, how she wished she could unload her burdens on him. His hair was straight and tied back, and his face was smooth and clean shaven.

"Nikki, we're not done," he said after they'd finished eating.

She eyed him warily. "What do you mean?"

"I mean, after last night, you don't expect me to just walk away from you. I'm going to find a way to get you out of here."

How could she tell him how much last night had meant to her? She didn't want him to know anyway. It would only cause trouble. "I'll come by tonight," was all she committed to. "What time?"

"I'll knock off about six."

"Okay."

He took a key ring from the peg next to where she'd taken the shell necklace and handed it to her. "This is the key to this house. Come anytime you want, Nikki. You can park the van in the back, if you want. Or did you already?"

"No, it's down the street. Thanks, Adrian. I'll see you tonight."

The bells on the door jingled as they always did when Nikki walked into the Garcia Gallery, a bit of familiarity in her strange life. Ulyssis smiled when he saw her, closing his checkbook and walking around the white counter.

"Hello, Nicolina. You look lovely, happy." He eyed her suspiciously. "What are you up to?"

"Nothing. Well, okay, something. But I don't want you to worry about me."

"It's that photographer man, isn't it? Didn't I tell you to stay away from him?"

"Yes, but I didn't listen to you, and see what happened?" She lifted her arms. "I'm perfectly healthy and alive."

"And in love," he said, touching his chin. "Oh, boy, do you have troubles, young lady."

Nikki leaned against the counter. "I know, but it's not the kind you think. Adrian Nash *is* Adrian Wilde, and he was the man who came in here. He's not working for Devlin, and he doesn't want to do me any harm. In fact, he wants to take me away from here."

None of that appeased Ulysses. "And do what with you? Nicolina, how can you be so foolish to trust him? You're thinking with your heart, a dangerous thing." He shook her shoulders. "Do I have to tie you up in the dark room until you come to your senses?"

"No, no. I have something to tell you that will change your mind." She told him about Adrian's experience with the lightning, seeing her life instead of his own, and then experiencing the horror of the explosion. Ulysses looked skeptical, but he could hardly deny the poignancy with which she told him what Adrian had seen and felt of her life. She didn't tell him, however, about their lovemaking.

Ulysses paced a little in the small shop, pinching his chin thoughtfully. "I don't know. I just don't know. But maybe this is a good thing, considering."

"What do you mean?"

"Maybe, if this man is what you say he is, it's good that he's here to protect you. I have friends who know Devlin, so I keep my ears tuned for you. I've heard something that might interest you.''

''About Devlin?''

''Yes. You know that brother of yours was always an idiot with money. I'm surprised he never bought the Brooklyn Bridge. Can you believe he's run out of the entire inheritance? One of my friends overheard another man yelling at Devlin in a restaurant for buying some high-rise office building in Tampa without getting this man's advice. Devlin thought it was a bargain. It's called the Madeira. I called a fellow gallery owner up there who runs in the real estate circles to find out what he knew. It was built three years ago, but before it was finished, the builder went bankrupt. Then some other company bought it, but they didn't do anything with it either. Now I know why. Apparently the building has serious structural problems, enough that it will have to be torn down and started again. Devlin owes the bank for the balance, the previous owner is nowhere to be found, and he's going to lose everything.

''My friend doesn't know why I'm interested in Devlin's dealings, but he knows that I am, so he kept listening to their conversation. Apparently this man, who my friend didn't know, offered Devlin a deal. If this man could fix the building problem, would Devlin agree to turn his business, LandCorp, over to his control. The two men didn't make a decision then, so I don't know what the outcome was.''

Nikki shook her head. ''I can't imagine Devlin turning control of anything over to anyone. He's been trying for that brass ring for years, and he's not about to let someone else grab it.''

''I thought that too. But if he didn't take that offer, then he's going to be desperately looking for money to bail out. He's already gone to all your family's friends begging for loans, but everyone knows what a loser he is. I'm afraid he'll start thinking about finding you if he doesn't get funds soon.''

Nikki shivered. ''If he hasn't already been looking for me. But if he hasn't found me yet. . . .'' She trailed off, because she could never be sure.

''What about this Adrian?''

''I know he's not working for Devlin. I've known him for three weeks now. He would have already told Devlin where to find me.''

''No, I mean, if he wants to take you away from here, and you trust him so much, then why don't you let him?''

''Because I feel safer here on the streets than I would anywhere else.''

Ulyssis shrugged, already knowing the argument was futile. She had survived for two years on the streets in the most unlikely place, and she would survive the next two years too.

''I know I'm always the bearer of bad news and concern, but please be careful. Trust no one, not completely.''

Nikki stopped by the shelter around noon, bringing Adrian two meat patties from the restaurant he seemed to like. The shelter looked completely different, covered in dust and filled with hard workers and rock and roll music. There was a palpable excitement in the air of people working together to save something they cherished. This was the only home many of these people had.

Adrian was positioning a cabinet in the kitchen when she found him. Even with the cool air coming through the open doors, he looked hot wearing his tank top. When he saw her standing there, he smiled.

''Time to break for lunch,'' he announced, though another man who seemed to be in charge grumbled that there wasn't time for lunch. Adrian's eyes smiled at her when he said, "Some things are more important than work, fellows."

Dave crawled out from beneath another cabinet in the far side of the kitchen, covered with white dust.

"Nikki! How are you doing?"

"Okay," she said, though she wasn't quite sure at the moment.

Dave turned to Adrian. "So, this is why you've been in such a good mood this morning, huh?" He winked at Adrian.

"Come on, let's go outside," Adrian said, taking her arm and pointedly ignoring the smirk on Dave's face. "Sometimes people are too nosy for their own good."

They walked around the back of the building next door where her van was parked. Crackers jumped up on Adrian's leg, his tail wagging.

"He sure likes you, considering . . ." She let the words trail off, but kept an eyebrow cocked.

"Don't even talk to me about that. I still feel terrible about the whole thing. At least he forgives me."

Her cocky attitude wilted. "I do too. And thanks for taking care of his vet bill."

"How'd you find out about that?"

"I asked when I took him back."

He shrugged, biting into one of the meat patties. "It was the least I could do."

After Adrian finished off his patties, with a piece left for Crackers, he sat back on her little bed, pulling her backward against his chest. With his arm protectively around her, she felt safe enough to tell him what Ulyssis had said.

That protectiveness showed in his brown eyes when he sat up and looked at her. "I want you to come back to New York with me. Now."

"I can't, and I won't. He's not going to drive me out of the only place I feel safe in. I just wanted you to know."

He took a deep breath, visibly calming himself down. "Okay. You're tough, you can take care of yourself. I have to keep remembering that. But if something happens to you . . ." He shook his head. "I'd blame myself for not packing you up and shipping you to New York."

"Adrian . . ."

He raised his arms in surrender. "I know, I know."

Crackers crawled up on the bed where Nikki sometimes let him sleep next to her. He curled up next to them, sighing before closing his eyes.

"I never liked animals much," Adrian said, stroking the pup's soft fur. "Maybe because I never had one, except for this cat I've been babysitting for a year. But this guy is pretty neat. If you want, why don't you just leave him at the house? That way he'll have more room. Of course, you could stay too."

Nikki absently petted Cracker's paw. "He would be happier there. So would I, but you know I can't stay."

"Tell me about Devlin," Adrian asked, surprising her by his sudden change of subject.

Nikki hated to even think about him, but she tried to remember what she could. "He was pretty much a normal kid, got into trouble, talked back to our parents, that kind of thing. He got into even more trouble after my father died ten years ago. He played with fire a few times, built those rockets I told you about, and nearly burned down the next-door neighbor's house. He was never particularly smart, but he wasn't dumb, either. I used to feel sorry for him, because he always pretended to be something he wasn't. He acted flashy and outgoing, but he was neither. I could see right through him, but maybe his friends couldn't. Or his so-called friends. I think they hung around with him because he bought them stuff, like liquor and concert tickets. It was sad."

"Were you and he close?"

"Never. He was mean when we were younger, and then we grew apart when he hit his teens." She remembered that strange conversation about not losing touch with each other a few months before the explosion. Why had he said that when he'd planned to murder her? "A couple of times he locked me in the wine cellar and didn't let me out for hours. This was when my parents were out and the staff was busy or off for the day. It was pitch dark, and I was so petrified. To this day I hate being in the dark."

Adrian stiffened. "He locked you in a cellar?"

"Told you he was mean. It was funny, but when he met Jack, he started acting like him. Jack embodied everything Devlin wanted to be: handsome, charming, completely sure of himself. Jack was also intelligent and clever, and after all the failures Devlin had suffered in his life, he clung to Jack in hopes of that success rubbing off on him. Devlin idolized him."

"What about you?" Adrian asked, leaning back on the bed.

"You jealous?" she teased.

"Maybe. Should I be?"

Nikki pulled her knees up and wrapped her arms around them, her back still against Adrian's chest. "No. He's nothing like you. Oh, I thought I was in love with him. I'm sure now it was infatuation. I dated him for about six months."

"Oh, so it wasn't serious."

"We were talking marriage." At his raised eyebrows, she added, "*He* was talking marriage. I wasn't sure, especially since I hadn't known him that long. He was very debonair, and very charming. I wasn't worried about him being after my money, because he had enough of his own."

"This was the guy who was pushing you?"

"Yes."

"How did you meet him?"

"Through my brother. Devlin met him at Bradley's. They became fast friends, and somehow the conversation turned to Devlin's little sister. The next weekend, Devlin talked me into going out, and we *accidentally* ran into Jack. I eventually forgave Devlin for setting me up without telling me. Jack and I hit it off instantly. Then he started talking marriage, and I wasn't sure. I told him I needed more time for a decision like that, and he reluctantly gave me another few months. Still, he kept pushing, dropping hints about other women who might like to marry a man like him and not make him wait. I didn't like being manipulated."

"Good girl," he said. "What was his rush, anyway?"

"He said he loved me and couldn't wait to make me his wife."

"What a charmer," Adrian said with a smirk.

"Then he did something else that bothered me even more. He asked to borrow money from me. He was always into some business venture or another, but he said his money was tied up and there was a hot deal he wanted in on. He told me all about it, some restaurant on the bay, and worked through the figures with me and everything. He made it sound great, like we couldn't lose. Jack said he wanted to have money of his own so we wouldn't live on mine, since his was so tied up. If he hadn't made it clear that he didn't want to live on mine, or to even touch mine, I would have wondered."

"Wondered about what?"

"Oh, I don't know. Jack said he had made himself a fortune, had homes here and there, businesses and such. But aside from his dressing nice and big talk, I never actually *saw* any evidence of that money. I had to take into consideration that to someone who didn't know me, I didn't look like I came from money either. He had a nice place, but nothing special. He said he was looking for a home here, but didn't care much where he stayed until he found the perfect place. Jack talked a lot about the estate where he'd grown up in France, the vineyards, his father's hating him. He talked about his money and investments, mostly in relation to when we got married. I hated talking about money. I figured I'd tell him eventually that I had five years before I inherited any money of my own.''

"How much did Jack want to borrow?''

"Seventy-five thousand dollars.'' It seemed like so much money now, but back then it was only a tiny part of the money she lived around. "He said he'd even sell one of his homes, if he thought he could do it soon enough.''

"Jeez. So what did he do when you told him you didn't have any money to loan him?''

"He was bummed. Devlin couldn't get in on it because Mother had just cut him off financially. He figured she owed him somehow. She kept most of her money tied up in investments, and Devlin's loans were not good investments. He'd started a music store, and it had failed miserably. By his fourth failure, she stopped loaning him money and demanded that he get his head straight and figure out what he was going to do with his life. She was afraid he was going to do exactly what he did . . . waste his inheritance away with his schemes, and his ideas kept costing more and more money.

"With Devlin, it was one thing after another. I knew my mother wouldn't give either Jack or Devlin a dime, especially since she didn't much like Jack. Something about him being too slick, having no real background. I wasn't about to ask for money. I had just started my own photography business and was proud that I didn't have to ask her for anything. I couldn't bring myself to borrow money from her.''

"Where was Jack from?''

"San Francisco. Originally from somewhere in France.

He was from an old family in the wine business there. His mother had married a wealthy immigrant, and he continued the business.''

"Did you ever meet them?''

"No. After he and I had talked marriage, I'd asked to meet his parents. I'm very . . . family oriented that way. He explained that he was the black sheep of the family since he'd scorned a strategic marriage that would have helped their business. Apparently there was no making peace with them.''

"Did they ask you about Jack while you were on the witness stand?''

"Just what my relationship was with him, the timing of everything that day. He wasn't a suspect.''

"He wasn't? I mean, didn't the police check him out?''

"Sure, he was a witness. But he lacked a motive. What benefit would my family's death have for him? I was only his girlfriend, not his wife. Besides, I was supposed to ride with him. I only rode in the Mercedes because Jack was running late, as usual. I thought you wanted to know about Devlin.''

"I do. But Jack is interesting too.'' He leaned over and gave her a quick kiss. "Thanks for bringing lunch by. I hear hammers going, so I'd better get back. See you at six. You're welcome to get there early and freshen up if you want.''

"Okay, thanks.''

He scrambled out of the van and walked back to the shelter, waving before disappearing into the building. Nikki sat there and watched him, wondering if he was really jealous of Jack. She wondered what Jack was doing now. Not enough to try to contact him. That part of her life was over, and she couldn't go back to any of it. In fact, her infatuation for Jack had been waning before the explosion anyway.

What she'd felt for Jack was nothing like the gut-wrenching, consuming feeling she had for Adrian.

Adrian made a couple of calls from the shelter, calls he could not tell Nikki about. Then he picked up some essentials for the evening ahead. He knew he had to touch base with Stanley, but didn't want to think about that now. Just the thought of dealing with his whiny agent made him want a cigarette. He realized then that he hadn't wanted one since Nikki had shown up the night before.

He thought about the conversation they'd had over lunch. Why had he been so curious about Jack? Maybe he was jealous, though it wasn't his nature. Then again, there had never been anyone is his life he cared enough about to be jealous over. It was Devlin he was concerned about, but his thoughts kept drifting to Jack, the faceless charmer who had almost stolen Nikki's heart.

His errands didn't take him as long as he'd figured, so he returned to the house early. It looked quiet from the outside, but when he walked inside, he heard the shower in the bedroom. He tossed the steaks in the refrigerator and walked into the bedroom, stripping off his clothes as he went.

Steam filled the bathroom, but he could make out Nikki's figure through the mist. She looked tantalizing. He slid the door open, and she started when he trailed his finger down the crevice of her spine, all the way down. . . .

He grinned like a wolf, but tried to look a little innocent by raising his eyebrows. "Oh, I'm sorry. I didn't know you were in here. I was just going to take a shower." Then she smiled too. "Mind if I join you?" Never mind that he had already taken a shower.

"No, not at all."

Her long hair clung to her wet body, reaching almost to her cute buttocks with the curls straightened. The shower that had seemed large enough before felt cozy and small. She held up a washcloth dripping with soap bubbles.

"Want me to scrub your back?"

He took her other hand and slipped a finger into his mouth. "I'd love it if you scrubbed my back."

Nikki closed her eyes briefly at the action, then pulled her finger from his mouth. "Keep doing that, buster, and you won't get that back scrub."

Adrian turned around, not even bothering to hide the surprised smile on his face. She slowly rubbed the soapy cloth down over his back and buttocks. Very carefully, she scrubbed every inch of his backside, then knelt down to wash his legs. After a few minutes, she slipped her arms around his waist and pressed herself against him. He pulled her arms tighter, amazed at how something so simple could feel so exquisite. After a few minutes, he turned around and pulled her into his arms. Their kiss was long and sweet; she was definitely no first-timer to that. Her hands slid over his soapy body, slipping easily over the slick surfaces.

She looked up at him as she trailed a finger down the center of his chest. "I've never taken a shower with a man before. Does that make me terribly naive?"

He snaked his fingers down her cheek. "I've never taken a shower with a woman either. Does that make me naive?"

She poked him gently in the stomach. "Oh, get out of here. You have too." But he saw in her eyes that she wanted it to be true. It was.

"Honestly, I haven't." He lifted her hair off her shoulders. "Taking a shower with a woman always seemed so . . . I don't know, serious. Domestic. So I never did it."

She smiled, a soft smile that made his heart jump. "What about now?"

He hugged her to him, burying his face in her wet hair. "This feels so right, it scares the hell out of me."

She squeezed him back fiercely, reminding him how

strong she really was. Their future was uncertain, even though their past had been intertwined. *What about now?* Adrian had never felt this way about a woman. Maybe it was because she was Madame Blue, or because her life was in danger. Whatever the reason, he knew he was letting himself get in too deep. And while he held her there in the shower, he didn't care.

Adrian soaped Nikki down and took precise care to clean every inch of her body. Some parts he did without the cloth, causing her to catch her breath beneath the touch of his fingers. Without any warning, she reached around and took him into her hands, caressing the length of him. He stood beneath the flow of water with her, kissing her as it flowed down all around them.

"Nikki, let's get out of here," he said breathlessly.

"No," she said, stopping his hand from shutting the water off. Instead, she turned it a little hotter. "Right here. A first time for both of us."

He kissed her again, fiercer this time. Hoisting her up on his hips, with her legs wrapped around him, he leaned her against the tile and glided into her. He felt no resistance this time, no pain on her end. Her eyes were closed, she had a smile on her lips as he gently moved inside her. Her fingers gripped his shoulders, and every time he pushed deeper, she gripped harder. He took pleasure in the way her breathing came short and quick, and the way she fit around him as if she had been made just for him.

When she shuddered, he felt every vibration. Just knowing that he could bring her such pleasure pushed him over the edge he'd carefully kept himself away from, and he let himself explode.

"Adrian, Adrian, Adrian," she murmured as he held her tight, trying to catch his own breath.

Just hearing her say his name like that sent another ripple of pleasure through him. They stood there until the water ran cold, and then he set her on her feet. He smiled wryly, though he was kicking himself mentally.

"You know, hot thing, I had birth control in the bedroom."

"Good," she said, pinching him on the cheek and stepping out of the shower. "We'll need it later."

Adrian grabbed a towel and lassoed her with it, pulling her back against him.

"What if you get pregnant?"

"I won't."

"How can you be so sure?"

"Because I had a reading when I was fifteen, and the psychic said I wouldn't have a baby until I was twenty-eight. This woman was supposed to be the real thing." Like Stella. Adrian pushed the thought from his mind. Nikki turned around in his arms, water dripping from her hair. "We'll be good from now on."

He tilted her chin up and just before his lips contacted hers, whispered, "You were good right from the beginning."

She kissed him ardently, smiling the whole time. If he ever thought he'd be kissing Madame Blue, holding her naked in his arms, making love with her . . . he would have thought he'd really lost it.

He towel-dried her hair, then walked her into the bedroom where a shimmering green dress was laid out on the comforter. She looked at it, then at him.

"What's this?"

"It's for you. Put it on."

"But I can't go out. Especially not around here."

"Who said anything about going out?"

She turned to him, and he gave her a smile. "You dog. You shouldn't have done this."

"Well, I've seen you in old clothes, and I've seen you naked. Now I want to see you dressed up. Put it on."

She slipped into it while he put on dress pants and a white shirt. Her eyes glittered as she twirled around, set off by the green of the dress. She was more beautiful than any model he'd ever photographed, complete with all their makeup artists and hair stylists. He picked up the camera on the dresser and snapped three shots of her. She covered her face briefly, then dropped her hands and smiled.

"It's beautiful," she said, twirling around.

"So are you. Dance with me."

"There's no music."

She moved into his waiting arms anyway, entwining her hand with his.

"Sure there is. Just listen with your heart, and you'll hear it."

Something inside her heard the music, moving her in perfect rhythm with his every movement. She looked up at him. "I hear it."

Chapter 13

How can you argue with a heart on a collision course with love?

Adrian derived more pleasure from watching Nikki eat the filet mignon than he did eating his own. Two years was a long time to go without prime beef. Or human contact. Her skin glowed and her eyes shimmered with contentment. He hadn't bought her any makeup because she didn't need it. Besides, he was used to seeing women made up to the max all the time; it was refreshing to see a woman dressed up without it.

She looked up at him from beneath her thick lashes, a quirky grin on her lips. "So, who *was* that woman who came up to us on the street that day?"

Adrian leaned back in his chair, resting his hands over his stomach. He didn't feel like talking about Rita just then. "A friend. She watches my cat when I'm out of town."

"A friend, hmm? What's her name?"

"Rita."

"Is she a model? She was quite beautiful."

"She's a model, but she has nothing on you, Madame Blue."

The name made her smile for a second, but that questioning look returned. "Are you seeing her?"

He shrugged. "We go out sometimes. That's all there is to it."

Adrian stood and extended a hand to her. She took it, and they walked into the living room, sitting on the couch where he had found Nikki sleeping. He didn't like the thoughtful expression on her face that creased her eyebrows. She looked at the ashtray sitting on the wicker end table.

"Do you smoke?"

"I'm trying to quit." There were two almost full cigarettes in the ashtray from a few days before.

Nikki leaned against the back of the sofa, gazing absently at his leg. She looked lost in her thoughts, or in her heart. Was she worried about Rita? Surely not. Nikki didn't appear to him as the insecure type. Not after what she'd been through in the last three years. He touched her chin, lifting it so that she had to look at him. Still, she looked downward.

"What's wrong, Nikki? Talk to me."

Her gaze slowly met his, full of some emotion he couldn't identify. "Adrian, I . . ." Her voice caught. "Make love to me. Please."

Like she had to ask. But he knew it wasn't the physical aspect of lovemaking she needed. It was the emotional part. Damn, that was all foreign to him.

He gathered her up in his arms and carried her to the bedroom. This time it was less frenzied than in the shower. When he laid her down on the bed, she clung to him, holding him close for several minutes. As he held her, he realized again how small and fragile she sometimes seemed. He wanted to hold her there safely forever. He wanted to take away all the pain of the last three years. Adrian couldn't do that, and she wouldn't let him take her away from this place. Nikki thought Devlin was so powerful that he could find her anywhere. Maybe he was, though that wasn't the impression he got from the man. Well, he'd soon find out.

When Nikki finally loosened her grip on him, he leaned over her and trailed a finger down the side of her cheek. It was damp. Tears glistened on her lashes. Her hand trembled as she reached up to touch the side of his face. He took her hand, the scarred one, and pressed it to his mouth, then kissed down the length of her arm until he reached her lips. Her eyes searched his, and he wished he knew what they were looking for so that he could give it to her.

"Adrian, I love you," she whispered.

And he gave her what she wanted, without hesitation. "I love you too, Nikki. I have always loved you." The words had come so naturally to a man who hadn't used them since adolescent hormone overload. So naturally, in fact, he wondered if he meant them as much as she did. Not that he regretted saying them after seeing the light in her eyes. No, he had meant those words. He felt them deep inside. They were more than right. And this was more than love. She had been in his heart for a long time. He ran his fingers down her damp cheek. "But why are you crying?"

Nikki shook her head, then pulled him tight against her and kissed him fiercely. He returned her fervor with his own, fearing that he might crush her under the power of his feelings. Her fingers quickly unbuttoned his shirt, then his trousers. He helped her out of that shimmering dress, feeling chills climb down his heated skin as her fingers stroked through his hair.

Adrian let her set the pace, following like a willing slave. It was a change he didn't mind. She took control, rolling him onto his back and sliding down on top of him. He kneaded her hips as she moved in a hard rhythm. And when she had taken what she needed, and they were both satisfied, she snuggled into the crook of his arm and fell asleep.

He was far too charged up to fall asleep, so he watched her breathe and wondered what it would be like to wake up with her every morning.

All the reasons he had for not opening up to a woman, for not having one in his life, seemed to vanish as he held Nikki in his arms. Opening his heart to a woman had never been an option before, but it was too late. Nikki had his heart as surely as a thief had broken in to take it. Except that he didn't want it back. He had hers to take its place.

But he wondered just what the future had in store for them. Tragedy connected their souls these past three years, and fate or God had put her in the background of his shot, brought him here, and wouldn't let him go back to New York without finding her. Yet, she wouldn't let him help, and she wouldn't leave for two years. No matter how safe he could convince her she'd be with him, he knew she wouldn't feel safe. Even if he could move his business down here, she still wouldn't be safe living with him. And he couldn't live on the streets for two years. So where did that leave him?

It was more than an hour before her eyes fluttered awake in the dim light from the dresser. He had been absently stroking her arm and staring at the ceiling when he felt her stir.

The first thing Nikki felt was Adrian's fingers against her skin, a rhythmic stroke that pulled her to consciousness. What had gotten into her, anyway? She already knew what it was, though. She needed him, desperately. Nikki wanted to crawl inside him and live safely there, not just for the next two years, but forever. If she had fit in nowhere else in her life before, she fit here. This was where she belonged. He loved her. She smiled at the memory of his words. And blushed at the memory of hers. Why had she told him that? The words had wanted to come out, had been pushing to get out since the first time they'd made love. As he'd looked at her and said them back, she knew in her heart that he meant them. But what good would it do?

When she'd looked at him sitting next to her on the couch, looking magnificent and sexy and strong, she realized how inaccessible he really was to her. He had a life back in New York. And Rita, the woman he didn't want to talk about. Nikki had two more years of hell here. Then what? She certainly couldn't ask him to wait for her. It all seemed so hopeless, and yet, she couldn't tell him good-bye, couldn't stop seeing him so he'd leave and get it over with. That meant waiting until he told her good-bye. The thought had ripped her heart apart, just as it did now. She wanted to obliterate those feelings by getting lost in their lovemaking. And she had, for a little while.

It was late, though she had no idea how long she'd been asleep. She shifted as she opened her eyes, and found him looking at her.

"Are you all right?" he asked, his voice a little hoarse.

No. "I'm fine."

He tilted his head. "Sure?"

She tried to smile, but only managed a half smile and a nod.

He touched the tip of her nose, looking thoughtful himself. "What do you want to do with your life? I mean, after this two-year sentence of yours is up?"

She looked at him, surprised by his question. "I want to start over someplace else. Do something with my photography. I hardly had a chance to succeed or fail before, and I can hardly call what I do now a career. I'll keep aside a little of my inheritance for that. Maybe Mother didn't like my photography, but I believe she wanted me to be happy."

"Of course she did. She probably never realized what her disappointment was doing to you."

Nikki rolled over and looked at him, bending her head forward just a little.

"What? What are you thinking?" he asked, intent on her every move.

She shrugged, looking away. "You'd probably think it was silly. I don't know, maybe it is."

"Why don't you try me."

She hesitated, meeting his gaze. "When I think about living in real society again . . . I get scared sometimes. It's weird, because you'd think it would be just the opposite. But I've been out of it for so long now, it seems foreign to me. Even the simple day-to-day events of a normal person's life have me fretting. A small part of me wants to stay hidden."

Adrian leaned forward and grabbed her arm, a fierce intensity in his brown eyes. "Don't be afraid, Nikki. You can't waste your life hiding. I won't let you, do you understand?"

She just stared at him, and he loosened his grip. Adrian seemed like the prince and the dragon all at once. Yet she wasn't afraid of him. No, because if she were to hide, it would be in his arms. If she let herself, she could well imagine burrowing into his life and never coming out. And then he'd get bored of her. Nikki threw off the thought. Thinking of a future with Adrian was dreaming again. In two years, who knew where he'd be? She didn't even know where he was now, not really. He was her protector, her savior. But he had a life back in New York City that was vastly different than hers. Rita might be his girlfriend, waiting for her prince to return.

They had both gotten caught up in the visions, life on the street, and the explosion they had shared thousands of miles apart. Even if he did love her, how serious was he? He wasn't hers, though strangely enough, she felt as if she belonged to him. His Madame Blue. Without thinking her hand reached out to entwine with his.

"And what about you? Where do you see yourself in two years?" she asked.

That intensity flared again as he reached out and touched her chin with his other hand. "You know, Nikki, I never thought about two years ahead, or even one. When I was younger, I thought of the future only in terms of my career. People came and went, and that was fine.

"Right now, you know what I see? Loneliness. I've been alone most of my life, but I've never been lonely. I never thought I was, anyway. I've seen lonely now. In your life, in Seamus's, Charlie's, everybody down there in the city. I don't worry about being homeless anymore, but their loneliness struck a fear even stronger. I want more."

His words didn't comfort her, though. If he realized his life was lonely, she couldn't be there to fulfill it for another two years. *Nikki, you knew when you met him that he wouldn't stay. You knew when he kissed you that falling in love would be futile. Yet you kept seeing him. I know, I know*, her thoughts answered back. *How can you argue with a heart on a collision course with love?*

LandCorp's offices were housed in a three-story building in downtown Palm Beach. It wasn't as impressive as Adrian thought it would be, but he figured they wanted to keep a low profile. He had spoken with Devlin on the phone about possibly investing in some new venture for which Land-Corp needed money. Adrian now kicked himself for going to see Devlin before, hoping that his completely different appearance, sans beard and bum's clothes, would throw Devlin off. And the accent, of course.

He couldn't tell Nikki about this visit. He'd promised not to talk to Devlin again. All he knew is that he loved Nikki, and he'd be damned if he was going to wait two years for her while she hid among the homeless. What he would find at this meeting, he wasn't sure, but he had to start somewhere. Finding out just how desperate Devlin was to get that money was a start.

Adrian checked himself in the reflection of the glass entrance before opening the door. With the dark suit he'd worn last night and his hair brushed straight and tied back, he looked the part he was going to play.

The offices were richly furnished, with an oak desk and dark blue chairs for visitors. The receptionist was a young, prim-looking lady in her midthirties. Her eyes widened with interest when she took him in.

"May I help you?"

"Sure. Name's Adrian Santucci, here to see Devlin Madsen," he said in a Brooklyn/Italian accent. "He's expecting me."

She smiled at him. "Yes, they are. Please follow me."

They? The other man in the restaurant maybe? His guard went up as he walked into a panelled conference room. Two men stood as he entered, businesslike smiles on their faces. Adrian shook hands with the tall blond man who was about his age. His handshake was firm.

"Hello. My name is Jack Barton. I'm the CEO of LandCorp. This is Devlin Madsen, the president."

Adrian tried not to show surprise at the name. Jack? Nikki hadn't said his last name, but this had to be him. So, Devlin had made the deal with the man, then. Yet, they were still looking for investors, evidenced by how quickly Devlin had agreed to the meeting. Devlin leaned forward, his grip soggy. His brow furrowed as he studied Adrian. Did he recognize him? It was too late now. Adrian had to keep up the charade.

"Please, sit down," Jack said. Jack, the CEO. He smiled, and Adrian could well imagine that smile charming someone like Nikki. "I appreciate you coming down from New York to talk with us about this investment. I understand that you . . . heard we needed some help.'' Jack glanced at Devlin. ''May I ask where?''

''You've heard of my uncle, Carlo D'Aprile, right?'' Adrian's confident smile gave way to amazement. ''You never heard of Carlo?'' He laughed. ''I thought everyone knew about Carlo. Anyway, he's got a large family operation up in New York, but he likes to keep his fingers all over the country, if you know what I mean. And he has a particular fondness for real estate. Uncle Carlo looked at that building, but saw the flaws immediately.'' Devlin blushed slightly, avoiding Jack's burning gaze at Adrian's words. ''Of course, when it sold for a price far beyond its value, he was more than a tiny bit curious about the transaction. Being that he's in Sicily right now taking care of some old . . . debts, he asked me to check it out.''

Devlin stood, face still red. ''The man was a scam artist! He could have fooled anyone. Even the consultant I hired agreed the building was sound, that the deal was good. He's gone too. The whole thing was a setup.''

''Devlin,'' Jack murmured, giving him a look Adrian couldn't see. Devlin sat down, kneading his fingers in his lap. Jack turned to Adrian, that smile intact. ''I wasn't involved or consulted in that deal, but it's my job to make the best of it. We have investigators seeking the man or men involved. Why are you here, Mr. Santucci? Certainly not out of curiosity.''

Adrian sputtered a laugh. ''Nah, not at all. Uncle Carlo, he figured you got bamboozled. Being a fine, upright kind of guy, he gets real generous when someone gets bamboozled, so he sent me down here to see what he could do to help you out, if you know what I mean.''

Jack's eyebrows raised. ''And how does he propose to do that?''

''By loaning you the money you need, how else? No bank's going to touch that building, but Uncle Carlo, like

I said, is feeling pretty generous. He'll loan you the money you need for a share of the building.''

"What kind of share?" Devlin asked before Jack could open his mouth.

"We gotta look at all the numbers before we can tell you that. As I said, Uncle Carlo is feeling—''

"I know, very generous," Jack finished. "So what exactly do you need?"

"I'll need numbers, lots of them. Background information on this company, what you need to blow that building to pieces and to make it pretty again. So, gentlemen, let's get to the bottom line here, which is always money. How much do you need to get this going?"

"Money isn't only the bottom line, but every line in between heaven and hell," Jack said, smiling to temper his words. "LandCorp made a bad decision." Jack glanced at Devlin. "But we can turn this into a moneymaking venture for all of us. We owe the bank fourteen million dollars. So far I've been able to allay their fears once word got to them about the building being useless. If we can assure them of plans to make the venture successful, we can quell their fears permanently. Our goal would be to rebuild and sell the building, which might get us forty to fifty million. I think that would be a nice, tidy sum for all concerned. I'll get you the necessary numbers." His blue eyes hardened. "So, tell me about this uncle of yours. Carlo D'Aprile? What kind of projects does he get involved with?"

Adrian met Jack's skeptical look square on, keeping his profile to Devlin as much as possible. "Let's just say Uncle Carlo likes to dabble in a little of everything: real estate, exporting and importing, even art."

Adrian was all but telling them outright that good old Uncle Carlo was Mafia. If Devlin and Jack weren't desperate, they'd turn Adrian right around and head him out the door.

Jack glanced at Devlin. "My partner and I will begin working on it right away. It might take us a couple of days." Jack and Devlin stood. "I'll be interested to see just how generous your uncle can be."

Adrian didn't stand, and the two men hesitantly sat down again. Adrian relaxed in his chair a little, as if signaling an end to the business part of the meeting but not the meeting itself.

"My uncle likes to know a little about the men behind the investment. Where are you from, Jack? What does your family do?"

Jack loosened his collar a little, but otherwise seemed composed. "I'm from San Francisco originally. My father heads a large corporation in Seattle."

That was interesting. No wine business? "What kind of business might that be?"

"Seattle West Insurance. One of the largest in the United States."

"I'm surprised you didn't follow in his footsteps. In our family, it's almost mandatory to go into the family business."

"Too boring for me. Give me these fly-by-the-seat-of-your-pants kind of investments, that's more my style."

"Your father was probably disappointed that his son didn't join him."

Jack shrugged. "He didn't much care what I did, Mr. Santucci. In fact, he would have been disappointed if I had joined him. I left home when I was seventeen and never looked back. What I've accomplished, I've done on my own."

Adrian tried to conceal his surprise. He may have been the black sheep, but for a different reason than the one he'd given Nikki.

Devlin's story coincided with Nikki's version, how Addington Madsen worked his way up in an industrial plant in Connecticut before buying it when he was fifty-two. Addington was an investment genius, making a huge profit when he sold the plant only five years later and retiring to Palm Beach. Devlin left out the fact that he hadn't inherited that genius, that he'd already lost the millions he'd inherited when his mother was killed.

Adrian stood up and shook hands with both men. "Call me when your proposal is ready." He patted his breast pocket. "Ah, shoot. Forgot my business cards." He reached for one of Devlin's cards, sitting next to his leather folder and jotted down the number at the rental house. "I'll be here for a few days."

Jack smiled, looking a little more relaxed now that the conversation was off his personal life. "Feel free to call if you have any questions."

"Yeah, I'll do that."

Just as Adrian turned to leave, Devlin finally spoke up. "I know you, now. You came by the house and asked for my sister, Nikki."

Adrian tried his best to look calm as he shook his head. Devlin was smarter than he'd given him credit for. "Who, me? Nah, I don't even know where you live, or who your sister is. You must have me mixed up with someone else."

"Are you sure? You look just like him." Devlin scratched his head, shaking it slightly.

"I'm sure. Good-bye, gentlemen."

Jack watched Adrian Santucci get into his Mustang convertible and leave, then walked back to his office with Devlin right behind him. He dropped into his leather chair and propped his new Italian shoes on the desktop.

"There was something about that man that bothered me."

Devlin nodded. "There's a *lot* about that man that bothered me. He's Mafia, I guarantee it. We deal with him and we'll end up in some concrete block. But the weird part is I swear it's the same guy that came up to my house about a week ago. It was those eyes.''

"You're sure?"

"Well, he didn't have that Italian accent, and his hair was different, but yes, it was him. Do you think he's been scoping us out?"

Jack stuck an ivory toothpick in his mouth, wondering the same thing. But where would he get Nikki's name in all this? "Ah, it's probably a different guy."

"It's the same man, I'm sure of it." Devlin sat down. "You didn't arrange this meeting, did you?"

"No, I didn't. This guy came out of nowhere. I know what you're getting at, but you already took the deal. Now you've got to trust me on it. If you'd talked to me in the first place, you wouldn't be in this predicament."

"You would have fallen for this guy too. He was good." Devlin stood, pacing in front of the desk. "Someday I'm going to make the business deal of a lifetime, and I'm going to do it without anyone else."

"Not while I'm in charge. You know the rules now."

"And you know I had no choice."

"Sure you did. But you're not going to regret this, Dev. I'm going to make both of us rich men. We might still find the schlump who sold you this lemon. But if we don't, then we'll find some other way to get out of this."

"Like maybe with this Carlo D'Aprile?"

Jack stared out the window. "Maybe."

Chapter 14

Do anything but betray my heart.

"Adrian, where were you today? I stopped by the shelter, but Dave said you had taken the day off."

He hated to lie to Nikki again. What would she do if he told her exactly where he'd been today? She'd be angry. Maybe even furious. But he couldn't lie to her, not anymore. The other alternative wasn't going to get him any brownie points either.

"I had some business to take care of, that's all."

"Business? With your studio, you mean."

"Something like that."

"Oh." She nodded, but he could see she didn't quite understand why he was being evasive. "Why didn't you tell me this morning?"

"I'd forgotten until I was heading down to the shelter." A tiny lie. He smiled, changing the subject. "How's it coming?"

"It looks almost done. They only have to put the shingles on the roof. The kitchen still looks a wreck, but Dave said it was only a few days away from being completed." She looked at him, as if trying to read his expression. He kept it straight, showing nothing of the guilt he felt inside. "Is anything going on?"

He pulled her next to him on the couch so that he didn't have to look into her eyes. "Everything's fine."

But she turned to him anyway. "Are you planning to leave soon?"

He could tell by the tone of her voice how painful it was to push those words out. His hands circled her face, and he said, "I want you to trust me, Nikki. Okay? No matter what, trust me."

"I do trust you."

"Good." He kissed her lightly on the lips, wanting to linger there longer. The perplexed look on her face stopped him from becoming more amorous. For now, anyway.

Nikki walked into the kitchen to start the chicken he'd brought home for dinner. She had arrived only minutes after Jack had called to set up another meeting for the following morning. That seemed awfully quick for them to get a report ready. Maybe they were going to tell him to forget it. That would make him feel a little more comfortable about Nikki's safety. That might mean Devlin wasn't desperate enough to kill for it.

Another alliance based on lies. This time those lies went both ways. Jack Barton had lied about his past. Either to Nikki or to Adrian, maybe both. More interesting, Jack seemed to be the man in charge, not Devlin. So Devlin had taken the bargain, sold his soul to the devil. But why would Jack agree to bail LandCorp out to take control of a company that seemed little more than a failing business?

From his second impression of Devlin, he didn't seem capable of enough smarts or passion to blow up his family. He had to remember that looks could be deceiving.

Adrian leaned his head back against the couch, delving deeper. Nikki was supposed to have ridden with Jack to the fair that day. Who knew that? Jack, and Nikki's family. Maybe someone who knew the family. Could that pipe bomb have been meant only for Devlin and their mother?

Still, who stood to gain from that? Jack wasn't married to Nikki, and she had five years before she could inherit more than a living allowance. Though there was a John Barton who headed the insurance company in Seattle, Jack himself seemed to have little more than an old Toyota and a rented apartment in Fort Lauderdale. A man like that didn't own houses all over the country, and he obviously wasn't still looking for that perfect mansion into which to sink his fortune. Adrian rubbed his forehead, the facts and lies crashing into each other.

"Is something wrong?" Nikki asked, walking into the living room.

Adrian stood up, wandering into the kitchen to help her with dinner. "No, nothing's wrong. I've just got a headache."

Even cradled in Adrian's arms, Nikki couldn't fall asleep. He was up to something. "Trust me," he'd asked. How could she trust him when their whole relationship had started out with a lie? He was gone all day from a job he seemed dedicated to, and all he said was that he was taking care of business.

It was more than that vague answer. He had been quiet all night, avoiding her eyes, making chitchat. It wasn't like him, or at least like the man she had come to know this past week. Adrian had moved away from her that night, not physically, but emotionally. Could it be that he was getting tired of her already?

Well, what did she have to offer him, anyway? A woman who was hiding for her life, living on the streets by day, sneaking back to his place at night to make love and have dinner. He would have to leave soon, and the pain that rumbled through her would rip her heart in half when he left. She was falling more in love with him every day, and he was falling out of love with her.

Nikki thought of the reflection she'd seen in the mirror that night before getting into bed. No makeup, no fancy hairdo. He was used to beautiful women posing on beaches in bikinis, not street urchins.

A sob caught in her throat, and she swallowed it back. She didn't regret a moment with Adrian, not even the ones where she was uncertain of him. Most of all, she didn't regret giving him her most precious gift. He had been tender, loving, passionate. A tear slid down to the pillow. She could feel his heartbeat against her bare back. When he breathed, she moved with him. Saying good-bye was inevitable, and every night she spent in his rented house put her in danger. She had to let him go. Maybe he would stay around another few days, or a week. She would be more in love with him, and he would be glad to be rid of her. No, she had to be the one to say good-bye, and soon. Tomorrow night.

When Nikki woke up the next morning, she was surprised to find Adrian facing her. He reached over and rubbed away the wetness on her cheek. She had dreamed that she'd awakened and found him gone. She'd tried to call his studio, but the number was disconnected. But he was there, looking at her with compassion in his brown eyes.

"Why are you crying, Nikki?" he asked, his voice thick.

"I had a bad dream. It'll be fine."

"Do you want to talk about it?"

"No. Just hold me."

He gathered her in his arms, giving her that instant feeling of security for which she longed. He kissed the top of her head, then her forehead, then across her wet cheeks. She sought his lips, warm and full against hers. Their tongues joined that intimate dance so naturally, as if they'd been kissing for years. Her hands slid around him, cradling his tight buttocks. Would any man make her feel this way again? Would she want anyone to?

His arousal pressed against her stomach, and his kisses became more insistent. She felt the heat rise from within her, reaching for him. Adrian's essence wrapped around her, filling her with warmth and love and energy. When he slid inside her, her breath caught. He slid his arms beneath her and pulled her up against him, continuing to move in rhythm. *I can hear the music, Adrian.* The shattering sunlight exploded inside her and she tried to remember how it felt when he wasn't there. His whole body tensed, then shuddered.

His breathing calmed, and he leaned down and kissed her gently. "Don't cry. I love you, Madame Blue."

"I . . ." Her voice was swallowed in the cry that threatened to erupt. "I love you too."

They took a shower together, standing beneath the water until the heat gave out. He held her, somehow sensing that she needed that so badly right then. Trust him. She did trust him. But she still had to say good-bye.

"Are you going to the shelter this morning?" she asked, dressing in her old garb.

"I'll be there. Meet me for lunch, okay?"

"Okay."

After Nikki left, she waited in her van for him to pass. He did, but he turned in the opposite direction than the shelter. What was he up to? She couldn't believe now that he was working for Devlin, but there seemed no other plausible explanation. No, he wasn't deceiving her like that. Nikki wanted to follow him, but her body wouldn't cooperate, wouldn't put the van into gear. His car disappeared around the corner and sped out of sight.

Adrian hated lying to her, hated himself for deceiving her. But he was determined to get to the bottom of her mother's death. More determined to free her from this two-year sentence she'd imposed on herself. If she doubted him now, someday she would thank him.

He walked into the LandCorp offices and told the receptionist he was expected. Jack seemed different at this meeting, not quite as charming. Was he suspicious of good old Uncle Carlo, or of Adrian himself?

"Hello, Mr. Santucci. I have to apologize. When I called you yesterday, I thought I'd be able to spend the whole night working on these numbers. Unfortunately something came up that prevented me from completing them. Then I realized I'd left your number at work, and by the time I got here, well, you were pulling in. How about tomorrow morning? I promise I'll have them done."

"I understand. Tomorrow's fine."

They shook hands. Adrian noticed that Devlin wasn't in this meeting, and seemed to be nowhere around. No matter. Jack seemed the mastermind behind LandCorp now that Devlin had given him control.

Nikki pulled up to the shelter, sitting in her van for a few minutes. Adrian hadn't gotten to the shelter until nine o'clock, and he'd been dressed in nice pants and a dressy shirt. Maybe he would tell her what was going on today at lunch. Her heart ached at the thought of losing him, but there wasn't any choice. They were doomed, and Adrian was still keeping secrets from her. She had to be strong and walk away, and she had to do it before it was too late.

A knock on the glass beside her jarred Nikki. Adrian leaned against the door, a sweet smile on his face. She opened the door and stepped out, slipping so easily into his arms. He stooped to her level, not letting her look away.

"You looked deep in thought. Is everything all right?"

"I'm fine."

They walked around to the van's side door and sat on the bed eating egg salad sandwiches. Adrian had mentioned once that he liked them. While he ate, he talked about how close they were to finishing the shelter and opening it again.

"I can't wait to see that inspector's face when he returns, ready to shut us down."

Us. Adrian had taken a real interest in the shelter. Soon it would be done, and then what?

"All the homeless people keep coming by every night to see if we're open yet. It's so sad. The blanket collection's been going well, though, so at least we can give them something to keep them warm at night."

She watched him talk, saw the excitement in his brown eyes. He was so damn gorgeous, so caring. She was going to love him forever, no matter what. At the moment, it seemed that she would never love another man the way she loved him. Just the thought of being back in the world, especially without Adrian, made her shiver.

"Are you all right?" he asked softly. "You've been awfully quiet."

She nodded, probably a little more vigorously than necessary. Putting on a casual face, she said, "I stopped by earlier, but your car wasn't here."

Instead of looking uncomfortable, he reached out and touched her chin. "Didn't I ask you to trust me, Nikki? Can you do that?"

She nodded again, but couldn't quite meet his eyes. Trust didn't come easily to her, especially with Adrian. Every time he touched her, every time he looked into her eyes, her heart ripped a little more. She couldn't take any more of this. Not another night with him, not making love with him. It hurt too much.

As if he could read her thoughts, he leaned over and kissed her. His lips caressed hers before his tongue slipped inside her mouth to seek its mate. She didn't want him to think anything was wrong, so she kissed him back. It was a sweet kiss, filled with the promise of much more later.

But she had already made a decision. She could not tell him in person. No, because then he wouldn't let her leave. Adrian had already told her he'd almost packed her up and shipped her back to New York to get her away from there. He wasn't going to let her slip off into the night. She had to write him a letter.

"Are you going to tell me what's bothering you?" he asked in that intimate tone that sent shivers up her spine.

"I'm all right, really. Maybe I'm coming down with something."

"The last time you said that, you stood me up." He smiled, but his words made her heart stop beating. "Why don't you go back to the house and get some sleep? I'll nurse you back to health when I get home."

"Okay." Her hand reached up to touch his cheek, already a little rough with stubble. "See you later." She hoped he didn't hear the thickness that had overtaken her voice.

Nikki drove to the house, composing the good-bye letter in her mind. She was also trying to figure out where she would go for a while. Last time Adrian had stuck around town when she had disappeared, but it would be different this time. She would explain to him that there simply was no other way, with no mention of his secret so-called business. She didn't want him to think he had to explain anything to her. Nikki wanted to make it all perfectly clear that it was hopeless and that he should leave.

Nikki parked the van behind the house, not taking any chances even though this would be her last visit. She walked in, greeting Crackers as he nearly ran to the door. He was only a couple of days away from getting his cast off. Nikki knelt down, and the pup tried to jump onto the shelf her legs made. She giggled as he licked her face and tickled her chin with his whiskers.

After trying to keep herself balanced, she toppled down to the tile. Crackers's tail zipped through the air as he nuzzled her. She rested her cheek against the soft fur of his back.

"What am I going to do with you?" Nikki had thought about it all the way home. She couldn't, wouldn't, take him to the dog pound. He deserved better than that. But she couldn't keep him in her van, as much as she had come to love his company. "I can't keep you. And I don't want to just turn you out to the streets again."

She held the puppy's face in her hands, looking at him. "Do you think Adrian loves you enough to take you home with him? If I ask him real nice in my letter, maybe? I know he cares about you, probably as much as I do. And he's already taken in some cat." Nikki felt a weight lift from her shoulders as she stood and searched for the note pad she knew Adrian kept around.

When she found it, she sat down at the table and took a deep breath. This was the coward's way out, to be sure. But it was the only way. She didn't think about the bleak future ahead of her without Adrian in it. Nikki wouldn't let herself hope that he might still be available in two years when she could inherit her money and give it away. She'd have two long years to wonder about him, who he was with, if he had fallen in love with someone yet. Two lonely years.

With a sigh, she started the letter:

Dear Adrian,

How do I write something like this? You'll hate me, I know, but please try not to. I know you have to go back to New York soon; you can't just stay here for the next two years trying to protect me. I can't keep putting myself in danger by coming here either. Even if I went to New York with you, I'd never feel safe. That leaves me with only one alternative. I have

*to get out of here before I become too attached to
you. Okay, it's too late for that. I have to leave before
I stop being careful because I want to be with you.
It has to be this way. I'm sorry I couldn't tell you in
person, but it's hard enough to just write this letter.
I hope you understand why I'm doing this.*

*Don't get mad at me—I left Crackers here. I can't
take care of him, and I can't bear to leave him at the
pound or put him back on the streets. Next time there
might not be anyone so caring as to carry him ten
blocks to the vet. I leave him in your capable hands,
hoping that you'll take him back with you. If you
don't want him, please find him a good home. I know
you care about him, and if you ever cared about me,
you'll do this one thing for me.*

*Never doubt that I love you. I've never loved any-
one the way I do you. Adrian, you've given me hope
for the future, and courage to face the world again
in two years. I hope that we can at least be friends
when that time comes. I'll know where to find you.
How could I ever forget? "Visions, Inc." Please
don't try to find me. It'll just make this harder for
both of us, and will do no good.*

I love you.

Nikki.

She folded the note and left it tucked beneath one of her
framed pictures in the center of the table. Tears filled her
eyes, and when she blinked, they spilled down her cheeks.
She could almost picture Adrian wiping them away with
his hand, but she shoved that thought away. Although he
would never understand it, she was doing this for him too.
If Devlin found her with Adrian, he might kill them both.
It was best for everyone. Now if she could only convince

her heart of that, she'd be fine. Nikki gave Crackers a kiss on his forehead and slipped out the back door.

The gray clouds above looked pregnant with rain. Adrian drove through the streets of Palm Beach, thinking of what he would say to Nikki. *Okay, forget about the present. What about the explosion?* She had been seeing Jack. In love with him. The thought nagged at him. Adrian was unaccustomed to having feelings of jealousy. But it was more than that. Jack had been pressuring her to marry him, and it sounded as if she was backing away from him. Playing devil's advocate, Adrian dismissed the idea of Devlin being behind the pipe bomb.

If everything had gone according to Jack's plan, Nikki would have ridden with him, and Devlin and Blossom would have driven together. They would have died together too. But Devlin conveniently forgot something, and then Nikki remembered the journal about her dreams. But what if Devlin and Blossom had died? Nikki would have inherited the mansion, both her father's and mother's money, plus any other assets he didn't know about. He knew she couldn't have planted the bomb. What about Jack? What did he stand to gain?

Nothing. Adrian exhaled a long breath. He wasn't named in the will, wasn't family. He'd lied about his past, either to Adrian or Nikki, but that didn't prove anything. His thoughts returned to Devlin. There had to be some piece of evidence, some thread the police missed. He was determined to solve this murder, but he needed Nikki's help. That meant coming clean with his visits to LandCorp, but he didn't care. No more lies. All he had to do was convince her that together they could solve this and free her.

The house was empty, a strange letdown with the electricity shooting through his veins. Crackers greeted him, but

Adrian had only enough time to pet him for a second as he scanned the public areas of the house. Maybe she was asleep in his bed. That thought kindled a warm feeling inside him.

He tossed his keys on the table and headed for the bedroom. The bed was empty, the sheets and blankets still rumpled from that morning. The bathroom was dark and quiet.

"Nikki! Are you here?"

Only the sound of Crackers's tail thumping against the wall. A thread of panic snaked through him, but he attributed it to his thoughts about Devlin. If he hadn't found her after all this time, chances are he wouldn't find her now. Then why did a panicky feeling pound in his heart?

"Nikki!" he shouted louder, but there was no response.

Adrian grabbed his keys off the table and started to turn toward the door when the note caught his eye. There was a heaviness in his chest as he pulled it from beneath one of Nikki's pictures. When he read the first line, the heaviness crushed him. She was gone. That's why she looked so sad when she'd met him for lunch. He slammed his fist on the table, sending the frame a foot up in the air.

He jumped into his car and headed back to the city where he had first found Nikki. Adrian didn't know why, but he had a bad feeling about this whole situation. Logically, she should be as safe as she had always been. Nothing about his and Nikki's relationship had been logical, though. Deep down, he had a feeling she was in more danger than she'd ever been in.

Chapter 15

*T*rust not your heart.

Everything was working as planned. Adrian had played his part perfectly, if unwittingly. And he'd buried himself. Sometimes people got in the way, like Blossom Madsen that Sunday afternoon three years ago. After all this time, he had Nikki within his grasp again. This time he wouldn't let her get away.

He cracked his knuckles while he waited for Nikki to come out of the house, then tailed her as she drove out of the city. If she had noticed him following, she'd given no indication of it. Finally, she pulled into an alcove between shopping centers and turned off the van.

Finding Nikki had been an unexpected surprise. He'd hardly had time to pull something together. No mistakes this time. So, she'd been hiding out among the homeless. Guess she thought she was clever. He'd hardly recognized her, what with all that drab clothing and her hair tucked beneath that god-awful hooded coat. But, son of a cocked gun, it was her. Maybe she slept at that shelter. He'd read about some renovations going on there, some mysterious business man funding the entire project. Was Adrian that mysterious man? Hell, the man seemed to be everywhere.

He had worked on the shelter anyway.

An idea slivered through the crevices in his brain. His lips spread into a smile. He pulled on a coat and walked over to a dilapidated phone booth that looked worse than the homeless bums in the area. He dialed information and got the number for the Lord's Shelter, then called there to ask who managed the place. Dave Watts seemed a personable man, eager to answer questions about the shelter's activities for a phony newspaper article. The man had a soft voice with sensible overtones.

Then he called Adrian Wilde's number. No answer. That's okay, he'd catch him later. He had a favor to ask.

Meanwhile he kept an eye on the small portion of the van that showed from the street. Everything had to work out just right. He was going to make sure it did.

The black clouds had long ago obliterated the sun, making it look like midnight instead of five. While he sat there, the sky shuddered with light and sound before the sudden onslaught of rain dumped from the heavens. Forty-five minutes since Nikki had parked. With the pouring rain, she wouldn't be going anywhere. Good. He had some things to take care of, and he couldn't afford to lose her in the meantime.

An hour later he returned, breathing a sigh of relief to find the van still in place. Walking to the phone booth again, he called the West Palm Beach Hardware Store.

"Hello, you still open till eight? Good, I need an order put together so I can just swing by and pick it up. Ready? A couple of four-by-ten-inch pipes, two caps, a pipe wrench, and, um, some needle-nose pliers. Got that? You'll have it ready for me at the counter? Great. Adrian. Thanks a lot."

He was annoyed at the thumping of his heartbeat, loud and steady in his ears. Practicing his voice as he dialed, he waited for Adrian to answer. He left a brief message on the machine with the number of the nearby phone booth. Since he didn't want to attract any attention, he stayed huddled in it until the damned phone finally rang. He gave Adrian the spiel he'd practiced in a hurried voice and hung up. Now he only had Nikki to deal with.

Her being in the van would certainly pose a challenge. But the storm would keep any potential witnesses from straying by, as well as cover any noise he made.

Holding the twenty-three-pound pipe inside his black raincoat, he walked across the street and around the back of the shopping center. A couple of bums huddled in the entrance of a store, but he knew they'd never recognize him even if they did remember anything about the night. The acrid smell of marijuana would probably ensure they'd forget about some black-coated character walking briskly through the rain.

He peered cautiously around the corner where the van would be faced. The driver's area looked dark. Only a dim light showed through the black curtain that separated the front from the body of the van. He could hear the faint sound of music, but nothing else. Thunder ripped the sky apart, but he was too focused to hardly notice. The lightning bothered him only because it showcased his presence for all to see.

He slid the metal bar beneath the hood latch, listening for the telltale click indicating he'd popped it. Just as he heard it, another sound sent him to his knees in front of the van. The sound of the side door sliding open. Why the heck was she going out in this weather? It just wasn't safe. He grinned at the irony of that thought, but waited for her to walk around and find him hunched there. Then he'd have to kill her face to face, and he didn't want to watch her die. He much preferred to miss the bloodshed and have death go on without witnessing it.

He heard the door slam shut, then footsteps splashing

through the puddles. Nikki dashed across the street to the diner, her coat pulled tight around her. The torrent of rain obliterated her before she even reached the sidewalk.

He smiled. This would be much easier. He could do this from the inside, where it would be right next to the driver. After all, he didn't want her to suffer this time. Nikki would be blown to bits before even realizing what happened. He broke into the van, stuffed the four-by-ten pipe inside the console between the two front seats, and hooked it up to the ignition. Even if Nikki did notice the water on the seat before it dried, she'd only think someone had broken in to steal something. She'd never think turning the key would end her life.

He whistled as he slipped through the rain back to his car, then headed toward West Palm Beach. He congratulated himself. Yes, it was a bit early, but he felt confident. This time everything was all worked out, most importantly with the one thing he'd left out last time: a patsy to take the fall.

The rain had been pounding for two hours now. Nikki sat in a small diner on the north end of town, sipping her third cup of coffee, absently missing the hazelnut brew Maryanna had made for her family every morning. Before the explosion. She had finally dried off, but the chill hadn't left her heart yet. Maybe it never would.

Rain always made her feel isolated, the rataplan on the steel roof closing her off from the world. But storms like this scared her. She always pictured her van tumbling with a river of rain, filling up with water. Fire was her first fear, but drowning drew a close second. Nikki shivered at the thought. This place would do fine, with its bright lights and activity, until the rain stopped. It had to stop sometime.

The thought pushed into her mind, no matter how hard

she tried to keep it away. She could be in Adrian's arms right now, cuddled against that solid chest of his. Safe and warm. Nikki closed her eyes, willing the impending tears away. By now he had read her note. Would he just give up on her and go home? Or would he look for her? She hadn't gone as far away as she'd planned because of the impending storm. But she doubted Adrian would be driving around in this weather. When the rain stopped, Nikki would scoot out of there and disappear.

A flash of red hair caught Nikki's eye as it tore past the front window. Nikki ran to the door and opened it, a gust of wind pulling her hood back and whipping her hair free.

"Ceil!" she screamed into the wind, seeing her friend dash away.

The woman stopped, the relief in her eyes evident as she saw Nikki. "They're chasing me!"

"Who?"

"The police! They think I was hooking." Ceil clawed at Nikki's sweater. "Nikki, I can't go back to jail. Last time I went there, they did terrible things to me!"

Nikki saw the raw fear in her eyes. "Okay, come inside with me. I'll buy you a cup of coffee."

Ceil's red hair was plastered to her head, and her whole body shook. As Nikki ushered her inside the diner, she saw a police cruiser approaching. Nikki walked behind Ceil, hoping to block her from the window. Just as they reached the table, a short, balding man walked up to them, a dishrag in his hands. He pointed at Ceil.

"I want you out of here! Out, now!"

Nikki tried to intercede. "Why? She hasn't done anything."

"Not this time, and that's only because she hasn't been in here long enough yet. Last time she took food off people's plates and scrounged the leftovers before the busboy could clear the tables. This place looks bad enough as it is without that crap going on. I want her out of here. You can stay, but she has to go."

Ceil looked like a child as she appealed with her large eyes. "I gotta eat, mister. Those people were wasting that food. It's a shame to waste food when some of us need it."

Nikki glanced at the front window. The police car drove slowly by. Ceil's body went rigid. .

"Can't she stay if I keep her at our table?"

"No. Get her out of here, or I'll kick you both out."

Nikki tossed a few dollars on her table, grabbed her coat, and walked outside with her friend in tow. "I know how to help you, Ceil."

Adrian combed every inch of the city, though he figured she wouldn't be there. Still, Nikki was good at being where you least expected her to be, so he searched the familiar areas before branching out in a gridlike system. If he had to comb the whole damned East Coast, or all of Florida, he'd do it. The feeling of doom grew inside him just as ominous as the thunderhead that rocked the sky above.

The north end of the city was the last part of West Palm Beach before he had to start branching out to other cities. What a task that would be, but he didn't care. The sense of urgency built inside him, but he had to believe Nikki was safe, wherever she was.

He knew that she faced storms like this all the time, that she was used to being on her own, but he grabbed at a small thread of hope that maybe she had returned to the house, or at least called. First he dialed the number and left a message on the answering machine.

"Nikki, are you there? If you're there, pick up the phone." He waited. "Damn." Then he dialed again and retrieved his messages. There was only one, and it wasn't Nikki. It was Dave.

"Hi, Adrian. Please call me right away." He gave a

phone number. Adrian didn't want to take even a minute from his search, but he dialed the number anyway. It sounded important.

"Sorry to bother you at home, but I need a favor. I've got a family crisis to deal with, and have to head out of town tonight. There are a few things we need first thing tomorrow morning, and West Palm Beach Hardware is holding them at the counter under your name. One of the guys is getting there at five in the morning to work on the kitchen, and he's going to need them. Can you stop by the store before eight tonight and hide the stuff in the bushes by the front entrance of the shelter?"

Adrian's mind picked through the conversation. A further delay. Dave sounded strange, but maybe it was the situation, the rain on his end, what sounded like rain on Dave's end.

"Is everything okay?"

"Uh, sure. I'll let you know what's going on in the morning. I appreciate it."

"Sure," Adrian said, though he wasn't. Dave hung up, leaving Adrian staring at the receiver. Who would be working at the shelter at five in the morning? Well, what harm could come in picking up whatever Dave thought they needed? Hopefully no one would steal the stuff. He reluctantly got into his car and headed back to West Palm Beach, trying to remember where the store was exactly.

Just as Dave had said, the package was waiting on the counter. Adrian peered inside, finding ordinary hardware items, though he was sure they had at least two pairs of needle-nose pliers. He paid the man and dropped the bag off at the shelter, nestling it in the bushes. Then he continued his search.

The rain wasn't helping. In reality, he could be driving right past her and wouldn't see her van if it was parked just right. He had driven down alleys and behind buildings, especially abandoned ones, just to make sure. It was making the search a lot harder.

A while later the rain finally lessened, making the all-night drive more feasible. A brightly lit diner on the left beckoned him with images of hot coffee, and he pulled over to get a cup to go. The cool air inside the diner raised goose bumps as it hit his wet skin. He walked past an empty table with a steaming bowl of chicken vegetable soup and a cup of coffee and headed toward the counter. He heard the sound of a door slamming shut, and glanced toward the restroom doors, expecting to see an angry person. Like the table with the soup, no one was there.

"Here's your coffee, sir," the woman said, handing him a large styrofoam cup. "That'll be a dollar."

He tossed his money on the counter and headed out the door. The lower level of gray clouds zoomed by beneath the black above it. The flash of brake lights across the street caught his eye. A brown van was parked in an alley. His heart jumped, but he was already running across the street, his cup of coffee dropping into the gutter unnoticed.

The sound of the engine starting made him run faster, but in that split second, there was another sound. An explosion. The van rocked, jerking sideways. A fireball shattered the windows and split the metal of the roof before spewing to the sky. He saw all this in an instant, not even realizing that he'd been blown backward by the force. He struggled to get up. A sharp pain across his forehead forced him back down again. *Get to Nikki*, his mind uttered. Pain throbbed through his head, pushing him farther and farther into the blackness that overtook him. He heard sirens. The roar of flames. Sirens getting louder. Before darkness took him, he saw what the van had looked like. Especially the driver's side. No one could have survived that.

*   *   *

God, please let her be alive. That was Adrian's first though as he rose from a black, dreamless sleep to consciousness. Had he been hit by lightning again, and lived through the memory of the explosion? Could he hope for that much?

Adrian blinked, letting his eyes slowly adjust to the bright sunshine that filled the room. He was in the hospital. The antiseptic smells and dull pain told him that much. He felt a little fuzzy as he held the details at bay until he could gain his bearings. Outside, he could see palm trees and the Intracoastal sparkling in the sun.

The light made his eyes close with the force of an iron box. Someone in the room closed the blinds. Adrian opened his eyes again, expecting to see a nurse. It was a man, about fortyish, dressed in a tan suit and tie. His light brown hair was parted far on the side.

"Adrian Wilde?"

He nodded slowly, feeling as though his head weighed seventy pounds. The movement brought back the throbbing ache that penetrated every nook and cranny in his brain. He ran his fingers across his forehead where it was most tender, encountering a thick bandage.

"I'm Detective Ted Sloan, Palm Beach County Police. I'm the investigating officer for the explosion down in West Palm Beach day before yesterday. I'd like to ask you a few questions if you're up to it."

Then it had been real, Adrian thought, that last bit of hope sliding through his fingers. And he'd been in the hospital for more than a day.

"Nikki?" he asked, his voice cracking. He cleared his throat. "Is she all right?"

Detective Sloan's gray eyes narrowed. "She was killed in the explosion."

"Oh God, no," Adrian groaned, closing his eyes and dropping his head back on the pillow. He fell into a great, black pit of despair. Nikki, dead. It couldn't be! Not when he was on the verge of freeing her. Not when he loved her. His heart squeezed, bursting from the pressure inside it. Why had he been having nightmares about her drowning when she'd died in fire? His agony had only a second to take hold when Sloan spoke again in a tone lacking sympathy.

"Your plan didn't work completely, though, Mr. Wilde. You're a suspect for the murder of Nicole Madsen."

His senses sharpened through the haze. "Pardon?"

"We have witnesses to the fact that you were seeking Nicole Madsen out. We obtained a search warrant for the house you're renting in Palm Beach, and found photos of her spread all over your kitchen table. Would you like to explain that?"

Reality was sinking in a little at a time. Nikki was dead. He pushed away the feelings that threatened to bombard him at that thought. The police thought he'd killed her. No, it couldn't be possible.

Adrian sat up again, this time fighting the dizziness. "I didn't kill her. I love her." The words came out, unbidden, straight from his heart.

"Loved her? Maybe you were obsessed with her, Mr. Wilde. Was that it? She spurned you and you decided to get even? Or maybe you thought you'd kill her so no one else could have her, just like some of the other wackos we've encountered.

"You're sick!" he spat out, but Sloan seemed unmoved. *Calm down, Adrian. Don't get yourself in deeper.* "It wasn't obsession." Or was it? "She didn't spurn me."

"According to a letter we found in your rented home, she left you."

He nodded slowly. "Yes, she left, but it wasn't like that. What would I gain by killing her?"

"Well, that's one thing I haven't figured out yet. But I

will, Mr. Wilde. I will. Or you could make it easier on yourself and just tell me.''

''I'm not admitting to anything I didn't do. Shouldn't you be looking into the first bombing? Surely you've figured out the connection.''

''I don't think there is a connection. Except that maybe you got the idea from it. Not very original, Wilde. It's the coward's weapon.''

''I've never been a coward, Sloan. Nor a murderer. But I have an idea of who did kill her.'' His head pounded as he spoke, but he continued. ''Devlin Madsen. He'll inherit Nikki's half of the inheritance. Jack Barton is his business partner in LandCorp, and they both desperately wanted to bail out of a bad investment. Have you even talked to them?''

''I've talked to them, yes. The brother didn't even know where his sister's been all these years. And he has an airtight alibi.'' The detective jotted down something in his note pad. ''We had a talk with Barton as well, though he has absolutely no motive for killing her. But funny thing is, they said *you* approached them about loaning them the money for this project, for some uncle. You gave them a false name. You don't even have the liquid assets to make such an offer. Where were you going to get that kind of money, Mr. Wilde?''

Adrian felt a chill wash over him. He had set himself up to take the fall, and Jack and Devlin had pushed him over the edge. How could he tell the police the whole story, starting from his visions to present? They'd never believe him.

''Why don't you just confess? It'll make the whole process a lot easier on you. Maybe you'll just get life in prison instead of the electric chair. I hear it's pretty nice these days, with color televisions and gyms and the like.''

''I didn't kill her,'' he said through clenched teeth. He

needed time alone to sort this all out.

"I have statements from several people that you were looking for Miss Madsen." Sloan looked at his notes. "Ulyssis Garcia, David Watts, and a few others. The story seems to be that you . . . dressed like a homeless person to find her. Is this true?"

"Am I under arrest?"

"Not yet. But I'm an optimistic kind of guy. We'll figure this all out. Consider that confession I mentioned earlier." Sloan looked so damn smug sitting there with one leg crossed over the other. He watched Adrian carefully as he spoke. "Here's what I think happened. You came down here a few years back and met Nikki, a young, beautiful heiress. Maybe things got a little hot, but you had to go back. Or maybe she lost interest. But you kept thinking about her, all that money, so you came back down. It could have been the money that obsessed you, or the woman herself, but you were determined to find her.

"You figured out where she was hiding, maybe from all those pictures on your table. Somehow you connected them to her and dressed like a homeless person to find her. You did find her, and won her trust—enough to get her in your bed."

Adrian lunged forward, but Sloan pulled out his gun and held it up for him to see. "Don't interrupt my story. It's very interesting. We found evidence that you'd had a woman in your bed, and the hairs on the bed matched the description of Miss Madsen's hair. We'll be running further tests on that."

Adrian felt sick inside. They had been looking at his bed, finding traces of sperm and hair. Nikki's hair. God, he wanted to puke. But he kept listening, because he had no choice.

"You obviously won the girl's heart, as you intended." Sloan pulled out a folded note, turning Adrian's stomach even more. Nikki's note in his slimy hands. "She fell in love with you. Everything was fine for a little while, or as fine as it could be in your bizarre situation. And then you met with Jack Barton and Devlin Madsen. You saw a good deal in the making and wanted to be part of it. I haven't yet figured out the charade of your uncle D'Aprile, but I'm sure I will."

Sloan shifted in his seat, the catbird seat, as indicated by his expression. "Maybe you figured you had Nikki in the palm of your hand, and if she married you, the money would soon be available to invest in this project." Sloan held up the note. "But she figured it out, didn't she? So she broke things off and left. But you weren't going to let it go, were you? So you looked for her, and then you found her. You were probably pissed by then, or maybe you had it out with her. So you got mad enough and planted the bomb. I'll bet you didn't plan on being there when it went off, did you?" Sloan nodded toward Adrian. "Nearly did yourself in too." He smiled. "And it's a good thing you didn't, because we wouldn't have the fun of prosecuting you. The break is going to come, sooner or later."

Adrian felt weak, light-headed. Denying it sounded lame. It looked bad, and he knew it. Juries convicted people on less circumstantial evidence. But, at the moment, he could scarcely think of himself. The emptiness he felt at Nikki's death overwhelmed him. The fight for his own freedom sagged.

"You're sure it was Nikki?" Who else would be in her van? But he just couldn't believe she was dead.

Sloan shifted uncomfortably. "Someone died in that explosion. It was a woman." The next words shot through Adrian like the metal shrapnel had. "There wasn't enough left of her to identify." He let the words sink in before adding, "Strangely enough, we couldn't even find any teeth. Miss Madsen didn't seem like the kind of person to let someone else drive her van. This was confirmed by the man the van is registered to, Ulyssis Garcia. He also identified a ring that was probably on the victim's finger when the van exploded, as evidenced by the blood on it. The blood type is the same as Nicole Madsen's, and what little we found seems to indicate it was her." Sloan tapped his gun on his thigh. "You hit your mark."

"Check out Jack Barton. He lied about his past."

"So did you, Mr. Wilde." He smiled. "Mr. Santucci. Or is it Mr. Nash?"

Adrian felt like a spider trapped in a web of his own making. "You've got the wrong man. Just check him out."

"He had nothing to gain by killing Miss Madsen."

"No, but Devlin did. With Nikki gone, he inherits her money, which they so badly need to save this deal. That's why I pretended to be an investor." He knew he should keep quiet, but he couldn't. "I wanted to find out just how desperate he was. Devlin has been trying to make a success out of himself his whole life."

"But he has a solid alibi, unlike you."

"Then check out Jack's alibi."

"Are you telling me how to do my job, Wilde?"

Adrian sensed the venom in the man's voice. "What did you find out?"

"He was home working on some numbers for a report he was giving to you in the morning."

"So he has no alibi."

"Not really, but he wasn't seen with the victim. He wasn't hunting the victim down. The pipe bomb was triggered when Miss Madsen started the van. It had to have been planted after she parked the van in the alley, roughly between four and the time it exploded. I don't suppose you have an alibi for then, Mr. Wilde."

"I was driving around." Looking for Nikki. "Anyone could have seen me."

"We'll check, just to be fair. We're always fair, Mr. Wilde."

The door opened, and another detective-looking man leaned into the room. "Detective Sloan." He nodded toward the hallway.

Sloan tucked his gun back into his jacket. "Don't try anything slick."

Adrian was already in jail. Devlin killed the one woman he loved, and now Adrian was going to pay the price for it. God, he wanted to die. Then he could tell her how sorry he was about everything. He wasn't sure how Devlin had found her, but he had the horrible feeling that he had somehow led him to her. How else would he find her now, after all this time?

He thought of the last day he'd seen Nikki—it felt like years ago—when she'd met him at the shelter and brought him egg salad sandwiches. If Devlin had followed him, and waited, he would have found her. Adrian pounded his fist on the bed, feeling the guilt descend upon him. Maybe he was responsible for her death, but he didn't put that bomb in her van. He would see the flash of those brake lights just before the van erupted for the rest of his life.

And that could be spent in jail, he thought as he remembered Sloan's words about getting him off easy. The electric chair seemed like the easier way out. He already felt dead inside.

The door opened, but it wasn't Sloan who walked in. This time it was the nurse. She was young and pretty, with short brown hair, and carried a blood pressure armband. Adrian started to sit up, despite the aches that roared through his body. The nurse stopped, her eyes wide. She glanced at the door, then back at him.

"Please don't move."

Adrian read her name tag. "You think I killed someone, don't you, Lorie?"

She approached slowly, her hands trembling a little. "I
. . . I don't know. I heard that detective talking to the doc-
tors. . . ." Her voice trailed off, but she took a deep breath
and slipped the cuff over his arm.

This woman was afraid of him because she thought she
killed someone. "I didn't kill her, Lorie. I loved her."

Her brown eyes locked with his, and he knew that everything that was in his heart showed in his eyes. He didn't care.

"It's not for me to say, sir." She pumped the black bulb,
squeezing his arm the way his heart felt squeezed.

He touched her hand softly, but she didn't jump. "I
couldn't have killed her. It would have been like killing part of
my own soul. That's where she lived for the past two years.
I had to lie to save her, but he got her anyway." Adrian removed his hand and let it drop beside him on the bed.

Lorie just stared at him for a moment, then shook herself
and continued pumping the bulb. After inserting the cold
end of the stethoscope, she released the pressure. "A little
low," she said softly, jotting it down on the chart.

"Lorie, will you do me a favor? There's a guy in town
named Ulyssis Garcia. He owns an art gallery, probably
nearby. Would you please let him know that there is, or
was, a dog in the house I was renting, and ask him to pick
him up and take care of him for now? Make sure he un-
derstands it was Nikki's dog, not mine. She loved that dog,
and I don't want him locked in that house starving while
I'm stuck here."

She nodded, jotting something down on the corner of the
chart. He held his arm out as she injected him with something. Adrian didn't even care what it was.

"Will I live?" he asked in a tone that indicated he really
didn't care.

"Yes. You'll probably be released in a day or so."

"What happened to me? I don't remember anything after
the initial blast."

"A piece of metal from the van flew through the air and sliced into your forehead. It was pretty deep. The force knocked you backward onto the street. There were five people who had run out to see what was going on who got hit with shrapnel."

"Are they all right?"

"None as bad as you. You were the closest."

He stared off for a moment. "I was running to the van, because I didn't want to lose her." His voice sounded distant, even to his own ears.

"I'm sorry," she said, and he knew she meant it.

"Sorry doesn't begin to sum up how I feel. Dead, lost . . ." He shook his head, because nothing came close. "There wasn't a body found . . . in the van?"

Lorie shook her head. "Just bone fragments. Not even teeth."

She looked away, then started to turn. As she reached the door, she paused. "I'll call your friend."

"He's not my friend. He probably thinks I killed Nikki too. Tell him that I didn't, will you? Most importantly, make sure he knows the dog is Nikki's. I don't want to see him put in the pound. His name is Crackers."

Lorie smiled faintly. "Crackers. I'll tell him." She took another step toward the door, then turned around again. "I'll be bringing your lunch in a few minutes."

Adrian's eyes filmed over at the memory of Nikki positioning Crackers in Seamus's baby stroller for a picture. It felt like a dream—*she* felt like a dream. And now she was no more than the images she had been in that tunnel.

A few minutes later Sloan walked back in, but even he couldn't darken a room already filled with black despair.

"Well, Sloan, any breaks in the case?"

He smiled, but there was nothing comforting about it. "Funny you should ask, Wilde. A young man from West Palm Beach Hardware just phoned in. He identified you as the man who purchased two four-by-ten-inch pipes the day of the murder. The same kind of pipe our investigative team found pieces of at the scene of the explosion. Adrian Wilde, you're under arrest for the murder of Nikki Madsen.''

Chapter 16

How cruel some are, to cast off a life for no other reason than greed.

Adrian started to sit up, but Sloan put his hand up to stop him. It didn't matter; with his head swimming, Adrian had to sit back again anyway.

"What are you talking about?"

"We also found another pipe matching the one you purchased in the garage of the house you're renting. You bought two pipes, one is in your garage, and we believe the other was planted in Miss Madsen's van."

"I didn't purchase any . . . oh, God, the bag I picked up for Dave at the hardware store."

"Who's Dave?"

"Dave Watts; he runs the Lord's Shelter. Check with him; he'll verify that he asked me to pick up a bag of items at the hardware store for someone who was coming in to work early that next morning. He had to go out of town on a family emergency. I hid the bag in the bushes at the shelter so whoever was coming in could find them."

Sloan was writing as Adrian spoke. "You're saying that Dave Watts asked you to pick up the bag with the pipes in it?"

"Yes. He called the order in, and I just picked it up. Call him."

Sloan left the room again, but somehow Adrian didn't feel any relief that the detective was checking out his story. A few minutes later Sloan returned, that cat look on his expression.

"Mr. Watts had no family emergency, made no call to either the hardware store or you, and had no worker coming that early."

"Did he check in the bushes? The bag must still be there."

"Yes, I asked him to check. Nothing. Nice try, Wilde."

Adrian wanted to scream, but he knew it wouldn't do any good. He had set himself up by looking for Nikki in the first place, then by posing as Adrian Santucci for Devlin. Now someone else was setting him up. His mind raced. What could he do?

"How did he know about Dave? The shelter?"

Sloan's eyebrows furrowed. "Who are you talking about?"

"Devlin Madsen. It had to be him."

"Why do you say that? I know he was arrested for the pipe bombing three years ago, but a jury acquitted him."

"He had them fooled. Nikki was afraid of him. He tried to kill her twice after the trial."

Sloan looked at his notebook. "I saw that in the file, but again, Devlin Madsen had an alibi for the attempted hit-and-run, and we had nothing to go on with the rattler. Maybe Devlin did have something to do with it." His gray eyes riveted on Adrian. "And maybe you're his accomplice. The only thing I've got to figure out is your connection with Devlin Madsen."

"I want to talk to my attorney." Hell, he only had a general attorney for occasional contract disputes. He would have to call Stan and explain the whole mess to him, and trust him to find the best attorney in New York. Then he would have to pray like crazy. Adrian hardly had the heart left to fight.

Sloan leaned back in his chair, obviously enjoying the struggle he saw in Adrian's eyes when he'd dropped the bombshell. "The only thing I couldn't figure out is, why were you running *toward* the van before it blew up?"

Adrian wasn't listening. He was seized by a feeling so familiar to him, a feeling he thought he'd never feel again. *Nikki.* She was alive, he knew it as he felt his own pulse surging. He saw the hospital parking lot blur by and felt Nikki's fear. Adrian quickly got to his feet and ran to the window.

Sloan reached for his gun at the rapid movement, in position to use it. "Wilde, there's an officer outside your door. Don't try anything."

Adrian thought of nothing, trying to focus in on Nikki. But it wasn't his psychic vision he saw now. It was Nikki, struggling as a man pulled her into a van and tore out of the parking lot.

"Get someone down to the parking lot, now! They've got her!"

Sloan was so irritatingly calm as he walked over to the window right after the white van veered out of sight.

"I don't see anything."

"They just took Nikki! Damn it, if you've got men down there, get them after the white van! It looked like one of those industrial types, real long without windows on the sides or back."

Adrian wanted to jump through the window, but it was several stories up. He turned to the door, but Sloan had his weapon pulled.

"What are you just standing there for? Get your men after a white van heading east. They'll find Nikki and the man who tried to kill her."

Sloan merely smiled. "Nice try, Wilde. And you just sensed somehow that something was happening and walked over to the window." He nodded toward the bed. "From there?"

Well, it would all come out in the trial anyway. "Yes."

Adrian wanted to push by the irritating man, shove past the officer who had brought the dastardly news about the hardware store, and get Nikki back. But he knew it was futile. He'd be shot down before he took five steps down the corridor. Even if by some miracle he made it outside, he had no transportation, and no skills in attaining a car without the key. Desperation mounted inside him. Nikki's life was in danger, and if her death became official, no one would miss her. Devlin could do anything he wanted to her, and he'd inherit the money.

When Lorie walked in with a tray of food, Sloan turned to her in surprise. Her widened eyes took in the gun and she started to back up. Adrian's instincts took hold, over-ruling sensibility and conscience. All he could think of was saving Nikki. He grabbed Sloan's gun and the nurse's arm at the same time. With a scream, she struggled, but he held the gun at her side. The officer rushed in with his gun at the ready, but he stopped dead when he saw Adrian with the nurse tucked in his grip.

Sloan held out his hand. "Come on, Wilde. This is crazy. We'll check out the white van, okay? Just let her go."

"No. You have your mind set that I killed Nikki, and nothing but the truth is going to change that. She's in trouble, and I'm her only hope." He turned to Lorie, who trembled in his grasp. "And you're my only hope." Turning back to Sloan, he said, "Let me leave, and she doesn't get hurt."

"You're not going to hurt her. If you're innocent, as you claim, then you have nothing to lose."

"Oh, but I do. I have Nikki to lose." He shoved the gun

into Lorie's side, making her yelp. "And don't doubt that I'll use it if I have to. Nothing will stop me from finding her."

Sloan motioned for the officer to move away from the doorway as Adrian edged closer to it. That wasn't good enough.

"Drop your weapon," Adrian ordered the second cop, and he slowly set his gun on the floor. With Lorie in tow, he edged to the bed and yanked on the phone. He pulled out the cord and tucked it in Lorie's deep pocket. Adrian kicked the second gun beneath the bed, out of their easy reach. *God, help me get through this. You know this is the only way.* Beads of sweat emerged on his forehead, and his body ached with every movement, but he showed them none of that. He stood tall and strong, holding Lorie tight against his chest.

"I'm sorry," he murmured in her ear, softly so the police wouldn't hear it. Then he pressed the gun to her side, causing her to wince. "If I don't get out of here safely, she dies." Sloan muttered a curse, but he looked concerned for the hostage. "Back up against the wall, both of you!" Adrian barked, and the men moved. What was he going to do to keep them quiet until he left the hospital? He thought of the cord in Lorie's pocket.

"Put your backs to each other," he ordered, walking closer. He kept Lorie in his arms as he worked to tie their hands together with the phone cord. Then, with the curly cord from the receiver, he tied their legs together and around the bedpost. Finally, he ripped two strips of material from the sheets and made gags out of them. Sloan's eyes never left him, and Adrian felt the man's anger.

He nuzzled the gun against Lorie's side again. "She doesn't get hurt if you let us leave here. Her life is in your hands, gentlemen. Keep that in mind."

When they reached the door, he took her aside where the

men couldn't hear him. When he saw his clothes in a folded pile on the counter, he stripped out of the hospital garb and put them on. "Lorie, I hate having to do this to you. Believe me. I won't hurt you, but I need your help. I've got to save Nikki. She's been kidnapped by the man who tried to murder her." At Lorie's widened expression, he added, "She's not dead. I don't know who died in that van. I want you to listen to me. I'm going to hide the gun, and you're going to walk right in front of me. Get your car keys, and we'll calmly walk through the hallway to the fire stairs and down to your car and then you're free to go. I'm just going to borrow it until I can reach a safe place." He held her arms, tighter than he'd intended to. "Don't screw up my chance to save her, Lorie. I'm her only hope."

She stood there staring at him for a moment, chewing on her bottom lip as she considered. Then she turned and said, "Follow me. I'll get you out of here."

Adrian was amazed by her smile as she passed her co-workers. She walked into the nurse's station and grabbed her purse. "I'll be right back," she said, the unnatural pitch of her voice the only indication something was wrong. Still, the nurses sitting there just nodded and went back to their paperwork. Lorie and Adrian headed down the hallway, walking as quickly as what looked normal.

"What did you give me a shot of earlier?" he asked as they walked through the fire exit door.

"It was a pain killer."

"Will it make me sleepy?"

She was two steps ahead of him, but turned and said, "Yes."

He had to get out of there before he started losing energy. He didn't even know where he would go from here. He would have to leave the car in one place, like a bus station, leading the police to think he took a bus somewhere, then head off in the other direction.

The parking garage was packed with cars, but Lorie went directly to a sporty little coupe. She handed him the keys.

"Lorie, I'm not going to take you with me. I'm afraid you'll get hurt." He looked at the car. "I'll try not to hurt your car either, but I can't make any promises. I will make it up to you, if I get out of this."

"Are you sure you don't want me to go with you?"

He raised an eyebrow. "You want to be a hostage?"

She shrugged. "It's the most exciting thing to ever happen in my boring life. Besides, you might get sleepy."

Without thinking about it, he pulled her close and gave her a quick kiss on the cheek. "Lorie, you're wonderful. But I'm not going to get sleepy. I can't afford to. Thank you for your help."

He got in the car and found a pair of sunglasses to slip on. Before he knew it, she'd run around to the other side and hopped in.

"You need my help just to get out of this garage. It can get pretty confusing. Go that way. Go on!"

He started the car and followed her directions, thanking God when they pulled out into the sunshine.

"You should drop me off somewhere else, so I'll have to walk back. That'll give you time to get away before they can question me and find out what car I drive."

He found himself smiling, shaking his head as he merged with traffic. She turned around and dug through piles of junk and clothing in the backseat. With a triumphant sound, she pulled out a Miami Hurricanes cap and stuck it on his head. Then she shuffled through the myriad items in her purse before coming out with four twenties and three crumpled fives. She handed them to him.

"What is this for?"

"For survival. I'll get out here. Go save your girl. Wait until the gals at the hospital hear about this!"

With that, she was gone. Adrian stared at the bills until

the light turned green and the car behind him honked. It certainly wasn't what he expected, kidnapping a woman at gunpoint and having her donate money to his cause. He found the same Goodwill Store that he'd visited earlier when he had decided to dress like a homeless person to find Nikki. That all seemed like ages ago, and now her life was in danger.

He sat back in his seat, Stella's prediction storming through him with sudden clarity. *You may bring her even more risk.* He had done that, by leading Devlin to her. If that prediction came true, then what of the terrifying nightmares that Stella said were a premonition? He had to get to Nikki before . . . the strangling feel of the water made him catch his breath, and he jumped out of the car.

He bought a couple of pillows, a change of clothes, and a few blankets with Lorie's money. He'd have to remember to reimburse her for this whole disaster—if he lived through it. Adrian only hoped that he'd have enough left to get him somewhere, anywhere. He'd never even taken a bus before, other than within the city, but he'd seen the advertisements for reasonable rates. The bus station was just where Lorie had said it would be. The sound of sirens made his blood pulse faster.

With his long hair beneath the cap, and a dark beard growing in again, he hoped he looked different enough from the composite drawings that would soon be circulating the city. And the cap hid the large bandage that was now seeping a little blood. Nothing was going to stop him from finding Nikki. Nothing, no one.

The shattering explosion and roar of flames, glass splintering—Nikki froze as she watched her van become a roaring inferno. It was her nightmare all over again, but this time it was Ceil whose life had been ripped away from her.

Fear paralyzed her as she stood inside the diner watching

the chaos through the window. Or what had been the window. The last few minutes had tilted her world—again. Nikki had given Ceil the keys to her van, telling her to drive around for a while until the police left her alone. She had been battling her own doubts that maybe Ceil was hooking to stay alive when she'd seen Adrian's car driving down the street.

How did he find me? she'd thought as she dashed inside the diner. He'd parked right out front and walked inside, as if someone in the diner had tipped him off that she was there. Nikki ran to the restroom and waited to see what he was doing. When she cracked the door, he had been standing by the counter, just about to look in her direction. Her heart had ached, pushing her to run into his arms, but she had remained hidden until she'd seen him walk out.

That's when the explosion rocked the building and shattered the large plate-glass windows facing the sidewalk. The glass fell away into a thousand deadly shards, making people scream and duck away. Nikki's heart had exploded inside her too. Adrian had been outside when it happened. She pushed herself to walk through the screaming swarms of people rushing away from or toward the ball of fire outside. It was as if she was walking through molten lead.

She saw the van first. Her van. Flames licked out of the front window where Ceil must have been when it exploded. *No, not Ceil. Why Ceil?* Then Nikki realized, as she made her way toward the shattered door—that horrible mess wasn't meant for Ceil. Who would have known that Ceil would have started the van? No, it had been meant for her.

Fear gripped her with deadly precision, marking her soul with its cold grip. She ducked away from the doorway, hardly able to breathe. People were screaming, and when she heard screams so near her, she realized they came from her own mouth. Her body trembled so violently, she could hardly think, much less move. Someone out there wanted her dead. Again. She searched for signs of Adrian. Oh, how she wanted to find him, make sure he was all right. A man rushed inside and screamed, "Call an ambulance! A man's been hurt out here!"

Without thinking about it, her hand reached out and gripped the man's arm. "Does he have long, dark hair? Is he . . . big?"

"Sounds like him. He's bleeding something terrible." He freed himself from her grip and returned to the chaos outside. Sirens wailed across the air as she pushed her way through the crowd. A swarm of people surrounded a man lying on the ground. She desperately searched for Adrian among those who were standing, but he wasn't there. His rental car sat just in front of her, covered in fragments of metal that were still aflame. *No, not Adrian too!* Fear and anger raged through her. Who had done this? Was he still here, making sure the bomb had worked?

Nikki battled with the overwhelming need to see Adrian and her sense of survival. She couldn't help him, but if he was conscious, she wanted him to know she was there and alive. And she wanted to make sure he was still alive. Nikki took a step in his direction when two fire trucks and an ambulance screeched to a stop several yards away from where flames still poured out of the van.

"Everyone clear the area!" one medic shouted, waving his arms madly. "The gas tank could explode any second."

The curious were pushed back, and the injured were helped to an area a safe distance away. Her heart sank as she gave up that last bit of hope that the man wasn't Adrian. She could see just enough of him to know it was. Two paramedics raced over to Adrian, led there by the man whose arm she had grabbed. If she went forward now, she would be highlighted for everyone to see. It didn't matter. She had to get to him!

As the crowd backed away from the scene, they pushed

her farther from Adrian. Within seconds, the paramedics had him strapped to a gurney and slid into the ambulance. She saw blood all over his face, horrifying amounts of it.

"Let me through!" she screamed, but the noise level was louder than she could ever be. "Please!"

No one even seemed to see her there. The ambulance raced off into the night, the siren becoming an eerie backdrop to the melee in front of her. People were sitting inside the diner, covering bloody wounds with their hands, rocking back and forth with the pain she saw on their faces.

"If there was anyone in the van, they didn't make it. No way," she heard one of the firemen say.

"Ceil," she whispered, her trembling hand covering her mouth. "I'm so sorry. He wanted me."

This was worse than last time. Mixed in with the excited chattering of those who had seen everything were the moans of those in pain. An older woman had a shard of glass sticking several inches out of her arm. "Ooh, take it out, please!" Another woman kept saying, "Don't pull it out! Let the medic do it, Gladys. He knows how."

Nikki closed her eyes a brief second. Other people got hurt this time. The fire sizzled as the firemen battled to put it out. Her eyes stung when she opened them again and stared at the flames. She was supposed to be in there. Then Devlin could inherit her share of the money. He could have the money, but she wasn't going to let him take her life too. Her survival instinct kicked in, and she found where she'd dropped her coat by the restroom door. Slipping the hood over her head, she ducked through the crowd, her shoes crunching over bits of glass. As soon as she got out of there, she would find a phone booth and call the hospital.

Several hours passed before the hospital would release any information on Adrian. The operator knew her voice by the tenth call. Nikki wanted so badly to go to the hospital, but she was terrified of leaving her safe cove on the outskirts of the city. She was drenched, shivering, but she didn't care. Nothing mattered if Adrian died.

"Ma'am, I show him as being in stable condition this morning. He's regained consciousness."

"Thank God," she said in a rush of breath. "And thank you."

She had to see him, to let him know she was all right. Yesterday newspapers had the explosion all over their front pages. Today she didn't even look. It was eerie to see her name as the deceased, but she was too afraid to come forward and correct the misunderstanding. Afraid? What an understatement. Terrified to the bone assessed it more correctly.

No one knew about Ceil, and no one would report her missing. Nikki had read that nothing but a ring and blood matching her type was found to tie the charred bones to her. The ring had been hidden in the glove box. They were surprised that no teeth had been found, but that didn't surprise Nikki—Ceil only had a few left that hadn't rotted out of her mouth. Maybe Ceil wasn't so bad off after all. Now she was free of that ragged body and lonely life of paranoia and sorrow. A tear slid down her cheek, and she wiped it away. No, it still wasn't fair for Ceil to die in her place.

Nikki had the whole day to think about the situation. All she knew right now was that she had to get far away from here. It was no longer safe for her. New York wasn't an option either. Her mind had been frozen in terror, but now it was thawing. She had a couple of things to do before she left. One was to see Adrian and let him know she was alive. Maybe he didn't yet know she was supposedly dead, but she didn't want to put him through that. She had to make sure he was all right. Then she would see Ulyssis and do the thing she detested, but had to do: ask him to get her another car. Living on the streets in her van had been one thing, but the thought of spending yet another night actually sleeping on the sidewalk petrified her. He was the closest thing she had to family, and she wanted to let him know she wasn't dead.

Nikki slipped into the hospital unnoticed. With her hair tucked beneath the hood and her jacket covering the clothes she'd been wearing since the explosion, she could pass for someone normal. She already knew what room he was in, so she made her way to the stairs. Whenever someone passed her on the way to Adrian's floor, she averted her attention.

A policeman stood in front of one of the hospital rooms, and she was startled to realize it was Adrian's. Why were they guarding his room? Was he in danger? Maybe the police thought his life was in jeopardy if he'd told them that he knew her. Her hand went to her mouth, and she turned away. What a mess. Nikki dashed to the stairway and made her way to the lobby. She found the phones where she could dial the rooms directly, but realized that maybe it was safer for her to call from outside the hospital. Nikki thought of going upstairs again, but decided against it. That officer probably wouldn't just go away. She would walk back to her safe place and call him again in a few more minutes.

The bright morning light betrayed the dark turmoil inside her. It was cool and breezy outside, and the wind pushed her hood back. She pulled it over her head again and walked along the rows of cars. After that, everything happened so fast. Nikki felt as if she was being plucked from one nightmare to another one.

A white van drove slowly beside her, but she kept looking ahead and walking. She heard the door open, and before she could quicken her pace, strong arms wrapped around her and yanked her backward. A sweaty palm covered her mouth in the same instant, but she was too startled to call out.

She was shoved into the open door of the van. When the driver jumped in behind her, she grabbed for the passenger door's handle. The van was already speeding through the parking lot, then pulling out onto the road. There was no escape.

Chapter 17

Who lies more—men or my heart?

"Nikki!"

The voice made her start, and she looked at her captor for the first time. She felt disoriented. The word would hardly push out from her tight throat.

"Jack?"

He looked as startled as she did as he kept staring at her between dodging through traffic. He reached over and squeezed her arm, a smile slowly forming on his face.

"Nikki, Nikki, Nikki. You're alive. I can't believe you're alive."

That was evident by the strange look in his eyes. "Jack, what's going on? Why are you taking me away from the hospital?"

"Your life is in danger. Someone tried to kill you, and they'll try again. You might not get lucky next time." His eyes widened, and his grip on her arm tightened. "You didn't see Adrian, did you?"

She wriggled out of his grasp. "No."

"Does anyone else know you're alive?" When she didn't answer right away, he said, "Nikki, I'm afraid for you. I don't want anyone to hurt you."

"Then please take me back. I'm safe where I am."

"Let me take you someplace where you'll be safer. Let me take care of you, sweetheart. That's all I ever wanted to do." His blue eyes grew hard as he stared ahead. "And you ran away from me last time."

"I didn't run away from just you, Jack. I ran from everyone."

He turned to her, that caring expression gone from his face. "You didn't trust me, did you?"

"It wasn't that I didn't trust you. I didn't want to put you in danger, that's all."

His eyebrow lifted. "Really?"

"Really. Now please take me back."

His fingers gripped the steering wheel. The nails were chewed to the quick, unlike the cool Jack she knew. "Don't you trust me now, Nikki? Don't you think I'll protect you?"

"It's not that. I've been protecting myself for two years now, and I don't want to drag anyone else into my problems."

Jack leaned forward while they sat at the light and kissed her. Not the soul-searing kiss that ignited her from the inside. Like Adrian's kisses. Jack's kiss was hard and demanding, just as it had always been.

"Nikki, I'm so glad you're alive."

She was relieved when the light turned green and he turned his attention back to the road. She didn't want to kiss him, didn't want to be around him. The shiver of panic trickling through her was probably her desperation to get back to Adrian.

"Who died in the explosion?" His voice was as calm as the eye of a hurricane as they continued to thread their way through traffic into Palm Beach.

"A friend." She couldn't bring herself to talk about Ceil.

"What was she doing in your van?"

"I let her drive it around sometimes when the police harassed her."

"That's too bad," he said, looking ahead.

"It was more than too bad. It was horrible. A lot of people got hurt when that bomb went off." She didn't know why her voice was rising so, but Jack glanced at her, noticing it too. The mansions of Palm Beach slipped by as they drove further in. The panic became a tremble that seized her insides and made her hands shake. "Jack, take me back to the hospital. Stay out of this." It came out as an order, but she didn't care.

He patted her hand. "Dear, don't worry. I'm going to take care of you. No one will hurt you again."

His words sounded hollow, but it was hard to tell with her heart pumping blood right next to her eardrums, pounding the century-old rhythms of a tribal drum. Maybe she was just overreacting. They were heading toward her old mansion, or maybe Adrian's house. A police car passed them, and Jack's hand tightened on hers.

"Jack, what is going on?"

"Trust me, darling." He smiled, but his words sounded much sterner than a request.

A cellular phone lay on the floor where she had probably kicked it when Jack shoved her inside. She reached for it and started dialing before Jack could do anything. It rang.

"Who are you calling?"

"I have to let Adrian know I'm alive." The switchboard operator answered, but before Nikki gave her Adrian's room number, Jack's hand snagged the phone from her and pressed the end button.

"I can't let you do that, darling." He dropped the phone between the seat and the door on his side.

She fought to keep the panic from her voice. "Why not? Why are you doing this?"

The gates of the Madsen mansion loomed ahead, and

Jack pulled right through. For a second, she was paralyzed with fear. Jack was taking her right to Devlin, the man who had tried to kill her. He parked the van and grabbed for her hand as she reached the door handle.

"Don't be afraid." He smiled, but Nikki saw an urgent gleam in his eyes. "I can't let you talk to Adrian, because he is the man who tried to kill you."

She wanted to spit in his face, but her throat was too dry to accommodate her. "Let me go! I'll never believe that!"

Without loosening his iron grip, he reached into the interior of the van and pulled out that day's newspaper, the *Palm Beach Post*. The headlines screamed the horrible lie: PREMIER PHOTOGRAPHER CHARGED WITH DEVASTATING EXPLOSION THAT KILLED NICOLE MADSEN. And in smaller print below: *Was it obsession that made Adrian Wilde resort to a gruesome murder?*

She threw the newspaper at Jack as if the flames in the photograph had reached out and burned her hand. "It's not true! He wouldn't do that to me!"

Jack leaned back against the door, but still held her hand in his grip. "He was there, wasn't he?"

"Yes, but he wouldn't try to kill me."

A trickle of sweat ran down Jack's neck and down the front of his chest. His white cotton shirt was damp beneath the armpits. Yet he looked so calm. "Why, because he told you that he loved you?"

"Yes," she said, the word barely above a whisper.

"Did he tell you that he'd come to see me a couple of days ago?"

"No!" An ache deep inside her widened to encompass her entire midsection.

"Yes, Nikki. He came to see me and Devlin at Land-Corp. He had a business proposition for us."

The ache spread to her limbs, her head. "No," she said, this time sounding more like a whimper. Adrian had gone to.two meetings, but he wouldn't tell her who they were with.

"The morning of the explosion, and the day before that."

No, she wouldn't believe that Adrian had set up that explosion. "You're lying." But he had the times right; the times Adrian had disappeared and wouldn't tell her why. "Trust me," he'd asked of her. Her eyes filled with tears, but she refused to shed them, to show Jack what he'd done to her.

"I'm sorry, Nikki." With his other hand, he reached over and touched her cheek. She jerked away before he made contact. His hand remained suspended in midair. "You loved him, didn't you?"

She didn't answer. Her hand was busy subtly trying to find the door handle. When she touched it, she grabbed hold and yanked it down. Nothing happened.

"It's locked, darling." He pulled her toward him. "You don't have to be afraid of me; I'm trying to help you. Let's go inside."

"No!" she screamed, but the van's windows were closed, and her voice was so thick, she knew no one had heard.

"Nikki, I'm sorry that I had to be the one to tell you about him. But you had to know, didn't you? I couldn't just let you waltz into the hospital and tell him that his plan hadn't worked. He might have killed you right there." With her face only a few inches from his, he leaned forward and kissed her, this time more gently. "Don't you remember, I loved you before you left me. I have always loved you, though I could never understand why you didn't trust me enough to tell me where you were hiding. I could have helped you."

"I didn't need your help. And I don't need it now." She felt numb, but there was something about Jack that made her distrust him. Maybe it was the tidal wave of betrayal that rocked her, making her doubt everyone in her life. "Just let me go. I promise I won't see Adrian, if that's what you're worried about. I'll just disappear."

"I'm afraid I can't do that. I'm not going to let you walk out of my life like that again, making me wonder if you're alive or safe. I want to take care of you, and I won't let you put yourself in jeopardy."

She glanced at the house sitting in front of them. "Then why have you brought me here?"

"Because Devlin isn't here. He's gone north to spend some time with friends, to overcome the horrible loss of his sister."

Nikki found a cruel laugh escaping her. "That's ridiculous! The police would never let him leave the state."

"Well, in truth, they told him to stick around in case they had any other questions, but he had an airtight alibi for the time during and before the bomb went off in your van. There was nothing to hold him in custody with, so they let him go. He left town this morning."

Nikki was baffled. Devlin had an alibi? If the bomb was triggered by the car's ignition, then it would have had to been put in during the thunderstorm, after she'd parked it in the alley. Something wasn't right.

"But he had to have done it."

Jack shook his head. "He didn't. He was at Bradley's most of the afternoon and evening, drowning his financial sorrows. Nikki, Adrian Wilde is the only suspect the police have. They're talking about it all over the radio, television." He flipped on the radio station. A news flash was already in progress, and her heart tightened even more.

"A source at the Palm Beach County Police Station just informed us that they have two witnesses to the fact that Adrian Wilde purchased the same kind of pipe that was used in the bomb. He—"

Nikki turned the sound down and closed her eyes, wanting to erase it all. Jack shifted after a few moments, reminding her he was there. His voice was soft as he spoke.

"You're just going to have to accept that he was the one who tried to kill you. But you're safe now. Let's go inside. Devlin won't be back for a week. He was on the edge of a nervous breakdown, and he couldn't stay around here any longer. I promise you that he won't come back and hurt you. Trust me, Nikki."

She looked at him with his earnest expression and boyish lock of blond hair hanging over his forehead. How could she ever trust anyone again? Somehow she had a feeling that Jack wasn't going to let her go. She wasn't sure why he had become so protective of her, but she sure as hell wasn't going to trust him. But for now, she would play along.

She glanced at the house, so hauntingly familiar. "But why here? Why not your house?"

"Because I don't want the help to see you and realize who you are. I don't want anyone to know you're alive until we can figure out what's going on and where you'll be safest."

"What about Devlin's help? Surely they'll tell him that I'm here?"

"There is no help anymore."

"No help? No servants, no maid? For this whole house?"

"Nope. Devlin doesn't have the money to keep it up."

Her gaze scanned the windows along the front. It looked dark, quiet. "Okay, I'll go inside."

He seemed to relax, then opened the door on his side and helped her out. "Good. You can freshen up, get some rest, and we'll catch up on everything that we've missed."

"We haven't missed anything," she said, following him up to the house. "How did you get a key, anyway?"

But the door wasn't locked. "Devlin asked me to take care of the house while he was gone."

The well-tended gardens in the courtyards on either side of the entrance were now straggly and malnourished. The rose bushes her mother had loved so much were nearly dead.

Inside, a thousand memories assailed her. Though the house was past its days of elegance, Nikki saw it the way she remembered: the white tile sparkling, the glass buffet laden with crystal bowls of punch and platters of hors d'oeuvres. Through the formal living room she could see the lanai and pool, all lit up at night when Blossom threw a party. If it was daytime, children would be splashing in the pool, causing rippling reflections to dance throughout the house.

"What's happened to this place?" she said, her voice almost a whisper.

The tile was dirty, the sheers over the windows were laden with dust, and the pool was a wretched shade of green. The house had been filled with plants, but now there only sat empty pots or nothing at all. Adrian had said her brother looked empty and sad. The house looked that way too. Maybe Devlin hadn't won after all. The thought brought her little satisfaction. It seemed as though he'd murdered their mother for nothing.

Jack had walked up behind her, and his arms threaded around her shoulders. "I'm sorry that you have to see it this way. But I want to keep you safe."

She turned, moving out of his embrace, and faced him. "You and Devlin are business partners? Friends?"

He shrugged, making it seem casual. "He needs someone to guide him. And he needs a friend."

"So you're the one who agreed to bail him out for control of LandCorp?"

He looked surprised, backing away from her a little.

"How'd you know about that?"

"I have my sources. But I didn't know it was you. Why? What's in it for you?"

Jack cocked his head, smiling. "Nikki, Devlin is like a brother to me. Sure, he's a nitwit sometimes, but I care about him. Think of me as a guardian angel of sorts. He makes mistakes and I try to fix them. Usually he won't let me fix them, but this time he's too mired in financial mud to resist."

"So what does controlling interest in LandCorp mean for you?"

"It means now I have the power to help Devlin, and to make LandCorp a successful company."

She was trying to get a bead on Jack and Devlin's relationship. Surely it would take a miracle to get LandCorp on its financial feet again. Why would Jack undertake such an endeavor? He'd never been the sacrificial type.

"But don't you have enough going on with all your other ventures? It just seems as though saving LandCorp was a losing proposition, and Jack Barton doesn't like to lose. Does he?"

His eyebrow bobbed up at that. "No, I don't. Why all the questions, Nikki?"

She gave him an innocent smile. "Just catching up." Then her expression became serious. "Jack, do you believe Devlin planted that pipe bomb, the first one? It was his idea for me to ride with them to teach you a lesson."

"No, he wasn't behind it. I think it was someone trying to get back at him for welshing on a deal. If he was behind it, he's smart enough to convince a jury and me that he's innocent. You still think he did it, don't you?"

"Yes." She walked to the sliding glass door, looking out to the ocean that always comforted her. This time not even the waves glistening with sun could temper the pain searing through her heart. Yet her mind was numb, filtering through the pain, groping for reason.

"Jack, I need to call Ulyssis. He won't tell Adrian or anyone else."

He turned her to face him. "Darling, if you want to stay safe, stay alive, you must let everyone think you're dead. Everyone."

"I have to tell Ulyssis. He'll be devastated."

Jack nodded. "Okay, but why don't you freshen up first? Then we'll call Ulyssis and tell him that you're all right." He pinched her nose gently. "Then we'll fix something to eat and figure out what we're going to do with you."

Jack walked upstairs with her, past the room that used to be hers. It was empty. When she paused, Jack stopped.

"He was so hurt that you'd testified against him that he got rid of everything. But your mother's clothes are still here."

Jack pulled her along to her mother's room. Nikki was shocked to find that the master bedroom looked exactly the same as she remembered it, and she realized that Devlin hadn't moved in. Surely he hadn't taken the mourning son bit this far, this long.

There were framed pictures on the wall of a young Nikki and Devlin. Her curls had been precariously corkscrewed by her mother for hours before that photograph had been taken, and back then Nikki tried to pretend that going through so much to look pretty was worth it.

A picture of her parents sat on the dresser, smiling through a layer of dust, not a care in the world. Back then, that was truly the case. They had plenty of money, two lovely children, a gorgeous house on the ocean, everything they could want. Her father, Addington, had been so handsome, so warm and loving. He wasn't as pretentious as Blossom; he was too busy working hard to make sure his family had everything they wanted. Much more than they wanted.

Nikki swiped at the tear that dripped down her cheek.

How had everything gotten so damned screwed up? And here she was, back in her own home, with a man she once thought she'd loved, wondering if the man she truly loved had tried to kill her. She was in a state of numbness, but the thought ravaged her heart again. Jack emerged from the closet with a pair of silk pants and a blouse to match. Nikki could remember seeing her mother in that outfit, though she'd probably only worn it once. It was burgundy, and Blossom despised dark colors.

She heard the water start, then Jack steered her inside the master bath toward the marble tub filling with bubbles. Nikki looked at him as if he'd lost his mind. A bubble bath? Now? Then she wondered if he was going to stay in the bathroom with her while she bathed. He lingered, staring at the bubbles as they rose higher.

"Jack?"

He started, then looked at her. "What?"

"Are you going to watch me?"

He smiled. "If you want me to."

"I'd rather you didn't."

He placed his hands on her shoulders. "Why didn't you ever let me make love to you, Nikki? I wanted to make you my wife, but you never let me please you in that most intimate way."

She moved away from his touch. "Because I was waiting for it to feel right."

"Why didn't it feel right?"

"I don't know, Jack. I don't know."

He seemed to contemplate her answer, watching her with those speculative blue eyes. She crossed her arms in front of her, signaling that she was not going to step into that tub until he left the room. After a moment, he turned away.

"I'll be waiting for you in the master suite. . . ." He glanced around before snatching up an old magazine from a rack by the toilet. "Reading this. Take your time."

She watched him disappear down the hallway and heard him drop down on the bed. Her parents' bed. It seemed strange that he had brought her here and was so guarded with her. She had thought about making that call to Ulyssis in private after her bath, but with Jack right there in the bedroom, that would be impossible. And Blossom had removed the phone in the bathroom after her father had died, wanting respite while in the tub.

Still, there were no doors between her and the bedroom, and Jack could easily hear her. Why was he sticking so close? Why, he could just peer down the hallway and see her in the tub.

The steam rising from the hot tub beckoned her, so she stripped out of her dirty clothes and sank into the bubbles. Even the hot water couldn't ease the ache in her heart at the thought of Adrian betraying her. It couldn't be true! But he had met with Jack and Devlin. Her eyes narrowed. What had they met about? What had Adrian proposed? She wanted answers, and she would get them as soon as she was finished with her bath. The biggest question made her heart stop beating for a moment. If Adrian had done the unbelievable and offered to kill Nikki for money, why hadn't Jack turned him over to the police? She shivered in the hot water, feeling more cold than she ever had.

Jack settled onto the bed, shifting on the hard mattress in an attempt to get comfortable. He heard Nikki's splash as she got into the tub. Hopefully she would stay in there for a while and give him time to think. He couldn't believe it—she was still alive. Alive. Jack had only gone to the hospital to try and get a scoop on what was going on with Adrian, maybe talk to him and see what he knew. And then he'd seen Nikki there. He remembered the way she felt in his arms when he'd come up behind her. Glancing down at his groin, he muttered, ''Is that worth six million dollars?'' But he could have both, at least for a time. Until Devlin returned.

Jack didn't trust keeping her at his apartment. The police may just come looking, though he couldn't imagine what for. With no motive, and no obvious opportunity, he had nothing to worry about. He still worried, though. Last time the whole operation had been screwed up. Marrying Nikki was out of the question this time. She was supposed to be dead, and she was worth more to him dead than alive. He wasn't going to take the chance that she wouldn't marry him. Besides, she was really in love with that Wilde guy. He grinned maliciously. Well, maybe not anymore. She'd looked pretty convinced when Jack had showed her the newspaper, and especially when she'd heard the radio broadcast. Everything was working wonderfully.

So, what was he going to do with her now? He could see that she wasn't going to let him talk her out of calling Ulyssis. Jack had no plausible reason for her not to, and she obviously trusted the man. Enough to tell him where she was. Why didn't she trust Jack two years ago? Heck, they were supposed to be in love. It bothered him more than it should. She didn't seem to know that he had been behind the original bombing, so why had she turned to someone else? He could have had her money long ago.

So, what was he going to do with her now? The answer was obvious. He was going to have to kill her. Damn, he hated messy one-on-one confrontations. But he didn't want to do another pipe bombing. His luck was bound to run out with someone recognizing him buying the pipe, even if it was outside town. He thought of walking right into the bathroom and shoving her beneath the soapy water, picturing her arms and legs flailing until they stilled in death.

That thought repulsed him, though. He didn't want to see her die, or deal with a dead body afterward. Maybe a fire. They might find remnants of a human body and figure out it was Nikki. No, she was already dead; best to keep her that way.

Jack walked out of the bedroom and wandered into Devlin's office. The knife that he used as a letter opener sat on the blotter. Jack picked it up, feeling the sharp tip. Filled with copper and coated with black zinc, the knife was strong enough to do some serious damage. The handle had a tiny ladder and a little man on top, matching some of the other art pieces in the office. Holding it against his leg in case Nikki had stepped out of the bathroom, he walked in and sat down on the bed again. Stabbing her held as little appeal as drowning her, but he had to have something in case she got out of hand.

Jack flipped on the clock radio on the white oak headboard. He spotted a pack of cigarettes and an ashtray. He'd smoke off and on for years, and a cigarette had enormous appeal at the moment. Finding a lighter nearby, he settled back and lit up, waiting for the calming effect. Instead, he nearly choked on the stale cigarette. He ground it out and put the ashtray on the dresser, waving away the cloud of smoke that surrounded him. The pack had probably been there from when Blossom was alive, since nothing else in the room seemed to have been changed.

His attention shifted to the radio as a newscast came on. The last two days Jack always listened to newscasts.

". . . escaped from his hospital room today, taking a nurse with him as hostage. They managed to escape the hospital in her car. Wilde later released the victim unharmed. Police found her car at the Greyhound bus station, and have verified that Wilde was on a bus heading to Panama City Beach. Although the police won't release any information, we believe that the FBI are setting up an arrest at the bus's next stop. We remind you that Wilde is armed and considered extremely dangerous. Anyone seeing him should notify the FBI immediately."

Jack sat up as if he'd been injected with air. Wilde was out, maybe headed for the panhandle. And maybe not. He searched the windows that looked out over the beach, almost expecting to see the man standing there. Jack shook his head and settled back on the pillows. If he were smart, he'd be hightailing it far from here, and it wouldn't be on a bus. The world thought Nikki was dead, and so did Adrian. He'd have no reason to look for her.

His thoughts returned to Nikki and what he had to do. If he could kill her and dispose of the body where no one would find it, then Adrian would be convicted for her murder, if they caught him, and that would be the end of it.

"Jack, I have some questions I want answers to."

He whirled around to find her standing there, wet hair dripping down the silk shirt. Turning down the radio, he tried to remain casual as she neared him.

"Sure, darling. Come sit down here with me."

"No, I want to stand." She lifted her head. "Have you been smoking?"

"No, why?"

"It smells like—" Her gaze rested on the ashtray with the partially smoked cigarette in it, and her eyes widened, then scanned the room. She shivered, then turned back to him, those eyes darker now. "Jack, what kind of proposal did Adrian come to you and Devlin with?"

"So, you believe me now? You know that he's dangerous, that he should continue to think you're dead."

"Just answer me, Jack."

"He told us that he knew Devlin would inherit a lot of money if you died, and he knew where you were. He said that if we cut him in on the project we were working on, he'd make sure you were never able to inherit that money."

Her expression was steely. "And what did you tell him?"

Ah, so she had been doing some thinking of her own while in the bath. "What do you think I told him? Not to touch a hair on your body, that's what I told him."

Her eyes narrowed. "Then why would he have blown me up? It did him no financial gain."

Ooh, she had him there. "I don't know why he did that. The only thing I can think of is . . ." Ah, yes. Her previous suspicion. "I know what happened." He injected a sinister tone in his voice, nodding his head sagely. "Devlin must have contacted him behind my back and taken him up on his offer. They probably worked together to make sure Devlin had an alibi since he was the obvious suspect. The bastard."

"So why didn't you go to the police when Adrian first contacted you?"

Hmm. "To tell you the truth, I was afraid. He made some pretty hefty threats if we went to the cops. You see the power behind the threats now, don't you? I figured if we didn't take him up on his offer that he wouldn't hurt you. After all, Devlin is only one your death is worth money to."

"And you, now that you're his partner."

"Well, technically, yes. But you know I'd never do anything to hurt you, don't you, darling?"

"What were you doing at the hospital?"

"That was just a coincidence. I was . . . visiting a friend. Appendicitis."

She stood there, absorbing every lie he'd told her. Did she believe him? She wrapped her arms around herself, a gesture he remembered her doing before when she was upset. Self-protective. Just when he thought she was going to sit down, she walked over to the phone and started dialing.

"Who ya' calling there, darling?" He was up in an instant, standing by her side. No need to get too hyped up.

"Just Ulyssis."

But he couldn't let her call anyone and alert them that she was alive. So his charade of protector, if she'd even bought it at all, was going to turn him into the monster she'd think he was. He wasn't about to let her ruin his chance to be a multimillionaire.

"Ulyss—"

He pressed the button on the faux marble phone. Taking him by surprise, she threw the handset at his head and ran. Jack didn't let the stars in his vision keep him from stopping her. As she started to run through the bedroom, he made a grab for those long, wet tresses and yanked her back against his chest. Before she could raise her foot to kick him, he slid the knife in front of her face. Her green eyes widened in terror as she recognized the curved camel blade Devlin used to open his letters, more of a piece of art than a letter opener or weapon. Still, it served Jack's purpose as Nikki's struggle instantly ceased.

"I'm sorry, Nikki. But you're going to have to die."

Frantic thoughts thundered through Adrian's mind, always overshadowed by one pulsing belief: *I can't let her die.* Every second of freedom was precious. He couldn't let himself get caught. Even if the police didn't shoot him on sight, he would rather be dead than know Nikki was dying and not be able to help her.

Adrian only hoped the police hadn't alerted the stations yet about the menace of escaped murder suspect Adrian Wilde. Nikki's life depended on it.

People milled about here and there in the station, some asleep on benches. Adrian took off his sunglasses and hat, tucking them into his back pocket. He walked up to the counter.

"Where can I go for seventy-six dollars?"

The heavy-set woman behind the counter eyed him, and

Adrian's heart pounded erratically. Had she been given a composite drawing of him yet? Would she turn around and set off some alarm, sending the police rushing in to apprehend him? He swallowed, trying not to let his anxiety show. She smiled at him then, making her cheeks seem even pudgier than they were. Her brown eyes scanned what she could see of him, and she seemed to be contemplating an unsuitable answer. Then she must have thought better of it, because she cleared her throat and glanced at a chart hanging to her right.

"You're in luck. We have some specials going on right now. When do you want to leave?"

"Now." He smiled, trying to inject power into that one word. He wanted the woman to remember him later.

She looked over at the chart again. "We've got a bus leaving in fifteen minutes, heading to Panama City Beach, Florida." The woman leaned back, a quirk of a grin on her face. "You running from something?"

"Yeah, the police." He conjured up his most charming smile, under the circumstances. "I'll take the Panama City bus. That's in the panhandle, isn't it?"

"Sure is." She processed the ticket, leaving Adrian with one dollar and fifty-two cents left. "You ever coming back?"

"Nope. It's north from there. Is the bus loading yet?"

"Yep. And if you ever come this way again, stop by and say hi, why don't you?"

He forced a smile. "Yeah, sure thing."

Fifteen minutes wasn't long enough to do what he wanted and get off that bus, but he had to take the chance. He couldn't wait any longer. Adrian walked across the parking lot and found the bus to Panama City Beach. He handed his ticket to the driver, who eyed it before gesturing for him to proceed. The bus was about half full. That would work fine. Even better, the last seat was still available. Maybe the fates were finally working for him. The young man in the seat in front of the last one was asleep.

Adrian made it a point to make eye contact with several people as he carried his bundle to the back. He settled the mass of pillows and blankets around him, pulling one blanket up over his head. He slipped out of the rangy, oversized sneakers he'd been wearing and pulled another pair out of his duffel bag.

The man in the seat in front of him lifted his head for a moment, then laid down again as he settled back into sleep. Adrian waited a few minutes just to make sure the man was really asleep again. Then he slipped on the cap, tucking in his hair, and put on the sunglasses. He took off the jacket he'd been wearing, but kept the black sweatshirt on. With the pillows and blankets arranged just so, and the sneakers at the bottom, it looked as though a man slept there.

With his whole new appearance, he quickly made his way back up the aisle, keeping his gaze straight ahead. He hoped that he looked like a man trying to make a last-minute call before the bus left. As Adrian made his way down the steps, the bus driver barked, "Hey! We're leaving in two minutes."

Adrian didn't turn around, but mumbled, "I've got to make this call. I'll make it back in time."

"Whatever," he heard the man mutter. "I ain't waitin' for you."

Adrian walked past Lorie's car and headed toward Palm Beach. That was the last chance he could take. He couldn't risk hitchhiking or being seen by anyone, even in his disguise. Not when he was supposed to be on a bus to Panama City Beach.

He knew the police would send bulletins to all area airports and bus stations, and hopefully the charmer at the window would recognize him. Then they would radio the bus driver, who would remember seeing such a man come aboard, and take a discreet look at the passengers behind him. There he would see the bundle of blankets that might conceal an escaped murderer, and the police would be waiting at the next stop. At least they would be preoccupied with busting him there and not concentrating on the local area while he looked for Nikki.

He walked into the men's room in a gas station and locked the door behind him. The medication was setting in, and he closed his eyes and willed the fuzziness away. Where would he start looking for her? *Concentrate, man.* Without thought, he sank to his knees. It was easier now. He could smell that soft, feminine scent of her, feel her skin against his and the pulse of her heartbeat as she slept in his arms. She was his, and she was in him.

Nothing came. The realization chilled him through. He couldn't connect with her. Maybe it was the fear and adrenaline pounding through his veins, or the medication. He had to believe that she was still alive, but where was she? Adrian realized that he didn't have a clue as to where to find her, and his time was limited. That strangling sense of his nightmare drifted through his mind. Devlin wouldn't have taken her to the mansion; that was too obvious. His thoughts started reaching farther out beyond the limited scope before him. Who knew the people involved in this sordid scenario? Devlin, Jack . . . Ulysses.

Adrian remembered how hostile the man had been, and now Ulyssis probably had no doubt that Adrian had done his friend in. Could he convince Ulyssis that Nikki was alive and needed their help? Time was slipping through his fingers, and going on wild goose chases wasn't going to do Nikki any good. The late afternoon rays stretched across the sky. He was going to have to take the chance that Ulyssis wouldn't call the police right there. Adrian patted the gun tucked into the waistband of his jeans. He wasn't a violent man, but he was prepared to do anything to save the most precious thing in his life. He shook his head at those words, but he didn't have time to analyze them as he made his way to the Garcia Gallery.

Chapter 18

A heart long deceived.

"Are you going to f-freeze me to death?"

Nikki shivered as she stared at Jack. While she was strapped into a chair with rope, he looked so casual leaning against the doorway to the wine cellar. Her father had been so proud of the thing, set at the perfect temperature to keep his precious bottles just right. It had been engineered and insulated to keep the cool air in, since they couldn't actually dig it into the ground. For Nikki, it had always been a dreary, scary place. Especially when Devlin had locked her in it a few times, just for laughs.

But this wasn't for laughs. Jack rested the tip of her brother's knife against his cheek, looking thoughtful. Where was Devlin? She knew he had to be part of this. Unless he really was up north.

"Freezing you into a popsicle is a possibility. But it's not how you die so much as how I get rid of your body. You see, you're already dead to the world. So your body can't just pop up somewhere, now can it? Nikki, it really would have been so much more convenient if you'd just died in the van like you were supposed to."

Anger boiled inside her. "Gee, sorry to screw your plans

up by not dying for you. Both times.''

He smiled, but there was nothing humorous about it. ''You did screw my plans up, but the first time, you weren't supposed to die. Everyone else was.''

A chill ran down to the tips of her fingers. ''What are you talking about?''

''Well, you might as well know. Blossom and Devlin were supposed to die in that first explosion. You, my dear, were supposed to be so grief-stricken that you'd marry me so I could take care of my little girl. And with all that money you were due to inherit, that would be very easy. Only you didn't wait for me, and Devlin forgot his stupid sunglasses.''

She felt another chill, helped more by the refrigeration. ''Devlin wasn't in on it? Just you?''

''No. So, you see, you had no reason to hide from him. Only he told you that he wanted to straighten things out between the two of you, and you took it as a threat and disappeared. At first I thought you had figured out I was behind it, so I found you and tried to kill you. You just don't die, do you? Then you really disappeared. If only you'd trusted me . . .''

''Then what? I'd be dead too.''

''No, I didn't necessarily mean to kill you after we married. Unless you didn't give me control of your money. But there was no you, so Devlin had to do. I've got him wrapped around my finger, you know. If only he weren't so stupid, he'd still have some of that money the lawyers didn't eat up. Then he went and bought this defective building. But I'm optimistic, you see. I saw an opportunity to make better. I made a deal with Devlin to give me control of LandCorp if I fished him out of the toilet. When he agreed, I knew that to do that, all we needed was you. Dead, of course. Then Devlin would inherit your share of the inheritance, and I would be in control of it. With that money, we could turn this building fiasco into a winner, and from there we'd become rich.

"You see, Nikki, I was never rich. No mansion, no servants, nothing. An apartment in West Palm Beach and a 1987 Toyota Corolla. That's all I had, aside from my style and a keen desire to get my hands on some money so that I could make myself the rich bastard I pretended to be. All those deals I told you and Devlin about were real; they were just engineered by someone else who had the money to accomplish them. All of my successes were on a small, much less impressive scale. I wanted the opportunity to make those big deals myself, and I needed you to do that. That's where Adrian came in.

"We all worked together to make sure we got your money for this project. Heck, you weren't using it. And then, after I think everything's worked out just fine, there you are in the hospital parking lot. I was there to talk to Adrian."

"You're disgusting. You'll burn in hell for what you've done."

"But until then, I'll make a ton of money. It'll be a lot easier to get investors when I have a nice chunk of it in the deal myself."

"Where did you get the explosives? Not everybody has the makings of a pipe bomb in his garage."

He drew the knife to his lips, pressing the flat part of the blade against them. "No, I don't suppose they do. But they're surprisingly easy to make; a little smokeless powder, some pipe, and a little electronics background, and voilà . . . a pipe bomb is born."

Her angry words churned out through frigid lips. "You're going to screw up, Jack. Somewhere along the way, you're going to mess up and someone will figure it out. Like finding out about your background."

He didn't look worried. "My background isn't easy to

trace, darling. I jumped around so much, doing different things at different companies, they'd never put together the total of two years I worked for an alarm company.''

"They're going to find out. I know they will." She didn't really believe that, but she didn't want him feeling so comfortable with murdering her.

"I won't screw up. I haven't yet. And you know what's so darn funny? Here you were all this time living right under our noses, and now you're in the most obvious place, yet no one is looking for you."

"I don't quite find the humor in it." She softened the edge in her voice. She didn't want to beg, but she had to take a chance. "Jack, if I married you now, and signed over the money to you as soon as I took possession of it, would you let me live? I mean, how could I ever prove all this, even if I did say something to the police, which I wouldn't?"

"Sorry, Nik. I couldn't take that chance. Don't think I like doing this. It's nothing personal. You're just worth more to me dead. Like your brother, I want to make something of myself. Only I'm smarter than he is. And it's true, you have to have money to make it. When Devlin inherits your money, I will have control of it. Before we know it, I will be a very rich man." He leaned over and pinched her cheek. "And darling, I will toast you when I make my first million."

"You're so kind. I hope someone poisons your champagne."

"Now, now. Don't get hostile. I told you it's nothing personal."

Her heart fell. There really was no hope. No one knew she was alive, Adrian might have been part of it . . . her heart ached at the thought of him. How could he have done this to her? She didn't want to believe it, but it fit too well. The meetings, his aloofness . . . heck, the police had him under arrest for her murder. There were witnesses to the fact that he had purchased the pipe needed. And the partial cigarette in the ashtray in her mother's bedroom. He had been there, plotting her murder along with Devlin and Jack. Right there in her parents' bedroom.

A tiny part of her didn't want to believe it, but she forced herself to face the truth. She had given her heart to a murderer. In fact, the only men she had ever cared about had tried to kill her. And her own brother had been part of it, if not the first time, then at least the second. Her life meant nothing but the money she was to inherit. She dropped her head.

"Then why don't you just get it over with?" Her voice sounded thick, strangled in her throat.

"I will. Tonight. I've got it all figured out." He glanced at his watch. "And we'll give it another half hour before we head out. The marina should be long closed by then, and we'll take a little cruise on the Madsen yacht. And then won't it be a pity that you'll fall overboard." He grinned, and she swore that a devil had possessed him. "And didn't I tell you not to wear those anchors? Tsk tsk."

She was going to drown tonight. The thought shot panic through her, but she refused to give Jack the satisfaction by showing it. She simply raised her head and said, "If God allows me, I'm going to put a curse on whatever project you're using my money for. I'll haunt you for the rest of your life."

His smile disappeared as his head snapped to the left. That wouldn't be Wilde, now, would it? "You just stay put, darling. I'll be back," he said, backing up and closing the door behind him.

The darkness shrouded her, and she sucked in a deep breath of panic. Would she see Adrian before she died? She thought of the ocean she had always loved looking out to, the very ocean that would take her life. Nikki took some comfort that it would be an old friend who would not take her life, but welcome her into its comforting arms. Yes, that's how she would look at it.

"God," she whispered, "let it be quick." Her mother had almost drowned when she was a teenager, and had told Nikki of the peace that enveloped her when she realized she was going to die. Then hands had reached in and pulled her to the surface. That wasn't likely to happen to Nikki. She only hoped it would be peaceful. "And God, please let me haunt Jack." She didn't want to think about Adrian.

Jack prowled the hallway, intent on the tiniest sound. The front door closed, and he heard a sigh as a bag was dropped on the tile foyer. A careful peek around the wall revealed Devlin standing there, his head cocked for noise too. The van parked out front probably tipped him off that someone was in the house, and Jack had no business being there. Damn, this complicated things a bit. Jack couldn't let him know he was there. How was he going to get Nikki out of the house now? He was going to have to get Devlin out of the way. Not permanently, of course.

Jack gingerly lifted a thick, ceramic vase from an ornate table. With it poised, he made a sound with his nail against the wall. Devlin's footsteps sounded in his direction. All Jack had to do was knock him out before Devlin could recognize him in the dark hallway. Just as Devlin rounded the corner, Jack slammed the vase over his head. Devlin's eyes glazed over, meeting his for just a second before he slumped to the floor. Hopefully, if he remembered seeing Jack later, he could explain it as some strange delusion. After he got rid of Nikki, he'd have to swipe a few things and make it look like a burglary.

Jack dragged Devlin's heavy form to the wine cellar door and opened it. Nikki's eyes widened at the body. He pulled it in and left it in a heap next to a row of wine bottles.

"Devlin?" she whispered.

"Yep. He almost ruined our little party."

She was staring at the still form. "What are you talking about? Is he dead?"

"No, of course not. How would he inherit your money if he's dead? He might have come in here and found you, and then it would be all over."

"He doesn't know about me?"

Oops. Jack had wanted her to think Devlin and Adrian were in on the scheme, just so he didn't seem like the only bad guy. But now he'd let Devlin's innocence out of the bag.

"No, he doesn't. He was actually quite upset about your murder, and that will work best as he processes the paperwork to inherit your portion of the money. When I find him in the cellar here, after getting worried when he doesn't report to work tomorrow, he'll tell me about some burglar who knocked him over the head. But we'd better get going now, before he wakes up and sees you there."

That phone call haunted Ulyssis all through the day. Even in the peacefulness of his home, he couldn't stop hearing Nicolina's voice. The strain was getting to him, that must be it. Surely he could dispel the uneasiness that grew within him. She was dead, even though his heart wouldn't allow him to accept that as fact. But that voice . . .

What would the police say if he told them what had happened? They'd think he suffered from dementia. Maybe he did. Nicolina had been like a daughter to him, and he was sure he was the only person she trusted throughout her horrible ordeal. That photographer had come into her life, stolen her heart, and then brutally killed her. Now the madman was on the loose. Ulyssis prayed they would catch and electrocute him. Not that it would bring his Nicolina back, but it would help to heal the anger in his soul.

The doorbell rang, and Ulyssis made his way slowly to

the door. He didn't even check through the peephole before opening it. He was sure that he was seeing things when that very man walked into his home. Surely he had conjured him up. The blood ran cold through Ulyssis's veins, but he managed to reach for the button on the alarm pad that notified the police they were needed. Adrian's words stopped him.

"Nikki's alive, and I need your help. You're my last hope."

Ulyssis knew Adrian had a gun. The hand poised for the button slowly dropped. Those words seemed preposterous, and yet . . .

"What do you mean she's alive? You killed her."

Adrian dropped his head for a moment, then looked up at him with pleading eyes. "I love her. All I wanted to do was protect her, and instead I led him right to her. But it wasn't Nikki who died in that van."

"Wait a minute. You led who right to her?"

"Devlin. He planted the pipe bomb, just like the first time. Think. He has the most to gain from her death. I don't know how he managed an alibi, maybe he had someone else do the deed this time. But she isn't dead. I met with Jack and Devlin because I knew about the building in Tampa and wanted to find out how desperate Devlin was to find Nikki, so I would know how to protect her. Hell, I should have kidnapped her and taken her back to New York with me like I'd threatened to. She would have been safe there."

Adrian crackled in a rush of energy, and his forehead was dotted with perspiration. Ulyssis couldn't deny the emotion he saw in the man's eyes. Was he a lunatic? A lunatic who made sure Nicolina's dog was taken care of?

"You said she is still alive?" Could he dare believe?

"Yes. Nikki and I are connected in a way that's hard to describe. Since the first explosion."

Ulyssis felt the blood drain from his face. "I know about the visions. She told me."

Adrian leaned forward. "Ulyssis, I saw her being kidnapped *after* the second explosion. This morning. I think she was coming to see me at the hospital, but someone grabbed her and threw her into a white van."

Ulyssis's hand went to his mouth. "Oh, my God. It was her, then."

"What was her?"

"The phone rang earlier today. It sounded like—" He shook his head. "But I thought it was my imagination."

"What did she say?"

"Just my name, and then she was cut off."

"When Nikki is in a highly emotional state, I can see through her eyes, feel what she is feeling. But they gave me medication at the hospital, and I can't seem to connect with her. You know Devlin better than I do. Where might he take her? Someplace near water maybe."

Ulyssis had to believe the love he saw in Adrian's eyes, the desperation to save her. He thought about calling the police, but still wasn't sure they'd believe him. And if Adrian was innocent, they might kill him on sight.

"There's an abandoned warehouse near the Intracoastal, one of Devlin's acquisitions. We can try there first. My car's in the garage."

A thumping, whining noise made them both look where Crackers stood only a few feet away. Adrian walked over and gave the dog a hug. Crackers went nuts when he saw the tall man, jumping up and talking in dog language. It was so much better than the plaintive whining Ulyssis heard day in and out.

"We've got to save our Madame Blue, Crackers. Then we'll be back for you."

Adrian turned back to the door where Ulyssis was waiting, and they jumped into his Jaguar and headed to town.

Adrian leaned forward, as if trying to make the car go faster. Ulyssis pushed the gas pedal further down.

Adrian's heart pounded faster than he'd ever felt it. The thought of her being held at some warehouse against her will pumped fierce adrenaline through his veins. For some strange reason, he pictured the sandcastle they had made together on the beach, and the princess in distress in the tower. Now he was going to be that prince come to save the fair maiden. If they made it there in time.

Adrian was rocked by a fear so deep and vivid, he knew it wasn't just his own. Nikki was still alive! And scared to death. Her heart beat rapidly, and her breath came in deep gasps. Dark images flashed in front of him, jerky and shadowy. Then he saw the back end of a large boat, a glimpse of letters before the vision disappeared.

"*Life's Too Short!*" he shouted.

"You got that right," Ulyssis said, taking a sharp turn.

"No, I see a boat, and that's the name of it."

Ulyssis turned to him. "The Madsen yacht. Addington, Nicolina's father, took me out on it a few times. Are you saying she's on the boat?"

"She's standing next to it." His throat tightened. "And Devlin's going to drown her."

Ulyssis had already turned the car around, making the tires screech into the quiet night air. "I know where the marina is."

Adrian didn't know if Nikki could feel him when they connected, but he concentrated. *Nikki, I love you. Baby, hold on, we're on our way.*

Chapter 19

The prince of my heart or the devil of my soul?

Nikki knew how those old pirates felt when they were told to walk the plank. Through her shoes she could feel the planks of wood that led to the Madsen yacht. The marina was long closed at this time of night, but Jack had expertly picked the lock that kept the gates closed.

Even at the late hour, the marina was an orchestra of noise, from the water lapping at the pilings to the squeak of boats rubbing against bumpers. She could have raised a scream to obliterate all those sounds, but her mouth was gagged with a handkerchief. Her hands were bound behind her.

Under the circumstances, Nikki could hardly remember having family parties on this boat. Jack walked her to where the yacht was docked. *Life's Too Short*, her father had named his favorite toy. How right he was.

Jack had a grip on her arm as he maneuvered the walkway down to the dock. Through the darkness and the pain and anger and fear that gripped her, she felt something else. Hope. Adrian. She shook her head, pushing it away. It was a trick, or her imagination. *Baby, hold on*, it seemed to say. She wanted that hope so badly that she couldn't help the tears that streamed down her face. What was there to hold on to?

Her life, that's what.

Rage filled her. She rushed at Jack, shoving him against the boat. Adrenaline pumped through her as she ran across the dock to the gate. But then what? She could hardly climb the fence with her arms tied, and Jack had locked the gates again. Find a place to hide! Crevices, nooks and crannies, and more than a hundred boats, there were plenty of places she could hide until the marina opened the next morning.

Jack's footsteps pounded on the boards behind her. "Nikki, don't make this harder than it has to be," he growled, his voice growing nearer. Fingers reached for her hair, tangling in it, pulling her backward until she hit the boards full force.

"Hold it right there!"

That rich voice blasted through her as though he had shot her with the gun he was holding. Adrian stood there, taking deep breaths, the gun pointed at them. But at who? Jack dropped the knife in his surprise. He grabbed Nikki and shoved her toward Adrian. With a quick twist of his body, Jack's foot slashed upward and kicked Adrian into the water. The gun flew out of his hand.

Nikki only had a second to realize Ulyssis stood there too. In one quick swoop, Jack grabbed the knife and pressed it against her throat. Then he jerked her to her feet and down the dock toward the yacht.

Ulyssis looked as horrified as she must have. Why was he there with Adrian? She wouldn't believe that he had been in on the whole thing too. As if expelled from a gun, he ran toward them with his arms outstretched, a high-pitched cry issuing from his throat. Jack shoved her down and lunged at Ulyssis with the knife, catching him in the upper chest. He dropped instantly, and Jack kicked him into the murky water.

Nikki followed Jack's smile to Adrian's gun balanced on the edge of the planks. She tried to shove herself at him, but he pushed her aside and grabbed the gun, aiming several shots where Adrian had plunged into the water. She screamed, but it came out as only a muffle. Jack tossed the gun in the water after wiping it on his pants.

He jerked her to her feet and dragged her back to the boat.

"Now you've made a mess of it. If you'd just come along peacefully, those men wouldn't be dead. And that means I'll have to dispose of them when I come back. I *hate* touching dead bodies." They reached the walkway, now poised for their entrance. "No, I don't have to do anything with them," he said in a lighter tone, shoving her along in front of him. "I'll just leave this knife in the water. The police will think Ulyssis tracked Adrian here and they had it out, with both of them dying." He gave a satisfied laugh. "Jackie boy, you just have it all figured out."

He dragged her with him to the steering wheel on the top deck. The engine wheezed a few times. Nikki cringed when it finally started. Jack held the knife to her throat as he maneuvered the large boat out of the slip. As soon as they cleared the marina, he kicked up the speed. He maneuvered through the choppy Intracoastal, then through the pass leading out to the ocean. The waves rose in great swells, dragging the boat down, then lifting it high on a crest.

"Almost there," he said, his fingers gripping the teak steering wheel. "Believe me, I want to get this over with as fast as you do."

She twisted her head and spit the gag out. Not that screaming would do her any good now. "You greedy bastard. I can't even begin to understand what a warped mind you must have to kill for money."

He patted her cheek. "No, I don't suppose you would

understand. You never even took advantage of the money you had. I thought you were incredibly weird that way, not wanting to be a part of it all, not indulging your whims. I was worried that you'd squirrel all that money away and not let me spend any of it when we were married."

"I never would have married you, Jack. Never."

"Doesn't matter, darling, now does it?"

"Adrian didn't have anything to do with this, did he?"

"Don't kid yourself. He just wanted it all for himself. I knew he'd try to double-cross me and sweet-talk Devlin into letting him control LandCorp. Now he's dead. Don't you think he got what he deserved?"

Nikki wasn't sure of anything anymore. Could she have been so wrong about Devlin? She looked at Jack, but could hardly remember being infatuated with him. Yes, she could be so wrong. Nikki didn't dare think about Adrian.

When she had looked at Jack, he was staring right through her. His eyes narrowed.

"You're right, you do keep haunting me. But you just had your last rescue. They're all dead. Devlin doesn't even know you're alive."

The black clouds become a nasty gray just as they started dumping water down on them. The wind picked up, whipping her hair around. They were the only ones insane enough to be out on the water that she could see through the black night.

Jack pressed the button that released the anchor, then dragged her down to the kitchen. It was fit for luxury, but like the mansion, it had been neglected too. A for-sale sign discreetly graced the window. Her fingers clawed at the ropes binding her hands. He turned around, and she stilled.

"Sit over there at that table. Don't try anything funny."

She didn't consider saving her life funny. She obeyed, still furiously working the rope behind her. Jack knelt down and searched the cabinets. One hand slipped free of the ropes. He eyed her, then went around the corner, pulling open doors down the hall.

"Stay right there, Nikki," he warned.

She was already on her feet, reaching for the fire extinguisher. When he suddenly appeared in the doorway, she slammed it down on his head and pushed him backward. His eyes rolled back, but she didn't take a moment to see if he was unconscious. She turned on the gas on all the burners with shaking fingers.

She could hear her heart beating through her head as she ran up the stairs and onto the deck. Rain pounded against her, and she grasped at the railing as she made her way to the Boston Whaler perched up high. The ocean was an alive and evil thing, foaming at the tips of the waves. She didn't even think about how the small dinghy would be tossed about in those swells. All she thought about was the flare gun she would aim at the yacht once she was a safe distance away. She remembered how her father had lowered the dinghy so they could reach some island or another. The electric winch whirred to life, and the boat started lowering. Just as she was about to step inside, Jack's voice bellowed out above the wind.

"Nooooo!"

He rushed at her, a wild gleam in his eye. The boat kept lowering. She'd never make it in before Jack reached her. Just before those hands shoved her out of the way, something moved between them.

"Oh, God," she uttered as Adrian knocked Jack off his feet. She didn't want to die by Adrian's hand. When she took a step toward the dinghy, she realized it was too low for her to even jump into without possibly getting knocked out of the boat.

"You son of a bitch!" Jack screamed. "Seems I can't get rid of you either."

Jack's voice was laced with violence, his expression sodden with hatred and rain as he stared at Adrian. Jack got to his feet and lunged. Both men flew backward onto the deck. The whole boat tilted to the side in the swells. Her thoughts were frantic. Find the flare kit. Radio for help. Get into the dinghy. The choice wasn't hers to make.

Jack swung a kick at Adrian's middle, knocking him against the side of the boat. Jack grabbed her arm, and yanked her toward him. She struggled, pulling her weight down. Rain and sea spray washed over her face, mixing with her tears.

"Please, Jack! No!"

He picked her up and threw her over the railing. Her stomach wrenched as she dropped down into the cold water. It swallowed her, washing up her nose, choking her. She reached the surface, searching for the dinghy. Safety and life banging against the side of the yacht. Too far. The current moved her away, rising up and down. She panted, swimming as hard as she could, using precious breath. A wave washed over her, making her cough up wretched seawater. Her body shivered, her arms ached. She tried to doggie paddle, keep her face above the surface. It wasn't working. She sank, came up in a panicked rush. *God, no! Please let me live!* Blackness surrounded her, the black of the sea and the world. Weak. Tired. Another wave taking the fight out of her. More seawater in her open mouth, down her throat. She closed her eyes. Fighting. So weak. Water all around. No more air. Oh, God.

Adrian's lungs constricted. The nightmare. But it wasn't a nightmare. Nikki was dying. That terrifying panic seized him. Would he die with her now that their souls were connected? Pressure constricted his chest. He sucked in a great breath, feeling the pressure ease a little. Or . . . he sucked in again, filling his lungs. Could he save her? Breathe for her?

Nikki! He could feel her heartbeat all around him.

Oh, God, I'm dying. I don't even know which way the surface is. Adrian? Is that you?

Yes! You're not dying, Nikki. He took a deep breath, filling his body and soul with it. Her panic eased a little. *Let me breathe for you.*

Yes, I can feel it! I can breathe! How? How is this happening?

Our connection. Stay with me, Babe.

Hands wrenched at his collar, and Adrian woke from the trance. He found Jack in front of him, a wild gleam in his eyes. Panic assailed him. Adrian sucked in another breath, getting to his feet, pretending to be groggy from the kick to his gut. Jack was trying to maneuver him to the railing. Another deep breath.

Hang in there, Nikki. I'm coming for you.

What's happening? I keep losing you.

When Jack tried to lift him over the railing, Adrian shoved him backward with every ounce of energy he possessed. Another deep breath. The porthole behind Jack's head cracked beneath the force. Adrian kept shoving him, giving Jack no time to regain his senses. Blood smeared the shattered glass. Adrian let him drop to the deck and climbed over the railing. He took a deep breath, scanning the roiling seas for her. The sight of her chilled his heart. She floated facedown a distance away.

Nikki!

I'm so tired. Let me sleep, just for a little while.

No, Nikki, you can't sleep. Stay with me. Breathe with me.

Something incredible shimmied through him at the thought that he could breathe for her. He slid down the rope to the dinghy and headed to where she floated.

Nikki.

No answer. He watched for her as a wave lifted him on its crest. His heart pounded inside him, harder than the rain and thunder. He cut the engine and nearly tipped the boat over reaching for her arm. When he pulled her into the boat, she felt limp and cold in his arms.

He could feel her heartbeat, inside him. His lips covered hers, wet and salty, and he pushed breath into her lungs. With a gasp, she sat up and pushed him away, sucking in breath after breath, coughing harshly. Her fingers still clenched his shirt. After a minute, she looked at him with widened eyes.

He smiled, sure his heart would burst inside him. "You're okay." She had to be okay.

Her breathing still came heavy, but fear remained in her eyes. She glanced at the yacht, drifting farther away. The rain had lightened to a drizzle. He started the outboard and put more distance between them.

"How did you get on the boat?" Her voice was heavy and scratchy from the seawater.

"I climbed back on the dock and jumped on the boat just as it left the slip. It took me a little while to actually climb aboard, but nothing was going to stop me from getting to you."

Nikki just stared at him, taking in the fire in those brown eyes as he looked at her. Was it really over? Was Adrian going to pretend he'd never consorted with Jack? Had he? The questions came at her from all angles, and she desperately wanted answers. She knew she couldn't believe him. Yet, she had breathed his breath. Down there in the water, when death beckoned her, Adrian's voice pulled her back from the blackness. Somehow, with water all around her, she could breathe. She shivered, overwhelmed by what he called their connection.

Adrian reached his hand out to her. "Come here. I just want to hold you, to know you're really here."

Nikki drew herself into a tight ball. The wind whipped her hair around her face, but she didn't move her hand to push it away. Adrian's hand remained in the air for a long minute before he let it drop.

"Nikki, what's wrong?"

The hurt she saw in those eyes pierced her heart, and she buried her face in her arms so she wouldn't see him. At the far end of the boat, Adrian couldn't reach her without letting go of the tiller. He didn't try.

"Nikki." His voice was more harsh now. "Don't be afraid of what happened. I . . . I used to think it was weird, but I got used to it. Remember I told you about getting hit by lightning and dying, seeing your life, and then going into your soul."

They heard a far-off scream. A tiny figure stood at the boat's railing. She saw something orange in his hand. "The flare gun!" she said in a rush of breath. He was going to shoot at them!

There was no point in trying to outrun Jack. Adrian could hardly zigzag though the swells to dodge the flare, either. He pulled her behind him as they heard the hiss of the flare. Nikki couldn't stop watching the spectacle of horror. Not the flare itself, but the source.

A spark had jumped from the gun, catching the gas released from the doorway next to Jack. The tiny spark grew as it swallowed up the gas on its way into the cabin. The explosion rocked the air around them. Just like the other two, she thought with a violent shiver.

Jack issued a scream of agony before the boat shattered in a burst of flames. Adrian covered her with his body, but Nikki could still hear flaming bits of wood sizzle as they hit the cold water around them. A second, smaller explosion sounded, and their bodies reacted in unison, cringing, waiting. More shrapnel flew through the air, landing close to the boat. A piece of splintered wood landed at Adrian's feet, smoking, but not aflame.

A few seconds later, they could hear only the roar of fire.

Adrian let her up, and they both looked at the portion of boat that still remained, burning in flames. This time there was no one to mourn for. Nikki could feel nothing but justice as she thought of Jack dying by his own hand. They both could only stare at the wreckage for a long time, and the anger and fear within her turned to numbness. Even with the occasional wave of heat drifting toward them on the wind, her body trembled.

Adrian pulled her close, his face only inches from hers. Like so many times, his fingers encircled her face. She wanted to move away, but her body wouldn't cooperate. It sagged in his arms. His eyes searched hers.

"Nikki, tell me why you're afraid of me."

Everything inside her ached. The warmth of his body enveloped her, and it took all her strength not to move into his embrace.

"I—" A sob tore through her, unexpected in its depth. "I don't know who to trust anymore." Her body shook, and she wrapped her arms around herself.

"Why don't you trust me?"

That voice was so silky smooth, and yet she heard the pain that roared through it. She couldn't meet his gaze, and concentrated on something just over his shoulder: the black smoke billowing up into the dark sky that matched the way she felt.

"Did you see Jack and Devlin b-before the explosion?"

She felt him release a breath. "Yes. I was going to tell you, but I didn't want to say anything until I had an idea of what we were up against with them. I realized that I needed to come clean with you, because you had insight into these two men. I just wanted to free you, Nikki. And find out who had tried to kill you."

She sniffed loudly, but still didn't meet his gaze. Her voice was so thick with tears, it was hardly intelligible. "Jack said you came to him with a proposal . . . to kill me for part of the building deal.''

Adrian turned her chin so she couldn't look anywhere else but at his face. ''Nikki, I know I lied to you. I felt that I had to. But I never meant to harm you.'' His voice cracked. ''Nikki, I love you. How could you think I'd do anything to hurt you? Jack must have followed me after that second meeting. Then he must have seen you. When I thought you were dead, I wanted to die too. And then the police thought I killed you.''

''I know. You bought the pipe used in the bomb.''

He closed his eyes for a moment before meeting her gaze again. ''It was a setup. Jack must have pretended to be Dave when he asked me to pick up some items at the hardware store. That placed me buying the same kind of pipe used in the explosion. And then, while I was in the hospital, I had another vision. You were in the parking lot, and Jack and Devlin kidnapped you. I knew I had to get to you.''

''Is that why you took a nurse hostage?''

''Yes.''

''Did you hurt her?''

His expression hardened. ''I would have done anything to save you. But I didn't have to. She believed me. Heck, she even gave me money and her Hurricanes cap. I didn't want to take her off the hospital grounds, but she insisted.''

''It wasn't Devlin who kidnapped me. I don't think he had anything to do with it.''

''I wasn't sure. He seemed like a puppet with Jack.''

''Devlin came to the mansion while I was in the wine cellar, and Jack hit him over the head and dragged him in there. He's probably still there. Jack had to admit that Devlin knew nothing about either explosion. I've got to let someone know he's in there.'' Her heart stopped for a moment. ''Is Ulyssis all right?'' She remembered the blood when Jack had knifed him.

''I don't know. I pulled him out of the water, but I

couldn't get help for him without losing you. He was conscious.''

"And what about you? Jack shot into the water."

"I was already swimming under the dock, intending to climb up on the other side and surprise him."

"And Ulysses. What was he doing with you?" She wanted to put the pieces together, but the lies kept interfering.

"I went to him for help, because I had no one else to turn to. Luckily you made that call to him, so he believed me when I said you were alive. Then I saw the yacht through your eyes, when Jack took you to the marina. That's how we knew where you were. There's more, but I'll tell you later."

The sound of a boat engine penetrated the air and wind, and they turned to see the coast guard approaching. Adrian said, "I hope they don't shoot me for kidnapping you or something."

Nikki moved away from him, waiting for the boat to take her to safety. She needed desperately to be alone and sort out her feelings and doubts. Too much had happened for her to just fall into Adrian's arms. Even if they had shared the same breath. Too many questions still lingered in her heart. Adrian didn't touch her again, except to help her onto the large coast guard boat.

"How did you find us?" she asked, nearly sagging into the neutral stranger's arms.

"A Ulysses Garcia called us from the marina."

"Is he all right?" both Nikki and Adrian asked simultaneously.

"We radioed the hospital to pick him up. He was talking, so he couldn't have been that bad."

During the ride back to shore, the authorities kept them both busy questioning them and checking their health. She told them to radio to the police that Devlin was in the wine

cellar as they listened to her breathing. They couldn't hear
any water in her lungs; she didn't tell them she'd been face
down in the water for more than ten minutes. She could
still feel that tingly connection when he'd spoken to her
just as she was about to die, and the way his breath had
filled her lungs.

Nikki took a breath, grateful to breathe, to be alive. She
couldn't bring herself to meet Adrian's eyes from across
the room, the man who had saved her life. Her heart felt
as if it had shattered into a thousand pieces inside her, and
at the moment, she just didn't care.

The last person on earth Adrian wanted to see when the
coast guard docked stood there waiting for them: Detective
Sloan. Ulyssis had explained what he could, but Sloan still
regarded Adrian with suspicion. Adrian didn't care at the
moment. He couldn't take his eyes off Nikki as Sloan
pressed forward and asked her some questions. Her arms
were wrapped around herself, and she was shivering beneath the prickly brown blankets the coast guard had given
them.

More than anything he wanted to pull her into his arms
and comfort her, but she had already stabbed him in the
heart once when she'd moved out of his embrace on the
dinghy. She didn't know who to trust anymore, she'd told
him. It was crazy, after all he'd done to save her. But he
could see it in her eyes, those few times she even looked
at him. Jack had brainwashed her.

"Please come with me, Mr. Wilde," a young, uniformed
man said, nodding toward the barrage of flashing red and
blue lights beyond.

Adrian numbly complied. He couldn't be under suspicion
of murder anymore, but he had fled the authorities and
taken a hostage. At that moment, he was sure nothing could
hurt him as much as Nikki's distrust.

The police station was a mass of confusion. Reporters clamored like ants all over the entrance, but the officers pushed their special party right through it without delay.

"Mr. Wilde, did you have anything to do with any of the explosions?"

"Were you after Nikki Madsen's money?"

If he'd had the energy, he would have growled at the reporters.

When they walked into the bright lights of the station, Adrian turned to the man at his right. "How is Ulyssis Garcia? Did he survive?"

"He'll be okay. The knife went into his shoulder. He'll be in pain for a while, but he'll live."

Adrian watched Sloan usher Nikki into his office and close the glass door behind him. She looked like a rag doll, limp and complacent, her long hair tangled about her face. Maybe she was just in shock. Maybe—Adrian shook his head. No, it wasn't anything like that. She just didn't trust him. Yet, no anger bubbled to the surface, no regrets. She had been through hell, and he had lied to her more than once. Adrian wanted to bust into Sloan's office and shake her silly, but that wouldn't solve anything.

The young officer led Adrian to another room, one without windows. "Detective Sloan will be in to speak with you in a few minutes. Can I get you anything? Coffee? Soda?"

"How about a cigarette?"

"Sure."

The man disappeared for a moment before returning with one cigarette and a pack of matches, then left Adrian alone. He rolled the cigarette in his fingers, then raised it to his nose. It didn't appeal to him anymore. Adrian dropped it and watched it roll off the edge of the table. It was nearly twenty minutes later when Sloan walked in. Adrian noticed a trace of smugness on the man's face, but he was too numb to let it bother him. Sloan stepped on the cigarette as he walked closer and took a seat across from Adrian.

"So why don't you tell us your version of the story, Wilde?"

Adrian leaned back, crossing his arms in front of him. The jacket one of the cops had loaned him only kept in the dampness that emanated from his sweater, but he wasn't cold anymore. Not on the outside, anyway.

"You want me to start at the beginning, or after I left you at the hospital?"

Sloan's lips curved upward. "Why don't you start at the beginning?"

Adrian didn't relish telling this man about his visions, but he supposed Nikki had probably spoke of them already. What did it matter anyway? He started with the visions, then the photograph, and moved forward from there, omitting the intimate details. Sloan had no business knowing more than he'd already figured out after scouring their bed with a magnifying glass.

When Adrian was finished, he asked, "Are you disappointed I didn't do it?"

Sloan crossed one leg over the other, smoothing out the cuff of his pants. "I just wanted the find the murderer, Wilde. It was nothing personal."

"That relieves me."

"But there's still the issue of taking the nurse hostage."

Adrian stiffened. "I'd do it again if I had to."

"Yeah, well. She's not pressing charges. In fact, she even confessed to helping you out." Sloan's mouth twisted into what could almost be considered a smile. "You must be one heck of a charmer."

"Lorie was smart enough to see that I wasn't a murderer."

"Yeah, well. We all make mistakes sometimes." Sloan stood, and Adrian knew that was as close as the man was going to come to apologizing. "You're free to go. There's some paperwork for you to sign. Officer Bernier will show you the way."

Adrian followed Sloan out of the room. His eyes searched for Nikki before his mind could tell them not to. She was still in the glassed-in office, talking to another officer. He was handing her a cup of coffee, but the cup remained in his grasp. Nikki was hunched into a ball in one of the chairs. Adrian moved closer to the room.

Sloan stepped up next to him. "Don't go in there."

Anger flared for a moment, reminding him that something was still alive inside him. "I need to talk to her."

Sloan placed his hand on Adrian's shoulder. It wasn't a restraining touch, but one to emphasize a point. "She doesn't want to see you."

"You're lying," he said, but he knew it was true.

"I'm sorry, but I'm not. That little girl is petrified. Give her some time. She's been through hell."

Adrian stood there for several minutes, his body rigid. Petrified. He couldn't feel her, couldn't connect. She didn't look in his direction. Once again, he was helpless to comfort her, to take her away from the hell that plagued her. Before it was fear of her brother, the horror of living on the streets. Now it was fear of him. He turned, following the female officer who was patiently waiting to lead him to her desk. Sloan remained there, looking at Nikki, then at Adrian before he turned away.

The sunshine and cool breeze embraced Adrian as he stepped through the back doors. He had one more stop to make before heading home. His life was far from normal, but he relished going back to what he had always considered part of his life. It was over. How long would it take to convince himself of that? Maybe forever. Maybe even longer.

Chapter 20

Will he ever leave my heart, and what will be left if he goes?

Nikki stood in front of the headstone in the cemetery. The cool breeze swirled around her heavy skirt, but her sweater and stockings kept her warm. Sunshine streamed through the trees, spotting everything with light. Her clothes smelled new, something she hadn't experienced in much too long. The allowance the trust fund had provided had been building up for two years, and when the mess was all straightened out last week, Nikki had taken some of the money and rented a small apartment in Fort Lauderdale. Buying clothes, makeup—it all seemed so foreign to her. Actually walking into a nice store, being looked at with respect and not scorn. It had sent her head spinning.

So she was taking it one step at a time. Coming back to Palm Beach was the biggest step. Before that morning, she hadn't talked to anyone from her past, except the family lawyer. She had stopped in to see Ulyssis a few hours before, and he had gathered her in his skinny arms and told her how glad he was to see her. It had felt good to be held, though it reminded her of other times, other people. . . .

She'd had a week to sort things through, but nothing was

clear yet. Nikki knelt down and put the bouquet of roses and carnations on the small grave marker. Engraved on the marble was *Ceil Whittaker*. Nikki had never known Ceil's last name. She had thought about giving her a fancy headstone, but that wasn't Ceil's style, so she'd kept it small and simple. Like Ceil herself.

"Ceil, I'm sorry everything worked out so horribly. Sometimes I think that you're actually better off now. I know that's a terrible thought, but you were so unhappy. I hope you can forgive me for that, and for everything. I only wanted to help you. You know that, though, don't you? You were my only friend down there on the streets. I'm going to miss you."

Nikki bowed her head and said a silent prayer for Ceil's soul. *Please give her mercy, dear Lord. She was a good woman, in her own distorted way. Maybe if someone had loved her, she would have been okay.*

Nikki walked over to where her mother's gravestone sat. It was the first time she would see it in two years. Blossom's stone was larger and more elaborate than Ceil's, more appropriate for her mother. Picking out that stone had been the hardest thing in the world to do.

"Mother," she whispered, tracing the edges of Blossom's name. "Dad." Her father's gravestone sat next to Blossom's. They had each other, at least.

"Mother, Adrian . . . Adrian once told me that you were probably proud of me, even if you didn't show it. The thought was preposterous, but I've had a lot of time in the last week to do some thinking. I do remember times, things you said . . . maybe you were proud of me, in your own way. I'm going to believe that, because it's all I have. I wished we could have gotten along better, but we were two totally different people. And you know what, Mother? We were both okay."

When Nikki knelt to place the second bouquet on her

mother's grave, she gave a startled gasp. A fresh bunch of yellow roses lay in the grass. She turned around then, and her breath caught in her throat. Devlin stood there.

"I saw you over here as I was leaving," he said quietly.

Nikki was surprised to feel none of the fear that always accompanied her thoughts of Devlin. He looked so much older than she remembered, and yet, his faint smile reminded her of happier times. He should hate her for blaming him all this time, for hiding from him.

Her voice was barely above a whisper; all her emotions were clogged in her throat. "These are yours?" She nodded toward the roses.

"Yes. I've been leaving a bunch here every month since she died."

"I—I haven't been here in two years. I was too afraid. . . ." She looked up at him, ready to encounter the bitterness that he must surely feel toward her.

"Of me," he finished for her, but there was nothing hostile about those words. "Don't cry," he said, lifting his hand, then lowering it again.

She didn't realize she was crying, but the wind chilled the track her tear left. "I'm sorry." That was all she could say.

"I'm sorry too. It was a misunderstanding."

He lifted his arms toward her, and nothing felt as right as moving into them. The years of fear and anger melted away as he squeezed her tight. Life was still scary, but maybe she would be all right. If only the huge empty ache inside her would go away. Some of it had been for Devlin, and some for Ceil. She didn't want to think about the rest.

When they finally parted, she smiled. "We have a lot of catching up to do."

"Yes, we do. I don't even know you anymore. Maybe I never did, Nikki. You were always so different from me. I think you were more mature than I was, and you were younger. Maybe that's what made me treat you so mean.''

"It doesn't matter. That's all in the past. I made a terrible mistake, and I almost lost my brother over it.''

He took her arm and tucked it beneath his. "Speaking of mistakes, what about Adrian?''

She looked at him, her heart twisting inside her. "What do you mean?''

"Have you spoken to him yet?''

She shook her head, too quickly. "No, I can't.''

"He came by to see me before he left for New York.''

Somehow she knew that's where he'd gone. Back to his life and career. And Rita. She wouldn't admit to anyone that she'd driven past the rented house in Palm Beach. The shelter was done now, but she hadn't had the guts to go inside. In any case, Adrian's car wasn't at either place, and the other day there was a minivan with Virginia plates parked in front of the house.

"What did he say?''

"He loves you, Nikki.''

She couldn't keep the startled look from her face. "He said that to you?''

"No, he didn't have to. I could tell. He said he was here to save your life, and that was all. He looked defeated.''

The pictures she'd tried so hard to keep at bay flashed through her mind like a movie. Adrian building a sandcastle complete with a maiden in distress, being held in his arms, making love in the bed, in the shower . . .

"But he's gone now," she said, more to herself than to Devlin.

"He said you knew where to find him.''

It was all so confusing. What did Adrian mean? Did he really love her? Or was he lost to her? She remembered most of all the hurt on his face when she wouldn't come into his arms in the dinghy.

"Do you think he was in on it at all?" she asked, though

in her heart, she already knew the answer.

"No. The police let him go, so they must have known he was clean. No, Nikki, I don't think he was in on it. It was Jack, only Jack."

Nikki couldn't picture Jack and Adrian consorting together, or even having a conversation. They were two entirely different men. She took a deep breath, then exhaled, hoping to dispel the tightening in her chest.

"Adrian asked me to take care of you." Devlin laughed softly. "As if my little sister ever needed someone to take care of her."

She turned to him. "I've trusted with my heart and been lied to. And I've feared with my soul and been wrong. I don't know what to feel anymore."

"You love him, don't you, Nikki?"

"Yes," she answered without thinking. But it was true. "Yes, I love him."

"Why don't you find out what you feel by going up there? I'll even go with you if you want me to."

A shiver assailed her body at the thought of going to New York, of seeing Adrian again. Would it be the same between them, after what she'd done to him?

"I have to go alone, if I go."

"Okay. You do what you have to. You've been doing that for a long time now anyway."

Adrian sipped his coffee, staring at the cityscape. There were twelve million people out there, and not one of them was Nikki. He couldn't get her out of his mind. Or his dreams. Not the nightmares he used to have, but luscious memories of holding her through the night, making love with her. His fingers tensed on the cup, and he forced them to relax before he cracked another handle. Sometimes as he made his way through the crowds of New York City, through the smell of hot dogs from the sidewalk vendors and the smog of the traffic, he caught an ocean breeze. It only lasted for a second, and he wondered if it was a vision or just an overactive imagination.

He took a deep breath, telling himself it was crazy to think about her. She was probably going on with her life, maybe hating him, or maybe just wondering if he had been involved in Jack's scheme. After what she'd been through in those last few days, he couldn't blame her. Not really. But if she couldn't trust him, then maybe it was for the better that they didn't see each other.

Life was good. The Calvin Klein shoot went better than he hoped, and they'd been understanding about his "personal business" postponing it. It hadn't taken long for word of the whole Palm Beach incident to reach New York. Adrian refused to talk about any of it.

He was taking his first trip since returning from Palm Beach two weeks ago. Waiting for her to call, he thought, shaking his head. No more waiting; he had a career to think about, and not much more. A week on Grand Cayman with Cindy Crawford would do wonders for his soul. Not that he cared much about being with Cindy personally, or anyone else. He couldn't even think about being intimate with anyone. It would be good just to get out and be with people.

"Is this her? Your friend in Florida?"

Rita held up the photograph of Nikki that had sent him down to West Palm to begin with.

"Yes." He knew Rita was dying to know more about the mysterious woman, but he didn't want to talk about Nikki. "Are you ready to go?" Adrian walked over to the leather bags sitting by the door. Oscar walked over, hoping for another escape. Adrian knelt down and scratched his head. "Bye, fuzzy fellow. Lucky you, another week with a gorgeous woman."

Rita cocked an eyebrow at him, but didn't say anything. Yeah, he knew he could spend a night, a week, a few years with that gorgeous woman. All Rita was getting from him was breakfast out for taking him to the airport and taking care of Oscar. And the customary dinner when he returned. She slid into the fur coat she had recently vacated when she'd gotten there.

"Is there some way to exorcise her from your heart?"

Adrian put on his full-length, black leather coat. "Rita, I told you, it's not up for discussion."

Her shoulders drooped. "Let me help you."

He shuddered, remembering saying those words to Nikki. "I'm fine."

"No, you're not. You're different. I think someone finally got to you, and you hate it." She glanced back at the photograph, shaking her head almost imperceptibly. "I'm glad. Because if she got through, then there's hope. Adrian, why do you think I've been hanging around all this time?"

He slung his equipment case over his shoulder and opened the door. "You hang around because you like the challenge." He smiled to temper his words. "I enjoy your company, but I never made any promises to you. Remember, there are some people who are meant to be together, and we are not those people. Don't wait for me. You'll be wrinkled long before I pop that question. Go find a man who'll give you what you deserve. And take Oscar with you. I won't have anyone to watch him, and I think I like dogs better. Come on."

"Dogs?" But she didn't ask any more questions as she followed him out the door.

Nikki stood at the door, her hand raised to knock. It had taken her over a week to gather the courage to come to New York. She had never been more scared in her life, even during those horrible moments with Jack. It was a woman who had authorized her entrance into the building. Her heart clenched inside her. What kind of situation could she be walking in on? After all, Adrian had every reason to hate her for not believing in him. She had only hoped and prayed that he would understand where she was coming from. But maybe he hadn't.

Maybe he had gotten on with his life like she could not. She took a deep breath. It could be the cleaning lady too. No matter. Nikki was there, and she wasn't leaving until she straightened things out with Adrian. If he was involved with someone else, or if his feelings had changed, then she would accept that and leave. But not until she apologized, and most of all, thanked him for saving her life. He had freed her, and reunited her with Devlin too.

Nikki had already decided she wouldn't throw herself at him, though her entire body seemed poised to do just that. She would be able to tell by those expressive brown eyes of his if there was anything left between them. A sharp pain shot through her heart at the thought that his eyes would be empty, cold.

She knocked on the door, exhaling a long breath to calm her nerves. The woman who answered didn't look like any cleaning lady Nikki had ever seen. In fact, Nikki knew this woman. She was the one who had walked up to Adrian on the sidewalk. Rita. She was tall and lean, with shiny black hair.

"Hello, Nikki," Rita said softly, moving aside to let her in.

There was a strange tension in the air, but Nikki stepped inside. Rita closed the door, crossing her arms over her chest. "You look different than in the picture." When Nikki gave her a puzzled look, Rita walked over and showed her the picture Adrian had taken of her by accident. The one that had led him to save her. Her heart's pace quickened. He still had the picture out.

Yes, she looked different. Her long hair was free, blush and lipstick tinted her cheeks and lips, and her long cashmere sweater looked far nicer than the shabby coat. Nikki sensed some kind of pain in Rita's expression. "I am different." She took the photograph, hoping the woman didn't see her hand trembling. "God, that seems like forever ago." A lonely woman standing on the beach wondering if she would survive another two years living on the streets.

Nikki realized that she was expecting Adrian to step out from some room by now. Except for a white, fluffy cat that peered at her from beneath a cut-glass table, the place seemed empty. She was glad that she'd left Crackers with the doorman.

"Is Adrian here?"

Rita shook her head. "He's on a fashion shoot in the Cayman Islands." She paused, seeming to weigh what she was going to say next. Her dark eyes studied Nikki, surveying her. "He'll be back tonight," she added in a low voice.

"I see." Nikki had to know, so she pushed the words out. "Do you live here?"

Rita hesitated, again seeming to weigh her answer. Well, what was it? She either did or she didn't. Or she wanted to.

"No, I just watch the place. . . ." She nodded toward the cat. "And Oscar while he's gone. He's gone a lot."

Relief flooded Nikki, but she understood Rita's position in all this. Rita wanted Adrian too.

"I'm sure he is. Perhaps I should come back later. It was nice meeting you, Rita. Again," she added, because it seemed proper.

Nikki turned, but Rita touched her shoulder, stopping her. "Why don't you wait here?" She shrugged, forcing a smile. "You're a friend of his. I'm sure he won't mind. He'll probably be home around nine."

Nikki smiled. "Thank you, Rita. I appreciate that."

Rita could only nod, holding her mouth in a tight line.

"Do you think he'd mind if I brought my dog in? I don't have anyplace else to keep him."

"Dog?" Rita said, as if the word were foreign.

"Crackers. He didn't tell you about Crackers?" Nikki felt disappointed. Had he forgotten the puppy?

Rita shook her head. "He likes dogs now," she said in disbelief. Then she focused in on Nikki. "He didn't tell me anything about his trip to Florida. He's like that. Well, he is with me, anyway."

Nikki appreciated Rita's candor. "You could say that he didn't tell me the whole story, either."

Rita slowly nodded her head, then looked around the apartment as if she'd never see it again. "I'd better go."

"It was . . . nice meeting you," Nikki said, but Rita was already stepping out the door.

Nikki brought Crackers up, along with her piece of luggage. She introduced him to the cat she barely knew, but Oscar preferred to view the puppy from atop the white refrigerator.

She looked around the apartment, searching for clues to the man she knew very little about. There wasn't much personal about the apartment, aside from framed photographs Adrian had probably taken. It was clean, and everything was in perfect order. No feminine touches, which was good. White carpet, modern kitchen. The strange part was that she felt at home here. Like she belonged here, in this apartment, in this city. The view of the skyline was magnificent, and Nikki stood at the window with her forehead pressed against the cool glass, watching the crowds swarm below. All those people, and he wasn't one of them.

She had seen the homeless of the city, bundled against the bitter cold. It amazed her that she had lived that life, even though it was only three weeks ago. She was going to help those people. But first she had to help herself.

Later, she snuggled onto the soft leather couch with a

photography magazine and waited for Adrian to return. That meeting had not left her mind for a moment. In fact, her whole future depended on it. Even with her freedom, her whole life ahead of her, and a nice little bank account with which to start a photography studio, it all seemed senseless unless Adrian was there to share it with her. How could she have been so stupid as to lose sight of that?

Rita had been unusually quiet during the ride back to his apartment. He was too tired to mind the lapses of silence between their small talk. When they reached the city, he asked, "Do you want to grab a bite?"

"No, that's okay. You're probably tired. I'm sure you're anxious to get home."

He was both, but her strange expression, and that melancholy tone in her voice had him worried. "Are you all right? Did something happen?"

She shook her head, too quickly, her lips pressed together. Well, he wasn't one to pry into people's personal feelings. Maybe she was just upset because he didn't invite her to join him, though she knew the rules on that from the beginning. He didn't have the energy to coax it out of her at the moment.

Rita stepped out of the car when they reached his building. She leaned against the door as he removed his bags. The doorman offered to help, but Adrian politely declined.

"I've got them, Fred, but thanks anyway."

"Good-bye, Adrian," Rita said softly before getting into the car. She glanced up at the building longingly before disappearing. Rita couldn't even see his apartment from there, what with the awning and all. He couldn't figure women out, and at the moment, he didn't care to try.

After a long, noisy flight, the silence of his apartment was comforting. At the same time, it felt lonely, and that feeling bothered him intensely. As he started to close the door, a strange noise made him stop. Thumping. A beige dog got to his feet and ambled over to him. Crackers. His heart started beating as fast as the dog's tail flipped through the air. On the couch, Nikki was sound asleep. It was like that first time she had come to him.

But this was a different Nikki. Her long hair was the same, and the peaceful expression on her face, but this was a classy woman wearing a long, black cashmere sweater, white stockings and just a touch of makeup to highlight her cheeks. Brown leather boots stood nearby, fringed with fur. He quietly closed the door, then removed his camera from his bag. Adrian never wanted to forget **this** moment, not even when he was a hundred years old. **He snapped** several photographs of her before setting down the camera.

Nikki's eyes fluttered open, and she sat up. Those beautiful green eyes searched his, and her lower lip trembled slightly.

"I—" She cleared her throat. "I hope you don't mind that I waited for you."

His first instinct was to pull her into his arms, but he remembered that last look of distrust on her face too clearly. Why was she here?

"No, of course not. Rita let you in?" No wonder she'd acted so strangely.

"Yes." She stood up, nervously smoothing down the black sweater that reached past her knees. She walked around the coffee table, only a few feet from him. "I came . . . to say that I'm sorry." She faltered on that last word, looking away for a moment. Then she met his eyes, and her voice was thick when she repeated it. "I'm so sorry."

Nikki seemed that fragile angel to him again, the one who had haunted his dreams. He couldn't stop the hand that reached out and touched her cheek, as he had done so many times before. She closed her eyes at his touch, leaning into his hand. Her hand covered his, moving it to her soft lips. She kissed his palm, her eyes searching.

"Nikki—"

She placed a finger against his lips. "Shhh." With his hand still in hers, she moved it down over her heart. His fingers grazed the soft curve of her left breast, but he didn't move his hand to caress her. Instead, he felt her heart beating through the soft sweater.

"Adrian, I—I love you. God, how I love you. I'm sorry I hurt you by not trusting you. I didn't know who to trust, everything was so confused. I was confused. Please understand . . . and forgive me. I don't want to lose you." Her eyes filled with shiny tears. "If I lose you now, nothing will have been worth going through. When I thought I was drowning, and I heard your voice, I thought you were an angel. That . . . feeling of being connected . . . is that what you felt these past three years?"

Adrian somehow found his voice. "Yes. Strange, awesome, spellbinding."

She nodded. "All of those, and more. You saved my life, but my life is nothing without you. I—"

Adrian pulled her into his arms, his heart ready to explode. His lips met hers in a hungry kiss, a kiss that would swallow her up if he could. Her arms slipped around him, and she pulled him closer yet. His fingers slid through her silky hair as his lips sought hers again and again. Was it possible to love a woman as much as he loved Nikki? It was more than possible. What they shared defied reason and reality, but there was no denying just how real it was.

"You're home, Madame Blue," he whispered between kisses. "Home."

Epilogue

Love is everything, and even better when you can share it.

Nikki Wilde walked up to the freshly painted stucco building and smiled for the camera before smashing the champagne bottle into the wall. The crowd cheered, and she felt like bursting inside. Adrian came up behind her, slipping his arms around her waist and nipping playfully at her ear.

"Remind me to never get you mad, sweetheart. You've got quite a backhand there."

She leaned into him, kissing the place just beneath his chin. "Darling, I have much better ways of punishing you than that."

Nikki looked up at the beautiful building that gleamed in the South Florida sunshine. The Ceil Whittaker Shelter, the sign proclaimed in clean, black letters. As soon as the trust fund had been released, Nikki had written a check to the contractor. Not that she feared for her life anymore. No, she wanted to do more with that blood money than just spend it. Besides, they didn't need it anyway.

Seamus stood in the crowd of people, along with several other faces she recognized. They were excited too. A woman stood nearby, tightly holding her young son's hand. He was already enrolled in the tutoring program that would get him up to speed so he could join regular school with the rest of his age group. His mother was signed up for the job training classes, computer technician, if Nikki remembered correctly. Their rosters were getting full already, and they had just opened that minute.

Adrian walked over to where Devlin held their little girl, Jodie. She wriggled her hands excitedly. "You don't even know what's going on and you're excited," Adrian said as he nuzzled her chubby cheek. When he walked her over to Nikki, she gave Jodie a loud kiss.

"Don't I get one?" he asked with a playful pout.

"Jealous?" she asked with a grin.

"Not if you give me some special attention later," he whispered in her ear.

All she had to do was take one look at him sprawled out on the bed, or even doing something as mundane as loading the dishwasher, and she lavished all the special attention on him that he could handle. And then some.

It was a completely different feeling that enveloped her when she looked at their perfect little girl. One look at her blond curls and Adrian's warm brown eyes, and Nikki's heart filled with love. That girl would never feel lonely, Nikki would make sure of that. And she would always know that she was an important part of her world.

Dave Watts stood by the door, opening it for her as she walked through. She'd been inside many times during construction, bringing lunch for Adrian on those days he was down in Florida performing manual labor.

"She's beautiful, Nikki. I can't wait to get things going!"

Dave rubbed his hands together, and Nikki hoped he realized how much work this particular shelter was going to be, much more than the Lord's Shelter.

Behind Adrian, the reporters followed, swallowing every word she said as she explained what the classrooms were for, the room filled with computer parts, and the nursery for the little ones. The lobby was filled with her framed prints that had garnered her respect and admiration in the finest galleries of New York and Palm Beach.

"Everyone who stays here signs a contract promising that they will help maintain the shelter, learn job skills, and keep off the booze and drugs. Even if they don't need a place to sleep, they have to make a commitment to learn. No slackers allowed." Nikki gestured for Dave to join her. "This is Dave Watts. He'll be running the place, coordinating the various duties, helping to place people in productive jobs."

A female reporter leaned forward, thrusting a microphone in Nikki's direction. "What made you put all this work and money into a homeless shelter, Mrs. Wilde? And who is the shelter named after?"

Adrian had wanted to name it after her, but Nikki knew in her heart who should get the dedication. He answered the first question, slipping his arms over her shoulders.

"If you look at her photographs, you'll understand why she did this." The cameras turned toward her collection. "She doesn't look at homeless people and see lazy, worthless bums. She sees people in unfortunate circumstances, down on their luck, people who have mental problems. No matter what has driven them to this life, they're still people. And they need help and comfort and love just like you and me."

"My life has been touched by some special people," Nikki said, turning to Ulyssis, Crackers at his side, Devlin, and finally Adrian. "I feel blessed that most of those people are here with me now. Ceil Whittaker died a terrible, unfortunate death. She deserved better than that. I couldn't help her when she was living, but I wanted to honor her memory. This seemed the perfect opportunity."

When the cameras were turned off, and refreshments were being served, Nikki pulled Adrian into one of the darkened rooms and slipped into his arms. "I can almost feel Ceil here. She's smiling."

"I'll bet she is."

"She would have liked you."

"I'm sure I would have liked her too."

Nikki's smile faded as she looked up at him. "Did I ever actually thank you for saving my life?"

"No, I think you were too busy apologizing for breaking my heart."

"Adrian," she said, leaning her forehead against his chest.

He lifted her chin up. "You've thanked me in so many ways, I can't even count them. And yes, you thanked me for saving your life."

"I owe you my life."

"And I want you to remember that. Because you'll always belong only to me."

She snuggled closer, closing her eyes and breathing in the scent of his aftershave. "This is where I belong, Adrian. Now, forever, even before we ever met. You were my prince when I didn't think I needed one. You not only saved my life, but you made me alive." Her voice became a whisper. "Thank you, thank you, thank you."

He kissed her then, taking her to that place where no one could ever hurt her again, where love triumphs always.

KATHLEEN KANE

The Soul Collector

A spirit whose job it was to usher souls into the afterlife,
Zach had angered the powers that be. Sent to Earth to live
as a human for a month, Zach never expected the beautiful
Rebecca to ignite in him such earthly emotions.
0-312-97332-2 _____ $5.99 U.S. _____ $7.99 Can.

This Time for Keeps

After eight disastrous lives, Tracy Hill is determined to get it
right. But Heaven's "Resettlement Committee" has other
plans—to send her to a 19th century cattle ranch, where a
rugged cowboy makes her wonder if the ninth time is *finally*
the charm.
0-312-96509-5 _____ $5.99 U.S. _____ $7.99 Can.

Still Close to Heaven

No man stood a ghost of a chance in Rachel Morgan's heart,
for the man she loved was an angel who she hadn't seen in
fifteen years. Jackson Tate has one more chance at heaven—
if he finds a good husband for Rachel…and makes her forget
a love that he himself still holds dear.
0-312-96268-1 _____ $5.99 U.S. _____ $7.99 Can.